LOST FRIEND FOUND

Zachary Ryan

ISBN: 1530786789
ISBN 13: 9781530786787

Andrew,
I hope this books
helps your heart open
up to love and joy.

"What I will do is promise you these days we share. I pray they're infinite, but if not, then I pray we fill them with all the love we have."

To Leah and Megan. I'm blessed to spend the rest of my life with two beautiful souls in it.

Huge thank you to Andrew Garcia for helping me edit this book. Also, thank you for being my moral support during this book and through life.

1

"I don't think being broken or damaged goods is a bad thing. I believe those are the most beautiful people in the world. They have sharp edges, but they're guarding something so pure. They give you all their heart and truly appreciate when they find joy. They survived the hardships and were able to smile again. It won't be easy for them to heal, but they cherish the journey. Everyone can be happy, but these people are the few who wiped the tears away and opened up again. Caleb never thought he was among the happy. He had a darkness to him, but he loved so much and so hard. Caleb gave you everything that his soul could. The world grew darker with his death, but it doesn't mean we won't smile again. Caleb, thank you for being the friend I've always needed. You were a brother and my foundation. I'll never truly appreciate all you've done for me."

I finished my speech. I looked around at the crowd of people. This was my best friend's funeral. He was gone and never was coming back. It was an odd sensation. Caleb and I had been on the rocks for a while, but it didn't mean the dagger to my heart didn't hurt any less.

I stepped away from the podium. I turned to look at the collage of pictures that were next to his coffin. Caleb's warmth was gone, and the body, that was unrecognizable, was closed to the world. I would never see his love splashed across his face again.

I saw the happy guy in those pictures. I saw us when we were in elementary up to college. We had always been there every step of the way until college. It never made sense to me the past four years of his life were a mystery. I don't think I'll ever get rid of regret in my heart.

Colby walked up to me and kissed me on the lips. "Colin, that was a beautiful speech." She smiled weakly. Her blonde hair was blowing in the wind, and tears clouded her blue eyes. "He would have loved it."

"It doesn't change anything. My best friend's gone."

She interlaced our fingers and gave me a gentle squeeze. "It's not your fault what happened."

"He was murdered."

She sighed. "You don't know that. It could have been an accident."

"Colby, his body was found in a fucking field with bruises all over. What do you think happened? He slipped and fell?" I could feel myself getting worked up. I wanted answers for what happened to Caleb.

She kissed me on the cheek. "I know you want all the answers, but we don't get them. All we can do is move forward. He wouldn't want you to feel like this. I'm going to go talk to your aunt." She gave me a weak smile.

Amy and Vince walked up to me. "That was a beautiful speech." Amy pulled me into a hug. Caleb got her brown eyes and soft features from her. "I still can't believe he's gone. How could this have happened?"

"I don't know."

"I knew it was stupid for you to separate in college. You both were always supposed to protect each other," Vince said.

"We were supposed to, but life happens."

Amy smiled weakly. "I just want my son back. I'm wishing that I could wake up from all of this. Are we horrible people to lose a son? What crimes have we committed to deserve this kind of heart break?" She asked.

Vince put his arm around her shoulder. "Amy, I told you to stop thinking like that. We're supposed to be strong."

She nodded and wiped the tears away. "I'm being a silly old fool."

"You're not old." I gave her a grin.

She touched my shoulder. "You've always been a charmer. You should have gone to the same school. We should have forced it."

"You know Caleb would have gone behind your back," Vince countered.

"He's right. Caleb was stubborn." It was weird using past tense when it came to Caleb. He was no longer a present.

"He got it from you, Vince. I hated how much he was so adamant about everything that he did with his life."

Vince chuckled. "You can't be mad at me for making him a strong, independent person."

"No, but you could have stopped being a pigheaded asshole."

"That's your son," Vince said lightly.

"Who is dead…" Amy made the situation come back into our minds.

Vince took Amy's hands. "I know, Honey. I know. Let's go see everyone else." He kissed her on the cheek.

Amy turned to me. "Please, come grab some of his things. You can have whatever you want. I know you'll find more meaning in a lot of it." I heard in her voice the amount of pain on her heart.

"No problem, Mrs. Moore."

People wanted to make sure I was okay. Sad reality is that I lost Caleb a long time ago. I didn't know the man that tragically died, and I don't know if I ever would.

I walked over to his casket and put my hand on it. I knew he was in there. His body and all the memories of us were held up in a wooden box. He had such a light and wonderment about him. He was someone special and a rare occurrence to this world. I'll never get why someone would do this to him. What happened in the past four years that caused his demise?

2

I looked at the past four years of my life packed into a dozen boxes. It was starting to hit me that I was moving home until the fall when I would start grad school. Sure it would be nice to get home, but I didn't know if I was ready to be surrounded by my past ghost.

I couldn't get Caleb's funeral out of my mind. I finished my finals and sat through the torture of graduation. I'm just happy to have three months to focus on Caleb's death. It had been two week, and people still were walking on eggshells around me.

"Earth to Colin. You with me?" Jimmy asked.

I blinked and turned to look at my roommate. He was wearing just a t-shirt and boxers. He was playing video games, throwing Cheetos in his mouth. Maybe that's why he was extremely fat. He even went by, "Jimmy the Fat Jew." He was proud of the title when we became roommates four years ago.

"Sorry, I've got a lot on my mind."

"Is it about your friend dying?" Jimmy asked.

"Yeah, I guess it's been really messing with me. Why would someone kill him?"

"Didn't they tell you it's an on going investigation?" Jimmy paused his game. He got up and stretched. His shirt lifted, and the hair on his stomach was starting to show.

I looked away from him. "I'm so glad I can get away from that view."

Jimmy laughed. He walked over and clapped me on the shoulder. "You get three months away from me before we start grad school. It's going to be the best two years of our lives."

"You said that when we became roommates."

"Did I steer you wrong?"

"More than you know." I rolled my eyes.

"You need to get out of this funk. We should take shots. I don't like when you're moody."

"My best friend just died."

"So?" It was silent for a moment. Jimmy shrugged.

I sighed heavily. I ran my head through my buzz cut. I felt the scar on my head and quickly retracted my hand. "I can't ignore it, Jimmy."

"Dude, he's dead. I don't understand why you're all upset about it. Yeah, you guys were friends years ago. I wouldn't be this upset if one of my childhood friends died."

It still amazed me how blunt Jimmy was. He didn't see the point of being around the bush with people. His parents had always told him about tough love. They thought it was necessary for him to have a backbone.

"Jimmy, he's dead. Can you show him some respect?" I snapped.

Jimmy raised his hands. "Sorry, I didn't know it was still a touchy subject."

"I was just at his funeral. Of course, it's going to be a touchy subject. Why do I room with you?"

"Because I'm the only one that puts up with your bullshit." Jimmy shot back. "You think going home is the best thing?"

"I just feel like I need to figure out what happened with Caleb."

"Colby okay with that?"

"She's actually thrilled were staying in our hometown. She was worried I would avoid Grandville all together because of Caleb's death."

"It's the sticks, though."

"We live in the sticks now."

Jimmy chuckled. "I would like to call this in the middle of no-where. It's not like we're far from the city."

"I guess you're right, but I need to be around everything connected to Caleb, minus our road trip in a week."

"You could always get a head start on first year of grad school."

I gave Jimmy a dirty look. Jimmy might have been a slob, but the asshole was a fucking genius. He actually cared about his grades. He got straight A's, minus an Art class that he decided we couldn't talk about.

"I rather not." My voice dripped with sarcasm.

Jimmy walked up to me and opened his arms. "Come give your favorite fat Jew a hug."

Jimmy and I weren't the type to hug anything out, unless we had been drinking whiskey. I was hesitant, but I finally went in for the hug. "I'll actually miss your pungent smell over the summer."

Jimmy smacked me upside the head. "I call it my aroma."

I rolled my eyes. "Whatever makes you sleep at night."

Jimmy then gave me a concerning look. "Just take care of yourself. I know you're going to be obsessed with your friend's death, but you need to relax. You always get stubborn and don't take people's advice."

It was moments like these that I truly could appreciate Jimmy for who he was. "I know. I just have a bad feeling about this. I need to know what happened to my friend. His life changed the past four years."

"Sometimes you don't get all the answers."

"That was oddly insightful."

Jimmy shrugged. "I can be wise sometimes. I'll see you in a week."

"Can't wait." I grabbed my bag. I had movers coming to grab the boxes later. I was going home to get the closure I needed before I started a new chapter of my life. I just didn't know where Caleb would fit in all of it.

3

I was nervous about knocking on the Moore's door. I usually walked right in, but that was high school. It felt like just a distant memory. It's the same awkward feeling when you sell your childhood home and visit it after you moved away.

Amy opened the door. "You could have just walked in. You didn't need to wait for us." She was drying her hands.

"I guess I didn't know where my place was in this home." I didn't know why I admitted that to her.

"Honey, you'll always be like a second son to us." She pulled me in for a hug. It felt good to have a mother's embrace. I hadn't experienced this in a long time.

"I just wish Caleb and I didn't drift."

"Don't we all." She gave me a hopeful smile.

She stepped aside to let me inside. "You know where his room is. All of his belongings from his apartment are upstairs. The police don't think it will do them any good." She stopped herself. "Sorry, I need to check on those cookies."

I could see that she was about to cry. I took in a heavy breath. Maybe I was the reason for Caleb's death? I could have changed, and he wouldn't have been alone. It's not right to have this guilt in my chest, but what else was I supposed to feel?

I walked up the stairs to Caleb's room. There were memories of us running around as kids and teenagers. I looked at the wooden door. There were so many dings and scratches from goofing off and being the friends we had been for twelve years.

I opened the door to boxes scatter across the room. I didn't even know where to start. Caleb's life was stored in these boxes.

I started going through the boxes looking at clothes, papers, books, and pictures. I saw faces and memories that I never experienced with him. I read poems of him falling in and out of love with guys that I had never been introduced to. I saw stupid notes and events that I wasn't with him for.

I threw the pictures across the room. I couldn't handle being reminded how much of Caleb's life I wasn't part of. "I know it's hard being in here."

I turned to see Vince standing there with a plate of cookies and milk. "Amy can't even come into this room without being upset."

"How can you?" I asked.

"My son and I had a great relationship. We called each other every day. We accepted him for who he was, but that doesn't mean he told us everything. I knew he was hiding things from us for a long time."

"I just wish I was more understanding."

"Or maybe he would have still been killed." He put the cookies down. "It doesn't matter what happens in our life. We could wish this or that was different, but that doesn't mean it wouldn't have the same result."

"That's a bit of a disappointment."

He chuckled. "No, it doesn't make things sound optimistic. It also makes you calm down about the mistakes of your life."

"I just wish Caleb told someone where he was going that night or talked to someone."

"Life doesn't give us what we want. It tests us to our limits. I wish I could still call myself a father, not be known as the man whose son was murdered. I hoped Caleb would be coming home with his boxes bitching about moving home. We can't..." He let the thought linger. "Anyways, here are some cookies. You know how Amy worries about you."

I smiled. "Thank you for giving me some understanding."

He shrugged. "I'm the adult. We give the youth our advice." He walked towards the door. He turned back. "I never lost any of my love for you that night. I know it was hard to adjust to Caleb coming out. It was a scary summer for both of you."

"I should have been more understanding."

He shook his head. "You were doing what you thought was right. You still loved and protected my son. It killed him, but I knew you weren't doing it in a vicious manner."

"It seemed like it."

"You'll learn with age that it's hardly a vicious thing. You didn't comprehend it, but you stayed his friend."

"But we didn't stay as close as we were."

"That's what life does. You both were growing up and naturally went separate ways."

"I missed him even before he died."

"I'll let you know he felt the same." He walked out of the room in that moment.

I was lost in my thoughts until I continued looking through his boxes. I found pictures and notebook of his writing that I wanted to keep. I found a USB and threw it in a box with the rest of the things I wanted to keep.

I looked at the box of memories that I was taking with me. I didn't know if this was supposed to be my goodbye to Caleb, but I couldn't deal with the fact that he was gone. I would never get to experience him light up a room again. We will never lie on his bed talking about our deepest secrets anymore. I didn't have someone that I would always count on. I lost a part of me, and I didn't know if it could be filled. I just wanted him back in my life.

I grabbed the box and closed the door to Caleb's room. I knew that I was dealing with a mix of emotions, and I just wanted every-thing to finally settle down. I don't think I could until I finally had closure with everything going on.

4

"You need to stop kissing me there," Colby said trying to push me off of her.

We were curled in my bed with sheets covering our naked bodies. "Why? I like kissing you there." I kissed her on the crane of her neck.

She laughed, and I could never stop hearing that laugh. She pushed my chest again. "You know that it tickles. I don't want Aunt June to hear us."

I rolled my eyes. "She's at work. She also knows what we're doing. She walked in on us before."

Colby looked at me. "I don't want to have a repeat. It was embarrassing."

"It was senior year of high school, of course it was embarrassing. We're adults now. We're supposed to be having sex all the time."

She rolled her eyes and got out of bed. The sun beat down on her back. She looked so beautiful. There was nothing about Colby I didn't love.

She turned to look at me. "You look like a stalker staring at me."

I leaned over and grabbed her arm. "I'm just admiring the woman I love." I pulled her back into the bed. I wrapped my arms around her and held her close. "I never want to lose you."

She sighed. "You won't."

"I can't believe he's gone."

She stroked my hands. "Colin, you can't blame yourself for what happened. It was a tragedy." It came out like a whisper.

"He was your friend too. Why aren't you upset?"

She rolled over to look at me. "He was the reason we got together. He made me forgive you after all the stupid shit you did in high school. He was one of my best friends, but he was your brother. You two were everything to each other."

"I failed him."

She touched the side of my face. "Sometimes we fail people."

"How do I get over this pain?"

"Maybe when you get closure." She gave me a chaste kiss. "I love you."

"I love you too."

"We have had our share of bumps, but we will always have each other. I don't see myself being with anyone else."

"Me neither."

"So put a damn ring on it. I'm not going to wait around forever." She smirked. She got out of bed this time and started putting her clothes on. "You need to go through all these boxes."

I got out and put on some boxers. I stretched. She was going through one of the boxes that I got from Caleb's house. "What's all of this stuff?"

I walked over. "It's what I got from Caleb's place. His parents thought that I wanted some of his belongings. It's just more junk. I don't want any of it."

"Then why did you take it?"

"I felt like I needed to. It would be rude to decline the offer. I didn't want to miss my chance to have some things of Caleb's."

"How philosophical of you?" She smirked.

I bumped her. "Shut up." I went through some of the pictures, shirts, and journals full of his poetry. "I just didn't want his writing to go to waste. I knew how much he loved it."

Colby picked up one of the journals and started flipping through some of the pages. "He was always good at creative writing."

"Yeah, he should have gone to our school. It had a better writing program. He would have loved it more."

"He chose to go somewhere else. That's not your fault."

"His exact words were, 'I want to go somewhere where people will accept me for being gay.'"

"It was a hard thing to adjust to." Colby always understood everything. She was compassionate, and I was too lucky to have her.

"He trusted me enough to tell me. What did I do? I rejected him. I told him I couldn't be friends with him because he was gay. How is any of this fair? He was a good fucking person, and he got murdered."

I walked over and sat down on the bed. Colby walked over and kneeled down in front of me. "You accepted him for being gay."

"It still didn't help."

"Colin, I'm not going to lie to you. You fucked up. That really upset Caleb. He would call me crying about it. He didn't know why his brother hated him so much."

I felt the guilt in my stomach. I wanted to curl into a ball and never talk to anyone else ever again. I was a monster. "I didn't accept him when he needed it."

"You're human. It happens. Stop beating yourself up, and you need to realize that. Colin, you did a horrible thing, but you aren't the first person. If I recall, I dumped my boyfriend because I knew you were going to ask me out."

"You didn't love him."

"And you didn't understand. We live in the south. We're not the forefront of gay acceptance."

"But he was my best friend."

"And you eventually came around."

"I just want to know what happened the past four years."

Colby stood up and walked over to the boxes. She picked up the journals. "It looks like you have your material right here. You have the whole summer to figure out who Caleb was in those four years. Why don't you get started?" She leaned down and kissed me on the cheek.

"I love you."

"I love you too." She walked to the door. She turned and looked at me. "Take my advice and figure out who he was." She opened the door and walked out.

5

Five Year Earlier

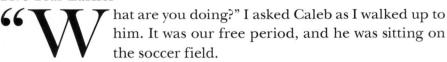“What are you doing?” I asked Caleb as I walked up to him. It was our free period, and he was sitting on the soccer field.

"I'm just writing for Mr. Welsher's class."

"I thought you had all your poems done for the rest of the year."

"Yeah, but I found new inspiration." Caleb didn't look up at me. He always got so engrossed in his writing that he didn't know what was going around him.

I sprawled out next to him. I closed my eyes and felt the warmth of the sun. "I could get used to this."

"Then you'll miss the rest of your classes," he said in a sarcastic tone.

"If I wasn't in a good spot right now, I would probably punch you in the arm."

"Who got you in such a good mood? Is it Colby? Did you guys do it behind the bleachers again?"

I opened my eyes and turned to look at him. He had a big grin on his face. "I'm never telling you anything ever again."

"Aw, but where is the fun in that? I love having dirt on you and Colby."

"So you can blackmail us to go on double dates with those horrible girls you try to date."

"I'm sorry about Chelsea."

I kept looking at him. "She ate with her mouth open. Her mouth open." I sat up. "What are you working on?" I leaned over to read some of his writing.

He quickly hid it from me. "I'm not telling you jack shit. You always make fun of me for my love poems."

I rolled my eyes. "I won't make fun of you, I promise."

"Not going to happen. Besides, you're worse with your poetry."

"He wanted me to write about something."

"You didn't need to write every poem about Colby. You could have talked about other issues going on."

I knew where he was going, and I didn't want to get into it. "Caleb, stop. I'm in a good mood."

Caleb turned and looked at me. "It's been twelve years. Aren't you upset or anything?"

"What do you want me to say? Yes, it still kills me that my parents are gone, but I can't just share my emotions as well as you."

"You haven't talked to anyone about it."

"I talk to you about it." I tried to defend myself. I wasn't great with my emotions especially about the car accident.

"You only talk to me when a bottle of alcohol is in your system." It seemed like he was judging me. I didn't want to get into this with him.

I stood up. "I'm not going to be judged for how I deal with my parents' death. I'll talk to you later." I knew he was going to apologize, but I just didn't want to talk about it. I wanted to act like nothing happened. People already knew the story, and I wanted to act like it was just in my past.

I tried really hard to stay away from my aunt's liquor cabinet. I was drunk. I've been drunk before, but this was a whole new level. It was twelve years since my parents died in a car accident, as we were driving to go camping. I was the only one to survive.

I banged on Caleb's door. "Caleb! Answer your fucking door. I need my best friend!" My words came out slurred.

Caleb opened the door. I saw the concern in his eyes. "Colin."

"My parents are dead. They died because I wanted to go fucking camping. I begged them to go. They thought we should have gone another weekend, but no, I backed them into a corner."

I felt the tears falling down my face. Caleb pulled me into a hug, and I broke down even more. I tried to keep the screaming to a minimum, but I couldn't. The pain in my chest was never going away. It never could.

"You had nothing to do with your parents' death. It was an accident."

Caleb pulled me into the house. I saw his parents at the top of the stairs. They both had understanding looks on their faces. I come here and broke down to Caleb, as he takes care of me.

Caleb escorted me to the kitchen. I sat at the kitchen counter just swaying back and forth. "You're so lucky. You have parents who love you. You have people that care for you. I'm alone in the world."

Caleb started making me eggs and handed me a glass of water. "You know that's so much bullshit. You have your aunt, Colby, and me. You're on the football team."

"It doesn't matter. They don't know how truly broken I am. They'll never understand how messed up I am."

He placed the plate in front of me. "I don't see a problem being broken. It makes us unique and helps us overcome things. We all have our demons we're facing."

"Yeah, what are yours?" I asked.

He opened his mouth but closed it. I saw the conflict on his face, but he didn't say anything. "We're talking about you, not me. Eat your eggs."

"You're my best friend, you know that."

"You're my brother. I love you."

I took a couple of bites. I felt my stomach flipping over. I could feel it coming. I got off the stool and ran to the bathroom. I started puking and my heart wasn't the only thing in pain.

Caleb was there, rubbing my back. "It's okay. I'm here for you."

"When will the pain stop? When will I be happy?" I looked at Caleb for the answers.

He shook his head. "I don't know. I don't think the pain will ever stop."

6

"Are you doing some light cleaning," Aunt June said as she walked into my room.

I was trying to finally get everything out of the boxes, things from my apartment and Caleb's. "I am, but it's been harder than it looks."

She sifted through some of the boxes. "It amazes me how much junk we accumulate over the years."

"Yeah. The guest room is your shrine for your shoes."

She rolled her eyes. "We won't get into that discussion because you still have all your trophies." She picked up the one I got when I was in tenth grade for just participating in a chess tournament.

I walked over and grabbed it from her. "All right. You win this round, woman."

She laughed and sat down on the bed. "How are you doing?" She asked.

I turned and saw the same look she gives me every time it's my parents' anniversary. "I'm fine. I have a lot of questions but I'm trying to survive."

"Colin, you like to keep things in. You want to avoid them."

"I'm not avoiding anything. I just have a lot going on. It's been a lot of things to process. I graduate college, my best friend is murdered, and I'm here now. It doesn't mean it's all going to click." I tried to keep my voice calm.

"Yes, I know it's been a hard couple of weeks on you, but you just need to grieve."

"How would you like me to grieve? I could just crawl into a ball and just let everything out. Would you like me to tell you the truth? I feel numb. I don't want to accept he's gone. Why was he murdered? Why did someone do that to someone who wouldn't hurt anyone?"

Aunt June got up and hugged me. "I know, honey. This world isn't very kind. It took my sister and husband from me, but it gave me you."

"How can you keep smiling?" I looked at her. Her husband died of cancer when I was three. Three years later, she loses her sister.

"What's the point of crying and being stuck in the past?"

"Shouldn't you have some hate in your chest?"

"Oh trust me, I have enough. I never got to fully appreciate my husband. We got married and the next year we found out he had cancer. Four years later, I buried him. Your mother got me through it. I lost my sister right after, but you got me through it."

"How?"

"Because you're so much like your parents." She lifted up my chin. "They would have been so proud with how much you have grown."

"I barely remember my parents. I remember people telling me how incredible they were."

"They would light up a whole room. They would understand and listen to people when they had problems. Your mother was a caregiver and made sure no one would be in pain. Your father loved to solve the problems of the world and figure out how he could fix things. They were a powerful duo."

"And now they're dead."

"But they're legacy is with you." Aunt June went through the boxes again and pulled up a picture frame. It was a picture of Caleb and I the summer after I lived with her. "I always loved this picture of you two."

"You and his parents always had to separate Caleb and I."

"You two would cry when you couldn't spend the night together. I swear you both were the same person."

"We found this secret treehouse in the woods, and I would make him watch out for other people."

"You guys would stay in that tree house for hours."

"You called the police on us because we fell asleep at the tree house one night."

We both laughed. "What was your nickname for him?"

"Scout."

"I hated how much trouble you two would get in, but it made you happy. You weren't this shy little kid anymore."

"I wasn't known as the kid who lost his parents. I wasn't a freak to him."

"He saw you for the person you were."

"Yeah."

"Maybe he wanted you to do the same." She placed the picture down. "I'm going to go start on dinner."

"I'll be down in a little bit." I smiled. I wanted to finish up a few things.

She walked out of the room leaving me with everything. I started going through Caleb's things again. I saw the journals filled with poetry. It wasn't giving me the answers.

After about an hour I got frustrated and threw it all back in the box. A USB fell out of the box. I forgot I even packed the thing. I didn't know what it was for and a part of me wanted to just chuck it in the box.

I walked over to my laptop and plugged it in. I clicked on the folder and it was a series of folders all labeled part one to five. "What in the world did he get himself into?"

I clicked on part one of the series. It was password protected. I felt like this was what I had been waiting for. I was praying this USB was going to give me the answers I needed.

I clicked on the hint that came with the password. "Tree house," I said out loud.

I thought about what Aunt June and I talked about earlier. How we would spend hours in the tree house away from the world. Caleb and I didn't care what was going on unless it happened in our bubble. It was the best summer of our lives. I typed in "Scout" for the nickname I gave him. The folder opened to a series of diary entries. I was hoping this would lead me to Caleb's lost years.

7

Dear Colin,

I don't want to sound cliché, but if you're reading this, then I'm dead. It's an odd sensation writing a letter alive when you know that when someone reads this your life is gone. I can never talk to you about these past years or ask you how have been. I guess we both were stubborn after that fight. Sure, we tried to keep in contact with each other, but it was hard. I was still hurting after the words you said. I was still destroyed by how angry you were. I'll admit my choice words weren't the best, but can you blame me?

I want you to know that I love you for everything that you are. I've never had a true brother until you. I saw that scared kid, and I wanted to be friends with him. Through the years, we had each other's back. I'm thankful you let me see your damaged soul. I wish you could understand why I kept it a secret from you.

I know that you carry a lot of guilt with you. I know that you'll blame yourself for what happened, but I did this all to myself. I knew what I was getting into. I knew that it could all end badly for myself, but I never saw myself grow-ing old. I never was going to have a happy ever after like you and Colby. I would be known for the short life. I'll be one of the "gone too soon" people. It's okay though, because I got everything I needed in my life.

I could have left these letters and diaries to someone else. I've made great friends since we drifted, but they didn't get me like you. They weren't my tree house best friend. They never full broke down to me like you did. I guess you were always the one that needed this more than any of them.

I hope you take care of your life, and I hope these give you the answers that I know you have. Colin, I never had a full happy life because you weren't there every step of the way. I never would be able to say that I got everything be-cause the piece that mattered the most was the person it was hardest to talk about. I love you, Colin, and I want this to be your closure.

Love,
Caleb

August 26th, 2011

I don't even know how I should feel right now. I'm moving into a new town without my best friend. I guess it's my fault or maybe it's his. I just wish that he didn't have to leave me alone here. I didn't know how much I truly needed him in my life. Sure, this is all about finding yourself, but I liked who I was, or maybe the world had a problem with me.

I looked around campus, and I saw all the freshmen looking for their dorms. I saw the confused and scared expressions. It made me feel refreshed knowing that I was one of them. We were all connected. We were bonded by the simple fact that we left our place of comfort to come to a new place.

Met my RA, and I knew he could be my first mistake. He had the surfer look, and I was attracted instantly. He was the male version of Colby. Colby, how much I missed her. I wish Colin and I hadn't fought. I didn't know if that meant I could never talk to Colby. How stupid would that be?

I quickly got my things, and I'm pretty sure he winked at me. I knew he was going to be bad news, but I relished in the idea of him. I wanted to explore my sexuality. I was tired of being in the closet. I've been in a cage far too long. I spent too much of my time focused on other's appeasement.

I walked into my dorm to my roommate already putting up posters. He was wearing a scarf and a beanie. He had gauges and jet-black hair. He screamed hipster. In an ironic sense, he seemed like the cliché roommate to have.

He turned around and smiled. "You must be Caleb. I'm Drew." He put out his hand.

I took his hand and shook it. "Nice to meet you. You moved in quickly," I awkwardly said.

"Yeah, I wanted to get it done and over with. I don't need to waste my time waiting for the reality to set in. I'm in college. I'm on my own."

I dropped my bags on my bed. "That's a quick way to realize things."

"You have to. That's how it works. College is all about getting out of your comfort zone. You need to accept that you will never be the same person ever again. All the people you left behind in your hometown will just be distant memories."

I didn't want to believe that. I didn't like the idea of leaving Colin in my past. Sure, we weren't on the right page right now, but he was my best friend. He would always be that, and years of friendship wouldn't be ruined because of a simple fight. It would take time for us to get back to being friends, right?

September 15th, 2011
I was looking at the campus map trying to find the library. Sure, I remember seeing it on the tour, but that was months ago. I was supposed to meet up with a kid in my class to work on a paper.

"You know you scream freshman right now." I heard a voice behind me.

It startled me. I turned to see Jack standing there smiling. I wouldn't admit I had a sex dream about him last night. It's not my fault he came back from his run sweaty as I was coming back from class.

"Is that a bad thing? You were a freshman last year."

He laughed, and I could melt. "Yes, and it's my responsibility to make you not stick out like a sore thumb."

"Is that because you like me or is it because I'm one of your residents?"

"Maybe it's a bit of both." He winked at me.

I blushed and looked away. "Thank you, but I think I got this."

"Oh really?" I looked at him with his arms crossed. "Where are you going?"

"The library."

"Where's that?" He asked raising an eyebrow. I wouldn't admit that it was super attractive.

"It's over there." I pointed to my left. I was praying I was right.

He laughed. "That's actually to campus safety, but you were close." He walked up to me behind me. He grabbed my arm, and I felt aroused. "You see that brown building," he said close to my ear.

I inhaled a shaky breath. "Isn't this a bit too close?"

"I don't think so. It's the best way to show you." I heard the flirting in his voice. "Do you see the building?"

"Yeah."

"It's right next to that building," he said. He stepped away from me, and I didn't want him to. I liked having his body pressed against mine.

I turned to him. "Thank you."

"Anytime." He smiled and walked away.

Jack and I had become close the past couple of weeks. He helped everyone find out where their classes were or counseled them when they were homesick. He seemed like he was just that friendly, but I wasn't certain. Was he flirting with me, or was he just being nice? I couldn't deny the arousal I felt having him behind me, and the yearning to turn to kiss him.

September 24th, 2011
Drew and I have been getting along pretty well. We decided to join the radio program, and it seems we have our little group of misfits. There was Cameron, she had half her head shaved and the other was dark red. Shawn was a shy poet. We connected through our writing. Then there was Beth, who connected with Drew on how much they hated mainstream music.

I didn't think I would actually like the radio station, but Shawn wanted to do a writers station. I had agreed to do it with him. It seemed that's all I had been doing the past month.

I was drunk stumbling because the radio station wanted to initiate us. I didn't think chugging beers and taking shots would make me feel bonded to this group, but it did. I was in love with my friends, but it didn't fill the hole that I had for Colin.

I pulled out my phone, and it dropped on the ground. "Fuck." I picked it up and stumbled while calling Colin. I knew we were avoiding each other, and I didn't like that. I didn't want that to be us. I wanted us to have solved everything. "Colin, please pick up. You're probably having sex with Colby as we speak. I hope college is going well. I'm drunk. Like really drunk. I'm more intoxicated than junior year after prom. God, I'm going to have a killer hangover in the morning, and you won't be here to share in the pain. I could bitch to my roommate, Drew, but I think he's sleeping with our friend Beth. They've been getting along. You would hate Beth, but she's awesome. I miss you. I just wish we could just forget about it all. I wish we could just be back to us. I'll talk to you later." I hung up on Colin. I needed to.

I felt myself wanting to cry when I got back to my dorm floor. I just wanted to forget about everything. I wanted to have a distraction. Isn't that what college is for? Isn't it supposed to make you forget about all your problems for four years?

I saw Jack walking down the hallway. He was in a pair of basketball shorts with a towel hanging off his shoulders. I have never been more turned on than right now. He shouldn't be walking around with abs like his. He had made everyone melt. I talked to him a couple of times. We've flirted, but it always stayed at that level. I wanted more. I wanted his soft lips on mine. I wanted his abs on me.

"Hey, RA Jack." I waved like an idiot.

Jack laughed. "You can call me Jack, you know."

"I kind of like the nickname. It makes you seem less like you're going to hurt me."

He rolled his eyes. "How drunk are you right now?" He raised an eyebrow.

I blushed and looked away from him. "I have no clue what you're talking about. I would never be drunk. I am sober." I probably screamed louder than I should have.

"Come with me." He pulled me by his hands, and I liked the sensation I felt when our hands were together.

Jack escorted me into his room. There was a pledge paddle on the wall along with other fraternity items. There were also pictures of him across the world and pictures with friends and family.

He assisted me to his bed before walking over to the sink and pouring water. "Here, just drink this."

I took a couple of sips. "Thanks, I needed that."

He came and sat down next to me. "You need to pace yourself. You can't just drink as much as you want. The older kids will want to see how much they can push you."

"Thanks, RA Jack." I saluted him. I can't believe I did that. He's never going to be attracted to me.

He laughed, and it was a nice laugh. I could hear him laugh all the time. He turned to me and placed his hand on my knee. "I'm glad you came tonight. I haven't been able stop thinking about you."

"Is that appropriate to say?"

"Same with you being drunk right now."

"I didn't think you were into me." All I could feel was his hand on my knee.

"Caleb, we've been flirting back and forth for weeks now. I've been waiting for you to make a move."

"I've never been with a guy. This is all new to me. Plus, isn't it wrong for us to start a relationship? You're an RA."

"It's frowned upon, but we can keep it behind closed doors. People don't need to know about this. This can be our dirty little secret." He winked.

I wanted to protest. I didn't want to be someone's skeleton in their closet, but Jack smelt so good, and I didn't want this to go away. I didn't think about Colin, or my family, or anything that was in my hometown. I was only focused on his lips.

"Okay."

We leaned together and kissed. It wasn't like kissing Tracy or Sarah. It was full of physical attraction. This felt like my first kiss. I was alive, and I never wanted Jack's soft lips off of mine. He pulled me closer to deepen the kiss, and he swallowed a moan that escaped from my mouth.

I don't know how long we kissed, and I didn't care. This is what college was for. It's a scary thought to know that this could be someone meaningful to me. Sure, I kept my walls up with Sarah and Tracy. I was an actor playing a foolish role. Jack saw through the bullshit even though we barely knew each other. He took something from me that I was a bit scared to give. The greatest excitement of it all was no one could take this moment from me.

8

I closed the laptop after reading a couple of the entries. I knew there were more, but I needed to process what was going on. Caleb knew he was going to be killed. He left this all to me, and he didn't stop any of this. Why didn't he go to anyone about it? Did his roommate know what was going on? Did this RA Jack guy have something to do with his death?

I had questions swirling in my head when Colby walked into my room. "Hey, babe."

I turned to see her smiling. "Hey."

She looked at me with concern in her eyes. "What's going on with you? You look like you've seen a ghost."

I pulled out the USB and handed it to her. "What's this?" She asked.

"It's all of Caleb's diary entries. He left it for me."

"What? Have you given this to the police?"

"I don't even know if it's evidence. I don't know what else is on there."

"Have you finished everything on here?" Colby walked over and put the USB back in. She started clicking on all the other parts. They were password protected as well, but I couldn't figure out the answers to the hints.

She got frustrated and closed the laptop. "You need to give this to the police."

"I want to figure it out on my own first."

"Colin, this could help them figure out what happened."

"You don't think I know that." I shouted at her. I could tell that she was a little startled by me. I sighed heavily. "I don't think he gave this to me to figure out who killed him."

"How so?"

"He talks about his first months at college. He talks about his first time making out with a guy named Jack. If he wanted me to know who killed him, then he would have told me right away."

"What do you think it's for?" She asked.

"I think he wants me to know the last four years. He wants me to know everything that I missed out on."

Colby sat down on my lap. She started scratching my scalp. "I think this is everything that you've been wanting." She turned and pointed at the laptop. "This is your chance."

"I don't know if I want to know anymore."

"Why's that?"

"It's going to make me realize how shitty of a friend I was."

She shook her head. "You have to stop thinking like that. You have your faults, but so did Caleb. You both were playing phone tag with each other. You need to read these letters and entries to figure out what happened."

"Will you do it with me?"

"Why?"

"He was one of your best friends. Don't you want answers?"

"Not as much as you." She cupped my face in her hands. "This is your journey, Colin. I'll be there every step of the way. I just don't want this to destroy you."

"I won't. I promise." I gave her a weak smile.

She leaned down and kissed me on the lips. "I think we should put this to rest right now. Your aunt wants us down for dinner. She didn't want to disturb you."

"I want to read a couple more entries before I eat. I need to know what happened after he kissed Jack."

"This is what I'm talking about. You're already obsessing. Let's get some food in you. We can worry about this later." I couldn't stop thinking about the entries during dinner and sex with Colby. I laid in bed still thinking about the entries until she fell asleep.

I got out of bed while Colby was sleeping. Caleb was right. She was an angel I was blessed to meet. I never knew how to appreciate her until now. I looked at her while she stirred. All she cared about were others. All she wanted was for me to be happy, and I'm thankful for that. She had the best qualities of Caleb in her, and it made his death a little less painful because I would be reminded of him in her.

9

September 25th, 2011

I woke up next to Jack. We didn't do anything that I remember. I felt this warm body stirring next to me. I rolled around to see his face. He was sleeping, but he looked so content. I looked at his soft lips and thought about how much we were kissing each other last night. I can't deny that I loved it. I felt alive, and I never wanted it to stop.

He opened his eyes to me looking at him. He smiled. "It's kind of creepy that you're staring at me."

I blushed and looked away. "Sorry."

He wrapped his arms around my waist and pulled me closer. Our legs were intertwined. "I think it's adorable." He leaned forward and kissed me.

I ran my fingers through his hair as our lips moved together. I enjoyed this moment because I felt truly wanted. Someone accepted me for the person I was, instead of this portrait they painted me as.

He broke the kiss. "I would love to keep doing this, but I have to go on duty. I don't need to explain to my boss why I was late."

I unlatched from him and started looking for my clothes. I looked in the mirror and saw the giant hickey he left on my neck. I touched it instantly. I saw him come up behind me and wrap his arms around my stomach. "I like it."

"People are going to ask who it was."

"Just tell them it was a drunk hook up. You don't need to tell people the truth."

"So I'm supposed to keep lying to people." I've become a pro of it.

He turned me around. "Caleb, you know people can't find out about us. I've wanted to kiss you since you first got here. I don't want you to think that I'm ashamed of you."

I felt like an idiot to think that he was. I knew that it was just people in my hometown that didn't care for me. He saw me as the person I was. "I know. I guess I'm not used to it."

"It's just frowned upon." I looked at him in the eyes.

He smiled. He leaned in and kissed me again. "I want to take you on a date. I want to see where this could go."

"I've never dated a guy before."

He intertwined our fingers together. "I know, and I like that I'll be your first. I'll be gentle and patient with you. It just has to be a secret. I'm not ashamed that I'm gay, but I could lose my job. It's only until the end of the year."

"Until the end of the year." I repeated as confirmation for myself.

He kissed me again, and I let him take me right then and there. I let him have my heart because I wanted to feel wanted. I craved the love that Colin and Colby had. I never was jealous of them, but it was a love that I always desired. "You better go. I don't want you to get caught."

I left his room holding onto this secret hoping that no one would find out. I left our safe place to enter the cold reality of this world. I was alone out of that room. I didn't have to think about having no family or Colin here. I may have new friends, but we didn't have the deep roots yet. They didn't know the demons I had.

October 3rd, 2011
"Someone looks nice," Drew said when he walked into our dorm room after his class. I was getting ready for my first date with Jack.

"Yeah, I have a date tonight."

"Is it with your mystery hook up?" Drew asked walking up to me. He pulled my shirt down. "It seems that they can't get enough of your neck."

"He likes to give me hickies." It stumbled out of my mouth. I never told Drew that I was gay or who this mystery person was. I always told him that he didn't need to worry about it.

"He?"

I turned and looked at Drew. I was ready for a fight. Drew and I had become close, and I thought this was going to ruin our friendship. "I'm gay." I felt my whole nerves taking over me. This was it. I was going to need to find a new roommate.

"Damnit."

"Are you mad?" I asked.

"I'm pissed." He threw his hands in the air.

"I'm sorry. I didn't mean to." It was over. Everything had been perfect the past couple of months, and I've been waiting for the shoe to drop.

He saw the fear and worry in my eyes. "I'm pissed I owe Cameron fifty bucks."

"What?" I was confused.

"Cameron and I had a bet to figure out if you were gay or not. I said you weren't, but you are."

"You don't have a problem with me being gay?"

Drew laughed, and it eased the tension in the room. "Caleb, I don't care if you have sex with unicorns. It's your life, not mine. My uncle is gay. He's fucking awesome." Drew walked over and pulled me into a hug. "Were you worried?"

"Yeah, I've had other people reject me for it."

"Those are good people to have in your life," he said sarcastically. "You need to realize that you have a support system that loves you. I wouldn't tell Shawn though."

"Why?" I asked. He didn't seem he was homophobic.

"He has a huge crush on you."

"He's gay?"

"Yeah, where have you been? It never comes up on breaks during your shows. How many nights have we gotten drunk together?"

I felt embarrassed. "We just talk about writers and share each other's poems."

"So, who is the lucky guy?"

I blushed and looked away. "I can't say. It's all new. We are trying to keep it a secret for a while."

Drew whistled. "Secret lover boy. Just make sure you wrap it." He pulled out condoms out of his drawer and threw them at me.

I looked down at them. This was his version of accepting me. "Thank you."

He looked and me a shrugged. "Caleb, we're friends. I will accept you for who you are. You're a good person, and I care about you. Have fun on your date, and I can't wait to hear all about it when you come back."

And just like that it was out in the open. There was no fighting, tears, or heartbreak. I came out, but it didn't matter. Life moved on, and I was thankful for that. It seems that maybe the real problem was Colin, not me.

10

October 3rd, 2011

He wanted to meet across town where no one would see us. A part of me enjoyed the secrecy. I wanted this all to myself before people started telling me that I was a fool for trying to be with this man. They would constantly remind me of the red flags, and I didn't need that right now.

I saw him waiting for me by a picnic bench, wearing a dark blue shirt with jeans. I was embarrassed for actually dressing up for this date. I wanted to turn back and run.

He waved. I was going to look like a complete idiot. He got up and walked over to me. I tried to get a "Hi" in, but he pulled me in for a kiss. It was the first time we didn't have to worry about wondering eyes. He didn't hold back. I loved the taste of his lips and the feeling of his arms around me.

I didn't know how long we stayed there kissing. We could have ended the date right then, and I would have been in a perfect state of bliss. It felt free being with a guy. I always wondered if being gay was right for me. In this exact moment, I knew this was me. I finally connected with my soul.

He released my lips from his. "I think we should get to the date portion."

I didn't open my eyes right away. I loved his voice. I laid my head on his chest. "How about we stay right here? I like this."

He chuckled and wrapped his arms around me and pulled me in tighter. "I'm sorry that we have to keep this a secret."

"No, I don't mind. I understand completely." I turned and looked up at him. "It's only till the end of the year, right?"

"Only till the end of the year." He reassured me.

We walked towards the picnic table holding hands. We sat down, and he produced a grocery bag. "Really? Not even a picnic basket?" I joked.

He looked upset. "I didn't have time to get one. I just wanted us to have something." He pulled out a bottle of champagne. "I figured you already ate."

"Yeah." Drew dragged me to get food with him before he met up with Beth for another sex session.

He popped the bottle and poured some into glasses. "This never happened because I could get in big trouble."

I took the glass and smiled. "It's our dirty little secret." I winked. I knew my life memoir's working title would be, "Dirty Little Secret."

"Good." He scooted closer to me and wrapped his arm around my shoulder. I leaned in to feel his body heat. We drank champagne and watched the evening sky. We didn't say anything, nor did we do anything elaborate. I thought that falling in love needed to be this grand gesture. I was realizing with Jack, it only mattered who had your heart.

October 31st, 2011

"I'm not wearing this." I looked at the stupid Aquaman costume that Drew forced me to wear.

Drew laughed. He was wearing a Batman outfit. "We're going as the Justice League."

I turned to him. "Why can't I be Robin Hood or Superman?"

"Because you look cute in blue." He winked.

I blushed and looked away from him. "I hate you."

"I didn't say that. It was Shawn."

"I told you guys that I have a boyfriend."

Drew rolled his eyes. "You keep saying that, but we haven't met him yet."

"We want to keep it between us for a while."

"As long as it's not a professor, I really don't care because if you're banging a professor, then I'm taking his class for an easy grade."

"I'm glad you're pimping me out." I looked again at my costume. I did look good in blue, but I wouldn't tell him.

Drew walked over and kissed me on the cheek. "I'll meet you there. Cameron needs help with her outfit."

"So you've moved past Beth now?"

Drew rolled his eyes. "Beth and I were just fucking. She's with Chester now."

I laughed because Chester was a junior. He was in charge of all the music we played on the station. He was a nerd who loved comic books and the reason we were the Justice League.

"Yeah."

"I'll see you in a little bit." He waved off, and I would meet him at the party.

I took a sip of my beer that Jack got with his fake id for me. I was starting to get the perks of dating him. I took a seat down at my chair and went through my Instagram. I saw pictures of Caleb and Colby at a party together. They were matching as a doctor and nurse.

I thought about all the parties we would miss together. I hadn't really talked to Colin in two months. We've been doing phone tag, but eventually, it has been generic text messages. I liked the picture.

I pulled out my phone and texted him. *"You guys look cute."*

"Thanks. Let me see you." He replied.

I took a selfie. *"I look ridiculous."*

"Haha, I'm going to have to agree with you. You're friends have corrupted you. Colby says you look good in blue."

I felt a little judged from Colin, but I just sucked it up. *"Tell her thanks. I'll call you tomorrow."*

"Can't wait." He replied, and I threw my phone across the room. I didn't like this feeling anymore. I had a great boyfriend and great friends, but why did I feel so alone? People that truly cared for me surrounded me, but it couldn't fill the hole in my chest. I just downed my drink. I tried to forget about it the rest of the night, but the loneliness kept coming back.

11

"Colin, have you been reading all night?" Colby asked me.

I turned to look at her. "No, I got up early to keep reading. I can't wrap my head around the fact that there are things in his life that I wasn't a part of."

Colby sighed and sat on my lap. She kissed me on the lips. It calmed my nerves. "You guys were growing apart. I know you don't want to accept that, but it happens. He doesn't know every little thing that has happened in the past four years."

"Like what?"

"Like the solid three months we broke up."

I stiffened. Junior year was hard for the both of us. We were freaked out about missing out on life. We took it out on each other, and we both needed a break to actually be young and single. I was miserable. "I guess you're right."

Colby turned to the last entry. "Caleb is letting you know now. He's giving you the chance to figure out what happened in those years with his diary."

"You're right." I knew that the diary entries weren't enough. "We need to go to Grover."

"What?"

"Caleb wouldn't want us to just read this. His friends are still there. They have two weeks left of classes."

"You're crazy."

"Colby, you know that I can't just let this go. Please." I gave her my best puppy dog expression.

She sighed. "Thank god my internship doesn't start for another three weeks." She stood up. "I need to go pack."

"Pack for what?" Aunt June asked.

I turned to look at her. "We're going to Grover to figure out Caleb's life."

She crossed her arms. "When were you planning on telling me this? You just got home from school a week ago, and you're off again."

I looked down. "It just happened."

She rolled her eyes. "Just make sure you're safe. Also, your friend Jimmy's here. He's raiding the fridge right now. I'm bringing him up." She waved me off and went to grab Jimmy.

"Why's Jimmy here?" Colby asked.

I shrugged my shoulders. Jimmy did whatever he wanted to. I had just grown accustomed to him popping in and out during the summer. His family was on the west coast. He needed a place here that made him feel like home.

Jimmy walked in with a sandwich in his hand. "Are you ready to go soon? I found the coolest places for our road trip."

I completely spaced out on Jimmy and I's weeklong road trip. I felt the instant guilt. We had planned it during finals week. I think it was the only thing that got me through. "Jimmy, I totally forgot. I've been so focused on the Caleb thing that it slipped my mind."

Jimmy shrugged his shoulders and sat on my bed. "Dude, we planned this for weeks."

Colby walked over and sat down next to Jimmy. "Why don't you come with us to Grover?"

I was hesitant about Jimmy coming. I loved the guy, but he wasn't the most sensitive.

"Why are you guys going to Grover?" He asked.

I knew it was stupid explaining it to Jimmy, but I already lost one best friend. "We're going to figure out the last four years of Caleb's life."

Jimmy finished his sandwich and wiped his hands on his shirt. "I'm in. As long as I don't have to hear you two fucking all night."

Colby rolled her eyes. "We thought you were gone."

"It was double experience weekend."

"Whatever that is." Colby got up and walked over to me. She kissed me on the cheek. "I'm going to go home and pack. We'll meet here in two hours to leave."

I looked up at her. "Thank you for understanding."

"Like I said before, he was my friend too."

She turned to Jimmy. "Please make sure you take a shower. I'm not dealing with unhygienic Jimmy ever again."

"We were watching a marathon of Supernatural. It was Bro-weekend. It's not our fault that you decided to crash it."

"My boyfriend hadn't answered any of my calls. What do you expect me to do?"

"Let him be a man and stop being such a wife about things."

She slapped him upside the head. "I hate and love you all at the same time."

He chuckled. "It's the Jimmy charm."

"I'll see you boys later. Jimmy, try not to give him any bad ideas. I want to go through this trip without any near-deaths or arrests." She called as she walked out of the room.

"Jimmy, you don't have to do this. I don't want to drag you into all of this mess."

Jimmy gave me a weak smile. "Colin, your best friend died. I know you would want to figure out what happened if I died too. You've never judged me for being the fat slob."

"I wouldn't say never." I gave him a small grin.

We laughed, and it eased the tension. "I want to be here for you during this. I know that there was always something missing in your life.

I was impressed with Jimmy and I's talks sometimes. He acted like a buffoon, but he was actually a giant dog. "Why do you never show this side to others?"

"Because I don't like opening myself up to people that don't matter. Why take your mask down for people that won't be here for the long haul." He got up. "I'm going to go make another sandwich before we go."

I turned back around to look at another entry. "Caleb, I'm done keeping these past four years a mystery." I closed my laptop and started packing. I didn't know what would happen in the next couple of weeks, but I just needed closure and my friend back.

12

"How did we get lost?" I asked trying to figure my way around Grover's campus.

"The map's not giving me anything," Jimmy said looking at the map.

Colby sighed and grabbed it. "I thought guys were supposed to be good at this."

"I play video games. Colby, you get into debates about politics. What do you do for fun Colin?" Jimmy asked.

"I read."

"Apparently not a map," Colby said.

I sighed heavily. "How the hell are we supposed to look for this place?"

"Follow the road north. We're looking for the Thompson Library. That's where the radio station is." Colby explained without looking away from the map.

"How do you know that?" I asked.

"I looked it up on our way here. Maybe if you paid more attention you would have known that."

"Damn, your girlfriend just fried you." Jimmy started laughing.

"This is not the time, Jimmy."

No one said anything until we found the building. We got out of the car and walked around campus. It was vaguely familiar. I came here with Caleb when we were looking at colleges.

We found the library and followed the signs to the radio station. We walked into a classroom size room with people around sipping wine while a guy was talking. "His favorite thing was to write, and he was so good at it. The world didn't just lose a great person. They lost a great writer. To Caleb, and how much he changed this world."

Everyone raised their glasses in cheers to Caleb. I felt like I didn't belong. They were grieving him in their own way, and I just had interrupted that. The guy made eye contact with me. "We have some visitors."

Everyone turned to look at us. "Everyone enjoy the rest of the party." People started talking among themselves while the guy walked up to us. "I was wondering when you were going to make it here."

"You know who I am?" I asked.

"There were pictures of you scattered across my dorm and apartment for the past four years. He talked about you all the time until the stories slowly faded, and so did you. I'm Drew."

"You're his roommate." I made the connection. He had tattoos and was growing a beard. I just imagined Caleb's description of him would stay the same, but in reality, it had been four years.

"He talked about me?" Drew asked.

"No, he talked about you in his diary entries." I didn't know if Caleb wanted anyone else to know about them.

"Huh." Drew crossed his arms. "It explains what he was typing on his laptop all the time. I figured he was writing a novel or something. Caleb always had a series of secrets."

It made me oddly comforted that I wasn't the only one that was left out of the loop when it came to Caleb. It seemed that he didn't trust anyone. "I guess you're right."

Drew turned to Colby. "I'm Drew."

"Colby." She shook his hand. It seemed there was some awkwardness between them. Colby was hesitant about shaking his hand. I thought it was odd, and I would bring it up to her later.

"And you are?" Drew asked looking at Jimmy.

"I'm Jimmy, the Fat Jew."

"The Fat Jew?" Drew asked.

"Yeah, it's a nickname my friends and I came up with. I've kept it ever since."

Drew laughed softly. He seemed warm and welcoming. "It's cool." He turned and we followed him down to the crowd of people.

Their gazes followed us all. Drew turned to everyone. "This is Colin, Colby, and Jimmy. They were childhood friends with Caleb." Everyone gave us a warm welcoming.

Three people came up to the front. One girl had black hair with purple tips. The next wore a black dress with a blue cardigan and had pearls. The last guy wore shorts and a t-shirt. He looked very timid.

"Colin, Colby, and Jimmy, these were Caleb's other close friends. The girl with purple tips was Cameron, the girl with pearls was Beth, and the guy who looked scared was Shawn.

They didn't look like anything I pictured. "I thought your hair was half shaved." I didn't mean to blurt it out to Cameron, but I thought I had them figured out in the entries.

She looked at him confused. "I haven't had my head shaved since first semester of college."

Drew turned to her. "He's reading Caleb's diary. I guess he's not far."

"Yeah, I'm only at Halloween 2011."

The group looked at each other. "So you haven't gotten to the professor yet?" Shawn asked.

"No, who is that."

"Shawn, it's not our place." Beth shot back at him. He kept his mouth shut.

"I never pictured you wearing those clothes." I admitted to Beth. "He said you were very anti-society and that we wouldn't get along."

She crossed her arms and rolled her eyes. "What did you think I would be a punk rocker? I would have tons of piercings and look like a pothead. That would make me fall deeper into those stereotypes, and I know that I need to get a real job. I don't care to be sucked into the corporate world, but I need to survive."

She had a lot of anger to her, and I knew that she was the type of girl that I would stay clear of. I just looked at her with my mouth wide open.

"Wouldn't that force you to still fall into other stereotypes?" Jimmy asked. I wasn't expecting Jimmy to say anything. I was impressed he kept it to the conversation at hand and didn't call her a stuck up bitch.

She rolled her eyes. "I'm not going to get into a conversation with a gamer about this." She turned and walked away.

Drew rubbed his head. "Just ignore her. She's going through a hard time. We're all still trying to deal with Caleb's death."

Weren't we all? I thought. He was my best friend since I was six. I knew him longer than any of them. Shouldn't they be consoling me, not the other way around? I was starting to feel that maybe this place was going to destroy me.

13

"What brings you here?" Drew asked sipping his beer. Drew, Cameron, Jimmy, Colby, and I were at the campus bar. "I need to figure out what happened with Caleb."

Drew smirked. "Don't we all? What's the real reason?"

"It's not fair that the last four years of his life were a mystery to me."

"Whose fault do you think that is?" Drew raised an eyebrow.

I clinched my fist. I felt Colby's hand on my knee. I took in a deep breath. "We both fucked up. I'll be the first to admit that. We were both stubborn, and it ruined us. I'm trying to fix that."

He sat back in his chair and crossed his arms. "Don't you think it's a bit too late for that?"

"Listen, asshole, I don't really need your help."

Cameron put her hand in the air. "Drew, stop being a dick. I know you were protective of Caleb, but so was Colin. We all want to figure out what happened. Can't we get along?" She asked.

"She's right. You both meant a lot to Caleb. There's no point in you two fighting." Colby added.

I sighed heavily. "I can put it to the side for now."

"Really, just like that?" Jimmy asked. "I've never seen you back away from a fight."

"Jimmy, do you think that's necessary?" Colby asked.

Jimmy raised his hands in the air. "I'll keep to myself."

"What do you need from me?" Drew asked.

I looked at him, and I knew he was trying to help. I guess it made things easier. I would never admit how much I was grateful for what Drew did for me. He protected my best friend, but he didn't do enough of it.

I finished my beer. "I honestly don't know. I'm trying to get through these entries, and I'm still lost."

"There's your problem right there. You aren't deep enough. You're trying to figure it out so quickly. You have four years of a person's life to understand and appreciate. You can't learn that over night."

"I want all my questions to be answered."

"You'll get there, but you need to read more." Drew stood up. "I can't help you until you've gotten further. You need to go back to your hotel and read." He walked away from the table.

"Well that was fucking helpful." I slammed my glass down.

"He hasn't taken Caleb's death really well. I guess it's the fact that Drew knew something was going on a week before he died. He blames himself," Cameron explained.

"You don't think I do?" I snapped.

"Colin." I could hear the worry in Colby's voice.

I turned to her. "I left him. We promised we would always be there for each other. Sure, that sounds like a stupid thing, but we planned on being together. This wasn't how it was supposed to be."

"I don't know you. I'm not going to say that I do, but you lost a great person." Cameron smiled weakly. "You can't put a fresh coat of paint over a broken wall and assume people will forget the damage."

I stood up and walked outside to get some fresh air. I saw Drew standing there smoking a cigarette. He turned and saw me walking out. "The conversation become too intense for you too?"

I chuckled. "Yeah, I just couldn't deal with the feelings."

He offered me a cigarette. "Thanks." My hands were shaky. I tried to light it a couple of times and gave up. "Nothing is going my way."

Drew scoffed. "What do you expect?" He helped me light my cigarette. "You came to the place where he became a stranger to you."

"Caleb was still the same guy I grew up with."

"That's your problem right there."

"What is?"

"You want him to be the same Caleb he was when he came here. He wasn't. He grew up, and he became the person he was supposed to be. Caleb changed. The Caleb I met four years ago isn't the one that died."

"I know that." I looked away from him. "I'm hoping to find that he didn't forget about me." I looked at the ground. "I don't want to be just a memory to him."

I felt Drew squeeze my shoulder. "Was he that to you?"

I looked up at him. "What?"

"A memory?"

I shook my head. "I could never forget about Caleb. I didn't understand him or react the way he wanted me to. We were both stubborn and hurt each other, but he was there for me. I wasn't a freak or weirdo. I was a human being."

"Caleb never lost that. He saw people the way they were and hoped to be. He would take the broken people of the world and make them better."

"Caleb never wanted to see people in pain. He loved all."

"And he loved you."

I looked up at Drew. There was softness in his eyes. "Really?"

"You were always talked about."

"Thank you."

"For what?"

"Being there when I couldn't." I didn't know much about Drew and a part of me hated him, but he took care of my best friend. He loved him like I did. He was right though. The Caleb he loved and the Caleb I loved were two different people. I just pray that I could love his Caleb.

14

Four 1/2 Years Ago

"Let's go to Grover." Caleb was showing me a brochure.

"Really? It's a small Liberal Arts School."

"They have a great creative writing program," he said flipping through the brochure.

"I don't know if that's for me."

"Colin, you need to figure out what you want to do with your life."

I shrugged. "I'm sorry that we all don't have great talents. I just know that I like solving mysteries."

"You do like figuring out everyone's problems. You always knew who the killer was. How about a criminology degree?"

"I don't know. Maybe I should figure out when I get there."

"Stop trying to avoid the fact that you're scared of failing your parents." He didn't even look at me.

Caleb sighed and closed the brochure. He looked at me. "Colin, I've known you for twelve years now. I'm not stupid.

"They can't have expectations because they're dead." I got up and stormed out of the room. I knew it was childish, but I didn't want him to analyze me.

I heard Caleb follow after me. "I get it. We don't want to fail people. We're so scared of trying to keep it in. We want to be perfect for the ones that we loved."

"Or the lack of."

Caleb smacked me on the side of the head. "You have Aunt June, Colby, and me. We're not going anywhere. You need to stop being an idiot."

"I just don't want to look like a fool."

"You won't be a fool as long as you're loved." He handed me the brochure. "Let's just go to see what it's all about."

I rolled my eyes. I hated how pushy he was. I just didn't want to think about my future right now. I wanted to forget about it all.

"Colin, look at this place. It's fucking beautiful." Caleb kept taking pictures of Grover. We were the only kids on the tour that didn't have parents.

I chuckled and rolled my eyes. "I think you're more excited about this tour than the actual tour guide."

Caleb blushed and looked away from me. "We could be room-mates. It would be so cool."

"Caleb, let's calm down for a minute. People are starting to look."

Caleb turned to me. "You don't seem really into this."

"It's not that. It's just." I paused, and I didn't know how to tell Caleb. "I found another college that I wanted to look at."

"Oh." Caleb's happy expression went somber. "Where?"

"Kuller University."

"That's two hours from here."

"Yeah, I looked into their criminology program. It's really good."

Caleb sighed heavily. "Now, you actually listen to me."

"You can't be mad that I want to look at other colleges. I want to try new things and explore other places."

"I thought we could do it together." I could tell that Caleb was about to cry. We've always talked about staying at the same college, but I realized maybe it was good if we separated. It wasn't like we couldn't still see each other.

"I know, but we're growing up. We can't always be attached at the hip."

"Here is the community center. This is where we have a variety of activities including our LGBT, Fraternities and Sororities, newspaper, and broadcasting," the tour guide said.

Caleb and I stepped away from the tour. People were giving us dirty looks, but I ignored them. I only cared about the anger that was seeping from Caleb right now. "Why can't you go here? We planned this out."

"Caleb, I can't go to a school that has a sub par program for me. This place is perfect for you, not me."

"It could be if you gave it a chance."

"You're liberal arts and everything that comes with it. I'm not. I'm mystery and figuring out puzzles. It's come to a point where our education differs now, and we have different needs."

"I just don't want it to ruin our friendship."

This is where I got angry. "Do you actually think we're best friends because of geography? Do you think that little of us?" I tried to keep my voice down. We were friends because we cared deeply about each other, not because it was convenient.

He recoiled. "No, I don't think that. I just don't want us to drift. I'm sorry. I guess it freaked me out thinking we would be going to two different places."

I pulled him into a tight hug. "I love you, and I won't let you go. You're my brother and best friend."

He looked at me. "Thanks, I needed that."

A guy walked up to us. "It's really refreshing to see a gay couple loving each other so openly on campus. It's why I love it here. We don't care about your sexuality as long as you're happy."

I stepped away from Caleb. "We're not together. We're best friends." I was a little offended that he thought we were gay. I didn't think I had a problem with homosexuality. I never knew anyone who was gay, and it wasn't like our hometown was crawling with them.

The guy blushed. "I'm so sorry. I just assumed."

"No, it's fine. I guess that's another selling point that they accept everyone," Caleb said. I didn't know why he felt like that was a selling point. Everyone loved Caleb and accepted him.

"Well, I hope you guys choose to go here. I'm late for class."

Caleb smiled and waved. "He was nice."

"Yeah, he was." I was skeptical about Caleb right now. He had hopefulness in his eyes that I never seen before. He was excited about this place, but after talking to the guy, he looked like he found his version of heaven.

"Let's finish the tour." He dragged me into the community center, and the rest of the trip was focused on Caleb finding where he would spend the next four years of his life without me.

15

We drove to our hotel and dropped off our things. "I'm going to need about a three-hour nap." Jimmy walked over to the bed and laid down on the bed. "This is everything I've ever wanted."

I laughed. "I'm glad that you're enjoying yourself."

Colby turned to me. "It seemed you and Drew got a better understanding for each other."

I kissed her on the lips and hugged her close. I would never be able to thank her for everything she has done for me. "Yeah, we did."

I leaned down and deepened the kiss with her. She moaned softly, but she put her hands on my chest. I separated myself from her and looked at her. "We can't have sex with Jimmy right there."

"I don't mind. I need something that isn't depressing to listen to." Jimmy's voice was a bit muffled from the pillow.

I rolled my eyes. "Fine, I won't love you any more."

She smacked me on the arm. "Shut up. What do we have planned for the rest of the day?"

"Well Drew invited us to go to some kind of bonfire they're hosting for Caleb tonight."

"That sounds like fun. I'm glad they're welcoming to us," I said. Colby walked over to her suitcase and opened it.

"Yeah, they seemed to like the idea of having other people that loved Caleb here."

"We should probably get some sleep. It's been a long day."

"I was planning on reading some more." I needed to know more about what was going on. I had to figure out how it all ends. It was like one of my own mystery novels, but I didn't know who the murderer was.

She walked over and kissed me on the lips. "Colin, you need sleep. We can figure all of that out tomorrow. We just got here. His friends want to take us out." She pulled me towards the bed.

We fell on the bed, and I pulled her in. I kissed her on the back of her neck. "I love you. Thank you for everything you've done for me."

She stroked my fingers. "I know it's been hard on you, but I'll never leave. We've been through too much shit to let you go through this alone."

I drifted softly to Jimmy's snores knowing, even though Caleb was gone, that I would never be alone. I think that's the best way to sleep.

"Why did we only get a twenty-four pack of beer?" Jimmy asked while we were walking to a clearing in of the woods.

"Jimmy, it's a kick back, not a party."

"Every situation could be a party." Jimmy laughed.

Colby groaned. "Why did we bring him again?"

"Because you love me," he said.

"Yeah, I do. I really fucking do."

I laughed as we got into the clearing. I noticed that the group was smaller this time. It was only Drew, Cameron, Beth, and Shawn. "Are we early?" I asked.

Drew smiled. "No, you're right on time."

"Where is the rest of the group?" Jimmy asked.

"The bonfire is usually just the core group. We survived all four years of college together. We went through heartbreak, loss, success, and happiness. Every year, we like to recollect and realize how close we got that year." Beth explained.

We dropped the case of beer and sat across from them. "That's really sweet," Colby said.

"It helps us get through the year. I think it makes us happier that we've kept our friendship." Shawn smiled. He was writing something down.

"What are you writing?" I asked. I've seen Shawn write a couple of times, and I've been curious about it.

"I write everything I feel. I learned this from Caleb. He wrote so much and so frequently. He wrote horrible things, but he wrote incredible things. I guess this is my way to keep Caleb's story alive."

"I never knew he had so much love here."

"Well you never were around. How could you?" Beth snapped.

I wanted to say something, but Jimmy beat me to the punch. "Caleb wasn't around either. I never met the guy, so how can you yell at Colin when Caleb did the same thing."

Beth was about to say something when Drew raised his hand. "We didn't come here to put blame on anyone. We came to celebrate his life." Drew opened a case of beer and passed a beer around. "Colin, do you want to say something?"

"Honestly, I guess I just want to say it's an honor to meet his friends. I know Caleb and I had issues where we couldn't agree with each other, but it makes me relieved knowing he wasn't alone." I paused for a moment because it was all catching up to me. "I regret losing Caleb. I regret so many things that I said, but I think that it makes it easier knowing he wasn't surrounded by hate or misunderstanding. I thank you all for that."

"We heard about you and wanted to meet you. He never spoke ill of you, and he always showed a fondness towards you. He loved you as much as you loved him. Life causes a lot of stumbles, but you figure it out along the way. We're blessed with finally meeting you even when it's under a difficult circumstance," Cameron said.

"Caleb always bringing people together." Drew laughed.

We joined in on the laughter, and I think that it made it all easy in the end. I had his past and present around me. The mysterious Caleb wasn't going to be just another one of the novels I loved to read. It would be my best friend that I would grow to love more.

16

November 25th, 2011

I looked at my outfit in the mirror. It was odd not having Drew there to comment on my date or what I was wearing. Thanks to the fact that no one was around there was some quietness. It was nice that my parents were okay with me staying for Thanksgiving.

I heard a knock on my door. I walked over to open the door to Jack. "You look good." I could see the hunger in his eyes to undress me.

I felt uncomfortable but thrilled to be wanted so badly by someone. "Thanks."

He pulled me into a kiss right there at the door. It was a tender kiss, but it meant so much. He wasn't worried about people catching us. We were finally out of the cage. We could actually be together, and that made me so happy.

"You ready to go?" He asked.

I tried to keep the stupid grin off my face, but it was becoming a problem. I just nodded. He grabbed my hand and towed me back to his room. He opened the door. I saw a bottle of wine, Chinese food, and a stupid rom-con on.

I pulled him in for a kiss. It wasn't anything special, but it was a moment. This guy took time out of his life to do something nice for me. I had always done these things for Sarah and Tracy, but they didn't appreciate me enough.

"What's that for?"

"Just being you." I played with the buttons on his shirt. "No one's ever done that for me." I locked eyes with him. I knew this was it. I could give it all up to Jack, and I didn't mind. He would be my first with a man, and I was okay with that.

He started unbuttoning my shirt. We tossed them to the ground. He guided me to the bed and kissed my lips, neck, and chest before putting me on the bed. He looked at me in the eyes. "Are you sure about this?" He asked.

I saw the concern in his eyes. I touched his face. "I've never been so sure in my life. I love you." I never meant to tell him, and it might have stupid to say it only three months into the relationship, but I truly felt it with him.

He captured my lips with his. "I love you too." He didn't give me any other words, and I don't think I needed more from him. It was all I needed to fill my chest and make me feel so alive.

He stripped every part of me, and I needed him to. I was truly naked in front of this man, and I wanted to open my soul up to him. We weren't just doing the physical act of fucking. We were making love. We were becoming one. I knew we were surrounded by complications, but not in that moment.

We could be who we were meant to be. No one was going to judge or punish us. The world revolved around us in this moment. He was slow and soft with me. Every thrust was brought with a gentle kiss to my head. I felt my heart open and pour out right in front of him.

I didn't care how quick it was because I would relive every moment in my mind. He pulled me close to him and kissed me again on the lips. I just stroked his face until he fell asleep. I continued to look at the man in front of me because he took everything from me. I just gave this incredible being my soul, and I never wanted it back.

17

December 19th, 2011

"Sorry, you can't come with me to our friend's Christmas party." I kissed Jack on the lips. We were getting changed.

He shrugged it off. "Don't worry we already had our Christmas." He kissed me again. "Over and Over again."

I laughed and pushed him off of me. I knew I was going to be late. "I better get going. They're going to think something's wrong."

We gave each other a chaste kiss. We didn't want to make a big deal that we wouldn't see each other for a couple of weeks. He was going back to California for the Holidays, while I was finally going home for the first time. "I'll see you when you get back." He winked.

"I can't wait. I love you."

"Love you too." He gave me another kiss before I walked out of his dorm.

Drew was walking down the hall when I exited Jack's dorm. "There you are. We were pretty worried you got lost."

I rolled my eyes. "Sorry, I was checking with RA Jack what we needed to do before we left."

He chuckled. "Just trying to be a good little tenant."

I hit him in the arm. "Shut up. Let's go." It had become a constant lie. Drew had his suspicions that we were hooking up, but I told him that I still was with the mystery guy. It was nice to know that my friends didn't care. They just wanted me to be happy.

We walked to Mitch's apartment where he was having the radio Christmas party. People were already drinking and in the middle of the conversation. I saw Cameron, Beth, and Shawn talking to each other.

Cameron looked up to see Drew and I walking in. "Finally. We thought you two had finally forgot about us." She walked over and kissed Drew on the lips. It was easy and carefree. I was looking forward to doing that with Jack. I wanted to stop feeling like I was in a cage. I got a taste of freedom, and I craved more.

Beth rolled her eyes. "God, I hate you two. You're both revolting."

"Are you jealous?" Drew raised an eyebrow.

It was odd that Drew and Beth had sex for a couple of weeks. It wasn't awkward, and there weren't any feelings. They always laugh it off. "Not the slightest. I'm going to go see if Mitch has anything stronger. I can't deal with you two." She walked away.

Shawn stood beside me laughing. "That's code for having sex with Mitch."

I turned to him. "You knew."

"We all do. We can't keep secrets from each other."

Drew turned to us. "That's not true. None of us know who Caleb's boyfriend is."

"And you won't."

"It's been months now. Shouldn't we know who has you feeling all lovey dovey?" She asked.

"Not if I'm going to turn into you guys." I didn't like that the subject was on me. I wanted to talk about anything other than the fact that I was dating our RA.

"Don't worry. They're trying to get me to date horrible guys in my English classes." It was nice to know that Shawn had gotten over his crush for me. We had become good friends and decided to take some classes next semester together.

"Are you planning on doing any writing this break?" I asked. I could see Drew and Cameron were bored of our conversation.

"I hope so. I want to finish this novel I've been working on. How about you?"

"I think going back to my demons will give me some inspiration." It would be the first time that I see Colin. I didn't know how I felt about it. I knew that we would probably fight, scream, and make-up. Maybe it would make things less complicated.

"I think that's the best way to move forward is getting rid of the problems holding you down."

I smiled. "I agree with you."

We couldn't continue our conversation because Johnny was stumbling around holding up a mistletoe. "Let's get some good kisses, shall we?"

He walked in front of Shawn and I. "Let's see it boys."

I was hesitant. I had a boyfriend. I couldn't cheat on him like this. Shawn saw my reservations. He leaned forward and kissed me on the cheek. I cared for Shawn more and more because he respected my boundaries. He understood me, and not a lot of people have done that for me in a long time.

"That was boring." Johnny walked away.

"Thanks." I smiled.

Shawn shrugged. "You would have done the same for me. Hopefully, we will get to meet your boyfriend soon, and you won't be put in this awkward situation." He gave me a weak smile and walked away. I had to agree with him. I just wanted to be in public with Jack. I wanted be proud to have him around my arm. Only a couple months left.

December 27th, 2011
I stood in front of the tree house that I shared with Colin for so many years. I guess we would never get the chance to resolve our issues.

This is where our friendship began, and it seems this is where it would end.

I thought I would get to see him while I was home, but it turns out he had other plans. I was an idiot to think that he would actually come here. I climbed up the tree and sat down. The years have done wonders to this place.

I saw the snow start to fall. It would blanket the land, and it would give it a sense of purity. I knew that I wasn't pure in the eyes of the Lord. I've been told over and over again that I was sinning.

I didn't think kissing and loving Jack would be so wrong. I just had too many complications in my life, and I just didn't know who else to call. My two closest friends were nowhere to be seen. I guess a cruise with the family was more important. I was left behind once again.

I picked up my phone and called the only person I wanted to hear from. It was so stupid that my only source of happiness was him. Sure, it was nice because he gave me what I've always wanted. "Hey."

"Hey, I'm surprised you called. I figured you would be with your hometown friends." Jack sounded happy to hear from me.

"Colin went with his girlfriend on a family cruise. They brought his aunt along too."

"I'm sorry to hear that. What are you doing?"

"In my childhood tree house watching the snow fall."

"That must be fun."

"It's extremely lonely."

"Wish I was there with you to warm you up."

It brought a smile to my face and heart. "Me too."

"Only a couple of months."

"Only a couple of months."

I heard voices on the other end. "I better get back to my family. I love you, and I'll talk to you later."

"Love you too and have fun."

I ended the called and wrapped my arms around my knees. I rested my chin on my knees and watched the snowfall. "Only a couple of months." I wouldn't have to be alone anymore. I would be loved, right?

18

January 5th, 2012

"You're back!" Drew said as he walked into the dorm.

I turned to smile at him. "Yeah, I was just ready to leave." Drew opened his arms to me, and I needed that.

"It's been quiet around here without you." I had to admit that Drew was the perfect roommate. I didn't know how much of my life had welcomed him.

He plopped down on the bed. "So how was home?" He asked.

"It was fine." I turned my back to him.

"Caleb, tell me the truth. I know when you're bullshitting me."

I sighed and turned around. "It sucked. I mean I loved seeing my parents and family, but Colin and Colby weren't there. I guess a part of me was hoping to fix things with them."

"Have you talked?" Drew asked.

The sad reality is we really hadn't. I'd got so caught up with my friends and Jack that I guess I forgot about him. Maybe this is what was going to happen when we go to two different places. I knew that I wasn't fully at fault. He was going out to parties with some heavier-set guy. I assumed we replaced each other.

"Not really. We've both been busy I guess."

"Do you miss him?"

"He was my best friend growing up. Of course, I miss him. Did you see your childhood friends?"

Drew got off the bed. "Yeah, it was nice reconnecting, but I'm happier here. It made me realize going home that I didn't fit in there. They all had secret jokes and moments that I wasn't a part of. I tried to bring up you guys, but there wasn't a point. We just disconnected."

"Aren't you sad?"

"Not really, it's what happens when you go off to college. I'll always have a special place in my heart for them. We will still be close, but there will be that disconnect from now on."

I truly understood what it meant to move forward with your life. I had changed since moving, and I thought we could keep it the same. I had a group of friends here that I didn't need to worry if I was replaceable with. We struggled together, and I needed that. Colin had his own thing going on. Maybe it was better this way.

"I guess you're right. I just didn't think it would happen to me."

"You're a writer. Do your characters always stay the same after a huge moment?"

"No, because it wouldn't make the character seem real."

"I guess you have your answer as to why we change."

January 11th, 2012

I knew seeing Jack would be different. He was finally getting back after being in California for the holidays. Almost three weeks apart, and I was about to lose it. Sure, we texted and called, but it didn't feel right like cuddling or kissing.

"Why are you so jumpy?" Drew asked. We were waiting for Jack for a floor meeting.

I shrugged. "I'm just ready to get this over with."

"Uh huh." I knew he didn't believe me, nor did I care.

Jack walked in with another guy. He was lanky, with red hair, and a tattoo on his left arm. "Welcome back. I hope you all had a good break. I'm going to keep this short. This is our new RA Ryan." Everyone gave him a hello.

I felt something in my bones that made me not want to get along with him. He turned and winked at Jack. Jack laughed and blushed. "I hope you all give me a warm welcoming like Jack has. It's been a pleasure, and I can't wait to get to know you guys further."

I could tell that Jack hung on every word that Ryan had said. It wasn't fair. This was my guy, and a stranger was taking him away from me. Drew leaned in. "Looks like Jack has a little crush on the new RA."

"I guess so." I tried to keep the defeat out of my voice, but I just couldn't do it.

Jack dismissed everyone and walked up to me personally. "How was your break?" He asked with a smile.

I couldn't smile for him. "Do you care? Don't you have a new boyfriend to flirt with shamelessly in front of me." I whispered so no one else could hear. I walked away from him because I just couldn't be around him. I was a fool to believe that I was something to him. I was an idiot to believe that we could actually be more than a secret behind closed doors.

19

"How goes the reading?" Colby asked as she walked over and kissed me on the lips.

"It's going. I'm starting to hate this Jack guy."

"Why's that?"

"Jack is playing games with him. He doesn't deserve it."

She raised an eyebrow. "What else is going on?"

I sighed and looked away from her. "We abandoned him. He came back that first winter break to make amends."

"When we went to the Caribbean?"

"Yeah."

"How were you supposed to know?"

"I should have. He was my best friend. I knew him inside and out. I should have figured out that he wanted to make amends with me before everything went to shit."

She cupped my face in her hands. "Colin, you had no clue what was going to happen. How could you be at fault?"

"I left him like everyone else."

"Who else left him?" She asked.

"I just..."

"Stop blaming yourself for everything." She stood up. "You can beat yourself up only so much. You made mistakes, and so did he. We came here to figure out what happened, not for you to throw yourself a self-pity party."

"But."

"No, 'but's.' Stop fucking blaming yourself. He chose his actions all on his own."

"How would you know?"

She looked hesitant to tell me. I was worried that she was keeping something from it. I felt it when she was talking to Drew. "I've been reading the journals."

I stood up and looked at her. "What?"

"He was my best friend too. I have a right to know what happens."

"That doesn't mean you go behind my back without me."

"You're keeping all of this from us. You can't do that. We're here to help you. When are you going to figure that out?"

"I'll tell you all you need to know. He kept these for me. This was our friendship, not yours."

She threw her hands in the air. "That's the problem. It was always just you and him. I was just the third wheel." She walked towards the door. She turned around. "I felt like I didn't get your love until we went to college."

"Colby, you know how much I love you."

"It was all words back then."

I stepped closer to her. I tried to touch her hand. "I'm sorry."

"I know that, but you can't make this your whole life again. I feel like I'm being put on the back burner again."

I pulled Colby in close and kissed her. "I would never let that happen. I love you too much."

She wrapped her arms around my waist and deepened the kiss. It was a quick kiss, but it gave us an understanding. "I already lost one person."

I understood where she was coming from. "I know. You won't. I'm almost done with part one."

"Have you figured out part two?"

I shook my head. "The password is his favorite poem."

"That's going to be tricky."

"I just hope it comes up soon or this will be the end of the road."

"I'm going to get us breakfast. Drew wants us to see the apartment, and he's going to take us out tonight."

I nodded. "Thanks. I'll read for a couple more hours."

"All right then." She walked out of the room. She had to take a backseat. I came here to heal my wounds with Caleb, not her.

20

January 14th, 2012

I knew who was banging on my door. I ignored it. I couldn't let him win. He was the reason that I've been crying the past couple of days. He's the reason that Drew and my friends have been worried about me. He doesn't care about me. I'm just someone he can toss to the side.

"Caleb, open the door before I use my own key." He threatened.

Why couldn't he just leave it be? Why was he fighting for me? I'm nobody. I sighed and got up. I walked over to the door in defeat and opened it up. "What?"

Jack looked distraught. He looked like he hadn't slept, and I saw the sadness in his eyes. "Can I talk to you?"

Why couldn't I just say fuck it and let it go? I moved to the side to let him in. "You have to be quick. Drew went to grab us food."

He closed the door. He grabbed my hand and pulled me into a kiss. I hadn't expect that, but I missed his lips with mine. It was filled with regret and sadness. I wanted to stay mad at him, but this felt right. This is what I've been hoping for since I got back a little over a week ago.

I deepened the kiss. I felt whole with his lips on mine. I broke the kiss. "This doesn't fix anything."

I saw the smug expression on his face. "I'm sorry that I flirted in front of you with our new RA. I was trying to be friendly."

"Do you know how bad that made me feel? I felt like I was just a cheap fuck you keep in the back of your closet."

He pulled me into a hug. I didn't know why that caused me to cry. "I never want you to feel like that. I know I fucked up, but I'm trying here. I just want it to be the end of the semester."

I turned and looked up at him. "Really?"

He gave me a reassuring smile. "Caleb, I wasn't lying when I told you that I loved you. I want this to work. I just can't standing hiding you anymore."

I knew I was pushing him away. I've got too many scars on my heart. I needed to realize he was one of the good ones. "Me either."

We couldn't finish the conversation because we heard Drew coming in. We separate, and I wiped the tears from my eyes. Drew walked into to see us standing there. "Hey, Jack. Did you come to see if our little boy was doing okay?"

I rolled my eyes. Jack laughed. "Yeah, I've noticed he hasn't been the same, and I came to check on him." He turned to him. "I hoped the talk helped."

I smiled. "It did."

"Well I better get back to my room. I have to be at the desk in a half an hour. See you guys around." He walked past Drew and out of the room.

"I hope he helped you fix those problems with your asshole boyfriend. I think you should dump him and go after RA Jack."

I was thinking about Jack and what he said to me. I blinked and turned to Drew. I got the tail end of what he was saying. "What?"

"He seems to like you. I think next year you should go after him."

"I don't think I have a chance."

"You never know." Only a couple more months until we could be open to the world. I was going to finally be with Jack, and no one could take that away from me.

February 14th, 2012
"Holy shit. Holy shit. Holy shit." I was pacing back and forth in my dorm.

"You're going to be fine."

I looked at Drew. "You don't know that. It could turn into a huge mess. We finally solved our shit, and now we're going on our first Valentine's date."

Drew rolled his eyes. "I think you deserve better."

"Drew, he makes me happy. Yeah, we've had problems, but we got through them." I just needed him to believe me that it would all work out.

"Fine, but I don't want him breaking your heart. You'll have a good time."

"What are you doing?" I asked.

"Seeing a movie with Cameron."

"Oh lala."

He threw a pillow at me. "Have fun freaking out. I'll see you later." He waved and walked out of the room.

I felt my phone go off, and it was Jack telling me to meet him downstairs. He brought his car back from California, and we were going somewhere for our date. I walked downstairs and walked into the ally between our buildings.

He greeted me with a kiss and a smile. "You ready for our date."

I couldn't help giggling like a schoolgirl. "Yeah."

He grabbed my hand and we drove off. I didn't know where we were driving because all I could focus on was the moonlight shine off his face. It was so beautiful and it revealed his imperfections. He had a series of freckles that I've never really noticed. His nose was a bit bigger than I thought. He had a scar on his right eye. He might have had all these flaws, but they were beautiful to me.

"It's kind of creepy you staring at me."

I blushed and looked away from him. "Sorry."

He rubbed my hand with his thumb and laughed. "I think it's cute."

I saw that we were going out of the city limits towards the lake. "Where are we going?" I asked.

"You'll see." He winked.

We didn't talk until we went up a dirt road and stopped in front of a series of steps that led to the beach. "We're going to the beach?" I asked.

He walked over and kissed me on the lips. This time he didn't rush or move forward with it. He just kissed me the way a person wants to be kissed. I felt the love and yearning he had for me.

"This is my favorite spot in the whole world. This is my gift to you. I want to give you a piece of my heart." He grabbed my hand and towed me towards the beach. We took off our shoes and walked hand and hand to the water. It was still February in South Carolina. It was warm but not warm enough. I knew in Virginia it was still snowing.

He wrapped two blankets around me while I had a sweater on. He laid another blanket down for us to sit down on. "Are you going to come share these blankets with me?" I opened my arms for him.

He willingly came into my arms and it felt nice to feel his body heat. I rested my head on his shoulder and closed my eyes.

I listened to his breathing and the crashing of the water on the beach. It was peaceful and what I wanted.

"Thank you for giving me a piece of your heart."

"I found this place last year when I was lost, and I had no clue what I was doing with my life. It gave me a sense of clarity. You're the first person that I've brought here."

I raised my head and looked at him. "Why?"

"Because you're the first person I've truly fallen in love with. I thought you were going to be some stupid little fling, but you took my heart."

I wanted to cry and kiss him right then, but I needed to give him my gift. I had been working on it for a couple of days now. I didn't know how to finish it until now. "I need to give you my gift."

"What is it?" He asked.

I pulled a little piece of paper from my pocket. It's the piece of my heart I want to give to you."

We'll be rebels of love
We won't let people take what we have
We will have our ups and down
But when I look into your eyes
I know my heart is in the right hands

I can't handle not kissing you
I can't handle being caged up
When all I want to do
Is show the world my love for you

But this world won't understand us
The world won't appreciate our love
But you're the one I'm walking through this with
We'll be rebels of love

I didn't know if it was all worth it
But when I look into your eyes
In the midnight sky
I know my heart is in the right hands

He didn't say anything when I finished the poem. He pulled me into a kiss, and I guess that's all I needed because I felt the tears streaming from his face. "Thank you for loving me the way you have."

"Thank you for giving me the chance to know what love really is." I closed my eyes and pulled him closer. We had our own complications, but we would get through it. We would be able to out of this cage soon enough.

21

March 7th, 2012

"When are we going to meet your boyfriend?" Beth asked while we were in the radio station drinking.

"Soon guys." It was going to be next week. Jack was going to tell them that he didn't want to be an RA next year. We could finally come out as a couple.

"I don't think he's real." Drew grabbed a slice of pizza.

I threw my crust at his face. "Please, you're just excited to find out who it is."

"It's very romantic. I love the idea of Romeo and Juliet." Cameron gushed.

Drew pulled Cameron close to him. He kissed her on the head. "I can be romantic."

Beth snorted. "Yeah, right. I don't think there is a romantic bone in your body."

Drew looked at me for support. I shrugged. "I hate to say, but she is right."

"Traitors, all of you."

We all laughed while Cameron kissed Drew on the lips. "It's okay that you won't give me a white horse or a fairy tale. I don't need any of that. I just need you."

Beth rolled her eyes. "That's disgusting." She got up. "I'm going to grab more beer. I can't see that anymore." She didn't have any jealousy in her voice.

Shawn scooted closer to me. "Are you nervous?" He asked.

I turned to him. "About what?"

"People finding out who your boyfriend is."

"I'm more relieved. I don't have to worry about us getting caught. I think it will be nice to not feel like the skeleton in the closet."

"You want to be wanted." Shawn grabbed my hand and squeezed it. "You're an amazing guy. You should be with someone that's equally as great."

I turned to him. "It would be easier with you. You get me, and we have so much in common."

Shawn shrugged. "We would be perfect together on paper, but nothing that's perfect on paper works out in reality. It's a sad life we live in." Shawn got up. He turned to look at Drew and Cameron who were kissing. "No one thought they would work. It should have been with Beth."

"What if it's wrong on paper? Does that mean I'm destined to fail?" I never wanted things with Jack to get to the point where we would be ruined. I loved him and the thought of losing him killed me.

"It's a bigger risk. As long as you respect each other, then I don't see it going anywhere wrong."

"I think we respect each other." I thought back to when Jack flirted with RA Ryan.

"You don't sound so sure," Shawn said.

I shook my head. "We respect each other. He loves me, and I love him. We know that our relationship is strong, and we discuss things together." I didn't know why I was defending my relationship.

"I just want someone to love you."

"Shawn, you'll find someone incredible."

"I did, but I'm waiting until he feels the same." He walked out of the room.

I turned to look at Drew and Cameron. I hoped RA Jack and I could finally have it. I wasn't so sure it would work out. We've had too many complications, and I was afraid there wasn't going to be hope for us.

March 14th, 2012
"What do you mean you're doing another year?" I screamed in Jack's room.

He raised his hands. "Can you keep it down?"

"Why should I? You worried that people are going to find out about your dirty little secret. I'm just a quick fuck." I was shaking, and I tried so hard not to cry. I wasn't going to waste my tears on him.

"The program is really good, Caleb. My parents can't afford all of my college, and I need this to help me."

"But what about us?"

He shrugged. "I don't know."

"This year has been torture. Do you get that? I've been praying that we could actually be together."

"I know."

"And you ruined that. I loved you. You were my first, and it's all gone to shit."

Jack tried to grab my hand. "Don't say that."

I backed away from him. "Don't you dare. How could you do this to me?"

"To you? Do you think I wanted to hurt you purposely? I had dreams and goals before you came into my life. I almost threw that all away to be with you. I'm sorry I don't come from a rich family."

"What's the supposed to mean?"

"I have three other siblings. All four of us had to figure a way to get through college on our own. This is how I'm doing it. You can't hate me for that."

"I don't hate you for getting an education. I hate you for making me believe that we could actually be something more than a relationship behind closed doors."

"Do you believe that?"

"I know that. I love you, but I can't do this anymore." I stopped myself because I needed to catch my breath. I couldn't be just someone's skeleton. I thought back to what Shawn had said. I needed to be respected.

"Don't." He pleaded with me, and it killed me to see the pain in his eyes.

I touched his face. "We had a great relationship. It was near perfect, but I can't be with someone who doesn't respect me."

"How am I not respecting you?"

"We've been together for so long, and you didn't discuss this with me. You just did it. I was looking forward to our future. We were going to be an actual couple, not one of dreams. We had everything going for us, but we won't work out. I always thought you saw me as your equal."

"You're making this a bigger deal than it actual is."

"Am I? Why didn't you ask me my opinion?"

"Because I didn't have to struggle about this. I knew I was going to do it when they offered it to me."

"Even though it would kill me that we would have to keep it behind closed doors for another year."

"I didn't make this decision because it would hurt you. I did this for myself."

"You still don't get it. I would have supported you. You put me back in that fucking cage, and you didn't give me an option. You forced me in there."

"Stop acting like I'm trying to attack you."

"Stop acting like I don't care."

"We can make this work."

I shook my head. "I care about myself too much to give myself false hope. I love you so much, but you went behind my back. You didn't ask me what I thought. That's the problem."

"I'm sorry."

"The damage is done."

I didn't give him a chance to respond. I grabbed my things and walked out the door. I had to keep it together until I got back to my dorm. I opened my door and I saw the worry in Drew's eyes. I just ran into his arms and let it all out. I wasn't crying about the break up. I was crying about what could have been. We would have had a beautiful relationship and a happy life together, but things don't work out as we want them to. It's what killed me most of all.

22

I looked at the last journal entry of the first part. His first big love had come to fail him. I never felt that pain before. Sure, Colby and I broke up junior year, but I knew we would be back together. She was the woman I was meant to be with. He never had that hope.

Colby walked into the room and kissed me on the lips. "What's wrong?" She asked.

"They broke up. Jack isn't the person."

She gave me sympathetic eyes. "Did you think he was?"

"I don't know. I just thought he would bring me some kind of answers. I'm stuck with no answers and no clue what the password to the second part could be."

She sat on the bed. "Have you asked Jimmy?"

"He said that he could do it," I said.

"Why don't you ask him?" She asked.

"Because he needs to figure this out on his own. He needs to know what his best friend wanted. It would be cutting corners. I know he would regret it in the end." Jimmy walked in and sat down on the bed eating a Slim Jim.

"Where did you get that?" I asked.

"While you were reading, and this one was looking at herself in the mirror."

Colby turned to him. "I don't look at myself in the mirror."

Jimmy laughed. "Yeah, keep telling yourself that, sweetheart."

She rolled her eyes. "Whatever. I got a call from Drew while you were reading. He wants us to come over and see his place."

"Why?" I didn't need to see Drew's place. I had no desire to be reminded that's where his friendship with my best friend bloomed.

"He thought it would help with Caleb." She got up. "It might help you figure out the second clue."

"Nothing in that fucking apartment is going to help me." I stood up. I didn't need everyone helping me. I just wanted to do this on my own. This was supposed to be my journey, not everyone else's." I stormed out of the room without talking to anyone.

I walked to my car and grabbed a pack of cigarettes I kept in there. I knew that Colby hated them, but I just needed to get some kind of stress out of my body. I light one and inhaled.

I saw Jimmy walk out of the hotel lobby. He walked over to me with a somber expression. "Colby is currently crying in the hotel room. You did a bang up job."

"Fuck you, Jimmy." I took another drag.

He put out his hand. I handed him the pack of cigarettes. He took one. "Remember when we first started smoking?"

"It was during finals week. It was this or drink."

"We didn't want to feel like shit taking our finals and forget everything we studied for." I paused and looked at the fog that was rolling in. "When did our lives become complicated?"

"What do you mean?"

"We used to have to just stress about grades, parties, and our future. Now, we're worried about who killed my childhood best friend."

"It's not my life, it's yours." He gave me an evil grin.

"You don't have to be here."

He clapped me on the shoulder. "You've been there enough for me. If I recall you had a bottle of Jack Daniels ready for me when my mom got cancer, and you were there with another bottle when she went into remission. We're there to support each other."

"I just don't want to go to that apartment. I don't want to think about how he..." I didn't finish the sentence. I knew it was a stupid reason anyways.

"Hey, you don't need to explain anything to me. You might need to go apologize to your girlfriend. She's only trying to help. Stop being an asshole."

"How else am I supposed to deal?"

"You've already lost one person, do you want to lose another?"

"No."

"Colby has been extremely understanding. She is as eager as you to figure out what happened. You think you're the only person who has issues. I don't even know the guy, but I'm wondering how everything went down. Stop being such a fucking dick and let people in."

It was the most that I had ever heard Jimmy scream at me. Sure, we've had our share of fights about roommate drama, but this was real life. He was calling me out, and I needed that.

"I'll go talk to her."

Jimmy smiled. "Good. I'll wait out here because I know you two will want some alone time." He raised an eyebrow.

"I really hate you." I laughed, and it was a nice touch to our conversation. I couldn't deal with what was going on, and I just needed a fucking drink.

I walked into the hotel room to Colby sitting on the bed crying. "I'm an asshole."

She turned and looked up at me. "Yeah, you are. You need to stop pushing people away. I get that he was your best friend. I get you think you have all this guilt, but we're in this together." She stood up.

"I'm just frustrated. I thought I would be able to figure out what the name of the goddamn poem was."

She kissed me on the lips and it made me feel at ease. She always knew how to bring me back to what was going on. "We need a night out."

"Do you think drinking will help?"

"I don't see how it could hurt. We've been so focused on finding out about his death we forgot about our own lives. I need a drunk Colin and fast."

"I would love to see Jimmy throw up everywhere."

"Should we invite Drew, Cameron, Beth, and Shawn?"

I knew that it was painful to see them and have them talk about the Caleb I didn't know, but it helped me feel like Caleb was there. "Yeah, I would like that." I kissed her on the lips. "Let's do it. We all need a night out. We all need to realize that we're still young."

23

"Is he going to be okay?" Shawn asked.

I turned to see Jimmy chug his second pitcher of the night. Jimmy was known for how much he consumes alcohol. I heard Colby chuckle next to me. "He's going to be fine. He drinks like this all the time."

I saw the sheer horror on Beth's face. "That just seems tragic. He might need a liver transplant."

"We tried to start a fund for him. We did get four hundred bucks for it," Colby said.

"Then we ended up using it on alcohol." I laughed at our sophomore year.

"Thank you for inviting us out with you." Drew sipped his beer.

"It seems pretty packed." I noticed there were people everywhere. I felt like an outsider.

"It's nice though. This was Caleb's favorite bar." Cameron passed around shots. "He loved that you could sit and talk to your friends or go dancing."

I finished my beer. We would always miss the plans for our twenty-first. We would never share a beer at the bar. I don't know why those moments really mattered. It was just a birthday and a beer.

"I guess I'll never see a legal-drunk Caleb."

"I'm sorry." I saw the guilt on Cameron's face.

"I wouldn't worry about it." I didn't want this girl to be stressed about her words in front of me. I knew that it was probably me. I was the one that was turning it back to how I would never get a chance to do so many things with Caleb.

"We came out to drink. He would have loved it, and I need a good ole fashion hangover tomorrow." She grabbed her shot.

We toasted to a good night and forgetting about our issue. Isn't that the point of alcohol? Colby grabbed my hand and towed me to the dance floor. We danced for hours taking breaks for shots and beers. I felt the buzz, and it was the first time that I actually seemed to enjoy myself in a long time.

Drew was dancing with Cameron next to us. Beth was getting into a debate with a guy she said she was friends with. I stumbled over to Shawn to ask him to dance with us. I didn't like how he was alone. "Come dance?" I asked.

He shook his head. "You don't really know me yet. I actually love being a wallflower."

"Why?"

"Because I'm a writer. I'm an observer. I enjoy watching my friends living in the moment because it's inspiration for my poetry and writing."

"Shouldn't you have that for yourself?" I asked.

"Sometimes, it's good to take the backseat. I've done so many crazy things in my life. The past four years, my friends have pushed me outside my box. I like to take these moments to relish them. I enjoy knowing how far I've come with amazing people."

I thought sitting on the sidelines was depressing. He should be able to enjoy his moments with his friends. I never saw the other side of the coin. "That's beautiful."

Shawn smiled. "I'm enjoying myself being here watching you guys. I can tell why Caleb loved you. You have his heart."

It was interesting because people told me that so many times. People thought that I loved like him, and I gave everything to everyone. I never understood that because love from Caleb was a beautiful occurrence. "Thank you."

Shawn smiled. "I have a poetry reading tomorrow. I think you should come."

"Why's that?"

"Because it will be like Caleb being there. We are half of him, and you are the other."

"I'll be there." I smiled and walked back to dancing with Colby. Shawn was becoming my favorite of the group. He was soft spoken, but his words could help a lot of people.

We continued to dance until Drew tapped me on the shoulder. I turned around to see him. "What's up?"

"You want to meet someone who destroyed your friend's heart?" He asked.

"Who?"

"RA Jack." Drew said with so much venom in his voice. I looked up to see who Drew was looking at. I saw Jack. He didn't have his long blonde hair. It was actually short. I saw the freckles and the imperfect nose. He looked older and was hand-in-hand with another guy. He seemed happy and confident to show off his love for someone.

"That's him?"

"Yup. I can't believe he's still here. Fuck him." He turned around and walked away from me. I could see he was upset, but I wanted to speak to him.

"Colby, I'll be right back. I have someone I need to talk to." I kissed her on the cheek.

"Okay, I'll go save Jimmy from hitting on those girls."

I walked up to Jack after he said his goodbyes to his boyfriend. "Are you RA Jack?" I asked.

He raised an eyebrow. "Do I know you?"

"No, but you know my best friend Caleb Moore."

Jack's smile went away. "You're Colin Wilson?"

"How did you know?"

"I've seen pictures and heard stories. It's finally nice to put a face to the name. I wish I got to know you when we were dating."

"You aren't ashamed of it, are you?"

"I guess Caleb has a different version of it all. I never was ashamed of him. I loved him with all of my heart, and it kills me that we broke up. He just dumped me without letting me explain myself. He didn't get that I was doing this to further myself in life. I knew it was hard on us, but I couldn't just give up the opportunity."

"Did you ever explain that to him?"

"I tried once." He paused. He didn't know how to say the right words. "He was an incredible soul, and he was the first and only guy I've ever opened up like that with. It destroyed me to hear he passed, but we lost touch years ago."

"Wouldn't you want to know how he's doing?"

"I learned that sometimes people just belong in the past. You will always have nice memories, but we just didn't work out anymore. I'll always have a special place in my heart for him. Why are you here, if you don't mind me asking?"

"I'm trying to figure out what happened the past four years of his life."

Jack smiled. "Well I'm just year one. I never knew what happened to him after that summer. I know he held a lot of guilt for your friendship ending. Did you ever make up?"

I shook my head. "No, I think it got worse over the years."

He smiled weakly. "I'm sad to hear that. Well I better get back to my boyfriend. It was good to finally meet you. Caleb loved you. I remembered he always had you on such a high pedestal. I wish you guys had made amends before his death." He walked away.

"Me too."

24

"I don't even know why we're here," Jimmy said.

"Because Shawn wanted us here. Stop being an asshole and enjoy." Colby looked like she was ready to punch him in the face.

We were at a small little coffee shop. Drew and his friends were front row while we were in the back.

"I want to know what he's going to read," I said.

"Maybe he'll do something for Caleb."

I stiffened. "I hope not."

Colby rubbed my hand. "I know."

I turned and kissed her on the lips. "Thank you."

"If I hadn't been puking this morning, I would vomit all over you guys."

I rolled my eyes. "Next time don't chug three pitchers of beer."

"It was light beer. It was fine."

"Not for our toilet." Colby mumbled.

I couldn't contain my laughter. This was easy, and it was what I needed. This is what I missed before Caleb's death.

The lights dimmed and there was a center spotlight on the stage. Shawn walked on stage. I could see he was a ball of nerves.

I saw that he felt reassured with his friends there. I was only there because of Caleb. Why did I want to root for Shawn? Why did I love the idea of Drew and Cameron? Why did I want to listen to Beth's crazy ideas? We weren't friends, nor were we ever going to be.

Shawn waved. "Thank you guys for coming out." He stumbled out his words.

"I know that I usually don't do these things. It's funny because a special guy in my life told me that I should get my words out there. He told me over and over again how special my words were, and how I could change so many people's lives. I guess that's why we were so close."

He wiped a tear from his eye. "He was taken away from us too soon, but he said that he wasn't surprised. He was meant to live this short spectacular life. I loved that about Caleb. He didn't believe that we should look at the negative even when he was alone and scared in the world. I truly loved him."

He took a deep breath. "I'm going to read the poem that he said was his favorite of mine. I just laughed it up, until now. Even though I wrote this poem, it felt like his. It felt like he was in my mind trying to teach me a lesson. I love you, Caleb. I loved you the moment I saw you during our first radio orientation, and I loved you even when you wouldn't have me. Thank you for always being there. Write for me while you're up there."

He opened the paper and started reading the poem. "It's called, 'Be Still and Love.'"

Be still count your blessings
Be still count the times
Your heart has fluttered
For someone so broken
That you love their cracks

Be still and kiss the tears
That were shed because of courage
Be still and love that soul who has captured you
Don't be afraid of the dark
Embrace all good that comes from them

Dance along the line of pain and pleasure
Take a sip of the high life
But don't forget it can all go away
Be still and love

Don't forget the warmth of their arms
Their tender kisses and their laughter
Be still and love
Because it can all go away tomorrow
Like the sun and our souls

Shawn finished the poem. I turned to Colby and gave her every-thing in a kiss. I never wanted her to forget what I felt for her in that moment and forever.

We separated from each other. She touched my face and smiled. "I love you too."

"Thank you everyone," Shawn said.

Colby clapped. "No wonder that was his favorite poem."

"Favorite poem." I repeated because it clicked with me. "That's the second key." I grabbed all my things. "I need to go. I figured it out." Colby looked confused. I gave her a kiss. "I love you. I'll see you later."

I walked out of the coffee shop looking forward to getting back to the hotel room. I had the second clue. I was one step closer to figuring out Caleb's life.

I got home and entered, *Be Still and Love* into the password. It opened the new entries. There was all another letter for me.

Dear Colin,

I see you met my friends from college. I hoped that Shawn would read that poem at the poetry reading. You're probably wondering how I knew about the poetry reading and everything else going on. It seems that's another mystery for you to figure out.

It's a bit of a powerful idea knowing what was going to happen next. I wish we could have drank with my friends while I was alive. I hope they're taking good care of you, like they did for me. I miss you, Colin. I miss all the adventures and memories we could have had. I guess this is better. This is how you can understand who I became. I'm still the person you grew up knowing. I want you to remember that.

Love,
Caleb

25

March 15th, 2011

"Can you please open your door?" I knew it was Jack. I knew he wanted to talk about last night, but I had no desire. I just wanted to completely forget everything he had to say.

"No, I don't see what we need to talk about."

I heard the door open. I turned to look at him. "That's an invasion of privacy." I yelled.

"I don't care. You're being ridiculous," he said closing the door. "I tell you that I'm staying as an RA, and you're giving up on us. You're going to dump me and think I'm not going to fight you on it."

"What do you want me to say? I've been feeling like a skeleton in the closet this whole relationship. You reaffirmed that by staying an RA."

"It doesn't mean that I stopped loving you. I have to do what's best for me."

"And I'm doing what's best for me."

"Caleb, please." He stepped forward.

I stepped back. "No, you don't get to put on those puppy dog eyes and think I'm going to be okay with you."

"I love you."

"But you don't respect me. I should have seen it all along. It's been written on the walls. That's the issue here. You decided to make a decision without talking to me."

"Let's talk now."

I shook my head. "No, I'm done. I love you with all my heart, but I know where this is going to go. It's a fucking major red flag. You did this without talking to me and then judged me because I don't understand. I get you have to pay your way through college. I get that you don't want to lose your job. I had to fucking do so much for you, and you did nothing for me."

"That's a lie, and you know it. It was my secret too."

"But you still flirted with other guys in front of me."

"I told you that I was sorry for that."

"It doesn't matter because I can't be with you." I laughed. "The sad part is that I'm moving off campus. I'm moving into an apartment next year. We could have been in the open."

"This shouldn't be an issue."

"It wouldn't be if you talked to me."

"Caleb, I want this to work out. Let's work it out."

"I need you to leave, so I can forget you."

"Caleb."

"I think he wants you to leave," Drew said walking into the room.

Jack and I turned. My skin went white. This isn't how I imagined Drew finding out. Jack nodded. "Fine, I'll leave. Caleb, I love you. I get that I messed up, but I want things to work out. I hope they will." He walked passed Drew and out of the room.

"So RA Jack was the mystery guy?" Drew asked.

I nodded. "Yup."

"He's still a dick, and he better let us get away with drinking in our dorm now."

I laughed. "Yeah, I'm his blackmail."

Drew walked over and pulled me into a hug. "I'm glad you dumped him out of respect for yourself."

"Thanks, but it doesn't help with the pain."

"I know, but I'm here when you need me."

I laid my head on his chest wishing it was Jack's. I wanted to fix things with him, but I knew in reality, we couldn't fix it. He didn't respect me or value my opinions. I couldn't be with someone that degraded me like that. I just hoped that I never felt like that with anyone else.

April 2nd, 2011
I had no clue what I was doing with my life. I had no feelings or emotions. I was numb. We only had a couple of weeks left of school, and I felt some comfort in knowing that. I wouldn't have to see Jack anymore. He would just be the first big mistake I made in my life.

I jumped right into studying. I didn't think about anything else. I was going to pull my shit together. I wasn't going to let some stupid boy ruin me. He tried to talk to me, but I ignored him. I blocked his number, and I tried to avoid the front desk as much as I could.

I was staring at the wall when Drew walked in with food for me. I wouldn't eat or sleep if it wasn't for him. It was nice having him know about Jack.

"How are you doing?" He asked.

I knew he was looking at me like I was broken. "I'm fine. I promise. I'm just trying to get through these finals, so I can go home." I packed up my bags.

"Or so you can forget about him?"

I turned to look at Drew. "Why does it still hurt? I'm the one that broke up with him. I'm the reason we aren't together. I could say it was okay, and we could be back together. Why can't I just move on?"

"Because you both have unfinished business. You want to believe that things could work out between you two. It's not fair that you had to go through that alone."

"I just want to stop feeling like shit." I felt the tears falling. I felt like an idiot for spending the past two weeks crying over that asshole.

"Thank god I brought reinforcement."

I raised an eyebrow. He opened the door to Cameron, Beth, and Shawn. They brought pizza and beer. They walked in and hugged me. I felt a swell of pride knowing they were my best friends.

"Guys, I need to get to studying. Thank you, but I can't."

"Bullshit." Beth grabbed my bookbag. "You're going to sit here and watch whatever stupid chick flick that you want to watch. We're going to get drunk and let you cry it out. It's what best friends do."

"Don't you have finals to study for?"

"This is more important to us." Shawn smiled while handing me a beer.

"We want to make sure you're okay. No final or grade matters right now." Cameron gave me a reassuring smile.

"As cliché as that sounds, it's true. We love you, and we're here for each other." Drew added.

"Besides, I want that asshole to come over here and try to write us up. I want to give him a piece of my mind." Beth laughed.

I looked at them. They could have been selfish and focused on their finals. They could have just called or texted to check up on me but instead they were here. They were letting me cry on their shoulders. This is what it means to find your soul-cluster.

May 6th, 2012

Finals were done. My first year of college was over, and I was able to heal. I was going on to my second year of college. I was closing this chapter, and I was hoping to keep this in the past.

I looked at my boxes packed and ready for my next adventure. I was moving into my new apartment the next day with Drew. We decided to stay here during the summer. I was planning on getting an internship at a publication house, while he was going to work.

"We're finally done." Drew threw his notebooks in the trash. "No more tests and exams."

"We still have three years left."

He waved me off. "Don't ruin my vibe right now."

I laughed. "What should we do on our last night?" I asked.

"Don't worry, boys." Cameron was at the door. "We're going on an adventure." She walked over and kissed Drew on the lips. It killed me seeing that sometimes because I couldn't have that with Jack.

"Get a room."

"We might eventually."

I rolled my eyes. "Where are we going? Are Beth and Shawn coming?"

"They're already there. We wanted this to be a surprise to you. We know you've had a bad couple of weeks, but we're going to make it up to you." She winked.

I was nervous walking through the woods. "I think this is a bad idea."

"Shut up. Where is your sense of adventure?" Drew seemed way more excited than I was.

"It was left at the entrance to the woods. Now it's complete concern. We might die out here."

Cameron laughed. "You'll be fine."

It was only a couple more minutes until we got to an entrance. Beth and Shawn had started a bonfire and smiled when we got there. "We were getting worried about you guys," Beth said. We all hugged and sat down around the bonfire.

"Why are we here?" I asked.

"Because we've been through so much together this year. Relationships come and go, but we will always have this. Each other." Shawn explained.

Drew handed me a beer. I looked around at the love around the bonfire, and I had love for them. "Thank you, guys. I came here alone and scared. I felt like I would never find the love I had with Colin and Colby. But in you four, I found something better. You accept me for whom I am. So thank you."

We raised our beers in the air. "Cheers to the first of many years together. We will fight, but we will love each other till the end of time."

We sipped our beers, and I knew that I would have them for life. I was closing my first year of college, and so much had changed. I didn't hide who I was anymore. I embraced it, and I would never be someone's skeleton in a closet ever again.

26

I left Colby sleeping in bed. I walked outside to the fog, and it was drizzling. I took out a pack of cigarettes and lit one up. I didn't know why I needed this to ground me. I didn't know why everything was swimming in my head. I just wanted all my questions to be solved.

"I'm glad you're up," Drew said.

I looked up to see him walking towards me. "Why are you here?" I asked.

"You left quickly last night. I was checking to see how you were doing." He lit his own cigarette.

"I'm a complete mess right now. I have no clue what's going on anymore. I can tell in his writing that he's not the same Caleb."

"He lost a bit of his light after Jack. He felt neglected. I thought it might have been from you, but I don't think it's that anymore."

I took a heavy drag. "It could be from the fact that he never knew his real father." Caleb had always kept that under wraps except the night he found out. They thought he should know before he went off the college.

Drew stared at me. "What?"

"His father left right when he was born. His mom said that he saw Caleb, realized he couldn't do it, and bolted. He sent money to help with college but never tried to contact Caleb."

Drew looked away from me. "He never told me that."

"He doesn't really talk about it. It hasn't been mentioned in the entries either. He talks about being alone, but I just assumed it was from me."

Drew gave out a broken laugh. "Daddy issues. It explains everything."

"What?"

"He did date his creative writing professor. I joked that he had daddy issues, but he quickly went quiet."

"The professor?" I wanted to know who this man was.

"It started sophomore year and ended junior year. They were close. He was like a mentor to him. You haven't gotten to him yet?"

"No, I'm at your first summer."

I noticed that Drew stiffened. "That was hard on us. We had never disagreed, but he went down a dark path. I've never seen that side of him. Jack broke him, but the professor destroyed him. It took a lot to bring him back."

I saw the pain in his eyes. Caleb was always put together for me, minus the nights he found out about his father and our fight. Caleb always wanted people to come to him with their problems, not the other way around. "I never knew about that."

"You know Caleb. He keeps it all in."

I looked up at the sky. "Why couldn't he just come to me sooner?"

"He was stubborn. He didn't want anyone's advice. During his downhill spiral he even said we were all fools to believe that we could actually care for each other."

"That's pretty fucked up."

"Like I said, Caleb changed. He became dark and cynical. He hurt a lot of people."

"Why did you stay friends with him?"

"After years of friendship, we knew that it was a cry for help."

"Did he ever get better?"

Drew sighed. "I thought he did until that final week. Caleb kept secrets from us. We didn't even know about Jack until after they broke up and then kept another relationship from us until it was killing him. We had no clue who took and destroyed his heart."

"He kept it all from you guys?"

Drew nodded. "We pressured him, but he said he could take care of himself."

"Did you ever follow him?"

Drew shook his head. "We wanted to give him his space. We weren't going to do that to him and ruin his trust."

"Bullshit. You knew something was wrong. You should have fucking followed him."

"You weren't here. You don't get a fucking say. You abandoned him long before we did. We were his friends. What were you? Another fucking reminder of how he wasn't loved. This could be all blamed on you." Drew snapped at me.

It was quiet for a minute. We looked at each other. "You don't think I know that?" I asked in a broken whisper. "I knew how much he wanted to be accepted and loved. I still left. Now, he's dead."

"I didn't pressure him enough. I thought he could figure it out all on his own. I knew he was going down this dark path, but I still believed he could do it on his own. I watched him fall to pieces in front of me, and I didn't do enough. Now, he's dead."

We confessed our sins to each other, but it didn't fix anything. I looked at Drew, and I understood him in this. He lost his best friend, and he was here to watch it happen. I left long before Caleb changed. I don't know if we could have done anything different to change the past.

27

June 6th, 2012

"What's that?" I asked looking at the package Drew handed me.

"It's your fake ID. We're going out."

I looked up at him. "What?"

"We're going out. You're twenty-two, and you're legal now." He walked out of my room into his.

I followed him. "You can't be serious." I pulled the ID out of the package. It had all the right information minus the year had been changed to 90.

He put on a dark V-neck. "Come on. We can't spend our whole summer vacation sitting inside. My job's going well, and your internship is fine. It's a Friday night. Let's celebrate."

I looked down at the ID. I had been dying to go out. All I've been doing is stalking Jack's Instagram. There were only so many nights I could cry myself to sleep. "I'm going to regret this."

"Yup." He nodded and smiled.

I sighed heavily and walked into my room to get ready for something I knew was going to be a complete failure. The thing though is I was looking forward to it. I was going home tomorrow for a couple of days. Colin finally texted me, and we were going to see each other. I didn't want to think about it. I knew it would lead to too many problems that I wanted to forget about.

"This is so stupid. No one is here." I was sipping on a beer at the bar with Drew. We had gotten into the bar with ease. Drew chatted up the bouncer like he owned the place.

"You're being dumb. There's a bunch of people here. You're just scared to meet new people."

"I'm not scared of meeting new people."

"Uh huh. I know you haven't been happy since Jack."

I stiffened. "I don't want to talk about it."

"Caleb, you look at his pictures all the time."

I turned to him. "I'm sorry if it hurts that he has already moved on to someone else." I finished my beer and slammed it on the bar. I stormed away from him. The picture of Jack kissing his new boyfriend, Marcus, was still burned in my brain. I was nothing to him. I didn't mean anything to anyone it seemed.

I heard Drew call my name, but I didn't want to talk to him. I just wanted to forget about everything going on. I needed a distraction. I didn't see where I was going and bumped into a guy, which caused his drink to fall on the ground.

I turned to look at him. He was dark skinned, lean, and his lip was pierced. He was wearing a tank top and I saw he had a couple of tattoos on his shoulder. "I'm so sorry."

He shrugged and gave me a winning smile. "It's all good. Just buy me a new one."

"I feel like I should get you some shots too."

He had a calming laugh. "James." He put out his hand.

"Caleb." I shook it. "I'm sorry again."

Drew walked up to me. "Is everything okay over here?" He asked.

I looked at him. "It's fine. I'll see you back at the apartment later." I didn't give a chance for Drew to respond. I grabbed James' hand and walked to another bar across from the dance floor. Drew had the expression of a kicked puppy, but it didn't change anything. He had no right to get involved in my life.

James and I got to the bar and took the shots and drinks that I paid for. "Who was that guy?"

"He's just my roommate. He's worried about me right now." I looked away from James.

"Why should he be concerned about you?" He asked.

I saw the sincerity in his eyes. I wanted to tell him to stop intruding in my life, but it was nice to have someone not judging my every move. "I went through a bad break up. He's seeing someone else already."

James touched my arm. "It's his lost. It's horrible going through a bad break up."

"Yeah, I guess I need a distraction." I looked up at James.

He raised an eyebrow. "A distraction, you say." He moved his arm to the center of my shirt. He grabbed a fist full and pulled me in for a kiss. Our lips crashed together because I had no clue what to expect. His lips were soft and full, but I couldn't help comparing him to Jack. There was no spark. This was all a physical encounter.

I was frozen for a minute until my head connected. This is what I needed to forget about everything. This was me moving forward with my life. Our lips moved together. He tasted like whiskey and beer, but I was thrilled. This was going to be a messy hook up, but there wouldn't be any feelings or disappointment to worry about.

He separated from me and had a grin on his face. "Shall we go back to my place?" He asked.

I nodded my head. He grabbed my hand and towed me out of the bar. I saw Drew talking to some guy at the bar, but I didn't care. My only concern was how quickly I could get James' clothes off.

He continued to kiss as we walked down the street to his apartment. We held hands, and I knew it was going to be an evening relationship. It was everything I needed. It was the good side, the rush that we all craved when looking for someone to love.

We got back to his place. I could hear the words in my head telling me to run. He kissed me and grabbed the hem of my shirt, pulling it over my head. He pushed me on his bed. My brain went on autopilot.

I felt him on top of me. I felt his lips on me, as he began to sprinkle me with kisses. I felt the sharp intake of my breath as he took off my clothes and left me naked. I felt my arousal I had when he took off his clothes. I felt his abs with my hands and how I wanted him on top of me.

I felt the sheer pleasure with every thrust and kiss. I felt the high I hadn't felt in a long time. I felt the connection we had when we locked eyes. I felt the sweat drop from his body onto mine. I felt it when he finished.

And then I felt the nothingness as he left me there to clean himself off. I felt numb as he came back to clean me off and cuddle with me. I felt his kisses as he curled up to me. I felt how wrong is was to be next to him in bed because this wasn't what I wanted. I felt how empty inside I was because I realized that no one loved me, and it killed me to know that.

28

June 8th, 2012

I came home to my mother hugging me. She was so thrilled to have me home. I shook the hand of the man that I thought was my father for eighteen years. I still loved him like he was. Why I couldn't just accept it and move forward? Isn't that what everyone does? We act like sharks or we end up dying.

I was lost in my train of thought until I heard a tree branch snapped. I turned around and saw Colin standing there. We both looked confused on what to do. His hair was grown out, and he looked chubbier than the last time I saw him. There we were at our tree house, face to face.

He gave me a weak smile. I couldn't do this. I couldn't be here right now. This was just too much for me. "Do you want to run too?" He asked.

"Why would you say that?"

"Caleb, I know you. I know when you look uncomfortable."

"You don't know me anymore. I've changed." I didn't mean to snap at him, but it just came out. I didn't like how smug he acted.

He raised his hands in the air as defeat. "I didn't want to come here fighting. I came here to fix things between us."

"Why? It's been almost a year since we've seen each other. It's been a year since we had that…" I didn't want to finish the sentence.

"We both said things we didn't mean. We both made mistakes in that conversation. I'm not proud of everything that happened."

"I came to you for acceptance. I came to pour my soul out to you, and you shut me off."

"What was I supposed to do?" I didn't want him opening old wounds. "Caleb, you dropped this bomb on me. I thought I knew you inside and out. You then tell me you're gay."

"You've always been there for me. You picked me up when I found out Vince wasn't my dad."

"That was easy."

"How was that easier than being who I was? I was told a lie my whole life. What do you expect me to do?"

"How did you think I was supposed to deal with it? I was told a lie when you said you were straight. You dated girls."

This argument wasn't going anywhere. "I just wanted my best friend to know who I was. I was nervous all of senior year about telling you. I thought you would reject me."

"I didn't reject you."

"You called me a faggot. How isn't that rejecting me?" I shot back at him.

He sighed and ran his fingers through his hair. He pulled out a cigarette and light one up. "You smoke?" I asked. He had always told me that he hated them. Who was this person in front of me?

"I only smoke when I'm stressed."

"We weren't like this before," I whispered. I didn't know if it was for him or me.

He gave me a weak smile again. "We used to be able to go to each other for everything. I would know who gave you that hickie." He pointed to the mark on my neck.

I tried to cover it up from him. I blushed and looked away. "I don't want to talk about it."

"Let me guess. One-night stand."

I heard a bit of judgment in his voice. "You don't get to judge me. You don't get to act like you're high and mighty. I'm sorry I didn't meet the love of my life."

"It doesn't mean you can just go fuck your way through people."

"You're opinion doesn't fucking matter anymore. You stopped being my best friend a long time ago."

"Then why the fuck are we here?" He screamed. He threw his cigarette.

"I thought we could fix us."

"It seems there's nothing to fix. We were friends in high school. It's been almost a year since we've seen each other."

I looked at my old best friend. He wasn't the same guy that I thought of as a brother. He wasn't my foundation anymore. He was just someone I used to know. "Could we ever get back there?"

He shrugged. "I don't think so."

"What's the point?"

"I don't know anymore. We're both stubborn assholes. Maybe that's our problem. We both want to be right."

"I want to forgive you, but I can't."

"Neither can I." He turned around and walked away.

"Is that it?" I screamed. He was walking away from me, just another person to toss me to the side.

"There's nothing else to talk about. We're done here. I'll always remember the good times we had before we fell apart. Maybe we will get there someday." He didn't say anything else.

I sat down in front of our tree house. I looked at all the memories that we shared in there. The tree house was falling apart. It was no longer the perfect escape from our outside world. We would never come back here to the land of imaginary. We had grown up, and we weren't together for it anymore.

29

June 17th, 2012

"Are we going out tonight?" I asked Drew as I slammed down my fourth beer of the night.

"How about we stay in?" Drew asked placing water in front of me.

I laughed at him. "What? You can't handle my tolerance?"

"Or you're becoming an alcoholic?"

I shook my head. I stood up. "Fuck you. You keep acting like I'm going to break. I'm fine. I've been having a great time."

"I don't believe you. You've been drinking, going out, and sleeping with random guys since you got back. What happened when you were home?" He asked.

I didn't want to explain that I couldn't look at my "father" or the fact that Colin once again wasn't there for me. How could I explain that to him? "Nothing for you to worry about."

I grabbed my wallet and keys. I walked out, ignoring his pleas for me to come back. I didn't listen. There was no point. I walked to the same bar I'd been going to the past couple of nights. The bouncer nodded at me. "Back again?"

"I've got nothing else going on."

He chuckled. "Make sure you don't get these boys' hopes up."

I gave him a grin. "I wouldn't plan on it."

I went up to my usual bartender. She handed me a beer and a shot of whiskey. I looked around at the crowd. There wasn't anyone that was peaking my interest. Sure, there were some guys that tried to talk to me, but they weren't up to my standards.

I needed something new and exciting. I couldn't get bored. I couldn't go back to my dark thoughts, or I was going to fail completely. I saw two guys dancing together. One of them was tall lanky with curly brown hair. The other was a bit shorter with dark brown hair. They both looked at me with hunger in their eyes.

They whispered to each other and made their way towards me. The one with curly hair smiled first. "You're cute. What's your name?"

I finished my beer to give myself some confidence. I had two guys approaching me. I had no clue if I could handle them, but this was exactly what I wanted. It scared me, but that's what made this even more desirable. "I'm Caleb."

"I'm Isaac, and this is Daniel." He pointed to the dark-hair guy. "We just saw you looking at us from over here." Isaac raised an eyebrow.

"I thought you both were cute." I admitted.

Daniel smiled. "We wouldn't mind getting you out there."

"I've never done this before." I wanted to play it cool, but I needed them to take control. Daniel smiled. "We know." He signaled for three shots.

We took the shots of whiskey. Isaac grabbed my hand and towed me to the center of the dance floor. "We prefer virgins." He winked.

Isaac grabbed me and pulled my back to his chest. He swayed me back and forth to the music. Daniel danced on me from the front. He wrapped his hands around my neck and we locked eyes. I felt Isaac's hands slide down my body.

"You need to let loose. We can't have fun if you don't let go." Isaac then bit down on my ear. It sent shivers down my spine and a moan escaped from my body.

Daniel moved his hands to touch my arms as Isaac started touching my ass. "We wouldn't mind seeing what else you have under these clothes." Daniel started kissing my neck.

I grabbed a fistful of Daniel's hair as I used Isaac's body for support. I had no clue where I was or who I was becoming. I was lost in the pleasure of it all. I was succumbing to my desires.

"Shall we take this back to our place?" Daniel asked.

I felt Isaac kissing me on the neck. I just nodded my head. They released me from their grip and towed me outside. "Good luck with that." I heard the bouncer yell out. I didn't know if it was towards them or me.

We walked a couple of blocks. I felt them groping me and looking at me as a sexual toy. I tried to contain my excitement. I was about to have my first three-way. I was about to enter a world that I've never experienced or thought of before. This was the ultimate land of lust and passion.

We got back to their apartment, a messy studio. They didn't waste any time taking off my shirt. Isaac took the lead and started kissing my chest. Daniel continued on the back. I felt their teeth nip along my skin. I inhaled and exhaled shakily. I tried to keep control, but there were so many emotions that I couldn't keep focus.

I felt my pants fall down and Isaac took me in. I tried so hard to keep control. I learned that I wasn't more than just an object. They were in control of me. I felt Daniel behind me. I felt him slide up and down.

Isaac finished, but he left me unsatisfied. He grabbed me and kissed me on the lips. It was harsh and abrasive. I tried to push him off of me, but I couldn't.

It clicked me with me that there was no love. This was a high for someone else. I thought about how Jack kissed, or even the other guys. They gave me some sort of hope for a future. They gave me the possibility of being a romance. There wasn't that here. I wanted to run. I didn't want this anymore. I wasn't meant for this.

"I don't want to do this anymore." I pleaded with both of them. I wanted to just go home. I tried to move my body, but they had me where they wanted me.

Isaac and Daniel were both prepping me. Isaac stood up. Daniel kept prepping me. "Don't be such a little boys scout. This is what college is all about. We saw it in your eyes. You're bored with your life. It must have been an ex-boyfriend. I'm assuming you wanted to be loved again."

"You want a distraction," Daniel said.

"This isn't for me. I was an idiot to think that I actually want this. I'm just some kind of toy to you. You don't care about me or love me."

Isaac put his arm on my shoulder. "This is a form of love. We have so many different forms. We were loving your body as you're going to love mine. You don't need to be so scared. It will be fun."

He didn't give me a chance to respond. Daniel bent me over. He spread my cheeks, and I felt him go inside of me. I moaned a mix of pain and pleasure. I felt how wrong this truly felt, but a part of me enjoyed this. I grabbed Isaac's waist for support.

I didn't think of what Isaac was doing before it was too late. I tried to protest but my words were muffled as Isaac was now in me. I felt them both thrust at me. I heard them moan and laugh. I felt their pleasure rising in their bodies. I tried to block it out. I tried to forget everything that was going on.

In that moment, I understood what it truly meant to be used. I was just dirt to them, and this wasn't what I wanted. I could feel them clawing at my body trying to get more. Wasn't this what I asked for? I was being desired, but it wasn't what I truly craved. I needed comfort and safety.

This was rejection. I wasn't meant for this life. This world was filled with darkness and abuse. I thought I could use this to forget about my father, Colin, and Jack. This was worse. I found kindness, but with these two, there wasn't any.

I don't know how long it took them to finish, nor did I care. I just wanted it all to be over. They separated themselves from me. "Didn't you enjoy that?" Isaac said.

"No, that was horrible." I felt wrong being naked in front of them. I didn't want to give them the satisfaction of seeing their conquest. I grabbed my clothes and quickly dressed. "Why would you ever do something like that?"

Daniel crossed his arms. "You seemed to enjoy it." He pointed to my crouch.

I didn't realize that I finished. "It wasn't worth it."

"You're one of those," Isaac said.

I was confused what he was saying. "What?"

They looked at each other. "You want true love. You want the romance. Boy, you're so naïve. There is no such thing."

"What about you two?" I pointed to them.

"We play with the dark side of the world. There are no emotions or kindness here. It's all sexual power when we bring in a third party."

Isaac and Daniel kissed each other. I saw how feral it was, but there was still a kindness of love. "But you two care for each other," I said.

They separated and turned to me. "We know that who ever we bring home that they won't be more important than each other."

"So no jealousy?"

Daniel smiled. "No, we're just getting this out of our system. We plan forever with each other, but we don't want to become boring."

"We want to make sure that we've crossed everything off our bucket list," Isaac said.

"But isn't that just using the third party."

Isaac laughed. "Isn't that what you were doing with the other guys you were sleeping with?"

"We know about you taking home all those boys. You were using them and then tossing them."

"It's why we thought you were perfect for this."

It was sad because I wasn't. I thought I was being this hotshot guy, but I was just looking like an asshole. I was a kid trying to play in the adult world. It made me realize that I still had so much to learn about being an adult and finding a serious relationship. College couldn't teach me that.

"We're having all the fun we want. You can leave now. I need to help my boyfriend out." Isaac didn't give Daniel or I a chance to respond.

He pushed Daniel on the bed and climbed on top. They continued to pleasure each other. I was intruding on them. Being with two guys didn't help me. It made things worse. I saw love in front of me, and I couldn't have it. They brought other guys into their beds, but they didn't with their hearts.

They weren't ashamed of themselves. Was I ever going to find that? Would I be able to trust my partner so much we could sleep with other beings. Would I be able to love someone and give them everything that they needed?

30

"I can't do this." I looked at the building. I just wanted to run away.

Drew grabbed my shoulders. "You're going in there. You're going to get help, or I'll kick your ass."

I looked at Drew in the eyes. "Thanks for putting up with my mess the past couple of weeks." I didn't know why he cared for me so much. Sure, I was there when he thought he failed his class, but he's been there for so much more.

He shrugged. "We've all been there. I almost didn't get into college because of my ex. I smoke and drank the first couple months of senior year. I didn't see the point. My guidance counselor helped me through it, and I got into here. You could say it's me paying it forward."

"I just don't want to feel broken anymore. I don't want to feel alone."

He pulled me into a hug. I didn't think I need it until he wrapped his arms around me and got the tears out of my eyes. We stood there for a couple of minutes to let me get everything I needed out of my system.

I stood back. "Sorry."

"Don't be. Jack fucked you over. I don't know what happened when you were home, but I'm not going to judge you for it. You got what you needed out. Go in there and get healed."

"I just don't want anyone else knowing about this."

"Caleb, it's between us. I've got you. Maybe this is for the best. You can put all your past bullshit behind you and actually love someone without feeling ashamed."

I pulled him in for another hug. "Thank you."

"No problem. I'll see you when you get done. I'll have a bowl ready for you."

I laughed. "Yeah, I can't do the hangovers anymore."

I walked up the stairs to the counseling building. I was tired of having these weights dragging me down. I wanted to forget all about my past and move forward.

I walked into the building and walked into the small room. There wasn't anyone else in there. I assumed it would be quiet since it was nine in the morning, and the office just opened up.

The woman smiled, and I filled out all the paperwork. I saw the door opened, and my stomach dropped. "You got to be kidding me," I mumbled.

Jack smiled as he walked into the office. He was talking to the secretary when he turned around and saw me. His smile dropped. "What are you doing here?" He asked.

I stood up. "I should ask you the same thing." I brushed past him and handed over the clipboard. The receptionist told me my therapist would be with me soon.

"You're a patient?"

"Yeah, I've been fucked over by some people lately."

"You can't be upset with me for what happened."

"I loved you. I still do, and I don't know why I do. I want to grab you right now and kiss, but I won't."

"Why not?"

"Because I need to have more self-discipline and respect for myself. I'm not mad that you chose to be an RA. You just never gave me a chance to tell you that I was moving off campus. We could have been something incredible."

He grabbed my hand. "We can be together." He pulled me into a kiss. It felt like old times. It felt like the poems I wrote, the nights on the beach, our first time, and saying I love you every time. Our lips moved together, but it reminded me of the bad. He didn't respect me, and I couldn't go back to that. I pushed him off of me. "I can't with you. You have a boyfriend right now. I'm tired of feeling like a skeleton in your closet."

"You don't have to be anymore. Caleb, I haven't been able to stop thinking about you. We can finally be something. We don't have to hide."

I shook my head. "That's the problem. You're choosing my life without me. You're once again not letting me have control."

"That's not what's going on here."

"I've had too many people take control of my life. I've had too many people disrespect me. I want to love me. I want to be able to control my life. Jack, I loved you, but I gave you too much. My world revolved around you. I kept you a secret not for me, but for you. I don't want that anymore."

"It could work between us."

I smiled weakly. "It won't because I'm not going to be the doormat you want me to be. I just can't do that for you." The door opened, and I saw my therapist walk out. "Have a good life. I hope your new boyfriend is okay with you having control because I'm not." I didn't let him say anything. I walked into the therapy session, and I smiled because it felt damn good to get that off my chest. This summer was me finally getting the dust to settle. It was going to be me getting what I really wanted.

31

I closed my laptop. I wanted to give Caleb a high five for telling Jack off. I didn't care for him. He didn't deserve Caleb's love, and I don't think I did either. I understood why I never saw Caleb after our tree house session. I understood why I needed to be put in the past now.

It killed me to know that he had to go through all those things alone. I wanted to punch Isaac and Daniel for causing him so much pain. I wanted to punch myself because I led him to do it. I remember that conversation. I was still so angry at him. We both were in the wrong in that argument so many years ago. Why couldn't we put our pride to the side? Why couldn't we forgive and love again?

I felt my phone go off, and it was Aunt June calling. I was surprised she waited this long to call me. I picked up the call. "Worried about me, are we?" I asked.

She sighed, and I knew she was rolling her eyes. "Still a bit arrogant, are we?" She shot back.

I laughed. It felt good to laugh, and I needed this back and forth. "How's everything at home?" I asked.

"Oh you know the same boring thing. I just now have to deal with my lazy nephew and all the things he left me to clean."

I felt guilty dumping everything and running. "Sorry, I didn't mean to do that. I just realized that I didn't belong there."

"Honey, I knew the moment after you got back from Caleb's funeral. You were trying to make sense of everything."

"I'm still trying."

"Did you honestly think it would be solved in the four days you've been there?" She asked.

"It's only been four days?" I laughed. It seemed longer. Maybe because I was reading four years of life, looking at the past, and trying to keep it all together.

"I'm worried about you."

"Why?"

"You're going to get too wrapped up in it."

"Aunt June, I need to figure out how he died. I can't just put it on hold."

"Have you cried yet?" She asked.

I thought it was such a bizarre question. "What?"

"Have you cried about Caleb yet?"

"We all grieve in different ways." I remember her saying that when I couldn't stop crying about my parents, but she hadn't cried herself.

"Don't give me that bullshit. I know you're avoiding the question." I could tell that she was getting annoyed.

"No, I haven't. I just don't have time."

"You need to focus on yourself. He's still going to be dead."

"Aunt June!" I snapped at her.

She sighed heavily. "I know. It's a bit messed up, but I just don't want you to obsess. This isn't your fault. I know you've heard this a lot, but you need to be reminded."

I loved her. I never wanted to lose her in my life. "I know. I'm learning more that he would have done this on his own."

"I just want you to take care of yourself."

"I love you."

"I love you too. I knew taking you in was a hassle, but it was the best decision of my life."

"Aunt June, I've made mistakes. I hurt him. I'm learning that now." I look back at the last couple of diary entries. He would have been fine if I loved him the way he needed. He would have been happy if I was his brother.

"We all wish we could step back and realize what we're doing in the moment. We can't step away from our lives. Our actions cause so many reactions. We hope to be a positive influence on people's lives."

"I wasn't for him."

"If you think one stupid fight will ruin all those years, then you're a fool. You're a good person who did a horrible thing. Everyone does sometimes."

I needed those words. I needed to hear that I made a mistake, but it didn't define me. I knew that Caleb didn't blame me for a lot, but I could tell how much it messed him up. I was at college missing him, but I was so distracted with my frat, Colby, and Jimmy. I guess I was lucky to have myself figured out. Why couldn't I have understood that sooner?"

32

Five ½ Years Ago

"Is it true?" I asked walking up to Caleb by his locker.

He was putting his books away. He turned to look at me. "Is what true?"

"You and Sarah broke up?" Colby had told me she needed to go take care of Sarah because she was crying.

"I don't know how you found out so quickly."

"I'm your best friend, and I had to find out from Colby."

"I was about to come tell you after class, but I guess we're doing this now."

I grabbed Caleb's hand. "Yeah, we're going to get to the bottom of this."

"I'm not a mystery novel."

"I don't care." I towed him outside towards the fields. I didn't care if I was missing math. I cared about Caleb. I needed to make sure that he was doing okay. "Spill."

"I wasn't happy with her anymore."

"Bullshit."

"How's that bullshit?"

"You don't date someone for two years and then all of a sudden break it off. There's something that you're not telling me."

He shook his head. "Why can't you take things at face value? Why can't that just be the story?"

"Caleb, I've known you for years. I know when to never take anything at face value. What's going on?"

"I just wasn't happy with her anymore. I felt like I was with her to make her happy or you guys."

I didn't like how he was assuming that I wanted him in this relationship. I wanted him to be happy with whomever he loved. I liked Sarah. She was better than Tracy, but he didn't need to stick with someone for the sake of us.

"Don't blame this on me."

"Excuse me?"

"I didn't tell you to date her."

"You and Colby set us up."

"On a blind date. You were still upset from Tracy. I thought you needed a quick rebound. I didn't think it would turn into a two-year affair. You liked her, right?"

"I loved Sarah. She was great."

"Then why end it?"

"I didn't feel anything for her anymore. I didn't feel the connection." He sat down and rested on the tree.

I saw the conflict in his eyes. I saw so many questions written across his face. Was Caleb going to be my next mystery I needed to solve? I sat down across from him. "What's going on?"

"Do you feel empty?"

"Excuse me?"

"Do you ever feel like there is a hole inside of you that seems you can't fill? Like you're just numb and alone?"

I knew about the pain he was talking about. It was an overbearing pain and darkness. You think there is nothing that can get you out of that hole and feel like you don't belong to your life.

"I got it with my parents. I would miss them and got rid of it."

"How did you get rid of it?" He asked.

I shrugged. "I had other things to focus on. I have a best friend like you, and I have my girlfriend. I guess that's really all I need. I found the love I didn't get from them. Why are you asking?"

"I just feel empty inside sometimes. I felt like Sarah's love wasn't enough."

"You have everyone around you. Your parents love you. Colby and I love you. What else do you need?"

"Colin, I want real true love. I want something that takes over me. I want to be so madly in love with someone that it's all I was meant to do. I want someone to love and destroy me."

"That's a bit psycho."

He sighed and got up. "I knew you wouldn't understand."

I quickly got on my feet. "I just don't get why you'd want to fall so hard for someone to break you."

"I just want to know that the love is real. You can't know the love was strong until they've broken your heart. I ended things with Sarah, but my life hasn't changed. I didn't love her enough. I don't want to be mediocre anymore. I want the real thing."

"Do you think you're going to get that here?"

He put his hands in the air. "I don't know. I just know that I'm not meant for her anymore. I'm not meant to be scared of who I am."

"Are you hiding things from me?" Caleb always came to me for all of his problems. It's what best friends do. I didn't understand this person in front of me. He was someone that had all these secrets and questions. Caleb was always an open book.

"Aren't we all keeping secrets? We all have enough skeletons in our closet that we don't want anyone to find out about."

"You're scaring me." I was worried about Caleb. He never was like this.

He gave me a weak smile. "I'm sorry. I just have a lot on my mind. I just don't need you to worry about me. I got it all figured out." He gave me a brave smile and walked away.

I had no clue what happened, but I knew Caleb was going through things. It didn't matter. He would eventually come to me for his problems. I would be there to fix it up. I would have my arms open, and I would love him regardless. It's what brothers do.

33

"Where are you taking me?" Colby asked as we walked down the street to the restaurant. I needed to get back to what I was before this mess with Caleb.

"It's a surprise." I smiled.

She gave me a skeptical look. "I don't like your surprises. They usually end in disaster."

"That was one time."

"It was sprinklers and a white dress. How could you not think it was horrible?"

"At least guys wanted to give you their numbers."

She smacked me on the side of the head. "You're such an ass-hole." I knew there was no venom behind her words.

We walked another block until we got to a country bar. Drew said it was fun, and he usually took Cameron here. Jimmy said he had some gamer tournament that he couldn't miss.

We walk inside and took a seat. We ordered our drinks and looked at each other. The place was set up like the inside of a barn. There was hay on the ground. The bar was made of wood and so was the stage where a country singer was performing. We were sitting in the back corner with candlelight.

"I feel like this is a bad idea," I said pointing to the candle.

"Why?"

"This place is made of hay and wood. This place could go up any second."

She rolled her eyes. "Way to kill the moment."

I smiled. "It's worth it looking at you in candlelight."

She blushed and looked away. "I know that was super cheesy, but thank you." She grabbed my hand. She started drawing circles into my hand.

"What are you thinking about?" I asked.

"Our future." She looked up at me.

"What about it?"

"Where are we going after this, Colin? We've been together for six years now. Are we going to get married?"

"I want to marry you, and I want to have kids with you. Nothing's changed."

"Then why don't I have a ring on my finger."

"Colby, I was planning on proposing after we graduated college. You know what happened? My best friend was murdered."

I saw the wave of guilt wash over her face. "I'm such a bitch."

I kissed her hand. "No, you're not. I know your mom is pressuring you to get married."

She laughed. "You would think that she would understand that we're focused on our careers, not our family right now."

"She's Polish."

She nodded. "I just don't want to lose this."

"Do you think I do? You're one of the only good things left in my life. I just need time."

She leaned over the table and kissed me on the lips. "I'll give you all the time in the world. I'm here as long as you want me."

"I like the sound of that." I raised an eyebrow.

"You really do know how to ruin a moment, don't ya?"

I chuckled. "I try." There was a calm quietness at our table. It was one of the favorite things I loved about our relationship. We didn't need to talk. We could sit and just enjoy the moment.

"Are you happy we came?" She asked.

"Here?"

"I mean to Grover. Do you think it was the right choice?"

"It's only been four days. I'm still trying to figure out who killed him."

"I don't think that's the point."

"I just don't like the idea that he lived this whole world without me. He has friends and memories and I wasn't there."

"So do you. You have rushing, brotherhood, college parties, our dates, making friends. You have a whole life without him."

"But he will never know how much I've grown since we said our goodbyes."

She touched my cheek. "Life doesn't give you everything you want."

"I hate knowing that."

"I hate accepting that."

I wanted nothing more in this world than to have Caleb back in my life. I don't think I'll ever feel complete anymore. My parents are gone, and my best friend is gone. Who else would I lose in my life?

"I know what you're doing over there. Don't go down that dark hole." Colby broke me out of my slippery slope.

"I don't know what you're talking about."

"You're thinking about who you're going to lose next."

"No, I'm not."

"Bullshit. You lost a lot of people in your life, but you've gained so many more. You can't continue thinking that this is all on you. This is the horrible part of life."

I smiled weakly. "You should have gone into therapy. You would have been really good at it."

"I'll continue with what I'm doing. I love you. We're in this together. I don't want you to think that you're alone."

"I know that. I love you too."

I leaned forward and we kissed again. She pulled me out of my dark thoughts, and I needed that the most. I love her so much that it hurt. I saw a future with her, and I couldn't wait to start it with her. I just needed to figure out this mess first.

34

August 25th, 2012

It felt good knowing that this summer all I did was focus on me. Drew and I spent most of the time smoking and going to the beach. It seems that all we've done is just connect, and we both needed it. He was my core, and he knew all my demons. We were just looking forward to the rest of our group to get back from their vacation.

"Do we tell them about me going to therapy?" I asked him.

"It's not their business. If you want them to know, then you can tell them. You really got over a lot of the shit, and you should be proud of that."

"I just don't want to be messed up anymore or feel like this freak."

"Have you ever felt like a freak with me or the rest of the group?"

"No."

"Then why would you feel like that now? Caleb, we're all messed up. We're all trying to get through things. We judge because we're trying to hide our own insecurities."

I got up and hugged him tightly. "I needed that."

"You're my brother. I'm not going anywhere."

We hugged again both of us tearing up.

I heard a click of a camera. I turned to see Cameron, Beth, and Shawn standing there with their phones out. "I knew my boyfriend would go gay this summer if I wasn't here."

We both separated and looked away from each other. Beth walked up and hugged me first. "I see you finally got some action. I'm so proud of you."

"Thanks, Beth. I guess I'm no longer a prude."

"I never thought you were." She winked at me.

Shawn came up to me next and we hugged. "I'm happy you're back." I meant it. I missed having writing sessions with Shawn. I couldn't talk to Drew about writing because he was as creative as a rock.

Shawn smiled brightly. "I thought I was the only one. I can't wait for our creative writing class."

"I heard the professor is great."

Cameron pushed Shawn out of the way. She hugged me close. "You'll never be broken again." She whispered into my ear.

I felt embarrassed because they heard our conversation. "I'm sorry."

She shook her head. "Drew was right. We're all freaks, but we're together for it. I don't need you forgetting that." She went and kissed her boyfriend. "I've missed you."

He smiled. "I'm glad you grew your hair. I have something else to tug at."

I felt extremely uncomfortable. "I'm so happy we have our own rooms now. I don't need to roll over to that again."

Beth put her arm around my shoulder. She put her other one around Shawn and pulled him close. "I do have to admit I did enjoy you trying to be discreet when looking at my ass when Drew and I had sex."

"You kept shaking it in front of me."

"I guess you do have a point." She pulled us closer together. "I'm waiting until you two get your shit together and start dating."

"I don't think it will happen," Shawn said. I heard the hurt in his voice.

I felt guilty. I didn't think he was ugly or we wouldn't have a great relationship. It was that I didn't want to ruin our friendship.

"I don't need to be fifth wheel." Beth kissed us on our cheeks. "Can we go to the beach now?"

"We're going to the beach?" I asked.

"Duh, we're getting our tan on before we have to be slaved to classes in three days. Fuck that." Beth walked into one of the rooms to change.

We spent the whole afternoon on the beach. We danced, swam, and tanned. I forgot all about the problems. I wanted to dry off for a little bit. Cameron walked up to me and sat next to me. "I never thought I would find happiness."

I turned to her. "What?"

"I was with an older guy. He was twenty-three, and I was sixteen. I thought my whole world revolved around him. I would skip school just to lay in bed with him. I almost flunked." She laughed. "I came home with half a shaved head. My parents freaked out. I eventually found out he was cheating on me."

"Do you regret it?"

"No, because he was my first real love. He gave me something no one else could. I kept my head shaved because I wanted a reminder that I fell hard for someone. I wanted to remind myself that it's okay to fall in love."

"Why are you growing it out?" I asked.

"Because I have Drew now. He's not perfect, but neither am I."

"You're perfect for each other."

"I wouldn't go that far. We have so many issues, but I love the asshole."

I looked at her. "Why are you telling me this?"

"Don't regret loving Jack."

"I never could. I just wanted him to respect me. I didn't want him having control over my life. We were perfect, but I could see him dictating my life. I couldn't have that happen."

She leaned over and kissed me on the cheek. "You're smarter than I was. Falling in love is one of the greatest joys in life. I'm grateful to have found it twice."

"I hope I do too." I saw how much Cameron admired and loved Drew. I wanted that for myself, and I believed I would get it. It was a nice comfort knowing that I would never have to go through anything alone.

35

August 27th, 2012

"I heard his class is the best. He has two best-selling novels. I wonder if he will sign my copies. He just understands the human soul." Shawn was gushing about our creative writing professor on our way to his class.

"I think you might have some kind of crush."

Shawn blushed and looked away. We took our seats in the second row. The classroom was small and could probably only fit about forty students. "I don't have a crush on him. I just want to be him."

"He can't be that great."

We saw a gentleman sitting next to us. I noticed his long brown hair with gray showing. He wore a button up and rolled up sleeves to reveal his tattoos. I noticed one of his tattoos said: "We sacrifice our sanity for love." I enjoyed the quote.

"Caleb, I can't believe you've never heard of him."

"I just don't see how he could be this great writer and teach at Grover. Shouldn't he be somewhere else?"

Shawn passed me a poem he wrote. I read the poem. It was about a boy falling for a girl that he couldn't have. He would hold her while she cried and wished he could fix all her problems. He eventually had his chance with her, but in the end realized that he didn't love her, but the idea of her.

"Isn't that a great poem? We can all relate."

I put it down. "Yeah, it's a good poem. I've read better. It seems he's trying too hard to be like the classics."

The man turned to look at me. He smiled. "Don't you think we're writing the classics for future generations?"

He had blue eyes that were so pure that they should be photographed. I've never been attracted to older men, but he gave me a reassurance I've never experienced before. My heart clung to him. I thought I knew what love at first sight was with Jack, but this was the real thing.

It took a minute and a nudge from Shawn to remember that I was asked a question. "There are a lot of people who think they write the great classics, but it becomes just a timely piece. We can't forget that."

"So what's the point of writing?" He asked.

"I think it's like a time capsule. We are writing about what's going on now, so future generations can understand our lives. The problem is that no one reads our work. They read the works of the people we read. Our education system doesn't believe in the present. They only look at the past. How can we evolve as writers if we are stuck in the past."

He smiled, and I knew that I was going to fall even more. "I like the way you think." He stood up.

"Where are you going?"

"I have a class to teach." My heart dropped. I just had a conversation with the professor without knowing it. "Don't be worried. I like what you had to say." He winked at me. I quickly looked at his hand and saw no wedding ring.

I stopped myself from the thought. He was my professor. We couldn't be together. I couldn't be someone else's dirty little secret. I wanted a relationship like Drew and Cameron's, but this would be my choice. I wanted him all for myself.

"Hello, class. My name is Jonathan. I won't be called Professor Lancaster. This is creative writing. It needs to be more informal."

He looked right at me. I wanted to melt away right then. "What's your name?" He pointed to me.

"Caleb."

"I like your idea of focusing on the present. We will be focusing on current writers, poets, and social activists. We will draw inspiration and write ourselves. I don't believe in the past. There is a reason that those books and stories are collecting dust in a library." We all smiled. "Shall we begin?" He asked. I never wanted to scream yes more than right then.

September 14th, 2012
"I think the point of the story is that we can love again. She lost who she thought was her soulmate, but she found this guy that made her forget about her first love," I explained after we finished reading a short story a girl in the class wrote. We were in a circle facing our critics.

"Do you think that this is relatable?" Jonathan asked.

"I want to believe that it's true. I don't want to look at my first love and think that's it for me. That would be a terrible ending to my life." I tried to make it as a joke.

Everyone in the class started chuckling. "Kelly came up with an interesting concept. We think our first love is going to be it for us. We put this person on a grand pedestal, but when does the magic go away?"

"When we find someone else." Shawn added.

"Or when we realize that they weren't meant for us," I said.

"But she loved her husband. It wasn't her fault he died at war. They would still be together now. It doesn't mean that they weren't meant for each other." A girl named Elizabeth argued.

Jonathan raised a finger. "You bring up an interesting topic. This world has so many roads and paths for us to follow. We choose one and then we wonder what would have happened if we chose the other. If this Ash didn't choose to be a soldier he wouldn't have died, but Daisy wouldn't have realized how much she loved him or how strong she was without him."

"Does that mean it's better to stay alone? We want to love someone because we think that's it. Should we just say 'eh' and risk losing that person for the potential of someone else?" I asked.

"It's the tragedy of the world." Jonathan looked at the clock. "Looks like our time is up. I need your critiques on this story by tomorrow morning. I might be a nice person, but I'll murder you if you don't give them to me." Everyone laughed as we packed up our bags.

Jonathan walked up to me and patted me on the shoulder. I felt his touch go through my whole body. I didn't like how much I stared at him and the sex dreams I've had about him the past couple of weeks. "I enjoy your view of love. You'll find someone else. You just need to be willing to let it happen." He walked out of the class.

I watched him high five a student leaving the room. I wanted it to be him. I knew there were so many red flags, but I didn't care. I wasn't going to let some complications control me anymore.

"I told you he was great," Shawn said.

"You have no idea." I wanted a real relationship like Drew and Cameron, but why couldn't it be with Jonathan. Sure, he was my professor, but we could keep it a secret. It would be an equal playing field. I didn't want people to think I was the student that slept for his grades, and Jonathan wouldn't want to be known as the professor who slept with a student. It was all a fantasy right now. It wouldn't turn into anything else.

36

October 1st, 2012

"**C**aleb, could you come to my office after class?" Jonathan asked.

The past couple of weeks we had been arguing during class. We disagreed on the themes and morals of my classmate's works. Shawn asked if I hated Jonathan, and I couldn't even fathom hating him. I loved arguing with him. It was the first time someone kept up with me. I emailed him excessively about story ideas or how I could work on a character's development. He was the first person I ever felt going to about it.

"Yeah, I'm free."

He smiled like he really wanted me to be there. "Perfect, I'll see you in ten minutes." He walked out of the room.

"No wonder you have an A," Shawn said.

"So do you?" I looked at him.

"But I'm not his favorite."

"I'm not his either."

"You guys talk all the time, and he emails you right back. It takes him a full forty-eight hours to get back to me."

"You subtly hit on him, and I've read your emails. I would need a couple of days to figure out what you were saying."

He rolled his eyes. "Whatever. I'll see you later."

"I'm not getting you an autograph."

Shawn laughed. "I already got it." I enjoyed seeing Shawn open up. He felt in his element when he was around creative people. He wasn't scared to show his work to everyone in this classroom, and that was because of Jonathan. He's the reason people were excited to show their work. It's why I never wanted this semester to end. I didn't want to say goodbye to this safety.

"What did you want to see me about?" I asked walking into his office.

He smiled at me, and I melted. "I just want to talk to you about your new story, plus your performance in the classroom."

I walked over to my usual seat. I never was nervous in here. It wasn't our first time having these types of conversations. He walked and closed the door. "This must be serious if you closed the door." I chuckled.

"Are you nervous?" He raised an eyebrow.

"I don't know. Are you going to be appropriate?" I didn't know why that came out of my mouth.

"Don't worry. I'm always appropriate during office hours. If you see me at a bar, then you can have your time with me."

"I'll have to wait another year." I enjoyed this back and forth. I wanted nothing more than to get up right then and kiss him. I felt my whole body crave him.

"I'll be looking forward to having a drink with you." He walked over and took a seat.

"Are you hitting on me?" I raised an eyebrow.

"It seems that this conversation has gone down a different path than I expected."

I felt guilty and ashamed. "I'm so sorry. I didn't mean to cross the line."

He smiled. "You never cross the line." I didn't know if he was hoping I was going to. He looked down at my paper. "I love your story. I enjoy the idea that these two friends never really knew each other. I assume that it's a true story."

"Why would you say that?"

"You can tell when a story is because life didn't work out the way you wanted it to. Writers sometimes use stories to get the resolution they've been fighting for."

I looked at the story 'Tree House,' and I knew that it was true. I wanted so many things to be resolved with Colin, but I couldn't be stuck on it. "I hope you enjoyed it."

"It's okay to be who you are."

"Or who I'm attracted to?" I asked.

He looked at me. He really looked at me, and our eyes locked together. "Who are you attracted to?"

"I feel like there are complications and problems. I don't know if the prize is worth the hassle."

"You never know until you try. Caleb, you're one of my favorite students. I've never met anyone student like you, and I want to get to know you more."

"Would that be over the line?"

"I don't know. Do you feel uncomfortable?"

I shook my head. "I've never met another human being that I've wanted to talk to before. I look at you during class, and the love you have for writing, makes me fall more in love with it. I just want to talk to you for hours and pick your brain."

He smiled. "I was hoping for you to say that. I would like to invite you to a book reading."

"Of who?"

"My good friend just published a series of short stories and poetry. I think that you would rather enjoy it. It's right up your ally."

"Would it be wrong?"

He chuckled. "We've been told being gay is wrong. We're already doing that. I don't see having you come see a writer as wrong."

I knew that it could be over the line. I knew that it could end disastrous, but there was something about Jonathan that I really wanted to know. He gave me the confidence and comfort I haven't had in a long time. I think maybe I could move forward, and it could be in his arms. I just didn't want it to fail me. I didn't need another disappointment in my life.

37

"I think Jonathan is the professor Drew, Cameron, Beth, and Shawn were talking about," I said while Colby closed my laptop.

"Why do you say that?"

"The way they bonded seemed extremely over the line."

"What was said?" She asked.

"They were talking about crossing lines, and it seemed that he was going on a date with him."

She looked at me. "Was there any mention of the professor being inappropriate?"

"No, but he had a crush on him. Jonathan looks like he's going to take advantage of my best friend." I felt my blood boil.

Colby kissed me on the cheek, and I was simmering down. "Someone is being protective. I just want you to know that it's over. This was three years ago. You can't be protective of someone in the past."

I turned and looked away from Colby. "That's not true."

She sighed. "I just want you to realize that he's gone. You can't change that," she whispered. "Remember we have the senior show-case tonight."

I turned to look at her. "The what?"

"Shawn asked us to come to the senior showcase. We're going."

"I want to keep reading."

"This isn't a mystery novel. This is a human being."

I looked at her. "He left me these for me to read. I know he's not a novel, but the answers are in here."

"It's sad when you want to be a detective, but you don't see the biggest clue. I'm taking a shower. I need you to get ready." She walked into the bathroom.

I didn't know what she was referring to. I knew I didn't want to fight with her. I knew it would be a good thing to go to the senior showcase. I was wondering if they would show off something of Caleb's. It was still weird hearing about this great Caleb, and I would never meet him.

I was sitting with Colby, Drew, and Cameron. Beth had work and Jimmy was still trying to get a code for his gaming. Shawn had fin-ished his short story and was awarded applause from the crowd.

I watched an older man walk on the stage. He smiled as he used a crutch to get on stage. I saw the sleeve tattoos and the sleek back hair, which was slowly turning into gray. He was Jonathan Lancaster. I didn't imagine him being Caleb's type. He was older and distinguished. He was only in his mid to late thirties.

He smiled, and I saw it. He looked like he had wisdom beyond his years to give you the confidence to make you believe in a false world. He looked like a con artist, and he took advantage of the ones that were confused in this world.

"I'm so happy to have such a huge turn out this year. I always enjoy the end of year showcase for the seniors. It's been such pleasure seeing these students become writers that they have the potential to be."

He stopped and wiped a tear away. Was he crying for Caleb? Was there something that I didn't know? I felt a hand on me knee. "You need to relax." I heard Colby say.

"No, it's Jonathan." I had so angry for a man that I didn't even know. I just felt something in my whole body want to scream that he had something to do with Caleb's death.

"Colin, you're being irrational. You don't know the man."

"Caleb loved that guy. They were close. You can't hate him when you don't even know him," Drew said. I could tell that Drew had admired him too.

"He can't be trusted."

"Caleb trusted him enough to sleep with the guy."

"What?" I looked at Drew.

He shrugged. "We didn't know about it until the end of junior year. They stopped after that. I told you this. This past summer was a rough one for Caleb."

"But you're okay with him now."

"Caleb got his peace with him. Jonathan had his own issues to deal with."

"I can't believe this right now. We aren't going to question this."

Cameron leaned over to look at me. "This is what Caleb was talking about you being judgmental. You don't have a right to make comments on his life. You don't know the full story. Jonathan loved Caleb a lot. How about you get to know him first?"

I wanted to snap at both of them. It was wrong, and they shouldn't be so nonchalant about it. He had sex with his professor. He was in a romantic relationship with an older gentleman, and no one saw a problem with it.

I looked back at Jonathan. "One of my favorite students of all-time passed away a couple of weeks ago. I had never met someone who was so bright, and he was going to change the world. He always questioned life, and I think people should do that. No one should be scared to know where this world is going. I loved my conversations with him, and he will be dearly missed."

I saw the devotion he had on his face for Caleb. I saw the love he shared. He wiped a tear away from his eyes. "I wanted to read a little excerpt from one of my favorite short stories that he's written. It's called, 'Tree House'.

We don't get the luxury of having others understand us. We aren't blessed with the world accepting us for all the flaws in our soul. I looked at my best friend, and I thought he would be one of the lucky ones. I looked at the life we built in that stupid structure in the trees, and I wanted to believe. Maybe I was the fool. Maybe I should have accepted the cold reality of this world. I don't get to be accepted. I don't get to be fully loved. Does that mean I'll never find happiness?

I refuse to believe that. I think in the whole world we're given those few people that make you feel better about yourself. I wasn't going to let this person in front of me have that control over me. Yes, he was my best friend, but he wasn't the controller of my life. I was. Sure, that's a bit cliché, but he had no clue what damage he caused in my life. What's the point of a life if you let other people choose it for you?"

It was silent in the room. I knew damn well those words were spoken to me. I knew that I had my own demons and made mistakes in my life. I'm proud that he got those words out on paper.

"Maybe, you shouldn't judge. Maybe you would still have a best friend," Drew said.

I didn't respond to him because apart of him was right. I didn't know if that upset me more or made me angry. I just wanted this trip to be over. I didn't want to keep going down this dark path. It was just old wounds continuing to be cut open.

38

"I don't want to meet him," I said while we were drinking champagne.

"No, we're going to meet him. He might give you some closure."

"You don't know that. This whole trip was stupid. We should have just gone home." I placed my glass down. "I'm going home. I'm done playing this stupid game."

I knew I was making a scene, but I didn't care. I just wanted to go home. I wanted to forget all about this. Colby grabbed my arm and pulled me to the side. She grabbed my face. "Stop being a baby. Yes, you were an asshole. Yes, that piece was about you. Did it make you look great? No, but who is shown in a positive light?"

"Caleb is."

"He was murdered. He had enemies. Don't beat yourself up. We came here so you can get closure. You're fucking going to get it. I'm not going let you feel like the villain."

"I'm the bad guy."

"Well turn yourself into the good guy. We're this far. You are going to figure out that third code. You're going to figure out who killed him."

I pulled her in for a chaste kiss. "Thank you."

"It's what I'm here for." She smiled. "Let's go meet him."

I turned to see Jonathan mingling with everyone. "Fine. Let's get it over with."

We walked over to Jonathan, who was finishing up with a couple of other students. "I really enjoyed the last story you read." Colby put her hand out to shake Jonathan's hand.

He smiled. "Yes, it was from one of my favorite students. Do you go here?" He asked. "I would have recognized you."

I balled up my fist. He was now hitting on my girlfriend. "I'm her boyfriend. I'm also that author's best friend." I snapped at him.

He looked at me with a smile. "Don't worry. I'm a married man." He showed his ring.

My heart dropped. He was married, and he had slept with Caleb. "What?"

"Yes, I have a wife and kids." He chuckled. "Who are you friends with?" He asked.

"Caleb. I'm Colin." He put out my hand. He was frozen for a minute. I saw the color in his face melt away. It was the response that I've been waiting for. "So you know who I am?"

He smiled. "I've heard about you. I didn't think that you guys were close anymore. I'm surprised to see you here." He played it off.

"I'm just trying to figure out what happened to my best friend the past four years. He left me some clues, and I'm here to figure it all out."

"He did tell me that you were into detective work."

"He talked about me?" I asked.

Jonathan smiled. "More than you know. Like I said, he was one of my favorite students. I saw him more of a friend than a student. He confided with me about a lot of things."

"I'm not proud of myself."

"Don't worry about it. I think we shouldn't be judged for our past actions. We've all made our fair share of mistakes."

"I bet you have." I mumbled.

Colby hit me. "Do you know anyone that could have done this to him?"

Jonathan looked away from me and to her. "I see you're his leash. I think he's going to need that in his life." He winked at me. "No, I think that's what makes this more tragic than anything in the world. Caleb was a bright soul that everyone loved to experience."

"Why would someone do this?"

"I think it's the mystery of the world. We can't harbor on answers we can't ever get."

"I don't believe that."

He turned to me. "Oh really?"

"I think there is always a way to find the truth. I think accepting that there are unanswered questions in the world means that you just give up. Truth gives you closure."

He nodded with me. "I can see how you will make a very good detective. Why don't you leave it to the real police."

I shook his head. "I want to do it myself."

"Or maybe you're here for more than just his murderer."

I raised an eyebrow. "What do you mean?"

"Caleb cared for you deeply. He saw you as a brother. I know you felt the same. It must be hard having to know the last four years of his life he became a different person."

"He was always the same person."

Jonathan raised a hand. "I don't think so. People grow in four years. He left his comfort and came here. He became someone that he needed to be. He still had the same heart."

"I want to believe he didn't forget me."

He smiled warmly. "He didn't." He pulled out a card from his pocket. "I would like to talk to you more. I think I can help you fig-ure out Caleb's life."

"Why?"

"I loved that man. I know it was probably over the line. What's the point of living when there are consequences? Call me. I would like to help you understand Caleb." He walked away from us.

I looked at the card. "Did that just happen?"

"Do you still want to run home?" Colby asked.

I looked down at the card Jonathan gave me. It was my next clue. "No."

39

October 5th, 2012

I heard someone whistle. I turned to see that it was Drew. "Someone looks nice." Drew raised an eyebrow. "Does someone have a date?"

I rolled my eyes. "I'm meeting with one of my professors. He wants me to see his friend read some of his work. It's not a date."

Drew walked in and sat on my bed. "It sounds like a date."

I grabbed my wallet and keys. "It would be inappropriate for me to sleep with my professor. I have some boundaries."

"You had a relationship with our RA all last year. I think your boundaries are a bit loose."

I knew he had a point. I tried to keep my thoughts about Jonathan on a professional manner. It was hard when he smiled, touched me, or just looked at me. I took in a deep breath. I couldn't get aroused in front of Drew.

"Nothing's going on. You need to stop letting your imagination get the best of you."

Drew chuckled. "Whatever you say. I haven't seen you that dressed up since you dated Jack." He got up and walked over to me. "I'm not going to judge you for your decisions. I just want you to have fun."

"I'm not dating him." I screamed as he walked out of my room.

"Whatever you say, lover boy."

I fixed my tie and maybe it felt like a date. He did imply that it would be nice to get to know me outside of the classroom. I was meeting his friend. Did this mean that he wanted to show me off?

I walked into the little bookstore that was a couple of miles from the university. It was where most of the upper classman went to get away from the toddlers as we were called. It was a nice place to find a vintage book and a good cup of coffee.

I walked into the coffee shop excepting to be shunned the moment I got in there. I looked around, and I knew no one here. This was a completely stupid idea. I should have said no. Why would I go to a place where I wasn't welcomed?

Jonathan saw me and waved at me. He looked like I made his day. I couldn't ruin that light on his face. I walked over and sat down with him in the front row. "You made it."

"Yeah, I've never been here before. I didn't think I was welcomed."

"Why do you say that?" He asked.

"I'm an underclassman. I thought only seniors were allowed here."

He had a full laugh, and I wanted him to laugh more often. "I still love the rules that go on around here. Everyone is welcomed here. Yes, it's the senior coffee shop, but they won't run you out of here."

"Are you sure about that?" I asked.

He leaned forward. "I'll protect you."

I liked him in my space. I could smell his cologne. I touched his biceps. I didn't know if it was forward. The people in the coffee shop were an older crowd anyways. "I'll need protecting from this world."

"Good. I'll protect and educate you." He turned back to the stage, but his hand was on my knee. This was extremely forward, but I enjoyed it. I put my hand on his, and he squeezed it.

I saw a gentleman come on stage. He was an elder man in his mid-sixties. He had gray hair and had to use a cane.

"Welcome everyone to my readings of short stories and poetry. My name is Paul Grady. I wrote this book a long time ago. It's so relieving to have this bitch out." People were laughing.

I enjoyed him. He had a wisdom that I wanted to know. I felt Jonathan's hand move closer to my thigh. He squeezed, and I let out a shaky breath. I saw from the corner of my eye an evil grin. I was fucked. I was going to go home with him, and I couldn't wait.

I had to remember I was here to meet one of his friends, not sleep with him. I refocused on Paul. He opened the book. "I want to start off with a poem that I wrote when I was on drugs in my twenties. I was so messed up that it was a cocktail of heroin, PCP, and weed. I should have died.

> *I'm truly running from the world*
> *I don't want to accept what I've become*
> *My parents hate me for who I love*
> *Isn't that a bit cliché?*
> *Shouldn't we live in a world*
> *Full of love, instead of hate?*
>
> *It doesn't matter anymore*
> *I resolved by distraction*
> *These are the only ones that love me*
> *I've been rejected by so many*
> *I'm truly alone in this world*
> *I'll die on this floor*
> *Knowing that my heart was hated by the world"*

There was a silence in the room until it broke into applause. I didn't know I was crying until Jonathan wiped a tear away from my eye. "I told you that he was good."

I turned to Jonathan. "Why are you doing this? Why are you being so nice to me? I'm a student. You're my professor. We shouldn't be doing this. Why aren't you more scared?"

He gave me a warm smile. "I learned from Paul that I shouldn't be ashamed of someone I've been attracted to. Caleb, your work made me fall in love with you. I want to get to know the writer behind those words. I want to understand everything that you have to say. Is this inappropriate? Maybe, but I don't care. You're a lost soul like me. I don't want to be alone in the world anymore. I want to be loved by you."

I touched his face. I just looked at him, and I knew that I could do this. I could fall madly in love with this guy. "Okay."

We turned back to Paul's readings. I felt Jonathan beside me and became at ease with the world. I accepted keeping this a secret because I didn't want the judgment. I wanted the purity to stay for a while.

I grabbed Jonathan's hand and intertwined our fingers together. I leaned into his weight, and he didn't seem to mind. We didn't worry about the consequences. We didn't have to explain our decisions. We could fall for each other, and we could be the souls we wanted to be.

40

October 24th, 2012

"I think that love letters are beautiful. I think we should write them more often." I looked at Jonathan. We had been spending a lot of time together. We would exchange books and story ideas. I told him about "Dear Love" by Patty Light.

"Why do you say that?" He asked.

"We're a world where texts and Facebook messages are counted as courtship. That's not courtship, that's just being lazy." Everyone in the room chuckled. "I want to feel like someone took the time and wrote me a letter. I know I would do the same thing. I want to actually know that I mean something to you, and I'll do the same for you."

"Like Alicia Key says, put it in a love song," Shawn added.

Everyone laughed. Jonathan looked at the time. "I think we should end there. I want you guys to continue reading 'Dear Love.' We will talk about this later on."

Everyone started packing up their bags. "Are you staying to talk to Jonathan?" Shawn asked.

I didn't want Jonathan to become my life like Jack did. I wanted to make sure I was my own person. "Nah, I was planning on going home. Did you want to come with?" I asked.

Shawn nodded. "I would like that."

I nodded at Jonathan, but I would call him later. Shawn and I started walking off campus to my apartment. "Did you mean what you said?" He asked.

I turned to look at him. "What?"

"That you think we should write love letters."

"Yeah, I want to feel loved. I want to actually matter to someone. I don't want a stupid text or comment. I know it's old school, but my parents did it the whole time they were dating."

"That's sweet."

I smiled. "My mom knew he was the one when he wrote her a stupid little postcard. She asked why he did it since they had just seen each other earlier that day. He said that he wanted to document their love, and many years later, they would read the letters together. They would remember how much their love has grown."

"That's extremely romantic."

"Yeah, I guess I get it from them. I've always wanted that love. I wanted to look at my past and know that I had something special with my soulmate. I wanted to believe that we were unique, and no one could take our love away."

"Sounds like a love ballad."

I laughed, but it was true. I didn't want to have a normal love. I looked at all these romantic novels and wanted that for myself. I didn't believe that we should half-ass something when it came to love. When you are head-over-heels, you should announce it to the world. You should give your soulmate everything you have, so they know you truly want them. I thought I might be able to get that with Jonathan. I just didn't know if he felt the same for me.

October 25th, 2012

"You have mail." Drew handed me an envelope.

"Are you sure it's for me?" I wasn't expecting anything.

"Yeah, it says your name." Drew rolled his eyes. "You get a letter and act like it's a big deal." He walked out of the room.

I laughed at Drew's response. I opened the envelope to see that it was a letter.

Dear Caleb,

You talked about in class that you wanted love letters. This was the way to properly court you. I agree with you. I'm able to write my feelings down on a piece of paper. I'm able to tell you over and over again how much my heart is drawn to you. It's scary to fall in love with someone so young, but you aren't young. You have an old soul that I've never experienced before. I knew the moment I met you that you were going to be special to me. It might be complicated for us, but it's our relationship. I don't want anyone taking this from us. I want the world to know our love when were ready for them to know. I can't stop thinking about you, and I hope you feel the same for me. I know there will be bumps in our road, but we will get through them. I hope you take me.

Love,
Jonathan

I had tears in my eyes. Yup, he had taken my heart. Those stupid words on this page made me realize he had me. I wanted nothing more than to kiss him, and it killed me to know that I had to be patient.

"Who was the letter from?" Drew asked.

I turned and wiped the tears away. "It's from a guy."

"Ah. Does someone have a secret boyfriend again?"

I shook my head. "No boyfriend."

Drew's smile turned into concern. "I just don't want to have what happened again with Jack. I know it messed you up."

Why couldn't he be in my past? Why couldn't we completely forget about him? I was happy with someone new. I was with someone who understood me. It was the first time in a long time that I truly felt loved.

"I'm not going to get there again."

"I'll be here no matter what."

I smiled. "Thank you for caring about me so much."

Drew shrugged. "We've got each other's backs. I'll be here if the asshole breaks your heart."

I laughed and looked at the letter. "I don't think you have to worry about that. He seems like a keeper."

"All right. We're going to the talent show. You want to come?" He asked.

"Yeah, I just need to write this, then I'll be set."

"Cool." He walked out of my room.

I pulled out a piece of paper and wrote my first, of hopefully, many letters to Jonathan.

> *Dear Jonathan,*
>
> *Are you stalking me? How did you get my address? I've never had someone write me a letter before, and I just want to say yes. I want to be loved by you, and I want to love you. It's been an incredible couple of months getting to know you. You get me more than others, and I'm grateful for that. I want to know everything about you. I want to understand you. I know it won't be easy for us, but yes. I want to try with you. I want to fail and be broken by you because you're the incredible person that has that control. So take me, and I'll never let go.*
>
> *Love,*
> *Caleb.*

41

November 1st, 2012

"Are you with me today?" I looked at Dr. Baer.

"What was the question?" I felt guilty ignoring her, but I was thinking about the letter I just got from Jonathan. He wanted to take me out. He wanted to take me away, so we could actually be ourselves.

"How are you today?" She asked softly.

"I'm conflicted. I'm sorry if I seem distracted."

"Is there something on your mind?"

I was hesitant to tell her. "Is everything that is said in here private? I won't be judged on it."

I saw the concern in her eyes. "I won't tell anyone unless it's you harming yourself or others. I'm forced to if it comes to that."

I shook my head. "No, it's not that bad."

"What is it?"

"I think I'm in a relationship with my professor." It felt nice to get it off my chest. Drew was on my case about the love letters.

"Ah, I thought it was going to be way worse."

"Isn't that bad?" I asked.

"Not really."

"What?"

"You were in a relationship with your RA. You like to keep these relationships hidden. You don't want people to hate you for the person you love."

"That's not true."

"Isn't it?"

"What are you talking about?"

"How are you and Colin? Have you talked to him?" She asked.

The truth was that we hadn't talked since we met up over the summer. "I don't want to be reminded of someone who couldn't handle who I was."

"Are you afraid of other people hating you? Colin isn't the first person."

I knew where she was going with it. "I don't want to get into it about how my father left me."

"But you love your step father, who you thought was your real father."

"Yeah, I love him so much, but it doesn't mean that I forgot about what happened. It doesn't mean that I can keep going forward knowing how much people have hated me."

"People don't hate you. You have a great friendship here. Drew was there for you during your dark time."

"I guess you're right."

She smiled. "I usually am." She was writing a note on my file.

"I just want to make sure that this is a real thing. I know we're already going to get judged because I'm a student, and he's my professor. I know that it doesn't make sense to other people, but it does to me."

"Isn't that all that matters?"

"I just don't want to feel alone in the world anymore."

"Do you?"

"Not with him." I felt the letter in my pocket. I got it right before I got to my session. I couldn't contain my smile.

"It's scary to be falling in love with someone that I barely know. I've known him for three months, but it's something so pure with him. I don't have to hide."

"Do you think he's hiding from you?"

"No, I don't believe so. We're connected and tell each other everything. I just believe that he's the one."

"That's a huge statement."

"I know that I look young and naïve. I shouldn't know what real love is. I'm twenty years old."

"I wouldn't say that."

"How so?"

"You've been through a lot in your life. You've learned to grow up. I think that your age is really just a number."

"Jonathan says that all the time. He found his old soul."

"His name is Jonathan."

"Yeah. He's something special. I get excited when he looks at me. I love when he calls on me. He's a great person to talk to."

She closed her book. "Enjoy it. You should not fear something like love. I just want you to protect yourself. Jack hurt you. You don't want slip and go back into that dark place."

I shook my head. I knew how to be careful, but I didn't think Jonathan would do that to me. I didn't want to believe that he could hurt me. He cared for me. He protected me from the doubts that I had. "I won't."

She smiled. "I guess we're done here. Always remember that this is your life. You don't need to appease anyone. Enjoy the feeling of love. It should never be forgotten."

"I don't think I will."

42

November 5th, 2012

"Do you love Cameron?" I asked Drew. We were sitting on the floor of the radio station smoking a blunt.

"Yeah, I've been with the girl over a year."

"When did you know you were in love?" I asked.

"Is this something to do with your new boy?" He passed me a blunt.

"Yeah, I think I love him." I took a hit. "I'm freaked out about it."

"Why?"

"Isn't it too soon to have these emotions?"

"He writes you letters all the time."

I smiled thinking about the letter I got this morning. It was a stupid letter riddled with stupid puns. "Yeah, he gets me. He knows that I'm this scared guy, but he makes me less scared."

"I don't think you should be so freaked out about how much time it took to fall for them."

"How long for you?"

"I think the moment I met her. I know it's stupid, but she was just this force that I couldn't get out of my mind. She stood up to Catherine during our first week. Who does that?"

I laughed. "Yeah, I could see that from Beth, not Cameron. Why did you sleep with Beth for that little bit then?"

"Because I wasn't ready for a serious relationship. I don't think I was ready for the love I could have for Cameron. I wanted the so-called college experience. I learned sleeping with Beth that all I really wanted in life was Cameron."

I took another hit. "I see that with Colin and Colby. They've been together since we were sophomores in high school. I thought they would have broken up by now because they haven't been with other people."

"Do you miss them?" Drew asked.

I looked at the ceiling. I remembered all the laughs in high school, the joy I felt to belong to a group, but I remembered the sting of rejection. I felt the tears stream from my eyes. "I want to believe that I miss them, but you can't miss something that caused you so much pain. It's like a bad relationship. You can't focus on the best parts of it, or you'll never move forward. You have to think about the reasons why it ended."

I felt Drew squeeze my hand. "It's okay."

"For the longest time, I felt like I was playing pretend. I didn't think I was going to be okay. I didn't think I felt like I mattered. It took you guys for me to realize that I am someone, and I shouldn't have people take that away from me."

"We're here for you."

I looked at Drew. "And this guy I'm with because I want to be. It's on our own terms. I'm not controlled by him."

"It's nice to hear that. I just don't want a repeat of this past summer."

I shook my head. "I'll never get there. I promise." I didn't believe that Jonathan could hurt me. Jonathan was so open to me. He had no secrets, and trusted me. We respected each other, and I could see this going the distance. I loved this man, and I just couldn't wait to be with him.

November 14th, 2012

"Jonathan has been making us read a lot of love stories lately," Shawn said. We were in the library finishing up our next round of short stories.

I knew what he was doing, and I had to admit that it was working. "I love the stories. I think they're beautiful."

"I bet you do."

"What's that supposed to mean?" I asked.

"You have feelings for the guy. I see the way you two look at each other."

I had to play it cool. I trusted Shawn, but I didn't want anyone to know yet. I wanted this to be something only I could have. "I don't know what you're talking about. I respect him."

"There's nothing wrong with having a crush on the guy. I've learned that crushes don't go anywhere." He looked at me and back at the paper.

I ignored his comment because I didn't want to get into it with him about that. "We're just mutually respecting each other."

"And you want to sleep with him." Shawn shot back.

"I can't believe you. Where did the shy Shawn go? I liked him better." I joked. I loved that Shawn has finally opened up to us. He never told us why he was so timid, and we never asked him.

"I've always lived on the sidelines. I don't want to do that anymore. I want to feel something."

"It's fun being on the field." I winked at him.

He blushed and looked down. "So you and Jonathan?"

"Nothing's going on. It's just student-professor relationship."

"Except he asked about you when you were sick last week."

I contained my smile. Jonathan had sent me roses plus three letters that day I missed class because I was feeling like crap. I didn't want to explain to him that I was actually hungover from a radio station mixer.

"I still don't believe you."

"He looks at you like you're his sun."

"I see what you mean by him being a great writer and professor. I'm on the same boat as you."

"I just wish he talked about me like he does you. I want to be recognized for my writing."

I grabbed his hand and squeezed. "I know, and he does. You're his second favorite student. You'll get your work out there. It's brilliant."

"Coming from you, who is going to be the next Mark Twain."

I laughed. "I don't think that will happen, but we can try."

I never knew why I couldn't have fallen in love with Shawn. He was smart, funny, and extremely sweet. Our relationship would be filled with love and words. I wouldn't have to be scared with him, but I think at a part of me enjoyed the danger. I liked the idea that it could all go down in flames tomorrow. It made me feel alive and loved.

43

November 18th, 2012

Dear Jonathan,

In this life, you experience some of the greatest people and some of the worst. I never thought my creative writing professor would be one of the greatest. I just never have had these kind of feelings for someone before. I just thought it was a stupid crush. I've gotten to know you for the past couple of months, and I can tell you that it's not a crush anymore.

You sit there and listen to me vent about my life. You give me poems and short stories that are suited perfectly for me. You took me to a reading of an artist that I now am obsessed with. We debate and argue because we're equal human beings. You make me a stronger person. You write me letters because you know how much they mean to me. Who does that? I've never met anyone like you, and I don't want to meet another person who compares.

I want to first thank you for listening to me during all of my conversations with Colin. You didn't have to listen or even care. It's so nice going to you about everything that I'm feeling. Thank you for being my anchor, my support, and my foundation. I thought I found that it my friends, but I found it in you. Jonathan, it's naïve to believe this, but I see a life with you. I love you, and it's not just three stupid words to me. I've fallen for you, and I don't want to stop.

Love
Caleb.

I was looking at the letter that I sent Jonathan yesterday. I hadn't heard from him, and I was worried. Maybe I came on too strong. Maybe he hasn't read it yet. I probably was fool. I shouldn't have said it. I needed to stop thinking like that because I believed in those words after our conversation two nights ago.

November 16th, 2012
"You seem upset," Jonathan said when he walked into the library to find me.

I looked up at him. "Why are you here?"

"I was finishing up grading papers, and I figured you were in here studying for midterms."

"More like being distracted by life problems." I closed my history book. I wasn't going to figure the dates of wars with everything swimming in my head.

"What's wrong?" He asked, and I could hear the concern in his voice.

"Why do you care? I know you're a really sweet guy, but you're my professor. We flirt and write letters, but isn't that all it is." I looked around. "It's wrong."

He smiled. "I am your professor, yes. Is it frowned upon? Yes. Is it illegal? No. I like you for being you. I have feelings for you that I haven't felt for anyone else. I'm not going to hide behind some bullshit because of it. I'll ask you what's wrong because there is a darkness in my life when you're upset."

He was good with words, and I fucking ate them right up. I sighed. "I hate you."

He chuckled. "I bet you do. Tell me what's going on?"

"It's my best friends birthday."

"Today's Drew's birthday?"

"No, my hometown best friend. His name's Colin."

"You never have talked about him."

"There isn't much to talk about. We had a huge falling out before I got to college. I told him I was gay, and he couldn't accept that. Words were said, and we haven't spoken since. I thought we would make up, but it hasn't happened."

"So what's the problem?"

"We planned to spend his twenty-first together. We planned on being there for each other in college. I know I have great friends here, but I have a piece of my heart missing. I don't want to feel empty anymore." I felt like a fucking fool crying in front of this guy.

He grabbed my hand and stroked it for a minute. "It's okay to be upset about losing a friend. We don't think we would ever lose someone that important in our life. You can't be upset because it happened."

"Why can't I just let it go?"

"He was one of the major reasons you've become the person you are. You should never be ashamed of that. You should never feel like you're a fool because you want to cry about losing a friend. I've lost a lot of good people in my life. It doesn't mean I forget about them, or the pain's gone."

"How do I get it to be better?"

"It takes time, but you focus on the good in your life. You relish in the friends that stick by. It's a sad truth, but we spend more time getting the approval of the people who don't cherish us than the people who would. We begin to realize later in life that people do come and go."

"I don't want to lose people in my life."

"It's part of it. You learn that there are souls in our life that stick with you through the long haul. We learn something from every single person. You have people for every phase of your life. He was part of one phase. It doesn't mean it tarnished his impact on your life, but it was time to grow apart."

"Could we ever get back to being us again?"

"Be hopeful. It's one of the magical things about it. Our hope and determination is what gets us by. Never lose that. You two will be friends again, if you fully have hope it will happen."

I took in every word that he said, and I knew Colin and I would be okay. We needed to be separated to grow up. We needed to be our own people before we could continue together. I had to hope for that. "Thank you for everything."

He gave me a smile. "It's what I'm here for. I'll let you get back to your studies." He stood up and waved. I watched him walk away from me, and I knew that I needed to tell him. I wasn't scared anymore about my feelings. He was this great character in this chapter of my life, and I wanted him to know that. I wanted him to have my love, and I wanted his.

November 18th, 2012

I was still patiently waiting, and I knew that maybe I spoke too soon. Maybe I should have just kept our relationship a slow burning instead of adding fuel to the fire. I couldn't go to talk to Drew because he was on a date with Cameron before everyone left for Thanksgiving Break. Beth wasn't the type to talk to about emotions, and I knew that it would kill Shawn going to him.

I heard a knock on the door as I was heading to the fridge to grab a beer. I would just get drunk and forget that all of this happened. I walked over to the door and opened it. Jonathan was standing there. "Jonathan, what are you doing here?" I saw the letter in his hand. I knew he was going to end it.

He stepped into my space. He pulled me in and crushed his lips on mine. It was a bit abrasive and took me by surprise. It took a minute for me to realize what was going on. I was kissing Jonathan. The man that I was in love with was finally kissing me.

I reciprocated the kiss and put my weight into it. His lips were soft on mine, and I let out a moan. This is what I wanted in life. I felt my whole body just melt into the kiss, and I had never felt something so pure or magical in my life. I felt alive, and I never wanted it to end.

I knew we couldn't sit in my doorway kissing for the rest of eternity. We had to talk about this. We separated and looked at each other. "You kissed me."

"I love you."

"You came here and kissed me." I repeated.

"I love you." He repeated.

"Why?"

He smiled. "Because I love you."

"Why?" I wanted to know what was so special about me.

"Because you insulted my writing the first day of class." We both smiled. "It's been downhill since." He pulled me in for another kiss, and I let him.

I was loved. I had someone that I never wanted to be out of my life. He came into it at an unexpected time, but I never wanted it to end. I never wanted to be out of his arms. This was the man I would spend the rest of my life with. It was a short amount of time, but I loved him. I wasn't scared to. He felt the same about me, and that's all I needed in my life.

44

I slammed my laptop. There was no way the second part could end like that. How could someone accept him sleeping with his professor? "No!" I screamed.

Colby looked at me. "What's wrong?"

"Caleb and Jonathan are together."

She looked at me confused. "We know this. Drew and everyone else knew this. Why are you saying it now?"

"No, I got to the diary entry when they get together. It's how the second part ends. I can't. No. I don't want to believe that he had a relationship with that man." I stood up and walked into the bathroom. I splashed my face with some cold water.

Colby walked over and leaned against the doorframe. "What's so wrong with him being in love with his professor?"

"The man was older than him."

"So?"

"That's disgusting."

"I can't believe you right now. How could you say that? Caleb was your best fucking friend. Do you think he would be okay hearing you say this?"

"He shouldn't have started a relationship with him."

"You don't get to control who you love." She screamed.

It was quiet for a moment. We looked at each other and there was anger behind her eyes. "What's wrong with you?" She asked.

"What are you talking about?"

"That man was your best friend. He would do anything for you. You would do anything for him. Why can't you remember that?"

"I can't get over it."

"Why not? Why can't you look past one thing you don't agree with? Why can't you accept that he was gay?" Colby looked me straight in the eyes.

"My father raised me to be against it. He told me that it's wrong to be a homosexual. I can't just forget that."

She sighed. "Your father was an asshole."

"You didn't know him." I snapped. I thought about all the times we saw guys walking together holding hands. I saw how much they were in loved, but my dad told me it was wrong. He said it was disgusting. I still believe his word is law.

"It doesn't matter. Your father shouldn't teach you to hate your best friend."

"I don't hate him. I just can't accept him being gay."

"Maybe that's why you guys could never fix your problems. You say that it was equally both your faults, but I'm starting to believe that it's you. Colin, you have always shown me so much warmth. I saw how much you loved Caleb, but I'm starting to see how truly dark you can be."

"Because I don't believe in homosexuality."

"You couldn't put your own prejudice aside for your best friend when he needed you the most. He was the only one that was friends with you growing up. I listened to the other kids when they said to stay away. You were the freak with no parents. He put that aside."

"He was a kid. He didn't know better."

She shook her head. "No, it was the type of person Caleb was. I don't care that he fell in love with his professor. I think it's beautiful. Everyone in this world should love the people they want it."

"He was sleeping with a married man. How is that right?"

"Caleb didn't know that, did he?"

I read and reread all the journal entries. There was no mention of a ring, a wife, or a family. He kept talking about how he met this incredible guy. "No, I haven't seen it."

"You need to stop judging him for being gay. You need to stop acting like it's a flaw. I think it's brave that he came out. He could have kept it in the close it forever. Caleb was more of a man than you."

"Because I don't accept it."

"No because he looked past his views to love someone for who they truly were. Maybe you didn't deserve Caleb as your best friend. Maybe you don't deserve me as a girlfriend."

"Colby, you can't say that."

"I don't know what you want me to do. You've become this horrible, judgmental asshole since we've gotten here. I thought this would help you. I thought this would bring you back to me. It's just driving you away. I can't do this." She turned into the bedroom.

I walked in there. "Colby, stop." She stopped before the door. She didn't turn around. "I'm working through my shit. I'm sorry that I can't all of a sudden change who I am because of how I was raised." I pleaded with Colby to understand. I knew I was an asshole, but I was raised like this. My Aunt tried to change this in me.

"My father was my whole world. He was my idol, and I lost him. I don't want to ever disappoint him."

"Do you think that being there for your best friend would make him disapprove of you?"

"A part of me does."

"Then you need a new role model." She opened the door and walked out.

I sat down on the bed with a heavy chest. I always believed everything that my dad said was the law. He had taught me right and wrong. He was a good man. People loved my parents and never spoke negative about them. How could he be wrong about this? How could he be a villain when he was my hero?

45

I was sitting in Jonathan's office. I was trying to imagine all the entries. This is where Caleb fell in love with the man that would eventually break him.

"I feel like we got off on the wrong foot." Jonathan put down his pen and looked at me.

I crossed my arms. "Why do you think that?"

"I think that you're still very upset about Caleb's death. Yes, we were close, and he talked about you. I know that the story I read must have been hard on you."

"You don't know me."

Jonathan raised an eyebrow. "I think I know you very well. You're a good person. You've always been there for people, but you have these views and opinions. You've been trying to adapt to a new world, and maybe that's the problem."

I tried to keep anger down. "You don't know me. Yes, I didn't get his homosexuality. Yes, I didn't take it very well. It's hard for me, okay?"

"Why can't you accept he had a different kind of love?"

"Because it's hard to change your views on something that you've been raised on since day one. You believe what your parents say is law."

"It seems your parents needed a teaching."

"My parents are dead." I snapped.

He raised his hands in defeat. "I didn't mean to judge. I do apologize for that. It's not why I asked you here."

"Why did you?" It was a question burning on my mind.

"You want to know who killed your best friend. Is that why you're here?" He asked.

"I want to figure out what happened to my friend the last four years of his life. Yes, we separated. I know that I still deeply care for him. He was my brother, and I didn't like that we had a falling out. I'm trying to understand him."

I didn't trust him, nor should have Caleb. Their whole relationship was built on a lie. I looked over and I saw him with his wife and kids. "You have a cute family."

Jonathan saw I was looking at the picture. He had a warm smile on his face. "Yeah, it's been great to have them back in my life. Two years ago, I was separated from them." He paused. "I made bad decisions without my wife. I realized that I loved her, and I wanted things to work out."

"Did you hurt people in the process?"

"I don't think they understood what it meant to have a family. Love is a beautiful thing, but there are so many different kinds of love. I thought I was looking for romantic love at my age, but it was my family love that I wanted. I never wanted that taken away from me."

"Do you feel guilty for things you've done?" I asked him. I wanted to scream out how could he have done those things to Caleb. Caleb had no idea how much pain was coming his way.

"Do you?"

"I'll always live with the guilt of rejecting my best friend."

"It's a hard reality when we reject someone. We try to tell them our side of things, but I don't think that could ever work out."

"How so?" I asked.

"People don't think like us. The only person who does is you. You could explain to them the reasoning behind your actions, but they won't get it. They haven't walked a mile in your shoes."

"So will people ever understand each other?"

"I don't think you can. We will always live in a civilization where people won't understand each other. We will always have miscommunication and misunderstandings."

"I just wish I knew him better." I looked down at my hands.

"We all make poor decisions. It happens, but you're here now trying to make sense of it all."

I looked back at him. "I don't think I'll ever make sense of it."

"You won't. You never were going to." He pulled out a stack of papers and handed them to me. "This is all of Caleb's writings he had given me."

"That's a lot of work."

He smiled. "I had him for three semesters. He took every single one of my classes."

"Sounds like he was your stalker."

Jonathan chuckled. "He was driven to learn from the best. He saw me as that. We had a connection and honesty to our relationship. I was his mentor, and you don't change that."

"What did you think of his writing?" I asked.

"I've never met anyone who had more talent or potential than him. He wrote stories that were specific to him, but also helped with everyone. The world lost one of the greatest writers."

"That's a grand endorsement."

"Why don't you read his work? You'll understand what I mean. I think after you read them you should come to one of my classes."

I looked at the papers in front of me. I was nervous and scared to read them. I always knew that he was a talented writer, but would our demons be splashed across the pages? I just worried that I wouldn't be able to handle them.

46

Did our friendship even matter? Why would he just reject me like that? I guess in the scheme of things you do have to be broken by people. I never assumed that my brother would backstab me. It seems we all have to be hurt by the ones closest to us. Maybe that's why I've become stronger and focused on the people that love me.

The words were echoing in my mind as I finished another beer. I couldn't believe how much I hurt him. I rejected him so hard that I was a villain in his life. Was it wrong to take your parents' view? They raised me, and they were taken away from me. I don't want to believe that they were horrible people.

I saw Jimmy walking into the bar. "I see you're already in your self-pity mode."

I rolled my eyes. "What are you doing here? Don't you have a tournament or something to get to?"

"Yeah, but when my best friend's girlfriend is worried sick about him, I'm going to find out what the fucks going on."

"I'm not looking for a judgment call. I just want to be left alone."

He sighed and walked up to the bar. He grabbed two beers and handed me one. "I'm not going to judge you. We've all had our rough spots. You knew that this was going to happen when you came here."

"Am I horrible person?" I asked.

I looked straight into Jimmy's eyes. I saw the concern in his eyes. I saw my reflection in his eyes. I looked like a mess, but it's what I felt. I didn't know if I could ever be put back together. No one has been able to fix my pieces like Caleb.

He sighed. "I'm not going to lie to you. You made a dick move. You can't change that. It's been four years. Why can't you move past it?"

"Because that fight changed both of our lives. That fight is the reason were here right now."

"The fight caused a lot of problems in your life. Even after all this time, you still hold him to such a high standard."

"He did nothing wrong. It was all me."

"It seemed it wasn't. You weren't the only one that said something during that fight."

"You don't know what was said."

Jimmy shrugged. "You're right. I don't know what happened, but you're still pressed on it."

"Fuck you." I finished my next beer. I wanted to just feel numb.

Jimmy didn't move. "You can't be angry at me because I'm calling you out on your bullshit. Colin, we came here for you to get closure. We were supposed to go on a guy's trip to travel the country. I wasn't angry giving that up for us to come here. Colby pushed her internship back, so she could be here for you."

"Why don't you make me feel more guilty?" I didn't want to be constantly reminded that people were giving up all this for me, and I didn't give them anything.

"You're not seeing the point."

"What's your point?"

"We care about you so much. You're not this villain that you think you are. You've always been there for me. You've made sure that all the girls who rejected me knew what they were giving up. You were there for me when my mom had cancer, dude. You and Colby have an incredible relationship. All I see is the love there."

"What do I do?"

"You need to move on. You need to grieve."

"I have grieved."

Jimmy shook his head. "I don't think you have. You haven't had time to really digest what's going on."

"My best friend was murdered. Someone thought he didn't belong here anymore. How can I digest that?"

"Saying it over and over again won't make you move forward."

I slammed the glass down on the table. People started looking at us. "I don't know how to move forward. What I do know is that I'm going to find the bastard that killed him."

"And do what?"

"I'm going to make them pay for Caleb's death. I'm not going to live in this world without Caleb. He was my best friend. He's the reason I survived our hometown. He took me in, and I never got to thank him for that. I never repaid him."

"Maybe this is your way of repaying him. You're here now."

"How can you repay someone whose dead?"

"Because you give them the chance to explain their life through their eyes. You understand the person for who he truly was. You're looking through all the bullshit for the soul."

"I just want it all to go away."

"It won't and never will." Jimmy got up. "I'll see you at the hotel."

"You're leaving me?" I looked at him.

He shook his head. He grabbed some of the papers. "I'm not leaving you. I'm giving you time with your best friend."

"It's a reminder that I was a horrible person."

"There might be a lot of hate in there, but there has to be love."

"Why do you believe that?"

"I've seen all sides of you, Colin. I know he had to love the friendship you had at some point. We wouldn't be here if it wasn't for that." He gave me a weak smile and walked away.

I picked up another story and started reading. *We were the best of friends and the worst of enemies. We were stubborn and never wanted to be wrong. We loved and fought. I don't think I met someone as strong as him, and I was thankful for him. He gave me the strength I needed to be the person I wanted to be. I know he never understood or accepted me for who I was, but he still gave me the power I needed to come out. I'll thank him for that until I die.*

47

Four Years Earlier

I didn't want to leave my bed. I wanted to have nothing to do with the world. Caleb's words still echoed in my head. He was gay. He had been keeping this secret from me. Why would he tell me this?

I heard a knock on my door. "I don't want to be bothered."

"I'm sure you don't, but we need to talk." Aunt June walked through the door. I felt a dip on my bed. I took the cover over my head and looked at her.

"I don't want to talk about it."

"I'm just making sure you're okay. I have no clue what you're talking about." I knew she was playing innocent. I wasn't going to fall for it.

"I'm not talking."

"What happened?" She crossed her arms.

"He told me he was gay."

"And?"

"And." I couldn't believe that it wasn't a bigger deal to her. "He's gay. It's wrong."

I felt a slap go across my face. "I raised you not to be a fucking bigot. You should know better than that."

I rubbed my face. "Dad said."

She shook her head. "I don't care what your father said. He was a good man, but he was an asshole. I can't believe he has you brainwashed to believe that it's wrong to love."

"But."

"No, buts. Caleb has always been there for you. You two have been through so much together. Do you believe that it's right to be rejected from being in love?"

"No."

"Then why would you cause so much pain to each other?"

"I don't know." I couldn't answer the question. "I just thought it was wrong. I was taught this."

She scooted over and grabbed my face. "You should never shun your best friend. It must have taken a lot of courage for him to tell you this. You need to apologize."

I felt the anger boil in my body. "Why should I apologize? He said some things that I didn't like."

"They couldn't have been that bad."

"He said he understood why my parents got into the accident. Why would they want a son like me?" I still felt the jab in my heart. He was the only one I trusted with my worries they left me because they didn't love me.

She sighed heavily. "You both did a number on each other."

"I can't be okay with him. He's changing, and I don't like it. We've always been on the same page, and now, I don't know."

"It's part of growing up. You don't want to miss out on each other's lives."

"I don't want to be the bigger person."

"You sometimes have to be the bigger person because the world needs good people. We need people to choose the right path, instead of the selfish path." She kissed me on the cheek. "I don't want you to lose a friend because of this." She got off my bed.

"What if I don't make up with him?" I asked.

"It will be one of your greatest regrets. I've never seen a friendship like yours. You don't want to lose that."

I nodded. "I just can't forgive him."

"Tell him that. Don't go into it trying to win the fight. Go into it trying to compromise." She walked out of my room.

I put my head back on my pillow. I looked at my ceiling. I didn't know what I was going to do. I closed my eyes hoping it was all a nightmare. He wasn't gay, nor my enemy.

I got out of bed and changed. I walked into the forest to be alone. I got to the tree house. It's where we had our last fight. *"I could never be friends with such a bigot."*

"I'm not a bigot. I was raised that it's wrong. I'm sorry that I can't agree with it."

"No wonder your parents left you. They would have been ashamed to have a son like you."

"Least I'm not a fag."

The words echoed in my brain. I felt the tears starting to form. I climbed to the tree house and looked at all the memories we shared over the years. It was supposed to be us against the world. I didn't know if that was true anymore.

I saw our little carving on the door. We will always be friends. We will always have each other. We will always be brothers.

I touched the carving. "I don't think that's true anymore. I don't think I can be your brother."

I knew it was easier because we were going to different colleges. Maybe that's why he was so persistent on checking out a new college. He had this all planned out. I just didn't want to believe that I was just nothing to him. I didn't want to believe that we could never get there.

I watched as a thunderstorm was coming. I didn't want to move. I didn't want to bother with anything else. I watched as the rain began to clean the surrounding area. We never got to fix the holes in the roof, and my tears mixed with the rain.

I never felt like an abandoned human being until now. I never felt like I didn't have parents or friends. I felt like the loser kid the first day so many years ago. I never wanted to feel like this. I blamed Caleb for this pain.

It's his fault that I'm like this. I can't accept that anymore. I agreed now. It was best we went our separate ways. I could never be a friend to someone who was strongly against my beliefs. He wasn't someone I needed in my corner. I wanted to believe that, and I had to. I needed it to move forward and put Caleb in my past.

48

"We've made it to the end of the semester. Hell, we made it to the end of the year." Jonathan looked out to his class. I was seated in the back of the room. I got a few odd looks, but I ignored them. Colby and I hadn't spoken much before I left.

I had no clue what I was doing here. I didn't know how this would help me with the next clue. All the hint said was it was the first story. I thought it was Caleb's, but it wasn't. I grew frustrated, but I think the hangover might be the cause of that right now.

"I want to talk to you before you guys begin finals. Some of you this will be the last time you'll be in a college setting. You will grow and figure out your life when you go into the real world. Some of you will go to grad school while others aren't close to finishing up your undergrad." He smiled. He walked around and sat down on the table. He picked up a paper.

"I know most of you took this class just to get rid of a Gen-Ed credit." The kids in the class started to laugh. "I just wanted to read this to the ones that actually truly care about writing."

"The short story, 'Windmills,' by Jonathan Lancaster is the debut from this writer. It shows how much inexperience this writer has. Yes, he has the potential to become a great writer, but with this piece of work it seems uncertain. He focuses too much on describing the surroundings, instead of focusing on the characters. I was rather bored with both of these characters, and I didn't see the point of this story. It seems the writer had no connection with Paul or Mary, and the reader was left wondering, do we root for them or hate them? I hope this writer gets into some creative writing workshops."

The class was silent. People didn't say anything. I saw the admiration in Jonathan's eyes. How could he admire someone that destroyed his first piece for work. "I read this to the class at the end of the year. I know some of my students continue to take my class, and I've grown a connection with them. I wanted you to know this piece of work."

He smiled. "It's interesting because this reviewer later on praised my writing. He has joked in interviews that it was his review that caused me to be a better writer. I didn't want to admit it, but it was this that made me continue to write."

"Why read us that?" A blonde hair girl asked.

"Because I want you guys to see that you will get ripped apart. You will want to crawl into a ball. You need to have a thick skin in this industry. I'll admit that this destroyed me."

I raised my hand. "How did you move past it?" I asked.

Jonathan smiled. "You get reviews that make you feel inspired. My next short story that I wrote was better than 'Windmills.'" He picked up another piece of paper. "Thank you for writing 'Chained.' I guess I've always questioned my place in the world. I never knew who I was supposed to be, or if I even mattered. I saw Matt continue to get beaten left and right for what he believed in. I saw how much courage he had to be who he truly was. I think that's what we all want to strive for in the world. It's what I'm going to do myself. I just wanted to say thank you for writing something so profound that I can believe and have hope for my life."

I saw a tear go down Jonathan's eyes. It was a beautiful review, and I now wanted to read some of his work. "I had to dig deep within myself to get what I wanted."

"Was it all worth it?" A bald guy asked.

"You'll always get the good and bad. You'll never have work that is fully hated or fully loved. You need to take the good with the bad. I just want to say thank you for an amazing semester and for some an amazing year. I do hope you continue to write. I want you to never lose your passion or love for writing. You should never be scared to write what's deep inside you. It's how the greatest writers get known."

People started packing up their bags to leave. They were shaking his hands and asking for thoughts on their pieces of work. Eventually it was just him and I in the classroom. "I'm surprised that you actually came."

"It's been a rough couple of days." I walked down towards him.

"How did you like the class?" He asked.

"I thought it was very educational. Are those real reviews?"

"Yes." He chuckled. "I couldn't believe my first story was destroyed." It hit me then that the clue was referring to Jonathan. It was 'Windmills'.

"Did Caleb ever hear the speech?" I asked.

"It would have been his second time." There was sadness in his voice. "It's still hard to realize that he's gone." He put his papers in the briefcase. He smiled. "He always wanted people to love his work."

"Wouldn't everyone?"

"I guess you didn't get the point. Caleb didn't get it his first time. It's not about everyone loving your work. It's about if you can stand by it. Who gives a fuck about everyone else?"

"Do you believe that?"

"I was destroyed when I wrote 'Windmills.' I thought I couldn't write anymore. I put my everything into it, but no one loved it."

"What changed for 'Chained?'"

"I wasn't honest with myself with 'Windmills.' I was keeping secrets, and you can't with writing. You have to fully expose yourself to the world."

"That seems frightening."

"You aren't a writer, so you won't get it. There's nothing wrong with that."

"What's the point of writing?"

"To help people. It's what Caleb wanted to do with his writing. He wanted to expose the dark depths of the human soul to the world. He wanted people to feel okay with their messed up minds and hearts. He wanted them to find safety."

"I caused him pain."

"But you caused him to be who he was. He didn't hate you for that fight. He was upset you guys couldn't get over it."

"We were both stubborn."

"That's the greatest flaw with our generation. We don't want to lose power. We don't want to admit when we've been defeated." He gave me a weak smile.

"I can't fix it."

"No, but you're trying to now. You're here to find closure here."

"I don't know if I will."

He picked up his briefcase. "I think you haven't hit the end of your journey. You'll get there." He walked out of the classroom. I knew I had the third clue, but I didn't know why he was helping me. He was part of Caleb's history. Maybe he needed his own closure for the guilt he had built in.

49

Dear Colin,

I know what you're probably thinking. How could I be sleeping with a professor? I don't think you have a right to judge me for my actions. I think writing these letters has made me realize how much we were different. I never could blame you. We were a series of misunderstandings. I didn't write those stories to bash you. I think I needed to make sense of it all. Jonathan taught me that. You've met him. I want you to see how beautiful of a soul he is. He picked me up and made me a stronger person. He made me whole, and I love him for that. I thank him for making me understand you more. I think we needed those four years apart, and I was ready to move forward. I was ready to be friends. I guess life has different plans for us. It's okay because you're learning about me now. Please don't worry about me. I knew about my choices, and I would make them all again. I experienced a love like I've never had before.

Love,
Caleb

December 3rd, 2012

I had no clue what to expect walking into Jonathan's class today. We hadn't seen or spoken since our kiss. I couldn't stop thinking about him during Thanksgiving. I couldn't stop wanting to tell him how much I loved him. I wanted to show him everything.

Shawn was walking next to me. "You seem nervous."

I looked at him. "Why would you say that?"

"You're fidgeting."

"I'm nervous about handing in this story."

"You've never been this nervous about turning in a story."

"I just have a lot on my mind." I snapped. I didn't mean to, but I didn't want to get into it with him. I wanted to see Jonathan. I knew he was rejecting me, and I wanted it to be over with.

"I'll keep to my business."

I sighed. "I'm sorry. I'm ready for this semester to be over." I wanted to forget completely about Jonathan. I would change my schedule, so I wouldn't see him again.

We walked into the classroom. Jonathan and I locked eyes. It was like time stopped. I felt my heart racing and everything in me had to control myself from not running to kiss him.

I looked away from him and took my seat. I couldn't look at him during the whole class. He respected me, and he didn't care that I didn't get involved with any of the discussions during class.

He ended class early. People started packing up their bags. "Are you coming?" Shawn asked.

"No, I need to talk to Jonathan about something."

Shawn shrugged. "I'll see you at your place later." He walked out.

Only Jonathan and I were left in the classroom. He walked over and locked the door. I wanted this to be private. "Caleb."

"We kissed, and I don't hear from you for two weeks."

"It's not like I heard from you either."

"But why?"

"Because I needed to digest what was happening. I haven't loved someone like you in so long. It scared me how I felt. I'm not ashamed of my feelings, but you need to know it took some time."

"What about now?" I crossed my arms. I could sympathize about needing time to fully understand what was going on with our emotions. I could never fault him for that. It took me months to finally figure it out.

He walked up to me. He pulled me in close and kissed me like he meant it. I've never felt more in love with someone than I did right then. I deepened the kiss and our hearts were displayed right there. We weren't scared about getting hurt. We just cared about showing how much we loved one another. I didn't know what would happen next, but I was looking forward to it.

December 22nd, 2012

Jonathan and I didn't see much of each other in the next couple of weeks. We continued sending each other letters, and we would call each other. I had to focus on finals and the holidays. My parents wanted to see me. I had finally accepted Vince as my dad. I didn't care if we don't share the same DNA.

I was re-reading the letter Jonathan sent me over the holidays. I was smiling as I watched the snow fall on our town. I was sitting in our side room with the fire going. It was one of my favorite spots in the world to just decompress. There were windows that looked out to the forest and a bit of the lake that was on our property.

My mom walked into the room and handed me a mug of hot chocolate. "I always seem to find you in here."

I took a sip. "I just get lost in here. I like seeing the forest. I'm glad we have these windows."

"Well, you designed the room. You have all your books. It seems this is more of your office than an actual additional room."

"Can you blame me?"

She laughed. "No, I can't. How is college going?" She asked.

"I'm the happiest I've ever been."

"Does it have to do with the boy you've been smitten about all semester?"

I turned to look at her all-knowing expression. "How?"

"Please, I know when my boy is in love. Who is he?"

"His name is Jonathan. That's all your going to get out of me."

She frowned. "That's not very nice. Why can't I know more?"

"Mom, it's still fresh. I want things to stay between us right now. I want something to be special before it's tarnished by others."

She grabbed my hand. "You need to stop worrying about what others think. This world is full of villains. You have to ignore them and live your life."

"I thought Colin was a friend."

"He is your friend. It's going to take time for you guys to get back to that. No one should take your happiness away."

"Mom, I love this man. I know it's complicated and people will judge me for it."

"It doesn't matter. You should love him no matter what. It's what romance is all about. Never forget how he makes you feel."

"What if I get hurt?"

"Your father rejected me. It destroyed me."

"But you seem so much happier now."

"Because I found a man that picked up the pieces. Vince put me back together, and I'll never forget that. Love can be your glue."

"I'm scared."

She leaned forward and smiled. "Let love scare you, destroy you, save you, bring you joy and become you. It's one of the precious gifts of the world. You should never forget to just let love do anything it needs."

He consumed my being with happiness and devotion. I felt inspired and open to life. He made me feel love like I've never felt before. I belonged to this world finally. I never wanted it to go away. He was the greatest experience in my life, and I wouldn't ever let him forget it.

50

December 28th, 2012

"It seems like Déjà vu all over again," Drew said walking into my room.

I was looking in the mirror trying to contain my nerves before I would meet up with Jonathan for our first date. I chuckled. "Yeah, it does."

He walked over and sat on my bed. "You're getting ready for a date with a guy that none of us know about. Don't you think that's a bit funny?"

"What's your point?"

"I just want this guy to do right by you. I know that Jack was an asshole."

I smiled. "Yeah." I looked away from the mirror and towards Drew. "I've learned my lesson from him. I want this to be kept a secret."

"Why?"

"Because I want to enjoy it before it becomes a problem. I want to have these butterflies without people ruining it with doubts."

"We don't want you to get hurt."

"Aren't I the one to make that decision for myself?"

He put his hands up. "I understand that. We're all here for you no matter what."

"Thank you. I just want this to work out. I thought that I knew what love was with Jack, but this is different. This is something life changing."

Drew got up and wrapped his arms around my shoulder. "It seems that you should be enjoying this more than any of us." He laughed. "Have fun and embrace everything. I'll see you when you get back." He winked and walked out of my room.

I was different this time. Someone else wasn't controlling me. I wanted this all for myself, and it made me believe that I could do this. I could actually be loved by someone the same way I loved them. There was respect here, and I never wanted that to go away.

"You look nice tonight," Jonathan said as we were sitting in a little Italian restaurant.

I blushed and looked away from him. I didn't want to tell him how beautiful he was with the candlelight shining on his face. "You know how to say all the right words."

"Or maybe they're truthful. Why don't you believe me when I say it?" He asked.

I turned to look at him. "I don't deserve you. You're this incredible being that I'm lucky to experience."

He grabbed my hand and kissed it. "You worry that this will end. You're so scared for tragedy."

"I've learned that there is always another shoe. I'm just waiting for it to drop."

"It won't with us. You need to enjoy the high."

"I enjoy the high very well. I think always waiting for the tragic end gives you a sense of appreciation."

"For what?"

"The small moments like these." I looked at him, and I never wanted it to stop.

"I'm not going anywhere. You can let go."

I shook my head. "I can never do that. I've been disappointed too many times in my life to actually believe that I can."

"Colin?"

"He isn't just the only one. My father also left me. It was before I was born. My mom met Vince, and he's been my father since. I didn't find out until last summer."

"I'm sorry to hear that."

"I guess I've lived with the doubt in my mind. Why would he leave me like that? How could someone not want me? I've grown accustomed to rejection."

"You can't think like that. I've known you for only a couple of months, and I've given you my heart. I want you. I crave you. I need you." He looked at me right in the eyes.

I inhaled a shaky breath. I felt alive. My whole being was in that moment. "I never want to lose you. It's scary to be this far in love, but I don't want it to stop. I'm in love with you, Jonathan Lancaster."

"I'm in love with you too, Caleb Moore." He leaned forward and captured my lips with his. My whole body was into this kiss. We've had these kisses before, but it didn't mean that they lost their power over me. I loved Jonathan, and I saw this world with him.

"We should get out of here," he said.

I nodded still in a haze from the kiss. We paid our bill and walked outside. It was a bit chilly, but I found warmth in Jonathan's embrace. We walked down the cobble street until we found a street that led to a canal. I put my hands on the railing while the moonlight bounced off the water.

I felt his hands wrap around my waist. I leaned back and used his body as my support. He kissed the side of my head and we stood there quiet for a moment. "I don't want this moment to stop," I said.

"I do."

I stiffened. "Why?"

He laughed. "Because we will have more beautiful moments than this."

"You're so hopeful for our relationship."

"It seems that someone has to be."

"Why do you find so much joy with us?"

"Because I've never loved someone like you. I've never found someone who could be my soulmate."

"Soulmate?" I didn't believe in soulmates. I thought we all had great loves, but soulmates were too much.

"I know you don't believe in them, but we could be. You never know what this world will give you."

I maneuvered, so I could look at him. "Are you telling me you've never loved before?" I couldn't believe this incredible soul has never had someone love him like I did.

"I have loved and been loved. I'm not a fool to believe that those are compared to us. Our love is what stories are inspired from. Our love is what people with broken hearts dream for. Our love is what we should share with the world and believe it's so pure."

I pulled him in and kissed him under the moonlight. I wanted to share our love with the whole world. He was right; this was just one moment for us. This would begin our story, and it was something that I wanted to continue to experience.

51

I walked into the radio station to get away from everything. I didn't want to deal with Colby or Jeremy. I just needed time to myself. I thought this would be the perfect place because this is where Caleb spent so much of his time. This is where he could go to think about his life.

I saw Drew reading behind the desk. "I didn't think anyone would be here." I figured people would be studying for finals.

He looked up and smiled at me. "How am I not surprised you are here?"

"What's the supposed to mean?"

He got up and walked around the table. "You're here to learn about Caleb's life. This is where he spent a lot of his time. This or his room writing, or with his mystery boyfriends." He laughed. "He seemed to work in a pattern."

"Were you always curious about them?" I asked.

"Who?"

"His boyfriends. It seemed that you didn't learn about them until after they broke up. Jack and Jonathan."

Drew shrugged. "I didn't see the point. I knew he would come to us when he wanted to talk about it. I thought it was rude to invade in his privacy."

"Even if it could have saved him."

"I think you're uptight." He turned to go looking through a drawer.

"I think that's a quick assumption."

"You've been here almost a week. I think it's a solid assumption." He pulled out a bowl and a baggie. "You need to get high."

I raised my hands. "Yeah, I'll pass. I'm trying to go into law enforcement."

He rolled his eyes. "You can't tell me you haven't smoked before. Aren't you a frat boy?"

I had to admit that weed was always around. I have taken a couple of hits, but it had been a couple of years since I got stoned. I sighed because maybe this could help me out. I needed to just relax. "I'm going to regret this."

"That's the spirit." He packed a bowl, and I took a couple of hits. We sat down on the floor with our backs against the desk. I needed this.

We sat in silence for a couple of minutes. "I was a shitty friend to him." I looked at the door that had a picture of Caleb, Drew, Cameron, Shawn, and Beth.

"I wouldn't think that. You both had your disagreements. You both came from different walks of life. It doesn't mean you were a shitty friend."

I looked at Drew. "Why did he leave all this for me? Why didn't he just give it to you?"

"I've only been around the past four years. I think maybe he wanted to get some kind of connection with you again. He knew that this would be important to you."

"I just miss him. I'm not talking about since he died, but for the past four years. I've missed my other half."

Drew wrapped his arm around my shoulder. "Losing a friend is losing a piece of yourself. You can never fully feel complete unless you have them back in your life."

"How do I fix it?"

"You learn about his life. You understand what he was going through before he died."

"How did you find out about Jonathan?" I asked.

"It was before Caleb broke Shawn's heart."

"They dated?" I never thought Caleb was remotely interested in him.

"It was right when Jonathan and him ended. He was so frustrated with people taking control over him. It was a mess. He saw Shawn and knew he could date him. Shawn has never stopped having feelings for Caleb."

"They would have been perfect for each other."

"Yeah, we all thought it. The problem is that perfect isn't for everyone. We don't love the person that would be the right fit for us. He chose Jack and Jonathan over Shawn. I think it comes back to feeling he didn't measure up to anything."

"He measured up to so much."

"We all know that, but he didn't believe that. It took him a long time to get confidence after Jack, and Jonathan killed it. Caleb really loved him."

"It's hard reading these diary entries, knowing that he had no clue. He was so in love with that man, and he was married."

"Imagine being here for the downfall. You don't know how many nights I had to hold Caleb as he cried himself to sleep."

I stiffened. "I don't think I can keep doing this."

"Doing what?"

"Trying to figure out the last four years. I don't think I want to keep going."

"Why?"

"Because I failed him. I've failed everybody. It's a constant reminder that I was a fool to believe that this would solve anything. It's causing too many problems. My life was great before Caleb died. I was going to grad school with my best friend. I was going to propose to my girlfriend. It's all shit now."

"I think it would have been a nice life, but you would have always had these doubts in the back of your mind."

"How do I keep moving forward without this guilt?"

"You need to keep the guilt, but there is a reason you're here. You have to figure out the ending."

"I just want him back."

"He's gone forever."

I took another hit of the bowl. "Gone forever." I had doubt in my voice. I didn't want to believe that he was gone. I needed to move past this doubt and solve all these questions.

52

"I don't want to show you this," Caleb said. He paused and looked at me. "Well, I do, but I'm nervous."

"Why are you nervous?" I asked. He asked me to come over to show me something.

"Because I don't want you to hate it."

I rolled my eyes. Caleb has always been dramatic, and this was one of the moments. "Caleb, you need to stop being such a baby." I grabbed the piece of paper.

Carter walked down the stairwell. He had no clue what was going to be there, but he was hoping it was some kind of closure. He knew that falling in love with her would cause too much pain. He needed to actually believe that she would stay with him, but he was a fool. Weren't all lovers fools? Didn't they all believe that they could make it in this world?

He continued to walk until he got to the door. He knocked a couple of times, but he didn't get an answer. He tried to open the door, but it was locked. He felt the tears streaming from his eyes. "Vanessa, you need to let me in. I was an idiot to think that I could be without you. I was a fool to believe I was happy without you."

There was an opening at the door. There was a maid standing there. "She's not doing well, Sir."

"I need to see her."

"I don't think that's necessary."

"Why not?" He balled his fist. "That's my girlfriend."

"The surgery had some complications."

"Complications?" Carter was worried that she might not make it. It couldn't happen. "We had the best doctor do the procedure."

"Sir, it's a grave surgery. There will always be complications."

"I want to see her. I need to see her."

"I don't think that's best." The maid tried one last time.

"I don't care what you think." Carter was fed up. He pushed past her. He saw a couple doctors standing around Vanessa. Carter pushed past all of them, and walked up to her. His heart dropped.

The color in her beautiful face was gone. The light behind her eyes was diminished. He saw no love or caring in her facial expression. All he could see was pain. "Carter, you aren't supposed to see me like this."

He grabbed her hands. There was no warmth in them. "I don't care. I needed to see you." He kissed her forehead. "You can make it through this."

She gave him a weak smile. "I don't think I will. It's okay though."

"No, it's not. I shouldn't have punished you like that. I shouldn't have tried to push my opinions on you. I'm sorry. We should have kept it."

She shook her head. "It doesn't matter now. We can't change the past."

"But I'm going to lose you."

She smiled. "I'll always love you. I'll love you until you meet me in heaven. I've loved every second with you. I will never forget you, Carter."

He felt his heart breaking as she took her last breath. He couldn't continue without her. He lost his delicate rose. He tried to control her when he should have let her be free. He should have admired her because now she was only a memory. He would never get her back, and he didn't know if he could continue to live. He only could live with the mistake of pushing her too far.

I dropped the piece of paper. I walked over and pulled Caleb into a hug. I tried to keep from crying, but it was extremely hard. That was too beautiful for words to comprehend.

He rubbed my back. "I'm assuming you liked it," he said to my chest.

"I can't believe you wrote that. How did that come out of you?" I asked.

"I was thinking back to our health class about abortions. I thought about when they first happened and the complications." He shrugged. "I didn't think it was that good."

"I'm glad that I get to prove you wrong. Caleb, that was fucking fantastic."

He smiled. "You're the first person I showed it to."

"Why?"

"Because we're best friends. I trust you."

"Thank you for showing me it."

He shrugged. "I just don't know if it's worth applying it for this competition."

"What's the competition?"

"It's where you can send your short story. The top ten get scholarships, and it will be published. Can you imagine something of mine being published?"

"I'm surprised that it's not published already. Caleb, you have the talent."

"You're only saying that because we're best friends."

I shook my head. "It doesn't matter. I would still tell you no matter what. You have to be confidant in yourself."

"I'm not ready for people to call me a fool to think that I could actually write. I just want to make it, Colin."

I pulled him in for another hug. "You will. I believe in you. You're going to change the world with your words. People won't forget about you. I know I won't."

"I never want to lose this."

"We won't. It's going to take a lot to break us up. I'm here for the long-haul."

53

"I figured I would find you here," I said walking into the library to find Shawn sitting there reading.

He looked up at me. "Are you stoned?" He asked.

I shrugged and took a seat. "What's it to you?" I crossed my arms.

"What do you want?" I could tell he was getting annoyed with me.

"I've been thinking about Caleb's writing. I've read all of his stuff that he gave me before..." I let the thought go. I didn't want to think about the fight. "I also read the stuff that was left at his house before he died.

"Do you think I have more of his work?"

"Shawn, I know how much you cared for him. You have to have kept some of his stuff."

"Why should I help you? I know you're the asshole that hurt him."

I wasn't getting anywhere with this guy. "Shawn, I know you had feelings for Caleb. I know you still do."

"I don't after what happened."

"What are you talking about?"

"You don't know." He looked me up and down.

"No, I don't. I'm only on the end of sophomore year. I'm almost there."

"Why are you here?" He asked.

"I'm trying to figure out who killed my best friend."

"The guy you had a falling out with right before you went to college. You both didn't get along during college, and you never resolved your issues with each other."

"Okay, what the fuck is your problem?"

"I don't like you."

"You could have fooled me."

"Just because I sit in the corner, doesn't mean I'm just oblivious to it all. I saw how destroyed he was about you."

"Because he wrote about it all in the short stories. There were things said in that fight that we both regret." I stood up. "Why don't you get to know me before you judge me?" I stormed out of the library.

I got outside and pulled out a pack of cigarettes. I didn't think that my conversation with Shawn would lead to that. He always seemed nice to me. I took a couple of puffs. I saw someone standing beside me. I turned to see Shawn standing there. "I'm not in the mood to keep fighting."

"Sorry, I shouldn't have snapped at you."

"Do you want to explain?"

"I get that everyone knew that Drew was super close to Caleb, but I was too. People keep forgetting that Caleb and I had a bond. I was messed up there for a little bit, but we still connected."

"And?"

"I'm tired of people forgetting how much his death really affected me."

"Do you want to talk about it?"

"It's pointless now. I'm just the quiet kid."

"I thought you were coming out of your shell."

He looked at me. "What are you talking about?"

I forgot that I was two years in the past. "Sorry, I've been reading Caleb's diary entries. He talked about how open you were. I could see it too. You seem to have reverted back to it."

"It's hard to keep the walls down after the guy you loved was using you."

"Caleb did that to you."

"How did you know?"

"You don't keep it hidden." I chuckled. "What happened?"

"He was this great guy I tried so hard to get over. I kept falling more and more in love with him for three years. I saw these guys take advantage of his love. It killed me because I wanted to be that guy, and I felt like I never would be."

"I never knew."

"No one did. I kept it to myself. I finally got my chance to be with him. He finally kissed me. We were finally on the same page."

"What happened?"

"He was in a rough spot in his life. I watched him fall apart, and I couldn't do that anymore. It killed me saying goodbye to him."

"Why did you do it?"

"Because I had too much respect for myself. It was better to have the idea of Caleb than the actual Caleb. It wasn't him that I was truly in love with."

"But you loved him for years."

"Yes, I did, but I couldn't handle his dark side. I never saw it until we became a thing. Love isn't about enjoying the good. Love is about loving every part of them. You have to accept their dark side as much as their good side. I couldn't do that."

"Do you regret it?"

"I'll never regret it because it made me hopeful that the person I'm meant to be with is still out there. I just have to be patient."

"What are you doing now?" I asked.

He smiled, and I saw the tears in his eyes. "I'm still mourning my first love. I'm still trying to realize that he's no longer here. I'm trying to put the pieces back together."

"How's it going?"

"I'm just the quiet guy. I've always stayed in the shadow. I finally broke free for this one special guy. He was the only man that could actually make me believe I'm better than I thought I was. I've never had that before. My parents weren't around, and I didn't make friends until college. He was the first person to get to know me, and he's gone."

I pulled him in for a hug. "He does that to people." Caleb took on the broken souls and gave them hope. It was something so special about him.

"How do I move on? How do I get the strength to be happy again?"

"I think we're all trying to figure out those answers."

"Why was he taken?"

"He gave his heart to the wrong person," I said, and it killed me to know it was the truth.

54

Dear Caleb,

I don't see the need to see each other today. I love you, and you know that. I won't cheapen our relationship with silly trinkets or the desire to be together today. We celebrate our love every day. I'll miss you today, but I'll see you soon to love you even more than yesterday.

Love,
Jonathan.

I was a little upset that he didn't want to spend Valentine's Day together, but I understood his point. I also didn't know how he would be able to top what I did last year. My Valentines with Jack was something special.

Drew walked into our apartment as I was sitting on the couch flipping through the channels. He had roses in his hand and a bag I presumed was for Cameron. "Why aren't you getting ready?"

"What are you talking about?" I asked popping chocolate in my mouth.

"Shouldn't you be going out with your boyfriend?"

I shrugged. "He thought it was cliché to celebrate our love on the day of love. I actually like not having to worry about the pressure."

"I'm glad one of us is having a good Valentines. It took me a whole fucking week to find a gift for Cameron."

"This is your second Valentines. Why are you so nervous?"

He sat down next to me. "The more I fall in love with the girl, the more I want to make it perfect."

"That sounds so beautiful." I laughed.

"So you're not upset about doing nothing tonight?"

"Not really. I'm glad I'm staying in. I called Beth and Shawn over to watch movies and devour pizza and chocolate. They should be here any second." I looked at my watch.

Shawn was the first to walk through the apartment. I didn't know how I felt about all of us having keys to our apartments. It was nice, but I walked into Beth's apartment one time to her having sex with a guy from her class. We needed to have boundaries.

"I brought over the movies." He dropped down a series of romantic comedies and horror movies. He looked at Drew. "Nervous?"

"Yeah."

"Beth said they were running a couple of minutes late. Cameron was freaking out about her hair." He rolled his eyes and sat down next to me.

We flipped through the channels until we were watching a cartoon. It was about a talking bear running a forest park. We got half way through the second episode when Beth barged in. "I will have to say that I'm a miracle worker."

"Why do you say that?" I asked. I turned to see Cameron walk in. She was wearing a tight lace dress. Her hair was now a dark black and curled. She was wearing little make up.

I looked to see that Drew's mouth had dropped. I closed his mouth. I leaned in. "This is where you give a compliment," I whispered.

"You look so beautiful." He stammered while getting up. He walked over and pulled her into a hug.

Beth rolled her eyes. "I didn't need to see that." She walked over and sat down next to me. "Why aren't you like that with your boyfriend?" She asked.

"He didn't want to cheapen our relationship by going out tonight."

Beth nodded. "I like him already. I told Alex that I didn't want to go out tonight. I thought it was rather stupid also."

"Alex was okay with that?" I asked.

"We had sex this morning. He was thrilled he didn't need to get me a gift or spend money on me, and he still got laid. I think he called me the best girlfriend."

Beth had met Alex in her ethics and politics class last semester. They spent the whole semester arguing with each other in the class, until finals when they were forced to work together. They ended up getting a C on the paper because they were too busy having sex.

"I applaud you." I smiled.

"I'm glad I'm not spending today alone." Shawn grabbed the popcorn.

"We're going to go," Cameron said.

I looked at her. "We will be back later." Drew grabbed his jacket.

"We don't need you eating too much food or drinking." Cameron pointed to all of us.

"I'm not cleaning up that puke." He put his hands in the air.

Beth rolled her eyes. "Shut up."

They said their goodbyes and walked out the door. "I'm not going to sulk tonight. We're getting drunk." Beth got up and walked over to the fridge. She placed three shots and a bottle of Jack Daniels on the table.

"I'm going to regret this, aren't I?" I asked.

"Probably." She handed me a shot.

We spent the night taking shots to all the corny lines and moments we wanted to cry to. Shawn ended up passing out during the third movie, while Beth was having phone sex with Alex. I walked into my room and closed the door. I dialed Jonathan's number.

"Hello?"

"Hey, baby. You sound so sexy." I knew my words were slurred.

"Are you drunk right now?"

"Yeah, why wouldn't I be? Shawn, Beth, and I are trashed."

"I can't talk right now."

"But it's Valentine's Day."

"I'll talk to you tomorrow." He seemed to rush me off the phone.

"I love you."

"Night." He hung up without telling me it back. I felt in the pit of my stomach the worry. Did he love me or was it all just a game? Did I mean something to him or was I just a fool? I wanted to cry, but vomiting distracted me. I needed to feel pain because it would be this or sadness. I didn't like this. I thought I had control of my life finally, but it seemed Jonathan was slowly taking that away from me. I didn't know if I could get it back or wanted to.

55

March 3ʳᵈ, 2013

"What do you mean you guys haven't had sex?" Beth asked. She was curled up to Alex. We were in our apartment smoking.

I shrugged. "We just haven't had the chance, I guess." I didn't think it was that big of a deal.

"You guys have been dating for months now." Beth rolled her eyes. "I don't know if I could wait that long."

"You guys have been banging since you both got together. That's how you two got together." I pointed between them.

"I wish we knew who it was. I mean why haven't you guys?" Drew asked taking a hit.

"We haven't found the right time. We're taking things slow. I can't believe you're pressuring me into having sex."

"I don't think we're pressuring you. We just think it's odd," Cameron said. I could tell she was trying to be delicate with the situation.

"Maybe, there are some problems in the relationship." Shawn shouldn't have an opinion in my sex life. He was rooting for us to fail.

"No, we have a great relationship. Things are great." I didn't want to admit that it wasn't fair that we barely saw each other lately. I thought maybe he was busy working on his new book.

"But you guys haven't had sex." Beth added.

"Yes, we haven't had sex. We're doing things the right way. I'm not with the guy because I'm fucking him. I like him for the person he is. I like that we're getting to know each other on a deeper level. I'm not going to be ashamed for that." I got up. "Fuck you, guys." I walked out of the room onto our balcony.

I just was fed up with people trying to butt into my relationship. This is why I didn't want anyone to know about us. I wanted to keep it a secret, so that I could actually enjoy it myself.

I heard the door open, and it was Cameron. "They didn't think you would get that upset."

"I'm just annoyed with them."

"Drew and I waited almost eight months before we had sex."

"Really?" I was surprised. "I've heard you guys in bed."

She blushed and looked away. "I'm not saying we didn't do other activities in the process."

I felt a little uncomfortable. "I didn't need to know that."

She glared at me with no heat. "You asked."

"Then why isn't Drew in there defending me?"

"I think he wants to know who this mystery guy is. He's worried you're going to have the same situation happen to you."

"It won't."

"Are you sure about that? Caleb, you're having a secret relationship without any of us knowing. You're avoiding talking about it, and it seems to control your life."

"There are some complications in the relationship. I'll agree with you on that. I want to keep this to myself. I'm tired of feeling judged."

"No one is judging you."

I crossed my arms. "Really?"

"Beth is a bitch. We all know this. She would judge you for wearing white. She's weird like that. Shawn just wants to be with you. I think he's being manipulative."

"I feel guilty talking about him in front of Shawn."

"Why?"

"Because I know how much Shawn cares for me. I wish I could be attracted to Shawn. I know being with him would make everything easier. I guess I liked the complications. I love knowing that it could all end tomorrow."

"You're trying to live through your short stories."

I laughed. "His name is Jonathan." I didn't know why I told Cameron about his name. I guess I could trust her. She was the only one that didn't seem to care or judge. She wanted the best for me. I knew she would keep it a secret.

"I like that name."

"Yeah, he's great. I've never felt so connected with someone before. I know that with Jack it was my first love. I knew that it would end, but I don't see that with Jonathan."

"You see a future?"

I nodded. "I guess it's why I don't want to rush things. I want to enjoy every single step getting there. I know we have forever with each other."

"That's beautiful."

"Thank you. I know people will judge us."

"Who cares about them?"

"You're right. I just don't want anyone else to know yet."

She pulled me in for a tight hug. "I'll keep this secret to myself. Thank you for sharing."

"I love you, Cameron."

I needed the day I could go out in the opened with Jonathan to come. I was worried it would be like with Jake. I didn't want this to fail, and my friends to be right.

56

March 10th, 2013

Jonathan and I were in his office. We were making out, but he stopped me when it went below the belt.

I sat down and frowned. He sighed. "What's wrong?"

"Why won't you have sex with me?" I asked.

He looked at me like I had grown three heads. "What are you talking about?"

"Sex. You and me. We haven't had it. Why?" I had been thinking about it for the past week. I tried to ignore the doubts, but I just couldn't stop the nagging feeling. It was so stupid for me to feel like this.

"Are your friends asking questions?" He raised an eyebrow.

"You don't get to do that."

"Do what?"

"Act like you're my dad. You're my boyfriend." It quickly came out. "Or whatever."

Jonathan laughed, and I hated that he was laughing. I didn't want this to be some kind of joke. He got up and walked over to the other chair. He grabbed my hand. "Do you want to be boyfriend and boyfriend?"

I sighed and crossed my arms. "Maybe." I didn't look at him.

I felt his lips at my neck. I tried to keep still. I laughed and pushed him away. "Yes, I would like to be boyfriend and boyfriend." I turned and captured his lips with mine.

I continued to kiss him until I realized what the issue was. "Why?"

"Why, what?"

"Why won't you have sex with me?" I grabbed his face, so he would look at me straight in the face.

"I want it to be special. I don't want us to rush it because were getting pressured. Are you happy with how things are going?"

"Yeah, I have no problems." It was true. I enjoyed us getting to know each other. Our relationship wasn't clouded by physical.

"So why are you coming to me now?" He asked.

"Because my friends got to me."

He leaned forward and kissed me on the lips. "Stop stressing out what your friends think. We will get there. You can't compare our relationship to others."

"I know. I just feel like I'm a chore to you."

"You aren't that at all."

"Why didn't you talk to me on Valentine's Day." I had still hurt feelings about it even a month later. I tried to keep it under wraps, but it constantly kept bubbling in my head.

"I knew you were drunk. I didn't want to talk to you then."

"Why?"

"Because I don't want to have an immature relationship with you. I want our relationship to be an adult one. I think getting drunk and calling each other is juvenile. We shouldn't stoop down to that level."

It was an attack on me. I was a constant reminder that I was younger than him by fifteen years. We were doing something a little wrong, and he didn't want to be reminded of that. I stood up. I kissed him on the lips. "Fine. I won't drunk call you."

He smiled. "I don't want to have rules. I don't want you to feel like you have to monitor yourself around me."

I nodded. I knew I couldn't, and I didn't want to go back here. I wanted to be something equal, but I had to swallow it up. You gave up things for love. Isn't that what you were supposed to do? Right?

April 7ᵗʰ, 2013

I was drunk. I couldn't think straight or keep my hands still. I was trying to call Jonathan, but I had the voice in my head. It was telling me that I couldn't do it. I couldn't call him because he didn't want an immature kid calling him. I cut back on my drinking the past month, but we celebrated. I got a story published in a magazine. It was a stupid little magazine, but it was something.

Jonathan gave me a bottle of whiskey. He said that when he first published "Windmill," he got a bottle of whiskey. He wanted me to celebrate. He encouraged me to drink, but I couldn't call him now. I'm drunk, and I knew he would be against me right now.

I sat on the side of the curb crying because things were a mess with Jonathan. There were rules, and I was back in the cage. I was tired of it.

I heard footsteps. I looked up to see Cameron standing there. I wiped the tears away. "I'm fine."

She smiled softly. "You wouldn't be crying if you were." She took a seat next to me. "What's wrong?"

"Where is everyone?" I asked.

"Drew took Shawn back to his place. I think Beth and Alex are fighting or having make-up sex. You never know about them."

"Why are you here?"

"Because you're my friend, and I'm making sure that you're okay."

"I told you I was fine." I wiped away another tear.

She kissed me on the cheek. "I would believe that if you weren't crying. What's going on?"

"I want to call Jonathan. I want to tell him thank you for the whiskey, but I can't. He thinks it's childish to drunk call each other."

"Why?"

I looked at her. I knew she would keep it a secret. I needed someone to tell. I couldn't keep this all to myself. "He's my creative writing professor." It felt like a joy to say it out loud. It made everything real.

"You're dating your creative writing professor?" She asked.

I looked at her. "I shouldn't have told you. You're judging me. Oh my god, I should have kept it to myself."

She pulled me into a hug. "It's okay. I'm not judging you. I'm not surprised."

I leaned back and looked at her. "Why?"

"Caleb, I could see you with an older guy. It seems to fit, but he shouldn't try to lock you up."

I looked at my phone. "I know. I love him too much to lose him."

"I'll keep your secret."

I smiled at her. "Thank you. I just needed to tell someone."

"I just think you need to realize that you should never be controlled by anyone."

I looked at her in the eyes. "He makes me feel like I'm actually someone. I feel so loved by him, and I never want to lose that."

"You have friends that love you. Love comes in different forms."

I smiled and leaned into her hug. "I just don't feel complete without him, and it scares me. I've given him too much, and I never want to deal with the downfall alone."

She stroked my arm. "You won't."

I don't know how long we stayed there, and I didn't care. I got to cry about the strains in my relationship. I didn't want to believe that someone couldn't love me. I didn't want to accept that Jonathan was turning into Jack or worse.

57

May 6th, 2013

"We made it," Shawn said as we were walking to class.

I laughed. "Yeah, we've hit the end of the year." It was an odd feeling being at the end of my second year of college. A lot had changed in this past year, but things stayed the same. I wouldn't have traded it for the world, and I'm grateful that I'm here now.

We all took our seats. "Hi, class. Welcome to the end of the year. It amazes me how far we have come along in the past semester, and some of you, this year. I wanted to read to you something that has helped other students in the past."

Jonathan picked up a piece of paper and started to read. "The short story, 'Windmills' by Jonathan Lancaster is the debut from this writer. It shows how much inexperience this writer has. Yes, he has the potential to become a great writer, but with this piece of work it seems uncertain. He focuses too much on describing the surroundings instead of focusing on the characters. I was rather bored with both of these characters, and I didn't see the point of this story. It seems the writer had no connection with Paul or Mary, and the reader was left wondering, do we root for them or hate them? I hope this writer gets into some creative writing workshops."

It was quiet in the room. I couldn't believe that he got a review like that. I would have crawled into a ball, and I wouldn't have wanted to talk to anyone. "Why would you read that to us?" I asked.

"This was my first review. I was divested. I didn't know how I could keep going."

"That doesn't make us feel safe about writing." I didn't want to hear that. I didn't want to believe those were the comments I was going to receive when I entered the writing world.

He laughed. "Caleb, I think you might want to hear the rest of the point of my lecture."

I crossed my arms. "I don't see how it could get better after that."

He picked up another piece of paper and read. "Thank you for writing, 'Chained,' I guess I've always question my place in the world. I never knew who I was supposed to be, or if I even mattered. I saw Matt continue to get beaten left and right for what he believed in. I saw how much courage he had to be who he truly was. I think that's what we all want to strive for in the world. It's what I'm going to do myself. I just wanted to say thank you for writing something so profound that I can believe and have hope for my life."

He put the piece of paper down. "The point is that you'll have people hate your writing, and you'll have people that will love your writing. You can't be scared or worried about this world."

"It's hard when you have an open heart to your writing."

He smiled. "I know, but you will do great things with your writing. I know a lot of you will. You have to believe in your writing and keep putting your heart out there."

I didn't want to look forward to the criticism. I was worried with my piece coming out next month. I was worried that people won't understand it or accept it. I wanted people to love my writing, but was it worth the negativity?

"I'm scared." I admitted.

He nodded. "It's good be scared. It means you care deeply for your craft. You should never lose that. It's what makes you a writer." I took those words to heart, and I never wanted to forget them.

May 10th, 2013
"We're here again," I said taking a sip of my drink. I looked around at Drew, Cameron, Beth, and Shawn.

Beth smiled. "Yeah, it's still the five of us." Beth and Alex had finally ended their odd relationship. They knew it was just physical, and there was no point in keeping it going if they would just fight and fuck.

"I like when it's just us. It makes us realize how close we all are." Shawn smiled raising his beer.

"I don't want to lose this." It had been a hard year for me. I've fallen in love again, and I didn't know if it was going to be worth it. I didn't know how this summer with Jonathan would go.

Cameron and Drew were going to Rome, Shawn was off to England, and Beth was going home. I would be here without them, but lost in my relationship.

"I can't believe we're all leaving." Cameron looked around.

"It's going to be quiet in the apartment," I admitted.

"It's only for two months. I'll be back in no time." Drew winked.

"I think it's good I'm staying here." I took a sip of my beer.

"You're only saying that because your boyfriend will be here." Beth wiggled her eyebrows.

I blushed and looked at Cameron. She had a fond expression on her face. It was nice going to Cameron about everything with Jonathan. It made things easier with my life and our relationship.

"It will be good for you to connect with your boyfriend. You won't have any distractions," Cameron said.

"Yeah, I think that's the best part. I just want this to work out," Drew said.

"So far it has." I admitted.

"Cheers to another year." Drew raised his beer.

"Another year." We all raised our drinks around the bon-fire, and we were looking forward to another year. I was half way through my college life, and I still had no clue where my life was going. I didn't know what to expect, or if I was ready for it. I felt comfort knowing I wasn't alone, and I had these people with me for the ride.

58

May 29th, 2013

"Where are you taking me?" I asked as Jonathan and I were driving down a back road.

He laughed and kissed my hand. "It's a surprise."

"I don't trust this."

He rolled his eyes. "Do you trust me?"

I looked at him in the eyes. School was over, and we didn't have to worry about anyone else. We connected on a deeper level. We got drunk and danced some nights. We would curl up on my couch and watch terrible movies. We would go to an author signing and debate the flaws of the book. I felt like I was in a real relationship.

I squeezed his hand. "More than ever." I looked back at the road. We were surrounded by forest and the sun was setting. "Why did you hate me being drunk?" I asked.

"I don't hate you drunk."

"You would ignore my calls late at night."

He sighed. "It took me a while to understand that I'm dating someone so young." I stiffened. He noticed. "I've learned that age doesn't matter with a human being. You're mature beyond your years. I've learned that now."

I turned to look at him. "Please stop being hot and cold with me."

"I'll try not to. I can't promise you that my doubts won't come back again. I can't give you certainty that I won't be an asshole again. I can only give you my heart."

"Okay." It was all I really needed from him. We weren't going to fit perfectly. We were different in a lot of ways, and it was going to show. I needed to understand and respect that.

We drove for another half an hour before we turned onto a dirt road. "I hope you aren't murdering me."

He laughed at me. "I'm not going to murder you. I love you too much to do that."

I turned to him. "Good." I smiled. "This would be too much work."

He turned to me. "Yeah, I wouldn't have driven all the way out here to do it."

It was another five minutes on the road until we go to a clearing. There was a small cabin right next to a lake. Woods surrounded it, and I couldn't hear anything but birds chirping.

He parked the car next to the cabin and got out. "Where are we?" I asked.

"This is my family's cabin. It was given to me once my parents retired. My sister moved to Oregon and didn't want it. I come here sometimes when I need to be by myself. I usually get writers block and come here." I walked down towards the lake. The woods open to a bigger section of the lake, and the sunset reflected on the water.

Jonathan came up and wrapped his arms around me. He kissed the back of my ear. "I wanted to share this with you."

I looked at the sunset and embraced the warmth from my love. I realized that this was another moment between Jonathan and I. "Perfect."

I turned my body around and looked at Jonathan. I've never see that kind of adornment before. I put his face between my hands and connected our lips together. We kissed as the sunset fell. We were in the middle of the woods just the two of us. We were inside Jonathan's heart, and I never wanted to leave.

May 31st, 2013
"What is taking you so long?" I was waiting by the door for Jonathan to get out of the bathroom. We spent all day yesterday hiking through the forest. We took pictures, and I only fell a couple of times. It was much warmer today, and we were going swimming.

"I need to put suntan lotion on." He screamed from the bathroom.

I rolled my eyes and sighed. "You're such a baby. You'll be fine."

He walked out of the bathroom with a coat of suntan lotion on. "You say that now, but when I get skin cancer, I'm blaming you."

I shook my head. "You're ridiculous."

He walked over and captured my lips with his. We stood there for a moment as our lips got reacquainted. He let go of my lips and slapped me on the ass as hard as he could. "God, you're an asshole."

He gave me a chaste kiss. "I'm your asshole." He laughed as he walked past me towards the water.

"That was extremely cheesy."

He waved me off as he started stepping into the water. I followed him. I got to the shore, and I was a little nervous. Cold water and I didn't really mix. He turned to me as he was waist high in the water. "It's fine."

I put my first foot in, and it was freezing. "No, it's not. It's fucking cold. I think I'm going to just stay up here."

He rolled his eyes. "Now who's being the baby?" He walked towards me. I saw the evil in his eyes. I was about to run, but he grabbed me by both hands. He then grabbed me by the waist and hoisted me over his shoulders. "I can't believe you right now. If you dunk me, I'll be the one killing you."

"You and what strength?" He turned and started going deeper and deeper into the water.

I tried to fight him. I kept lightly hitting him on the back, but it caused him to laugh even more. The deeper the water got the more my body got acquainted with the water. "I fucking hate you."

"Aw, I thought you loved me."

The water was shoulder length, and I was pretty much covered. "Let me go."

"Okay."

I didn't get a chance to object before he went under the water and took me with him. The cold water was a quick jolt to my body. I stood up and looked around for him. "Where did you go, asshole."

I looked around, but I couldn't find him. I then felt hands on my arms. "I'm right behind you." He pulled me into a hold.

I tried to get out of it. "You really are a dick."

He turned me around. "See? It isn't that bad."

I put my hand on his chest and splashed him with water using the other. He started coughing. I just laughed. "See? It isn't that bad."

He grabbed me and dunked me under the water. We spent the next couple of minutes splashing, dunking, and swimming away from each other. I couldn't remember the last time I had this much fun and how freeing it was. I didn't have to stress about people seeing us. I could actually be with my boyfriend.

We eventually gave up and swam together. We tangled our bodies together and wrote a peace treaty with our lips. We spent the day in the water, tanning, and grilling. I never left his side, and I didn't want to. I had to cherish every moment of this because I couldn't keep this forever. The other shoe would have to drop, and I would be ready for it.

June 3rd, 2013

It was our last night before we had to go back home. He started teaching summer classes in a couple of days, and I had to get ready for my own classes. I think taking on another major was probably a stupid idea, but I thought maybe psychology would help with my writing.

He told me to go away for a couple of hours. I had no clue what he was doing, but I knew it would be romantic.

I walked until the sun started setting. I knew I gave him plenty of time. I walked into the cabin. There were roses and candles leading to the bedroom. I couldn't even keep the tears in. I just let them fall. I followed the roses and candles to the bedroom. Jonathan stood there in a suit. Candles and roses surrounded him.

"Jonathan." I broke out.

He put a hand up. I noticed the piece of paper in front of him. He lifted it and started reading.

Dear Caleb,

Life is filled with so many wonderful moments. We experience: happiness, sadness, tragedy, joy, and, if we're lucky, love. I never knew with you that I could be this deeply and madly in love. You challenge me, and

I've never had that before. I'll admit that I was scared what you could do to me. I tried to keep my distance from you. My heart ached every second I was away from you. You've given me so much, and I never want to forget you. I love you now and forever. I know it's too soon to propose, and I won't. What I will do is promise you these days we share. I pray they're infinite, but if not, then I pray we fill them with all the love we have.

Love,
Jonathan.

I didn't give him a chance to ask him what I thought. I closed the space between us. I pulled him into a kiss. I gave him my whole being because this was what a great love was. This is what he talked about when he said stories were made from us and broken hearts dream for this. I found my forever.

We locked eyes and the world was still. The world was wondering what our next move would be, and I already had a feeling. "I'm ready."

"Me too." He captured my lips with his, and we took everything slow. It was like my first. He kissed me every time he took a piece of my clothes off. I did the same respect to him. We gave each other patience as we began exposing ourselves to each other.

He continued to care for me as he placed me on the bed, opened me up, and took care of my body. I wasn't nervous or scared about my inexperience. I knew Jonathan wasn't looking for the physical aspect of it. We were connecting as beings.

He positioned himself with me. He looked me in the eyes as he ran his fingers through my hair. "Do you want this?" He asked.

I touched his face. "I've never wanted this more than anything else in this world. I love you." I put my heart in those three words.

He nodded. "I love you too."

Sex with Jonathan was everything I needed or imagined it to be. He took his time, and it was like color was being added to my life. I knew we were giving our everything to each other, but we found comfort in that. There was no one that was holding back or that kept a wall up. We were honest with each other, and it's why I'll never forget that moment with Jonathan.

He was right. We couldn't promise each other infinite time. We didn't know what the future held for us, but we could have the present. We could make every day filled with the love we had, and I never wanted to waste a moment without him. We were finally on the same page, and I relished every single second of it.

59

June 18ᵗʰ, 2013

Dear Jonathan,

I can't stop thinking about our trip to the cabin. It's become a problem that I haven't been able to sleep with-out you in my bed. This summer has already been every-thing that I've ever wanted. I want to thank you for those few days alone with you. I know that I can't be selfish and ask for more, but I didn't want it to end. When can we go back?"

Love,
Caleb.

June 21ˢᵗ, 2013

Dear Caleb,

I know. I can't seem to get you out of my mind. I told you that we would have sex at our own time. I do hope that made you realize we aren't like your friends. We beat to our own drum, and we should never forget that. I just pray that you realize my love for you. I never want you to forget it.

Love,
Jonathan

June 25th, 2013

Dear Jonathan,

I have a problem with your snoring. I'll admit it to you in a letter so you have proof of it when we fight. Yes, I did tell you that I thought it was kind of adorable. I'll admit I do like watching you sleep, but you snore so loud. You better get me a pair of earplugs, if you plan on staying more nights at my place.

Love,
Caleb.

June 29th, 2013

Dear Caleb,

I told you over and over again that I snored. I don't see how this is any of my fault. We will not get into this fight. I think you need to accept that I have a snoring problem. I don't complain about you always cracking your knuckles. I think that's gross, but you don't see me being upset about it. We just need to accept our flaws. I still love you.

Love,
Jonathan.

July 5th, 2013

Dear Jonathan,

I wish you were with me last night watching the fireworks. I went with a couple of the people from the radio station that stayed around here. All I could think about during the lights in the sky was the sunset we watched the first night at the cabin. I wanted nothing more than to kiss you like all the other couples. I knew you had another engagement, but it didn't make the hurt in my heart go down any less. I don't want you to feel guilty for it.

Love,
Caleb.

July 8th, 2013

Dear Caleb,

I told you over and over again how sorry I was that we couldn't be together. I promise you that I'll make it up to you. I know how you feel. I watched the fireworks, and all I could think about was you commenting on the show. It pains me to know you were surrounded by couples when your boyfriend was towns over. I love you, and I never want you to forget that.

Love,
Jonathan.

July 14ᵗʰ, 2013

Dear Jonathan,

You made up for it big time. I can't believe you showed up with roses and the new James Holiday book. I didn't even think the book was out yet. I'm not going to lie and tell you that I've spent all week reading it. I'm pretty sure my classes are going to suffer, but I don't care. It's the best series in the world. I don't know how you did it, but you've swooned me. I am swooned.

Love,
Caleb.

July 16ᵗʰ, 2013

Dear Caleb,

I'm happy to hear that you love the book. I figured you were busy in the book and couldn't talk to me. I can't believe I tried to steer you away from the book with sex, and you still didn't budge. I can't believe I'm dating such a book nerd. I guess we can relate since I've got a pile of books I want to get through. It's hard dealing with these kind of kids. I can't wait until the new year starts. It will be students who actually want to be there.

Love,
Jonathan.

July 24th, 2013

Dear Jonathan,

It's our last week alone together. Drew and Cameron come back next week. I can't believe this summer is almost over. I just wanted to thank you for everything these past weeks. I'll never forget this summer, but I know I can look forward to what's coming up next. You've meant so much to me, and I love you. This is just the first summer of many. I believe in that. We will get our forever together. One of us has to believe in that.

Love,
Caleb.

60

Dear Caleb,

I don't want you to ever forget this summer because I won't. I got to spend almost every second with the person I truly love. We needed this to reconnect, and we're stronger this semester around than we were last. We have the confidence in our relationship, and I believe in that. Yes, it will be harder to stay away from each other, but we will get through it. You need to focus on your dreams and your future. I would never want to take that away from you. You need to spend these days with your friends because you won't get these back. I know I'll be around when we're older with our family. I want you to be your age and make stupid decisions. I'll never judge you or control you. I can promise you that. I love you.

Love,
Jonathan.

I held the letter in my hand, and I couldn't stop reading it. Drew and Cameron were going to be back any minute. I thought that I would be sad to have them back because that meant my time with Jonathan was over. It was the opposite. I missed my friends, and I was ready to have them back. I wanted my support system back, so I couldn't float too much away.

I heard the door open. "Honey, we're home," Drew said.

I walked out of my room and there was Drew and Cameron. Drew looked like he had gain some weight, and his man bun finally was in full swing. Cameron looked skinner, tanner, and she was actually blonde.

I ran up and pulled them both into hugs. "It's good to see you both." It felt like a part of me was finally back.

Drew laughed as we separated. "I told you he would miss us."

Cameron rolled her eyes. "Whatever." She looked at me. "How was your summer?" She asked.

I thought about the time with Jonathan, and I couldn't keep my smile to myself. "I'll never forget it."

I saw Drew looking me up and down. It then clicked in his head. "You finally got some with your boyfriend."

I blushed and looked away. He pulled me in for another hug. "I'm so proud of you."

He was shaking me back and forth. I looked at Cameron and saw worry in her eyes. "Yeah, we had sex. It was great. You can let me go."

He let me go. "I can't wait to hear all the details. I need to pee first." He walked out of the room and into the bathroom.

Cameron and I stood there for a minute, not saying a word. "So you and Jonathan had sex?"

I nodded. "He took me to his cabin on the lake. It was" I paused. "I can't describe it."

I saw the fondness in her smile. "It seems like you really love this guy."

I couldn't see myself being with anyone else. He had this hold over me, and I never wanted him to let it go. "Yeah, I really do."

She pulled me into a hug. "I just hope you know what you're doing."

I tightened the hug. "I do, Cameron. I never want it to end."

"If it does, we will be here for you through it all."

"I know."

Drew came back out of the bathroom. "Let's hear all about it." Drew pulled Cameron and I to the couches. It's how we spent the rest of the night. We swapped summer stories while drinking a couple of beers. It was good having them back, but I couldn't get the image of Cameron's worried expression out of my mind. Was I too blinded to see that this would only end is disaster? Would I just get heartbroken again or worse? I didn't want to have these thoughts, but it seemed they never go away.

61

I closed the laptop and took a minute to digest everything that was going through my mind. How could Jonathan love Caleb so much and then dump him for his wife and kids? How could he keep that big of a secret away from him? Do we really know the person we're in love with?

I saw Colby walk into the hotel room. "How goes the reading?" She sat down on the bed and crossed her arms.

"It's been very eye opening."

"Has it helped you with your issues?" She asked.

I sighed. I knew it had been intense with us, but I didn't want to continue this way. I didn't want this trip to cause problems with us. "I'm trying."

"Are you? All I've seen is you judge and make comments about his life."

"He fell in love with his professor. He had no clue about Jonathan's wife or kids. He was so oblivious that it scares me."

"Why?"

"What if you have kept things from me?"

She stood up. "We've been together for seven years now. What do you think I've kept from you?"

"There were three months last year where we weren't together. We've never talked about it, but I want to."

She shook her head. "No, we're not talking about that. We promised that those three months stay between us."

"Are you telling me that you're guilty of something?"

"I'm not having this argument with you." She stood up and tried to walk to the bathroom.

I grabbed her arm. "Tell me what happened."

She looked at me. "I almost slept with someone. I started to get feelings for a guy, but I realized that I still fucking loved you."

"Was it someone I know?"

She was hesitant, and I could tell that she was keeping something from me. "No." She ripped her arm out of my grip. "Why does it matter?"

"I don't want any surprises."

"What's this really about?" She asked.

"We've been together for so long. I don't want to get bored of each other."

Colby grabbed the side of my face. "We've been through too much shit to disrespect each other like that. I would never have sex with someone else." She walked into the bathroom and closed the door.

I rested my head on the door. "I'm an asshole."

"We know."

"I don't know what's wrong with me."

She opened the door. "There's nothing wrong with you. Why can't you realize that we're different than Caleb and Jonathan's relationship?"

"They had this epic romance."

"Are you saying we don't?" She asked.

I was fumbling over my words. "That's not what I mean."

"No, you're talking about struggling through pain. Yes, we have had a pretty easy relationship. We balance each other, but they destroyed each other."

"It was beautiful to read."

"Yes, like a romance novel. The problem is that it was all a lie."

"What?"

"He lied to Caleb the whole time. He used Caleb's worry to his advantage. He made sure that Caleb was dependent on him. Jonathan was nothing more than a con artist." She leaned forward and gave me a chaste kiss. "We don't need all the gimmicks."

"I just don't want to be lied to."

She shook her head. "I promise. I love you."

I pulled her close and kissed her on the top of her head. "I love you too." I believed in her. She was the only person to calm me down, and I think that's what I needed. I knew Colby and I weren't Caleb and Jonathan. We shared a mutual respect for each other. I don't think they did, and it's what failed them in the end.

62

"Why didn't you have a girlfriend in college?" I asked Jimmy as we were drinking. Colby went out with Cameron and Beth. She said I needed bonding time with Jimmy.

He shrugged and drank his beer. "I didn't see the point in dating. I saw how much of a roller coaster you were with Colby. I see it now."

"We're fine."

He looked at me like he wasn't convinced. "I've noticed the tension between you the past couple of days. Shit, I've noticed it since we got here."

"It's hard with everything going on. I can't just put it all to the side."

"You shouldn't be putting it all on her."

"I'm not, okay?" I finished my beer. "I just have no clue what's going on lately."

"With?"

"Caleb loved this guy so much. Shit, Jonathan seemed like he loved him. How could you just keep the fact that you're married with kids a secret."

"Maybe he was having issues with his wife."

"I've always been open with Colby. I've never kept anything form her."

"Really?"

"Why are you surprised?" Was it such a shocking thing to be honest all the time?"

"You've never told her a lie."

"I didn't see the point. I didn't want to have a secret hanging over my head. It's funny that people think it's shocking to always be honest."

"Maybe that's what happened with you and Caleb?"

I glared at him. I wanted to yell at him, but he was right. "I guess you're right."

"How are you on that subject now?"

"Homosexuality?"

"Yeah."

"I have so many conflicts going through my mind. I thought it was this disgusting thing, but I look at Caleb. I watch his journey those years, and I see the love a man can have for another man. I think that people should love others."

"So you accept it?"

"I think I do. I think the problem is that my father was so against it. He was a good person."

"Good people can do horrible things too."

"I know. I look at Caleb, and I just don't see why someone would kill him. I look at the relationship with Jonathan, and I see how much joy he has."

"The problem is that you don't know who killed him."

"What if it was Jonathan?"

"Do you think that?"

I shook my head. "I don't know. I just have a bad feeling about him."

"I'm wondering why his friends never told the police about his relationship with Jonathan."

I had my suspicion about that too. If they knew about Caleb's relationship with Jonathan, then how come they didn't bring it up during their interviews? "I know. There are so many holes in every-thing. I just don't get anything anymore."

"I'll be right back." Jimmy got up and went to the bar. He grabbed a couple more beers and brought them back to the table. "You were a mess when your aunt came to the apartment and told us that he died."

I took a sip of my new beer, and I thought back to when that bomb was dropped on me.

Two Months Ago
Jimmy and I were playing video games. We were slightly buzzed, and we were trying to forget about the horrors of finals coming up. I wanted to be over college. "I fucking hate you."

Jimmy laugh. "Suck it up, bitch. You're horrible at this." Jimmy killed me again. I slammed the controller down. "Don't be such a baby. It looks like you're going to be paying for our road trip."

I took a sip of my beer. "I can't wait to go."

He nodded. "It's only a couple of weeks left. We'll be on the road, and we can forget all about fucking school."

"Until August."

I glared at him. "Way to ruin the mood." We laughed, and there was a knock at the door. I walked over and opened the door. Aunt June was standing there completely destroyed. "Aunt June?"

She didn't say anything. She pulled me into a hug. "I love you."

I felt a knot in my stomach. Something happened. I tightened my grip on her. She was all I had, and I was praying that she hadn't died. "What's wrong?" I asked without looking at her.

"I don't know how to tell you."

I pulled her apart, and I looked at her. "Are you okay? Is Colby okay?"

She nodded. "Yes, honey, we're both fine. I haven't seen Colby. I thought you should be the one to tell her this." She looked at Jimmy. "Do you mind?"

He got up. "Yeah, I'm not dealing with this." He walked away into his room.

"What's going on?" I asked.

"I love you."

"I know."

"There are some things I can't protect you from." She touched my face.

"I know this." I didn't know where this was going.

She paused, and I could tell she was struggling telling me. "Caleb is dead." She said it slowly, and her voice broke.

"What?"

"They found his body in a field."

"What?"

"It was this morning. They're saying it's a possible homicide."

"What?"

"I'm so sorry." *She pulled me back into a hug. I couldn't believe that Caleb was gone. He was murdered of all things. Sure, we haven't talked in two years, but it didn't mean that my love for him was gone. He was like my brother, and now he was gone.*

I separated myself from her. *"Do they have any leads? Any possibilities who it could be?"*

"It just happened."

"It doesn't matter. Did they talk to his friends?"

She touched my cheek. *"Honey, you need to let the police figure it out. You need to grieve."*

I shook my head. *"No, I don't. I need to figure out who killed my best friend."* *I was about to storm out of there and drive to his college.*

She grabbed my arm. She looked me in the eye. *"You're not going to do anything. You're going to let this digest, and you're going to grieve. You will tell Colby, and you both can be together during this. You're not going to push your feelings away, Colin."*

I shook my head. *"I can't just sit here when my best friend died. I should have been with him. I should have protected him."*

"It's not your fault."

"It doesn't matter. I need to find out who killed him. I need to kill the son of a bitch. They can't get away with this."

Aunt June pulled me back into her arms. *"You need to worry about yourself. You need to grieve and let it go."*

The words were still ringing in my head thinking back now. I laughed. "I should have taken Aunt June's advice."

"Have you even grieved?" Jimmy asked.

"I don't have time. I'm trying to find out who killed my best friend." I took a sip of my drink. "I'll get him back. I just need to know what happened."

63

"Why didn't you tell the police about Jonathan?" I asked storming into the radio station.

Drew, Cameron, and Beth were eating. "Well hello to you too." Beth stood up. "I didn't know anyone could just barge in here."

"Answer the question."

"You really don't get to come into here demanding things when you have no clue what was going on."

"He was murdered. His ex-boyfriend was his professor."

Beth walked in front of me. "You don't get to accuse us of anything. He was devastated when they broke up."

"That doesn't change that you never told the cops."

Drew stepped in front of her. "What good would it have done?"

"He could be the reason he's dead."

"Why haven't you gone to the police?" Drew asked.

"I don't know the full story." I admitted.

"But you came in here attacking us. When will you stop being an asshole?" Beth asked.

"Beth, that's enough." Cameron walked over and rubbed her back.

"No, you've been here for over a week looking down on us and Caleb. Wasn't he your best friend? I can't see how Caleb, this sweet caring guy, could be friends with such a dick like you." She stared at me.

"I'm trying to understand, okay? It's why I'm here."

Beth shook her head. "Jonathan was a good guy. Yes, he did a fucked up thing by keeping everything from Caleb. We saw how happy he was those two years with him. Even after they broke up, he still had him on a pedestal. So no, we didn't tell the police."

"Do you have any idea who could have killed him?" I asked.

"No, but it doesn't matter," Drew said.

"Why?" I looked at him.

"What does it matter who killed him? He's gone. We've accepted it. Why can't you?" Drew looked me in the eyes.

"I can't believe you guys. You act like you are these great people of acceptance, when you let him die. You killed him."

"You know what? Fuck you. You have no clue who we are." Drew stormed passed me out of the door.

Beth slapped me across the face. "You don't get to judge. Caleb was right to get rid of you." She followed suit.

It was just Cameron and I. "You really know how to clear a room."

I chuckled. "Why didn't you leave with them?"

"Because they have their own demons about his death. All four of us do. I know you're still trying to grieve."

"Why didn't you say anything? You knew longer than anyone. Why didn't you expose his secret?"

"It's not my secret to tell. Drew was right. It doesn't change anything. He's still gone. I think we all can accept that Jonathan could have done it. We can't understand why a man who loved him so much would murder him."

"Do you know if they saw each other after they broke up?"

She shrugged. "I'm not a hundred percent sure, but I had my suspicion. Caleb was all over the place right before he died. He had a lot of anger in him about the break up. He was lied and cheated to. He loved Jonathan with all his heart, and he thought Jonathan felt the same."

"Why did he have to fall in love with his professor?"

"Because love is a fucking asshole. Love doesn't make you happy sometimes. It can be the worst experience in your life. Caleb loved with all his heart, and it's what probably killed him. Caleb didn't do anything half-ass."

"Yeah, isn't that true."

"He wanted this great love, and he thought he got it in Jonathan. I don't know what happened to Caleb. We all want to believe that Jonathan didn't do it. We want to believe that man didn't cause him anymore pain than he already did."

"Why don't you hate me?" She was willing to talk to me. I've gotten so much heat from the other ones. It didn't make sense that she was willing to help me.

"Because you were his best friend. He saw good in you, and I have to believe that there is a reason he left you with his final thoughts. We all deserve the right to closure. I think this is your way of it."

"I don't know if I'll get it."

She shook her head. "You can't get closure when you only know half the story. I think you need to figure the rest out." She placed her hand on my shoulder. "We don't hate you, and we've had our time to grieve. Don't judge us for our actions, and we won't judge you for yours."

"I just want him back." I didn't look at her.

"We all do, but we can come together as friends. It could be the next best thing. You just have to let us in." She walked past me and out of the radio station.

I stood there lost in my thoughts because I just couldn't process how they didn't go to the police. I tried so hard to not judge or make assumptions, but it could have solved his death. I can't just avoid his murder. It seemed the more I went down this path that I was the only one who was trying to find his murderer.

64

I stood outside my liberal arts building nervous about starting another year. It was my junior year. I was here, and I didn't know how I felt about it. Two years ago, I had been a lost and confused. I'm now in love with my professor, I have great friends, and I no longer thought about Colin. We've completely gone our separate ways, and I think that it's for the best.

I was oddly comforting knowing where to go. I saw the lost freshman trying to figure their footing. I got to Dr. Delilah's office. I knocked on her door. "You don't have to be so nervous," she said.

Dr. Delilah was my advisor for this year, and she was also the one I was interning for. She was a gentle woman that believed in everything Victorian Era. She was in her mid-fifties, but she didn't look older than her mid-thirties, minus the gray hair.

"I guess it's scary to think that I'm going to be your TA this year."

She rolled her eyes. "You've always been humble." She moved to the side to let me in. She took a seat behind her desk. "I'm surprised you didn't want to shadow Professor Lancaster. He wrote you a glowing reference."

I couldn't tell her that we wouldn't get anything done. We would probably spend the whole time sleeping with each other. "I thought it was a good idea to get a different writer's perspective."

"Mr. Wheeler couldn't stop talking about it during our advising meeting."

I laughed. "Shawn has a huge crush on Professor Lancaster."

She shook her head. "Students and their obsession with the professor fantasy."

"What do you mean?"

She looked at me. "It's pretty obvious that people only want to be with a professor because they don't have their own father figure."

I got uncomfortable. "Do you believe that? Can't you just want to be with an older male because they like the maturity?"

She shrugged. "I guess, but I don't think it could be that way. I think it's daddy issues." She looked down at her paper. "We have a lot to get over with. Why don't we focus on that?"

I didn't want to believe that I was with Jonathan because I never knew my father. Dr. Delilah didn't know my past or my relationship with Jonathan. I loved him, and I had to keep that go-ing. I had to believe that I was madly in love with him because of the being he was. I swallowed up my worry and focused on what she was talking about.

September 10th, 2013
"We are back in full swing, and we can't wait to hear from you guys this semester. Remember to mail us your submissions, and we will read them on the radio. Thanks for always tuning into Freedom Writers Radio," I said to close out the show.

Shawn and I high fived after the beginning of another semes-ter as co-host. "It feels good to be back from London. It's been hard to get everything back into the swing of things."

I smiled. "How's working with Jonathan?"

"It's the best." I saw Shawn light up. "He's been helping me write, and I can't handle how good my writing has gotten."

"Yeah, he's mentioned you've gotten better."

"You guys talk about me?" He raised an eyebrow.

I had a mental freak out. I couldn't tell him that we got din-ner last night. "I passed his office to Dr. Delilah's, and we caught up."

"Is it hard that you don't have him this year?" He asked.

I shrugged. "I understand he only teaches beginners and se-niors in the program. I'm not going to lie and say that I don't miss him. It was refreshing having him last year."

"Yeah, it's weird not seeing you in class. I'm surprised you didn't get paired up with him."

"I just wanted something different." I think that it hit me that I really did miss him. We talked to each other, but it was becoming sporadic. We still wrote letters, but they were becoming longer times between. I was focused on my future. He couldn't blame me for that.

"Yeah, I guess you're right."

"He had turned into my safety blanket. I could always go to him with my writing. I think it's weird not having him there as a voice."

"You know that you could always go back to him. You can still ask him to look over your work."

"Yeah, maybe." I just wanted this summer to be back. I wanted to be back on the lake just the two of us. Why did we have to come back to our responsibilities? This was worse than an actual break up. I couldn't just be with him. I just wanted to wake up curled in his arms, but I couldn't because Drew was back. I was tired of the complications once again.

"You okay?" Shawn asked.

I looked at him. "Yeah, I've got a lot on my mind."

"Problems with the boyfriend." I could hear the joy in his voice.

I shook my head and forced a smile. "We're great. It's all about balancing." I didn't want to force a smile with people. I didn't want to keep it all in. I just wanted to tell people the real issues behind the smile. I guess it was still Jack all over again. This time is that I was deeper in love, and there were bigger consequences.

65

"*H*ey, sorry I can't make dinner. I have a department dinner that I forgot about. I'll call you later. I love you.*" I read the text from Jonathan.

I sighed. "Well fuck." I had already been waiting twenty minutes for him. I just slouched down in my seat.

"What's wrong?" Cameron asked.

I turned to her. Drew was in the shower getting ready for their date. "Jonathan cancelled on me."

"Why?"

"Department meeting."

"I'm sorry."

"It's fine, I guess. I just hate the fact that he continues to do this. We continue to fight about never seeing each other. We had an incredible summer together, but we've been growing apart this past month. I barely see him." I felt the tears starting to form.

She pulled me into a hug. "I'm sorry that you're going through this. It's not fair."

"Shawn, Beth, and Drew have been asking what's been going on. I have to put a force smile on and tell them that I'm fine. I hate lying to them. I know I have you now, but I feel alone."

"It's not fair that he keeps putting you on the back burner."

"I understand that we both have responsibilities, but I'm trying here. I just miss him."

"I love you, and we're here for you. I think maybe you need to talk to him. You shouldn't feel neglected after this summer. I guess he thinks that he will always have you. He shouldn't take you for granted."

I looked at the hope and concern in Cameron's eyes. I wish I could believe that it would all work out. I've never had anyone fight for me. I've always been the person that is convenient. When was it going to get easy for me? When was I going to have a happy relationship?

September 24th, 2013

I knew this was a bad idea the moment I drunk stumbled into the hallway to Jonathan's office. He told me he had to work late tonight. We were supposed to just grab a fucking drink. I was twenty-one. I left my pre-game to come see Jonathan. All I got was a quick happy birthday from him.

I knocked on the door. Well I banged on the door. The door open and Jonathan was standing there confused. "Caleb, what are you doing here?"

"It's my birthday. I want birthday sex." I couldn't even process how not sexy I was being. I just wanted to be loved by him.

"I'm working."

I crossed my arms and pouted. "I left my birthday party to come here and have sex with you."

"Caleb, you're drunk. You need to go home."

I shook my head. "No, I'm not going home. I love you."

"I'm not dealing with this right now."

I felt the tears fall down my face. "Why? What happened to us? What happened after the cabin? Do you even love me?"

I saw that Jonathan was fighting himself internally. He didn't respond back to me right away, and it was enough of an answer. "Never mind. I'll leave." I turned to walk away.

"Caleb, wait." He grabbed my arm.

I ripped it out of his arms. "No, you don't get to pull me around like a fucking yo-yo. I'm not your plaything that you can toss to the side. I thought we cared for each other. I thought there was respect. You get back to me when you can properly love me." I left him with that.

I didn't want to remember this night. I wanted to forget about this horrible birthday. I stumbled back to my party that was still in full swing. Beth saw me first. "Where have you been?" She asked.

"It doesn't matter." I tried to keep the tears from coming out, but I was too drunk to even keep control.

"What did he do?" She asked.

"He doesn't love me anymore." She pulled me into the bathroom. She grabbed some toilet paper and sat in the bathtub with me.

"What happened?"

"I went to his office to have sex with him. I asked if he loved me, and he couldn't respond to me." I didn't care who knew now. I just wanted to feel better.

"Office. Who are you dating?" Beth asked.

I looked at her, and it was time to tell people. "I'm dating Jonathan Lancaster, my old creative writing professor."

"What?" I saw the shock on her face.

I laid my head against the cool tile. I need to keep control. "Cameron knows too. I've kept it a secret for obvious reasons. He rejected me."

"When did this all happen?"

"It's been going on for almost a year. He rejected me."

"How?"

"It just happened. He rejected me." I felt the tears fall, and I felt myself growing tired. I remember saying he rejected me before I fell asleep against the tile and Jonathan's face after I asked him if he loved me.

66

October 1st, 2013

I walked into my apartment. I was still trying to forget about my birthday from a week ago. I've been avoiding Jonathan and been trying to just stay in Dr. Delilah's office. He had been texting me periodically apologizing, but it doesn't matter. I just couldn't face him right now. He was probably going to break up with me.

I saw Drew, Cameron, and Beth standing there. "This can't be good."

"We love you," Cameron said.

"Is this an intervention?" I asked.

"You're sleeping with an asshole who keeps rejecting you. Damn straight this an intervention," Drew said.

"Who told him?" I looked between Cameron and Beth.

Cameron raised her hand. "Beth freaked out to me. I told her that I knew. We both figured out that it was time that we brought Drew up to speed."

"Why isn't Shawn here?" I asked.

"Did you really want the guy that's in love with you and your professor to know you both are sleeping together?" Beth crossed her arms.

"You do have a point. So what's this all about?"

"Your birthday. You freaked us all out," Drew said.

"I was drunk. I made an ass of myself and threw myself at him. That was a mistake." I tried to play it off.

Cameron walked over and pulled me into a hug. "Caleb, you were crying. I've never seen you so destroyed."

"I was drunk." I tried to push her off of me.

Beth walked over and pulled me into a hug. "I sat in that bathroom with you for hours, Caleb."

"I'm sorry that it sucked, but I love him." I screamed at them.

"No one is telling you that you can't love him," Cameron said.

"We're just telling you that you deserve better," Beth said.

"Why?"

"Why, what?" Beth asked.

"Why do you guys care? Why is it so important that I'm happy?"

"Is that a valid question?" We all looked at Drew. "Are you that fucking stupid?"

"Drew." Cameron tried to put her hand on Drew.

"No, I'm not having this conversation with you again. We're your best friends. We love you. We've been through shit together, and I don't care if you don't believe us. Yeah, I know your best friends from home really fucked you over, but we aren't them."

"It's hard, okay?" I didn't know how far I would push them before they ran away. I found everyone's buttons, and it seemed that I enjoyed pushing them.

"Why?" Beth asked.

"Because I've had so many people fail me before. I don't want to believe that I can get joy. Colin, Jack, and I think now, Jonathan. I don't like losing people, but they keep leaving me." I looked them in the eyes.

"We're not going anywhere. You need to accept that," Drew said.

"How do I get to be okay with Jonathan?" I asked. I walked to sit on the couch. "How do I still love him when he destroys me? How do I get to be happy when he controls that? When did I lose my control for my own damn life?" I screamed.

Cameron and Beth walked over and sat down on either side of me. Drew was in front of me. "We can't control other people's lives. We can only control our own," he said.

"I'm a fool because I want it to work."

"It can still work out," he said.

"How?"

"You need to focus on yourself," Beth said. "Alex and I thought we were going to be something. We realized that all we had was a physical relationship. It was pointless to stay together."

"Were you sad?"

"It's why I went home. I needed to recollect myself."

"I just want to stop feeling like a fool."

"It doesn't go away." She laid her head on my shoulder.

I was surrounded by support, but I didn't feel loved. The person that mattered was the one that was destroying me right now. Why couldn't I focus on the people that made me feel like a complete person? Why couldn't I find someone to love me back?

67

October 4th, 2013

I was sitting in the library working on a short story for Dr. Delilah's class when I saw a figure standing next to me. I looked up and saw Jonathan standing there. My heart dropped. I've been avoiding him since the intervention. I looked back down at my story. "I don't have anything to say to you."

"Talk to me."

"No."

"I messed up."

"I don't care."

"Please." I looked up when I heard the pain in his voice.

I looked around to see that no one was standing around us. I stood up. "You don't get to be the one that has been hurt in this situation."

"I've been an asshole."

"You've been an asshole since school started. I haven't seen much of you the past month." I grabbed all my stuff and put it in my bag.

"Where are you going?" He asked.

"If we're going to talk, we're doing it somewhere else." I stormed past him towards his office.

I took my seat and crossed my arms. I heard the door closed. He pulled my chair so we were facing each other. "I'm sorry."

"I don't care."

"Talk to me."

"Why should I?"

"Because I love you."

"Bullshit." I screamed.

"Caleb."

"Jonathan." We stared at each other. I wanted to punch him and kiss him.

He sighed. "I'm trying to fix this."

"You rejected me."

"You wanted to sleep in my office."

"Because I haven't had alone time with you since school start-ed. I get that we're both busy, but we've be so disconnected."

"I didn't mean for this to happen."

"I want to be loved by you. I want those days in the cabin. Did you mean those words in the letter?"

"Of course I do." He closed the space and his lips crashed onto mine. It was a messy kiss at first, but it felt right. It felt good to have his body on me after so long. I felt complete, and I started to have forgiveness towards him.

He let go of me. "Do you forgive me?"

"Don't ever do that to me again." I stared at him. "I won't be lied to or disrespected. Jonathan, I love you. It kills me to love you, but I can't do this hot and cold with you."

He grabbed my hand. "I know. I'm trying to get better at this. I love you."

I pulled him in for another kiss. "I love you." I would be an idiot to think that this solved everything. I knew we would still have our faults, but I thought that we could get through it. Love would get us through it.

October 18th, 2013
I was pacing back and forth in my apartment. I was waiting for Jonathan to get here. The past two weeks have been wonderful between us. The letters started up again, and we were connecting.

I could tell that my friends were still a little worried that he would still play me, but I refused to listen to them.

Drew agreed to give me the place. He went to Cameron and Beth's apartment for the night. He gave me one last pep talk before he left. I took his words with a grain of salt.

I heard a knock on the door. I opened the door to Jonathan wearing just jeans and a t-shirt. It was the first time since the cabin that I saw him without a suit or button up on. I pulled him in for a sloppy kiss.

We kept peppering each other with kisses until we fell on the couch. "I missed you."

"I missed you too." His arms trapped me in, and he looked at me. "How was your day? Did Drew believe you?"

I nodded. I couldn't and wouldn't tell Jonathan that my friends knew about us being together. I knew he would break up with me right then. It was a perfect situation. I would keep my relationship with Jonathan, and I would be able to tell my friends. I still couldn't tell Shawn.

"Yeah. He didn't want to ask questions after I told him I had a study group. He assumed I was getting laid."

"You're terrible at lies."

"Apparently, it worked." I kissed him. "It got you over here."

He chuckled. "It did. It's nice to hold you in my arms again." He pulled me close to his chest.

I enjoyed his heat. "I've missed this. I don't want to go that long without seeing you."

"I know. I just have been going through a lot of shit."

"Do you trust me?" I asked.

"Why do you ask?"

I turned around to look at him. "You can always tell me what's going on with you. I want to know what issues you're going through."

"I know I can."

"Then why have you been distant? Why haven't I heard from you since the summer ended?" I wanted answers.

"It's been hard to love someone again." He grabbed my hands. "I've been used before. I dated this woman for a long time. I thought she could be the one for me, but she ended up playing me. She cheated on me so many times, and I put walls up. I believed that I couldn't get that again."

"What changed?"

"You insulted my work."

I blushed and looked down. "I feel so sorry for that."

He laughed. "I just wanted you to know that I've been back and forth with it. I deeply care for you, and I love you. I don't want you to forget about that. I can only apologize for the mistakes that I've made and promise that I'll try."

"I guess it's all I can ask for."

"Good."

I knew this high would go down. I knew he would break my heart again. It was wrong because I accepted it. I loved him too much, and it felt so right being with him. I would take the pain because it would kill me more to lose him.

68

October 21st, 2013

"How are you and Jonathan?" Cameron asked while she was cooking Drew and I dinner.

"We're fine. We've been seeing a lot of each other lately." I looked between them. "Thank you for helping out."

Drew shrugged. "I know that you would do it for me. I just want you to be happy. I just don't want him to hurt you."

I shook my head. "Every relationship has issues." I didn't want to admit I saw the look Cameron and Drew shared between them. "I just think that we're getting on the same page. I love him, okay?"

"No one is telling you that you can't love him. We're just hoping that you don't lose yourself again."

"I won't."

"Caleb, I saw what happened when you and Jack broke up. I saw how destroyed you got because you loved someone."

"Are you saying I can't love anyone?" I asked.

They shook their heads. "It's not what we're saying." Cameron had a weak smile on her face.

"We're just protecting you. We don't want you to get hurt because of some asshole who doesn't know how to take care of your heart."

I grabbed their hands. "Thanks. I needed that."

"Now that we got that out of the way, why don't you two set up the table?" She asked.

"Or you could do it?" I asked.

She leaned over and smacked me upside the head. "I'm the one cooking. You two assholes can set the table."

I rolled my eyes. "Just go with it," Drew whispered.

"I heard that."

We laughed as we set up the table. There was a knock at the door. I looked at Cameron and Drew who both had a confused expression on their face like me. I walked over to the door to open it.

I opened the door, and it was like a ghost had appeared. She looked the same, but it had been two in a half years since I've last seen her. My heart dropped to my stomach because I saw how devastated she looked. I didn't know why she was here, but I feared the worst. Colin was dead, and she was here to tell me. "Colby?" I asked still trying to process why Colby was at my door.

69

I slammed my laptop shut. Colby saw him. Colby lied to me. She told me she had never seen him between high school and his death. Why would she do that? I looked at the date on the journal entry. It was day after we broke up.

She walked into the hotel room with take out for everyone. Jimmy followed her. "How's everything going?" She smiled at me.

It killed me because I didn't know how many secrets were hidden behind that smile. "You lied to me."

"What are you talking about?"

"You fucking lied to me." I screamed standing up.

Jimmy looked between us. "I better let you both work this out."

"No, I need you stand here to be a witness to her bullshit."

"What are you talking about?" She looked completely lost.

"You saw Caleb after we broke up."

It took only a minute for realization to flash across her face. "He wrote about it, didn't he?"

"I'm surprised that you didn't read it when you went behind my back. I can't believe you."

"I didn't think it mattered."

"Really? I asked you if you saw him, and you said no."

"We had broken up. I was destroyed. I needed my friend."

"I fucking don't care about why you went to see him. I'm pissed you never told me."

"I'm not proud of the three months we were separated."

"You're trying to avoid something. Colby, what else happened?"

She had tears down her face. She shook her head. "You're letting these fucking diary entries break us up."

"No, it's from my best friend."

"Ex-best friend. You didn't even talk to him for four years. You two were fucking strangers. You pushed him away like you're pushing me away."

"I'm not pushing you away. I'm trying to figure out why you would lie to me about seeing him."

"Because it doesn't matter." She screamed. "I'll never be proud of that time. Why can't you just move on? Why can't we just go home and focus on our future?"

"I'm sorry that I'm trying to find out who killed my best friend."

"No, you're doing this because you feel guilty of what happened four years ago. You're trying to make up for it." She stood up and got in my face. "You need to get the fuck over it."

"Colby, I never thought I couldn't trust you."

She threw her hands in the air. "It's why we broke up the first time. You thought I was cheating, while you were getting close to Bekah Dulling."

"Bekah and I were just friends."

"Except she was in your fucking bed in."

"She was drunk and needed a bed to crash. Jimmy can account for that."

"He didn't sleep with her." Jimmy quickly added.

"It's like you said. It doesn't matter. It's the fact that I didn't believe you." She grabbed her purse. "I don't regret lying to you about seeing Caleb. He was my best friend too."

"What else am I going to find out, Colby?"

She walked to the door. "Does it matter? You're going to find out in your fucking little journals. You're going to take Caleb's side over mine. Caleb will always be number one. You tossed him to the side. I guess it's my time." She opened the door and slammed it behind her.

I screamed and punched the desk. I felt pain surge through my body. I sat down, angry about everything going on. "I don't want to fucking be here anymore."

"That's not true."

"This whole fucking trip was a stupid idea. Why do I even care who killed him?" I grabbed the USB and threw it across the room.

Jimmy sat on the bed. "Colin, why does it matter that she saw Caleb?"

"Because she could go see him. She could walk in and out of his life without harm."

"You can't blame her for that."

"I don't."

"What is it?"

"She probably told Caleb about everything that happened to us. We were both in messed up spots in our lives. I'll admit that we were freaked out about being together. It doesn't mean that she can keep this from me."

"Why don't you talk to her?"

"No, I'm done with her bullshit. She keeps making me look like the bad guy." It was true. She caused problems while we were on this trip. She went behind my back to read the journal entries, and now, she lied to me about seeing Caleb. Did I even know Colby anymore?"

"You can't mean that."

I stood up. "I need a fucking drink. I need to forget about all of this." I walked towards the door.

"Colin, you can't solve all your problems with drinking."

I turned to him. "It worked in the past."

"This isn't college."

"Jimmy, fuck you. I need my fun slob of a roommate. I don't need my best friend."

"I'm not going to waste both of our time. Talk to Colby."

I shook my head. "What's the point? She might lie to me again."

"Stop being an asshole."

"When will people learn that I'm the one that keeps getting hurt in all of these situations." I opened up the door and walked out of the room. I was done with all of pain I was getting. I was learning that this trip was ruining everything for me. I just didn't know what to do anymore. It scared me.

70

I walked outside to see Colby standing there, smoking a cigarette and crying. She turned to see me standing there. "I hate
when you smoke these things, and I'm here myself smoking."
She gave out a weak laugh.

"Why didn't you tell me?"

She threw the cigarette on the ground. "I don't want to get into
this with you."

"Why not?"

"What do you want me to say? I'm completely destroyed about
the fact that we broke up. I had to run to the guy that already caused
us enough problems."

"How did Caleb do that?"

"I was always the sidekick to you and Caleb."

"We were best friends."

"I was your girlfriend. I always felt like I was number two until you guys ended your friendship. I hated Caleb."

"He was one of your best friends."

"He was, but I still had jealousy towards him. I still resented him. I know that doesn't make sense. I didn't like how I had to turn to him for when we were down. You both had so many issues on your own that I knew it would add more."

"What happened in those three months?" I asked again. She needed to stop dodging the questions.

"Caleb helped me a lot during that time. I can't lie and say I didn't miss him. Caleb was so kind, and I knew it would kill you to know we got our friendship back."

"What?"

"Caleb and I fixed us. We realized it was between you two, not us."

"Did you know about Jonathan?"

She shook her head. "No, I knew he was dating someone, but I didn't know it was his professor."

"Did you talk to him before he died?"

"We talked here and there until his death."

"Why would you keep that from me?"

"To protect you! I thought it was better for you to think that he rejected both of us. I didn't want you to feel alone."

"When were you going to tell me?"

"I was hoping never. I thought maybe after college you both would grow up and fix your problems. I didn't know he died. I didn't know he left those entries. I didn't know he would talk about me."

"I can't believe you would keep this all from me."

"I know it was wrong, but I did what I thought was best. You can continue hating me for it, or you can read the entries."

"I want to hear it from your mouth."

I saw her cry again. "What's the point? My words don't resonate as much as Caleb's. He has more power over you. I could sit here and tell you, but it would just be words."

"Colby, that's not true."

"You're blinded to the truth. You loved him like a brother. He was your idol, and you were his. I've never seen a friendship like that, and I never will again. It just sucked being your girlfriend because I had to compete for you. In a sick way, I was happy you two ended your friendship. I got my boyfriend all to myself. And now, I lost you again to him. I just hope you come back to me."

"What does that mean?"

"Read the rest of the entries. Learn what happened during those three months. Find me when you're done." She walked away from me, and I couldn't handle it. I was losing Colby all over again, but this time it was all her fault. She kept this from me. I needed to know what happened.

71

October 25th, 2013

"Colby, what are you doing here?" I asked. I prayed that nothing happened to Colin. I knew we didn't talk anymore, but that didn't mean I was over him.

She wrapped her arms around me and began to cry. "Colin and I broke up."

I pulled her closer to me. I was a little relieved that he wasn't dead. "Colby, I'm so sorry to hear that. What happened?" I asked.

She released me and looked at me. "I was an idiot to come here. I should go."

I grabbed her hand. "No, we should talk."

She nodded. I escorted her into the living room. I noticed that Drew and Cameron made themselves disappear. I was thankful for that. I would introduce them but at a later time. We sat down on the couch. "What happened?"

"We've been fighting so much lately. We've been stressed about school and our relationship has suffered. I went to his apartment to surprise him. He was having a couple of friends over. I was so pissed that he was having a party without me. He's been so focused on his fucking fraternity. I walked into his room and there was this fucking bitch in his bed."

She took a deep breath. I saw the tears continuing to fall. "Did they sleep together?" I asked.

She shook her head. "No, he didn't. She passed out in his bed. They were friends. It didn't matter. I didn't believe him, and I went off on him. We got into this huge fight, and he ended it. He said he couldn't handle how unhappy we've been lately."

"I'm so sorry." I knew Colby and I had our own issues, but I knew how happy she was in love with Colin.

"I didn't know where else to go. I thought that I could go to my sorority sisters, but they didn't understand everything we've been through. The only person I could think of was you."

"Why?"

"Caleb, you're one of my closest friends. I know we drifted because of you and Colin. I know I hated you for a while because you were taking my boyfriend away from me. I was number two in his heart. I shouldn't be so fucking selfish. You two were best friends before I came into the picture."

"Colby, it's understandable."

She shook her head. "No, it's not. Caleb, I had no one else to go to. I realized how much you meant to me, and how much I missed you."

It was nice to hear Colby say all those things. I realized that we had a big drift between us that didn't need to be there. I pulled her into a hug. "Thank you for saying that. I guess I missed you too."

"Do you mind if I stay here for the night? I just don't want to go back to my place to all that."

I rubbed her back. "You can stay here as long as you want."

I was oddly grateful that Colin and Colby broke up because it gave us a chance to fix our friendship. Maybe this was a good thing. I don't know. Maybe it could lead to me fixing things with Colin.

October 26th, 2013

I woke up the following morning thinking about the night before. It seemed more like a dream than reality. Colby was on my couch sleeping. Colin and Colby broke up. Colby wanted to be friends with me. It was an odd sensation because I wanted to be friends with her. I just always knew her as Colin's girlfriend. I could finally know her as Colby.

I got out of my bed and walked out of my room to the living room. Drew and Colby were sitting on the couch drinking coffee.

"Hey, guys."

Colby gave me a weak smile. Drew got up. "Someone slept in."

I shrugged. "I didn't hear my alarm. I see you two are getting along." I looked between them.

Colby giggled and took a sip of her drink. Drew rolled her eyes. "I said good bye to Cameron, and I woke up Colby. We sat here for the past hour talking."

"Yeah, I wouldn't think about it too much." She placed her cup down. She got up and walked over to me. She kissed me on the cheek. "Thank you for letting me crash on your couch."

"Are you going to stay here for the weekend?" I asked.

"If you don't mind. I just wanted a nice piece of home." She wrapped arms around me. "I missed your birthday. I think we should drink." She winked.

"I'm going to regret this."

Drew laughed. "I like the sound of that. I'll see you two love-birds later. I'm going to get some more shut eye." He waved us off before he entered his room.

"What did you two talk about?" I asked.

She shrugged. "Relationship problems. He needed my advice on stuff. He needed a girl's perspective. I guess Beth isn't a good girl to talk to about it."

I laughed. "Yeah, she doesn't do fuzzy stuff. You really want to stay?"

"I meant what I said about fixing our friendship. I know that it's probably odd timing since Colin and I broke up, but I'm not going to lose you, Caleb. I've missed you too much. I didn't realize how much you mean to me until now."

I pulled her into a hug. "I'll show you my life for the past two years."

We spent the whole day going to the radio station, walking around campus, and her meeting the rest of the group. It seemed that the group really enjoyed her. We ended up at the college bar grabbing some drinks.

I sat next to Colby as she ordered rounds of shots. Beth and Shawn looked confused. Drew was enjoying every minute of it. "Where's Cameron?" I asked.

He shrugged. "She didn't really want to come out. She wanted to be left alone. I didn't see an issue with it." He wasn't looking at me. He was watching Colby laugh and dance while getting us more shots.

"You went to high school with her?" Beth asked.

"Yeah, she was dating Colin."

"I can't see that," Shawn said.

I looked at him. "Why?"

"Because she's so nice and a lot of fun. What we've heard of Colin, he seems like a total ass."

"He never was when we were friends."

"Guess he's gotten worse. They broke up," Beth said. I didn't really care to talk about Colin. It was now a wound for Colby and I. I just wanted to enjoy my time with her without tarnishing it.

Colby stumbled up to the table. "Why are you guys sitting down? We should be dancing. Let's dance."

"I'm good on dancing. I'd rather sit here," Shawn quickly added.

"I'll dance with you." Drew winked at her.

I heard Beth groan. I turned to see her roll her eyes. "Of course you would. I'll dance I guess." She looked at me. "Only if you go dance."

I grabbed a shot. "I guess I have no option here."

Colby grabbed Drew's hand, and they walked to the center of the dance floor to dance. Beth followed, not looking pleased. I turned to Shawn. "Why don't you want to dance? You've been out of your shell for a while now."

He shrugged. "I know, but I sometimes like watching my friends dance. I enjoy seeing them happy because it's what brings me joy. I like to sit back and enjoy the scenery sometimes."

I nodded. "Okay. I'll see you in a little bit." I got up and walked to meet up with the group. I saw Colby and Drew dancing together. It seemed innocent, but it was on a very fine line.

I pulled Beth close to me to dance. "I don't like her," Beth said.

"Why?"

"Because I don't like what she's doing to Drew. She's been here a full day, and he's already crossing the line."

I saw what Beth was saying. They were dancing and smiling. I thought it was harmless. I didn't see anything over the line yet. "She's just looking for attention. She just got out of a relationship. I wouldn't put it against her."

Beth sighed. "I know. I just don't want our little group of friends to be ruined."

"Do I have to choose between them?" I asked.

She shook her head. "Not yet."

We danced, and I watched Drew and Colby. I saw how close they were getting. I was happy to see Colby smiling, but I knew it would break Cameron's heart if she saw it. I didn't want to lose my old friend, but did this mean I had to give up on my friends who have been here for two years?

72

Dear Caleb,

It's okay that we haven't seen each other on the week-ends. I know your helping your friend with everything going on. I miss you, and I'll patiently wait. I know you've done the same for me the past couple of months. I don't want to hold it against you. I love you, and I can't wait till we can get away for a weekend.

Love,
Jonathan.

I smiled reading the letter again. I've spent the past couple of weeks with Colby. I know that it's been helping her get through everything. I've been worried to watch her grow closer with Drew. She promised me that there was nothing going on between them. They were just connecting about relationship problems.

"You have a smile on your face," Colby said while taking a bite of her salad.

We were sitting on my couch just eating before we figured out what we were going to do for the night. "It's nothing."

"Who is the letter from?" She asked.

"Can you keep a secret?" I asked her. I didn't want it to get back to Colin. I had to make sure I could trust Colby.

"Caleb, what you tell me will stay with me. I won't ruin your trust."

"It's from my boyfriend. We've been dating for over a year now. It's crazy, but it's been going really well."

She squealed and pulled me into a deep hug. "I love the fact that we can talk about this. Wow a year. Things are pretty serious."

"Yeah, I love him. We write each other letters all the time. I know it's super cheesy. We have this incredible relationship. It was rocky a couple of months ago, but we've gotten our footing again."

She nodded. "It's hard when you don't have the right balance. I think that's why Colin and I ended. We lost our footing, and we couldn't get it back."

"How are you holding up?"

"I feel like a huge part of me is gone."

I grabbed her hand. "We can talk about it."

She shook her head. "I don't want to talk about it. I want to drink. I want to have fun. I want to completely forget about how I failed our relationship." I saw the tears begin to form in her eyes.

I grabbed her into a hug. Her salad fell between us. "We don't have to talk about it. We can just have fun. We can avoid it until you're ready."

"Thank you. Let's go drink." She got up to walk in the kitchen to grab a bottle for us.

That's how we spent the night. We took shots and avoided the whole subject. We caught up on each other's lives for the past two years. We talked about our twenty-first birthdays. I avoided telling her about Jonathan, and she didn't mention Colin at all. We knew it was walking on eggshells, but it was nice. She was right. It was good to have someone from home here. It made me realize how much I've grown.

December 6th, 2013

> *Dear Jonathan,*
>
> *It was so nice spending the day in my apartment watching movies. I forgot how great it felt having you in my arms. I wish you could come snowboarding with us this weekend. I know that you're busy with finishing up papers before finals begin. I'll miss you, but this will be a nice distraction. I've seen the glow in Colby come back, but I'm worried that she'll go back to Colin. She's been attached to Drew, and I don't feel comfortable with it. Cameron keeps her distance now, and it's*

become a whole mess. I'm stuck in the middle. Beth avoids the group now too. It seems that the only people left are Drew and I. Shawn wants to keep out of all the drama. He's been hanging out with this guy Dylan for a while. He seems to really care for the guy. I hope it works out for them. I love you, and I'll see you when I get back.

Love,
Caleb.

"Are you writing your boyfriend a letter?" Colby asked walking into my room.

"Yeah, I wanted to send him a letter before we go."

She smiled. "That's so romantic."

"Or it's rather pathetic," Drew said walking into the room.

Colby rolled her eyes. "He's just being an asshole. We should get on the road. It's going to take us eight hours to get there."

I put the letter in the envelope. I grabbed my stuff. "I'm sad the rest of the group didn't want to come."

Drew shrugged. "Cameron and Beth have been such bitches lately. It's also been good seeing Shawn have an interest in someone else besides you."

It was a weight off my shoulder. I've met Dylan, and he's a good fit for Shawn. I hoped it works out between them. Yeah, it seems it's us three." Was I replacing Colin with Drew? Was Colby doing the same?

"I don't want to cause problems with your group of friends." I saw the guilt on Colby's face.

Drew shook his head. "That's nonsense. They can live. I'll pack up the car." He walked away from us.

Colby looked at me. "Are you happy that I'm here?" She asked.

"I want you here." I couldn't deny that it felt good to have our friendship back in tact. The past two months have been incredible. I just didn't know if it was worth me losing Cameron and Beth in my life. I just hoped that she found her balance and could go back. I wanted my friendship with her, but I realized how much I have changed.

December 7th, 2013
"I've never been more worn out," I said as I dropped down on the couch in the ski lodge waiting room.

Drew and Colby laughed. They were curled up next to the fire while I was sitting across from them. "You both are getting cozy."

They looked at each other and blushed. "It's been nice having someone here," Colby said. She looked at her cup. "I'll go get us more hot chocolate." She got up and walked away.

I looked at Drew. "What?" He asked.

"You're cheating on Cameron."

"With your best friend."

"It doesn't matter. Why are you doing this?" I asked.

"Cameron and I have been rocky for a little bit right now. We're taking a break from the relationship."

"What?"

"Yeah, we freaked out about how much we're in love. We didn't want to miss out on what college has to offer. We thought we should give each other some space. She's been going on dates. Your friend and I are in the same situation. We're both lonely, and we don't want to lose that comfort."

They were in love with someone that couldn't reciprocate. "What about Cameron?"

"Colby is great and everything, but I'm madly in love with Cameron. Colby is madly in love with Colin. It doesn't matter what happens. We're going back to them. We're just giving them the time to get their head out of their asses." He chuckled.

It made me feel better knowing that they weren't going to be an item. Colby came back and handed me a cup of hot chocolate. She looked at me. "Thank you both of you. I've needed these past two months. The break up with Colin really killed me."

"Are you saying we aren't going to see you again?" I asked.

She shook her head. "No, I want to keep coming, but I miss Colin. I want him back, and it kills me we haven't spoken." I saw the pain in her eyes.

Drew wrapped his arms around her and pulled her close. "I'll be here until you don't need me."

She depended on his warmth. "Same."

I watched as the fireplace light shine on their faces. I watched my two worlds collide, and I realized that I didn't want it to continue. I didn't want my worlds to collide. I realized that I needed her to go. She needed to stay in my past because my present meant more to me. Did that make me a horrible person?

73

January 4th, 2014

"He texted me," Colby said.

I turned to her as we were watching movies on my couch. I needed a weekend to just relax. Colby had come down to visit for New Years. Jonathan said he couldn't be together for the holidays since he was going out of town. I was upset, but it didn't kill me. I realized how much Colby was a healthy distraction.

"Who?"

"Colin."

"Really?"

"Yeah, he wants to talk. He says he's misses me. It's been almost three months, and he's had time to think about everything."

"Do you want to see him?" I asked.

She nodded. "It's been great being here for the past couple of months, but I've been avoiding him."

"Are you happy with him?"

Colby let a tear escape her eyes. "I've never loved someone so strong as I do him. I know this was a case of nerves. We were planning on forever with each other. I think at our age that's a burden. It takes some time for you to realize that's a blessing you get to have forever of happiness and love. I want that with Colin."

"What does that mean for us?"

"Caleb, I love you. You're my best friend, and I don't want that to change. I can tell how much you've changed since I've been here. I've seen how you've grown with this group of friends. I just think it's time for me to go back. I know once we graduate that things with you and Colin will work out."

"Do you believe that?"

"He misses you. He brings you up subtly. I know how much he hasn't been himself. I think you just need to give it time."

"Where do we go from here?"

"You and Colin had so many secrets. You had your own little stories and inside jokes. This will be ours." She winked.

I'm happy to know that we've been able to get our own friendship without Colin. "Thank you for everything. It's been good to have a friend from home back."

She smiled. "I'm here for you. I don't want us to go radio silent. I want us to keep having this friendship." She got up, and we hugged. I knew that we could continue having talks, but it would be from a distance. She was going back to figure out her problems and issues. She was working on getting her forever back. It made me realize that I was fighting for my forever with Jonathan.

January 5th, 2014

"Thank you everyone for having me for the past couple of months. I know that I really haven't gotten to know all of you, except Caleb and Drew. I didn't mean any harm in anything I did. I just don't want there to be hard feelings," Colby said to the group.

We were having a little going away party for Colby. She didn't know the next time she would be back, and I was okay with that. I wanted to get back to normal. We all needed to go back to our problems.

We hoped for her to come back. I noticed Cameron and Colby walk out of the apartment. I started walking. Beth grabbed my arm. "Let them talk."

"Are they going to kill each other?"

Beth shook her head. "No, they need to talk. Cameron and I don't hate her. She wasn't stealing Drew. They just were there for each other when their spouses failed them."

I nodded. "I'm glad that they aren't going to hate each other."

"I honestly feel like this will be put in the past. We're just going to act like we never met her."

"Really?"

Beth shrugged. "I don't see us ever seeing each other. She's getting back with Colin. I think you and Colin won't make up."

"Why's that?"

"You've grown in the past two years. You're not going to let anyone bully or belittle you. I think it's something he'll have to get used to." She shrugged.

She walked away to go talk to Dylan and Shawn. Drew walked over. "It's good that they're back."

"Who?"

"Cameron and Beth. I didn't know how much I missed the bitches." He pointed to Beth.

I laughed. "I don't like us being separated."

"It won't. We know how much we mean to each other."

Cameron and Colby walked back into the room. Drew walked over and grabbed Cameron for a passionate kiss. Colby walked over to me. "I survived."

"I can see that. How was it?"

She turned to look at Drew and Cameron. "It was a good talk. I can see where Cameron is coming from now. It's nice to know that there is hope for my relationship with Colin."

"I'm going to miss you."

"I know. Thank you again for everything."

"I love you."

"Caleb, always take yourself. I know that you're in this great relationship that needs to be kept behind closed doors. I'm happy you're in love. I just don't want you to ever lose this light. It's something I've always admired about you."

"Thank you."

"I'm looking forward for Colin, you, and I to finally be reunited. It will be like old times."

It gave me hope to have those quick moments down memory lane. "Like old times."

74

"I think I've messed up," I said to Aunt June once she picked up the phone.

"What did you do?"

"I freaked out at Colby."

Aunt June sighed. "What did you do?"

"Colby went to see Caleb. It was when we broke up. I freaked out because she kept it from me. Why would she keep it from me?"

"Did you ask her?"

"She said she wasn't proud during that time. I read the journal entries about her and Caleb. She talked about how much she loved and missed me. I didn't enjoy the fact that she got close to Drew."

"Did anything happen?"

"I don't think so. They just were using each other for the attention."

"I don't see the problem."

"Why would she lie to me?"

"She's allowed to keep secrets. It's between her and Caleb."

"Why couldn't she tell me?"

"Colin, you need to realize that they weren't trying to be against you."

"They were replacing me." I read that in the journal entry, and it killed me. They were trying to put me in the past. I thought we actually cared for each other. I would never replace Colby or Caleb. I knew we had issues. I still had a special place in my heart for them.

"Colin, you hurt them. You broke up with Colby, and you rejected Caleb being gay. You can't be upset that they bonded over it."

"Am I that horrible of a person?" I asked. My best friend and girlfriend bonded over how much I hurt them. They wanted Drew to be the better version of me.

"Honey, you're not this horrible person. You just made some mistakes. It's part of growing up."

"Did Colby ever talk to you about being second to Caleb?" It was something that was bothering her in the journal entries and now.

"Honey, Caleb was your best friend. You two did everything together. I'm not surprised that she felt like the third wheel. I noticed a little resentment she had towards him. They were only friends because of you, and I could understand why she was upset about it."

"This whole trip has been a mess. I want to come home."

"The door is always open. I think you'll regret coming home. You need to finish this out."

"Why would they all act like nothing happened?"

"Who?"

"Colby, Drew, Cameron, Beth, and Shawn. They all acted like they didn't know each other. Colby and Drew were weird in the beginning, but now it's like they played me."

"You're missing the point."

"Which is?"

"Caleb, it was a dark time in Colby's life. She probably asked to keep it a secret. She knew that you would be upset. She knew how much you missed Caleb, and she ran to him. Who did you run to during your break up?" She asked.

"I ran to you, Jimmy, and my frat brothers. Why couldn't she run to her other friends?"

"Maybe because she needed someone else's perspective. She needed a person who knew you the best."

"She could have told me. I wouldn't have been mad. I would be upset, but I would hope that it would build a bridge between us. It could have changed all of this if she told me this."

"I don't think it would have mattered. You and Caleb needed to grow separately. I don't think Colby would have made a difference.

You're changing and accepting now. Maybe this is the only way for it to actually happen. This was probably how it all was supposed to go down."

"I don't want to believe that I'm meant to have this hole in my chest."

"I know."

"I just want my friend back."

"Colin." Her voice broke, and I could tell that she was crying. "He's gone."

"I don't want to believe that." I would figure out what happened. I'd fully understand Caleb after we went our separate ways. "I need to fix things with Colby." She was the love of my life, and I couldn't lose her. I wouldn't. I needed to make amends with her before we went down two separate paths.

75

Five Years Earlier

I climbed through Caleb's window. He turned around to see me climbing in. He slammed his laptop shut. "What are you doing here?" He asked.

"I had sex."

He rolled his eyes. "And you couldn't tell me later?" He asked.

I sat on his bed. "Colby and I had sex for the first time."

He looked me up and down. "Holy shit you had sex."

I couldn't stop myself from shaking. I had so much adrenaline coursing through my veins. "Yeah, it was everything that I had hoped it to be."

"Really?"

"I love her. I really do."

"We know this, but what changed?" He asked.

"She was patient with me."

"And?"

I shook my head. "You don't understand. I was so freaked out that it was our first time. I've never been naked in front of someone before."

"Too much information."

I rolled my eyes. "I thought I couldn't get it up."

"That must have been humiliating."

"It was. I thought that this was going to break us up. She sat there completely understanding. She told me that she was freaked out too. We talked about everything."

"She wasn't mad?"

"No, she wasn't. We thought maybe we should give it more time. She wanted to make sure that I was ready for it."

"But you guys had sex." He had a confused expression on his face.

"I looked at her and realized that I could do it. I was safe and comfortable with her. It didn't matter about if I was good or big for her. It was the fact that we love each other so much we want to take it to the next level."

"And you did."

"Yeah."

"How was it?"

"Caleb, I hope you find happiness and love like this. I hope you find someone that just takes your whole being. I want you to fall deeply in love with someone that your whole existence was made to find that special person."

Caleb smiled. "Do you mean that?"

I nodded. "Yeah, I love that girl. I really do. I've never met anyone that could ever match with me like she does. I don't ever want to find someone else. She's it for me."

"But we're so young."

I shook my head. "It doesn't matter. I know she's it for me. I just want to tell her for the rest of my life that I love her." I couldn't wait for Caleb to find a girl to feel like this with her.

76

I was hoping that Colby was going to be at the bar. I prayed that
Jimmy had got her to come. I had to apologize. We couldn't
keep fighting. My Aunt was right, we all made mistakes.

I walked into the bar searching around her. I found Colby. I
smiled until I saw that she was with Drew. My heart dropped. The
words came back to me. *Was I replacing Colin with Drew? Was Colby
doing the same?*

I walked up to both of them. Colby was crying, and Drew was
holding her hand. "What the fuck is going on?" I asked looking at
them.

Both of them looked up at me. Drew separated his hands. "It's
not what it looks like," he said.

"I don't care what it looks like." I knew they weren't crossing any
lines, but I didn't enjoy the fact my girlfriend was going to Drew of
all people.

Colby turned to look at me. "He's just consoling me on our
fight."

"The fight where I couldn't trust you. It looks like the fight didn't do you any good."

She stood up. "He went through it with Cameron. I was asking for his advice."

"I'm not trying to get involved in your relationship."

"But you're doing a great job of it. You were involved two years ago. Shouldn't you be focused on your own relationship?"

"My relationship is fine. Cameron and I got through our shit. Maybe you need to do the same." Drew shot back.

Colby got between us. She looked at me. "Can we not do this here?"

"You don't get to dictate my life anymore. You've been replacing me with Drew."

She shook her head. "No one is replacing you."

"That's not true. You were doing it two years ago. You, Caleb, and Drew were the three best friends in the whole world."

"It wasn't like that," Drew added.

I looked at him. "My best friend wrote over and over again how much of a better friend you were than me. I saw how you accepted him being gay. I saw you being there when I couldn't."

"He can have more than one best friend."

I shook my head. "Not when he was replacing me." I turned to Colby. "You were doing the same thing with Drew. Drew's the better man."

"Colin, you're being ridiculous."

"Am I?"

"No one could replace you. We talked about you all the time. We knew how much you meant to us."

"But I was an asshole."

She grabbed the front of my shirt. "I was a bitch. We were horrible people. Caleb said some horrible things. He was fucking his professor. He wasn't a saint either."

"But you were replacing me." I looked her in the eyes.

She grabbed me by both sides of my faces. "Maybe I was. Maybe he was too. We both were hurt by you."

"I-"

"Let me finish. We hurt you too. You don't think that you replaced Caleb with Jimmy. You don't think you didn't sleep around when we broke up."

"I didn't."

"I know you slept with Bekah."

"I was drunk and-" I tried to explain to her that it was a drunken mistake. I told her once we got back together. I was blacked out, and it felt wrong. I knew sleeping with Bekah wouldn't make me forget about Colby. It made me realize how much I loved her.

"Colin, I'm not holding it against you."

"Why?"

"Because I know you eventually won't hold this all against me."

I gave her a confused expression. "We both needed some comfort and attention. It was all Drew was for me. I never cared for him."

"Why are you here now?"

"Because he has a bit of Caleb in him. You don't understand how much I went to Caleb with our problems. He was always able to bring me back. He's the reason I didn't go down a complete spiral those three months."

"You could have come to me." It was once again me being replaced.

"I can't go to you if I'm fighting with you."

"She just needed some advice. I guess I remind her of Caleb. It wasn't anything harmful. I wouldn't make a big deal of it. We were all close to Caleb. He loved you like he loved me." Drew put his hand out to shake.

I looked at Drew, and I had so much rage in me for him. Caleb didn't love us equally. Caleb had been my best friend for fifteen years. It wasn't the same.

I balled up my fist and punched him right in the face. "Colin!" Colby screamed as Drew backed up.

I saw Drew's anger. Drew charged at me, and we fell into a table. I continued to punch Drew in the face as he did the same to my face.

"He was my best friend." I screamed getting him one more time.

"You need to grow the fuck up." It was the last thing I remembered before Drew's punch knocked me out.

77

I woke up extremely groggy. I heard the beeping noises and realized I was in the hospital. I opened my eyes, and it hurt. My
whole body felt like it was trampled on. My vision got clear, and
I saw Colby sitting there.

"Hey." My voice was a little cracked.

She looked at me and smiled. "Hey." She got up and kissed me
on the lips. It was a gentle kiss. She ran her hand through my hair.
"You're a fucking idiot."

I chuckled. "Yeah, I was waiting for that."

She took a seat. "Colin, we were just talking."

"I know. I just freaked out because of what the journal entries said."

She shook her head. "I read those journal entries. It's back to
what I said. I said over and over again how madly in love I was with
you. You believed Caleb's words over mine."

"He's been there for me."

"So have I. Colin, who do you think has been here the whole time you needed to grieve? Who do you think puts up with your bullshit?"

"I'm sorry."

She shook her head. "It's not going to fix anything."

"Why are you here?"

She looked offended by the question. "I can't believe you even need to ask that question. Colin, you have my heart. I'm planning to spend the rest of my life with you. You need to remember that."

I grabbed her hand. "I don't want us to continue to fight."

"Do you think I want to?"

"I don't know how to fix any of this. I don't know how to make this all better."

"Colin, we've been going back and forth like this for the past week. It's becoming exhausting. This trip is supposed to be helping you get through your shit, not destroy us."

"You don't think it's taken a toll on me? I've had to digest four years of a person's life. I have to accept everything they've done. I've had to deal with my views on homosexuality, me failing my best friend, and me failing you. It all came crashing down."

"And you got into a fight with Drew."

"I don't regret doing it."

"I know you don't."

"How's he doing?"

"He's fine. He just needed a couple of stiches. Cameron came to pick him up. He's not pressing charges. The cops want to talk to you, eventually."

"That's going to be great. He's just the fucking saint."

"Colin, shut up. You did this."

"I'm the one in the hospital bed." I didn't know why I wasn't getting any sympathy.

"Do you think I should be acting like you're the victim?"

"No, because all I've been is the villain."

"You never were the villain."

"It seems like it. It's written all over the journal entries."

"His best friend rejected him. Do you think you would be happy if he rejected me?"

"No."

"You need suck it up." She stood up. "I can't keep doing this."

"Are you ending it?"

Colby shook her head. "I'm not abandoning you. You need to work on that. I'm not trying to run out of here. I love you too much to do that, but you need to work on yourself."

"How can I do that?"

She grabbed her purse. She pulled out my laptop. She sat down on the bed next to me. "You need to finish these."

"I don't want to." It was causing too many problems. I just wanted to completely forget about this.

"I don't care."

"Colby, that's caused all of us problems."

"I guess you need to keep going to figure out why we started this in the first place."

"I don't know if it matters anymore." What was the point if I was going to lose everyone?

"You can't just give up. It means all of this was pointless. It means the problems that were caused from this would have been for nothing."

"I don't want to lose you."

"You're not going to lose me." She handed me the laptop. "I've realized that this trip was meant just for you."

"What about you? What about us?"

"I'll still be here. I'm not going to go anywhere. I think you need some time with you and Caleb. I think you need to actually reconnect with him. Read his words. You need to follow this journey."

"And us?"

"Colin, this is just a bump. We will get through this." She got up and kissed me on the lips. "I love you. I'll be here when you need me."

I understood why she was doing this, and I had no problem with it. Maybe she was right, this whole thing was supposed to be just me. I had so much unfinished business with Caleb. "I love you. I never want you to forget that."

She gave me a weak smile. "I know." She walked out of the door and left me with my thoughts. It was odd because now I knew what Caleb was talking about his first year of college. I was alone, and I didn't like that feeling. I didn't have anyone right now. I had journal entries and so much pain in my chest. I was going to figure out Caleb, and I was going to move forward with my life.

78

February 19th, 2014

"What are you working on?" I asked Jonathan as I walked into his office. It was nice knowing that things were getting back to what they needed to be.

He rubbed his face, which I thought was extremely cute. "I'm stressed out with this work."

"What work?"

"My agent wants me to have some of the new manuscript done sooner than later."

I closed the door. I walked over and kissed him on the lips. "Is there anything that I can help you with?" I asked.

He laughed. "That's cute."

"What is?"

"You think you can help me with my writing."

"Yeah, you said that I'm talented. You rave about my writing all the time."

"Yeah, but this is a whole different thing. This is for the big boys."

I was a little hurt that he thought so little of me. "Are you saying that I'm not a good enough writer?"

"Don't put words in my mouth."

"It's what you're implying." I backed away from him.

He sighed. He got up. "I don't want you to think that. I would never say you're writing is just subpar."

"Are you proud of me?" I asked.

"Yes, I think you've shown extreme potential at being an incredible writer."

"Are you happy I got into *The Writer?*"

"It's the student based publishing magazine. It's not that hard to get into it." He gave me a hard chuckle.

I tried to suck up the pain that was going through me right now. I couldn't be around someone that would say that to me. "I'm going to go."

"Don't do this."

"No, I'm not going to sit here and be degraded by you."

"Caleb, you're being emotional. You can't take everything to heart."

I would never be ashamed of the fact that I believed so much in everything I put all of my heart into. I knew that it was foolish to believe that people would give me the same strength. "No, I'm never changing that about me."

"You can't be upset with me giving you my honest opinion."

"I have potential, but it's a joke right now. I should stay at the kiddie table."

"Caleb, I'm an established author. You still have your training wheels."

"You could have just said no."

"I did, but I'm not going to mock you by not telling you why."

I smiled. "I wish you did. I wish you could sugar coat things. I wish you could give me some kind of respect. I guess that's just a fantasy in my mind." I walked towards the door. I didn't look at him. "Jonathan, I've always admired you for being such an inspiration to young people. Where did that go?" I didn't give him the chance to respond. I opened the door and walked out of his office.

February 20th, 2014
I started throwing all my writings away. I was crying, and I needed to just completely forget about writing. This man I was completely in love with was bashing me for it. Was I good enough? Did it even matter anymore? I was just playing in a fantasy according to Jonathan.

"What are you doing?" Shawn asked.

I looked up at him. I wiped the tears form my eyes. "I'm throwing away all my writings." I threw more in the trash bag.

He grabbed the bag and writings out of my hand. He sat down with me. He looked me in the eye. "Why?"

I looked away from him. "Shouldn't you be on a date or something?"

"I'm meeting up with Dylan in a little bit. He has to finish up some homework."

"That's good."

"What's going on?" He asked.

"What do you do when your hero lets you down? How do you try to suck up what the person you love says?"

"What happened?"

"My boyfriend told me that I'm not good enough to be a writer. He thinks that I'm just this joke." I grabbed another piece of work and ripped it up. I let myself cry. "I'm just an amateur."

He grabbed my hands. "No, you're not."

"Apparently, you're the only one that thinks that."

"Caleb, look at me." Shawn shook me.

I looked up at him. "Am I just playing pretend?"

"I've never read someone's work so honest. I've never experienced writing like yours. Why are you letting this buffoon do this to you?"

"Because I love him." It was a stupid reason, but it was the reason so many people have given before. You let the person you give your heart to control your life. Their opinion has heavier weight.

"No one should make you feel this way. I've never met a writer like you."

"Even Jonathan?"

"Fuck Jonathan." He screamed. "Caleb, you're this incredible being that we're lucky to be around. You put so much of you on those pages. You should never be scared of doing that."

"I just don't want to fail."

"We're all going to fail, but we have each other for the road."

He grabbed my writings. "I'm going to keep these until you're ready for them." He stood up. "You shouldn't throw them away."

"I'm going to fail." I looked at him.

"We all will." He grabbed the papers and walked out. I was sitting there surrounded by the work that I was so proud of. I picked up a piece of the writing. It was one of the pieces I submitted to *The Writer*. It was getting published. I reread the poem. I was proud of it, and I was tired of feeling like shit. Why couldn't Jonathan just love me? Why did he need to put me down?

February 25th, 2014

> *Dear Caleb,*
>
> *I love everything you've written. I didn't mean what I said. I feel like it was all a big misunderstanding. I don't want us to fight. I don't want us to continue to be back and forth. It seems this whole year has been us trying to find balance. When can we have it? I want to be the one that inspires you in a good way. I want to be the reason you love writing, not against it. I shouldn't have taken my anger out on you. I love you too much. I want us to be together. I want us to be a supportive system for each other. I want forever with you. I want to live up to my promises last summer.*
>
> *Love,*
> *Jonathan.*

I reread the letter before entering Jonathan's office. I hated how much he used his words to get out of a problem. I knocked on his door.

He opened the door. "I see you got my letter." He moved to the side to let me in.

He closed the door. I turn around and looked at him. I was about to open my mouth, but I didn't get the chance. He closed the space and crushed his lips on mine. My anger for him melted away because God, I hated how well he kissed.

"Jonathan." I got out with a shaky breath as he attached himself to my neck. I grabbed a fistful of his hair.

"Don't deny it. I'm sorry." It was words I've heard too many times before.

I pushed him off of me. He gave me a hurtful expression. "You can't just kiss me and tell me how sorry you are anymore. You have to prove that you will continue those promises. I'm not going to be some stupid fuck boy to you."

"I love you."

"Love. It's supposed to be supporting and making the other partner feel like they belong. This is supposed to be a team. I don't feel like that with you. You insult me and make me feel like a joke."

"I never wanted you to feel like that. I take you for granted all the time, but I never want to lose you. I love you so much that it hurts."

I grabbed both sides of his face. I saw the tears fall down his face. "Jonathan, I'm here as long as you need me. I'm not going anywhere. You just need to respect me. I've been disrespected so many times. I don't want to continue."

He nodded. "I won't."

I leaned forward and gave him a gentle kiss. Maybe there was hope for our relationship. I knew we were still figuring each other out, and this is what this whole year has become. We've been testing our boundaries. I just was wondering when it would get easier.

79

I knocked on Jonathan's door before I walked in. He looked up from papers and smiled. "I'm surprised I haven't seen you sooner."

I chuckled. "It's been a rough couple of days."

"I can see by the bruises on your face. Do I even want to know?" He asked.

I shook my head. "I don't think that's a story for now."

"Please sit down. What can I do for you?" He asked. "I don't have much time. I have to go pick up my son from school before his soccer practice."

"How old is he?" I asked.

"He's seven. I also have a daughter who is five."

"Wow." It made things even harder. I looked at the family photo again on his desk. "You guys look so happy."

"Yeah, my wife insisted I had a picture of the family on my desk. I just wanted to keep my private life private."

"Have you and your wife always had a great relationship?" I asked.

Jonathan looked at me skeptical. "That's an odd question to ask."

"My girlfriend and I are going through problems right now. I just want to know if you go through rough patches, then you can get through them."

He looked convinced. "Yeah, we did for the past couple of years. I felt like she was growing distant from me. I thought we were getting divorced. I needed to be loved, and I had so much love to give."

Caleb was just someone he was using for the meantime. "Did you ever find someone in that rough time?"

"I think in the end, we all make mistakes. I'm not proud of the past couple years of my life, but I'm madly in love with my wife. She's been there since I was first publishing. She never gave up on me. I think I lost focus of that. It was when I didn't see my kids all the time that I realized I couldn't lose them. She threatened a divorce."

"Really?"

"Yeah." He laughed. "She thought I was cheating on her, so she threatened to take it all away from me."

"What happened?"

"I grew up. I stopped living in this fantasy that I created. I think love does conquer all, but it needs to be with the right person. I was fighting for someone, but they weren't whom I was meant to be with. I was meant to be with my wife. We had a true love that can't be mimicked. It took me a long time to get there."

"What about this other person?"

"I think they were extremely hurt, but it's part of life. I wish them the best. I did truly care for them, but I think it was wrong for me to lead them on the way I did."

"Have you spoken to them?"

He shook his head. "No, I don't think they could ever forgive me for my actions."

"Do you regret it?"

"I think sometimes I do. I think that you make mistakes, and you never want to hurt anyone. You never want to be the cause for people's tears. I knew with my wife that's what I was doing. I was hurting her and my kids. I couldn't do that anymore. I couldn't relive my twenties."

"How big of you."

"I'm not proud of everything I've done. I saw the joy I brought that person. I will admit that I used them. I was looking for attention. I was looking for someone to give my love to. I think it was a bit rash."

"How so?"

"It was right when Cheryl and I were fighting. We hadn't had sex in months. I think life got to us. She was working on so many cases. I was working on a new novel and balancing my classes. We were also focused on our kids. It seemed that we lost ourselves in there."

"So you had an affair?"

"Yeah, I did. This spitfire came into my life. I've never met someone so strong or mesmerizing as this human being. They could light up the whole room, and they could truly love you without even really knowing you."

It was Caleb. I saw the love Jonathan had for Caleb in his eyes. "Why didn't you stay with them?"

"Like I said, you have to be an adult. You have to stop living in this Disney kind of love."

"Are you saying you two were always happy?"

He laughed. "Oh fuck no. We fought all the time. We both made mistakes in the relationship, but it didn't matter."

"Why?"

"Because I knew it was going to end. I kept falling into these fantasies. I told them over and over again I've never found love like them before."

"Was it true?"

"Yes, but I think I implied something more than it actually was. We were a different kind of love, and I thought I was truly in love with them. I promised forever with them. I gave them hope that we would make it."

"Why?"

"Because I didn't want to be alone. I had two people I was in love with. I know I'm a horrible man. I know that you can call me an asshole or a piece of shit. I felt like that ending it with them, but I knew I made the right decision."

"Why?"

"Because I would always regret letting my wife go. I would always regret losing my family. Family is a love you never can live without. You can have this passionate love with a person, which I had, but it doesn't compare to family. I get to go home to kiss my wife and tuck my kids in bed. I don't think I was ready for that. I had cold feet. I wanted to have one last great love, but it wasn't worth losing my family."

I wanted to hate Jonathan for hurting Caleb, but I understood him now. I got to see his side of everything. I think maybe that's why it is hard for me to believe that it all ended the way it did. I could see the love in Jonathan's eyes about him losing Caleb, and I didn't think he could kill him.

"Thank you."

"For what?"

"Giving me advice." I stood up.

"I don't know how I did that."

I shook my head. "It doesn't matter. I got what I needed. Thank you."

"I hope it helps you find closure here."

"It did." I walked out of Jonathan's office. I knew Jonathan better, but it still didn't answer the question. How did it all end between them? How do they go from making up to ending? It was something I needed to continue. I had Jonathan's side. I needed Caleb's.

80

March 13th, 2014

"Why aren't you with your boyfriend?" Beth asked when I sat down with her.

I shrugged. "He said he had some conference to go to. He said it was super last minute."

"Is that true?"

I sighed and took a sip of my beer. "I don't want to get into it. Can't we just watch the movie without me getting the third degree?" I didn't want to talk about how once again Jonathan was bailing on me.

"You haven't been happy."

I didn't look at Beth. I just focused on the TV. "I've been stressed with my internship, classes, and other things."

"And the fact that your boyfriend is being a piece of shit to you."

I slammed my beer on the table. "Can't we just drop it? I don't want to have this discussion with you."

"Why not?"

"Because it's the same discussion I've been having for months. It's the same speech I get over and over again. It's exhausting."

"Why don't you end it?"

"I really wish I could."

"Why can't you?"

"Because I'm madly in love with him. I can't just say my goodbyes to him. I want to believe that I don't need him, but it kills me to know that I do. When I'm with him, it feels like I don't have a care in the world. I believe that I'm actually being loved," I said.

"You don't think we love you? We want the best for you."

"I want to believe it's with him."

"Why can't you see it's not?"

"When you love someone you turn away from how it's going to blow up in your face. You truly believe that you can fix it all with love. Love isn't some magical power. It's a cure that destroys you."

"I don't believe that," she said.

"What do you believe in?"

"I think that when you find real good love that it is magical. You just have to go through a lot of shit to get to it. You protect your heart because that one person will break through it all. They will understand the struggle and will cherish every second with your heart."

"Are you saying that he's just a wall?"

"Honey, if you don't know that now, you're in for a really rude awakening."

Maybe Beth was right. It was just all a bunch of bullshit. It seems all we do was fight and make up. I know that's what relationships do, but it's not healthy anymore. It's become toxic, and I don't know how to get out of it.

March 21st, 2014

> *Dear Caleb,*
>
> *It seems we've hit another impasse. I don't know how to fix this one. Yes, I know that I've been failing you. It's coming to the end of the year again, and I'm being pulled a million different directions. I guess sorry doesn't cut it anymore. I know you're ignoring me. I know you've become tired of everything I've done. How do I fix it? Or should we say we had a good run? Please talk to me? Please, let me know."*
>
> *Love,*
> *Jonathan*

"Does he think I'm stupid?" I asked looking at Drew and Cameron. I took another shot of tequila. "I mean. Come on, dude. We've been fighting so fucking much. We can't seem to just catch a break.

"Why don't you just end it?" Cameron asked.

I shook my head. "No, we're going through a rough patch. We're just trying to figure it out. The summer will work. It's only a month and a half away. We're almost there." I took another shot.

"Caleb, you can't just pray the summer will make everything better," Drew said.

"Yes, I can." I looked at them. "You have no clue how great last summer was. We just truly bonded, and I need that back." I let a couple of tears fall.

"Maybe you can't have it," Cameron said. She grabbed my hand.

"Why can't I have what you guys got? You two went through a rough spot a couple of months ago. You two got through it. Can't I have the same?"

Drew and Cameron looked at each other. "Drew and I did go through a rough patch. We did have an emotionally fucking hard time. We got through it because we both wanted it to work out."

"Jonathan wants it to work out." I picked up the letter. "See, he says it right here."

Drew grabbed the letter. "When will you realize that this is all bullshit? He wrote a letter, that's cute. It doesn't matter!" He screamed. "He doesn't love you."

I recoiled a little bit. "That's not true."

Cameron grabbed Drew's arm. "You need to lay off a little."

He shook his head. "I can't when I'm watching my best friend fall apart." He turned to me. "You're falling apart. I don't even know who you are anymore. When are you going to realize that he is a piece of shit?"

I stood up. "You don't get to judge me for my actions. I know that he hasn't been the best, but you weren't here for the high. You weren't here when it was great. You don't get to judge." I walked away and slammed the door. I just didn't want to deal with that anymore.

I lay in my bed and started to cry. I knew Drew was right. Jonathan was a piece of shit, but I wanted to believe that he was still that good person. I wanted to believe that he still loved me, and he wanted to be with me.

I heard the door open. Drew walked in and closed the door. "I'm sorry for snapping."

"It's cool."

I felt the bed dip. He rubbed my back. "I don't want you to feel like I'm trying to attack or judge you. I just really am worried about you. I saw how you were with Jack. I just don't want you to fall apart again."

I pulled Drew into bed with me. He responded by wrapping his arms around me. "I hope this isn't weird for you," I said.

He chuckled. "I'm surprised this hasn't happened sooner."

"I just don't want to be alone anymore."

"Caleb, you're not alone."

I pressed my head to his chest. "I know. I just don't want to be in pain. I want to be happy. Will I ever get that?"

"Caleb, you're the only person in the world that I know who deserves it."

"So why can't it happen?"

"It will happen. Hope for love." He pulled me closer and rubbed my back. "Hope for love."

I fell asleep to Drew continuously saying hope for love in my ear. I prayed that I would get it. Maybe it wasn't with Jonathan, but I needed to believe that it was still out there for me.

81

April 4th, 2014

"I love you too." I heard Jonathan say to someone on the phone. He hung up to see me walking in.

"Who was that?" I asked.

"My sister."

"You have a sister?" He has never mention family in the past year in a half of us dating.

"Yeah, I guess it's never been brought up before." He looked extremely nervous.

It just didn't feel right with me. "Why are you acting weird?" I asked.

He got up and walked over to me. He kissed me on the lips. "I'm not acting weird. I'm just wondering where all these questions are coming from.

I rubbed his back. "I guess we just don't know everything about each other. I just thought I would ask questions. I didn't know it was like putting you on trial."

He kissed me on the lips. "I think some things need to be left in the dark.'

"Family?"

"I didn't mean family. I just meant in general. You can ask me anything you want." He kissed me, but it felt like he was just trying to dodge the question.

"I love you," I looked him in the eyes.

"I love you too." He kissed me again. Maybe I was the one causing the drama. Maybe I was the one that was trying to find another problem in our relationship.

April 5th, 2014
"I think my boyfriend is cheating on me," I said to Shawn and Dylan. We were grabbing beers.

Dylan took a sip of his drink. He looked at me with his blue eyes. "Really?"

Shawn touched his arm. "Caleb, you've been going up and down about this guy. Why are you still with him?"

"I love him."

"Have none of your friends met him?" Dylan turned to Shawn. "Isn't he the one that bailed on you on your birthday, has made you feel like shit this whole year, and played yo-yo with your feelings?"

"Dylan." Shawn glared at him.

I took a big sip of my drink. "Yeah, that pretty much seals it for me. I'm never going to tell you guys anymore of my relationship problems."

"I'm sorry." Dylan felt guilty. I couldn't be mad at Dylan's puppy dog expression. He was extremely adorable. He looked like a little child now with his buzz cut hair.

"It's fine. I wouldn't really worry about it."

"I think what Dylan is trying to say is that you should break up with the dude. He doesn't seem like a good catch for you."

I felt uncomfortable talking to Shawn about this. I knew he was with Dylan now, but he kept looking at me like I was the true prize. "Maybe you're right. I'm probably just making all of this up in my head. We're good right now, but I think we need to have a problem. I always feel like we need to have a problem."

"Why's that?" Dylan asked.

"I think it comes from the fact that I'm used to being in a fight."

"Which isn't healthy," Shawn added.

"I kind of figured that out." I snapped at him. I got up. "I'm just not feeling up to this. I have so much going on in my brain. I'll see you later." I waved them off and walked outside.

It was starting to get cold, and it was nice to see the sunset. It reminded me of the sunset on the lake. Too bad that was never going to come back. Too bad I was never going to get those memories again. I would be surprised if Jonathan and I lasted that long.

"Caleb." I turned around to see Dylan walking out the door.

"Why are you here?"

"I wanted to talk to you privately. I really haven't had much time in the past couple of months."

"What's up?"

"I know that Shawn is in love with you. I know that you want to go to your friends for advice, but I need you to stop telling Shawn about your boyfriend."

"He's over me. He's in love with you."

Dylan gave me a soft smile. "I wish he was in love with me. I see how he looks at you. I don't get that look."

"Why are you with him then?" I asked.

"Shawn has been so kind to me. We're both trying to move past something together. We're together because we can't be with who we really want. Max doesn't talk about his girlfriend to me because of respect. I would like to ask the same of you."

"Shawn is my friend."

"He might be, but he's in love with you. You can't keep doing this to him."

I felt guilt surge through my body. "I didn't mean to."

"I know you didn't, but you need to stop. Caleb, I have no hard feelings for you. I know how much you care for your friends. I just want you to stop. I do hope everything works out with your boyfriend." He smiled and walked back inside.

It was turning into a complete mess of a time. I was hurting Shawn, while trying to fix my own pain. Was this the vicious cycle? Was I going to pass my pain off to someone else? Were we ever going to be happy?

April 9th, 2014
I walked into Jonathan's office. I wanted to surprise him. I was going to take Dylan's advice. I needed to make things right with him. I had to stop trying to find problems in our relationship because I was scared.

I sat at Jonathan's desk. I knew he was finishing up a class. I looked around bored because I didn't think it would take too long. I knew he usually had either really horrible papers in his drawers or candy. I hadn't eaten, so it would be perfect.

I opened one of his drawers to find a stack of papers and a Snicker. "Fuck yes."

I pulled out the papers and the Snicker. I noticed there was a ring in the drawer. I picked it up. "What the?" I asked looking at the ring.

"What are you doing here?" Jonathan asked.

I looked at him looking at me. I saw how angry he looked. "I was bored and hungry. I thought I could wait here until you got off."

"So you went through my stuff?" He walked over and grabbed the ring and papers.

"I've done it before. I didn't see a problem."

"I don't like you going through my things anymore."

I got up, and I was a little stunned by his reaction. "Can we talk about it?"

"Caleb, that was a breach of my privacy. You don't see me going through your things."

"You do it all the time when you sleep over. You found my poems about you." I shot back at him. I was mortified, and he thought it was adorable.

"It doesn't matter. That's really disrespectful."

"I'm sorry. I didn't mean it." I tried to show my guilt on my face.

He sighed. "It's okay." He walked over and gave me a chaste kiss.

"What's with the ring?"

"It's my colleagues. He lost it, and I found it. I just threw it in there until I can give it to him later."

I didn't want to believe him. I thought this was another lie, but I needed to keep positive. I needed to believe the words that were coming out of his mouth. I had to trust him. I couldn't get suspicious or our relationship was going to fail.

I kissed him on the lips. "Okay."

"You believe me?" He asked a little surprised.

"I'm tired of fighting. I'm tired of feeling like we're having issues. I believe you." I wrapped my arms around him. I gave him another quick kiss and laid my head on his chest. "I believe you," I whispered.

82

I walked into the radio station, and I knew it was walking into the lion's den. I saw Drew, Cameron, Beth, and Shawn all stare at me. "I'm not here to fight. I want to talk to Drew."

"Really after what you did to him?" Beth was in my face.

"In my defense, I'm the one that ended up with a concussion."

"After you started it," Drew said.

I sighed. "Look, I'm not trying to fight. I just need to talk to you. It's all I'm asking for."

"Guys, can we have the room?" Drew looked at his friends.

They grabbed all of their stuff and walked out. Drew leaned against the table. He crossed his arms and looked at me. "You can talk."

"I'm sorry for overacting and punching you. I'm also sorry I've been an incredible asshole."

Drew shrugged his shoulders. "I'm not surprised. It's hard coming into a situation where you're kind of hated. I guess Caleb did a great job poisoning the well."

We both chuckled. "I just didn't like how I was portrayed. I know I did some messed up things, but I didn't know I hurt him that much."

"Colin, you need to move on. It happened, but he still cared for you. You wouldn't be here trying to figure out who killed him if you didn't still care for him."

"Yeah, you're right. I've also seen how much he cares about you. You taking care of him when he really needed it. It's getting bad."

"Last year was rough on the guy. Where you at?"

"April."

"Which means you're only a couple more entries away from when he meets the wife."

"He does?"

"I'm not going to ruin that surprise for you."

"I just still can't believe he went through all of that. Jonathan was a piece of shit to him. I wanted to yell at Jonathan for all he did, but I understood him. I got why he did it, and I don't get why I'm okay with it."

"Because you've been the villain and the victim before. We all saw both sides of the coin."

"Did Caleb?"

"I don't think he took himself out of the situation. He was so hurt that Jonathan lied to him the whole time. He tried to get that love back with Shawn, but it didn't work. I think he eventually wanted Jonathan to feel the same pain."

"Do you know if he ever got even?"

He shrugged. "He died. He ended up murdered in a field. I don't think that matters anymore."

"Why?"

"No matter who killed him, he's still dead. We still lost him. We can figure out what led up to him dying, but it won't change the fact that he's gone. It's a cold reality we all have to accept."

"I guess I haven't accepted it yet."

"I don't think any of us want to accept it." We were both silent for a moment.

I looked at him. "Colby and you never did anything?" I asked.

He shook his head. "No, we were just friends. It was nice to have someone I can go to for advice or even a distraction."

"It's funny. That's what Dylan called him and Shawn."

It seemed that Drew wasn't surprised with my statement. "It's what we all saw it as. Shawn wasn't over Caleb in any sense. Dylan came into the picture because his ex-boyfriend started dating this girl Amy. Dylan wanted his boyfriend back, but it seems that Max was over him."

"They were okay with it."

"I think as long as you accept what it really is, then you both can find some kind of comfort and happiness."

"I don't want to lose Colby."

"I don't think you will. I just think you need to go talk to her and fix things."

"Maybe she was right, I needed to do this on my own."

"I don't think you would have made it this long. You would have given up a long time ago."

"How do you figure?" I asked.

"It's like an emotional roller coaster in two weeks. I think it would make anyone snap. She balances you. She makes you come back to reality. You two work very well together."

"So do you and Cameron. I'm happy you guys worked out."

He chuckled. "I figured Caleb talked about us in his entries."

"I'll give them to you once I'm done."

He shook his head. "They weren't meant for me. They were meant for you. I think it's best if they stay with you."

"No hard feelings?" He put out my hand.

"I probably would have done the same." He shook my hand.

"I need to go find Colby."

"I hope it works out."

I smiled. "I think it will. I have faith that we can get through it. I don't want to have a tragedy like Caleb and Jonathan."

"Jonathan's wife was the problem. Jonathan keeping secrets from Caleb was what caused them to end. He didn't respect Caleb, and Caleb needed that. Caleb's relationships wanted to control him, and I learned that he shouldn't be controlled. He should be admired.

"I believe that." I said my goodbyes and left. It was one apology I needed to make, and I left thinking we could have a friendship. We loved and cared for Caleb. It was the only connection we really needed.

83

I knocked on our hotel room. I wanted to give Colby privacy. The door opened to Colby standing there. "I'm surprised to see you here."

"I'm sorry."

"I'm not supposed to see you until you're finished."

"I'm sorry."

"Colin."

I stepped forward to get rid of the space between us. "Colby, I love you. I've never loved someone more than you. You keep me sane. You've put up with so much of my bullshit for so many years. I never want you to feel like number two. I never want you to feel replaceable. It would kill me to lose you. I love you now and hopefully forever."

"Colin," she said before she pulled me in for a kiss. The kiss was gentle, but it was filled with remorse and forgiveness.

"Fucking finally," Jimmy said.

Colby and I separated. I blushed and looked away from him. "Sorry."

"I wouldn't be. You both needed to stop being stubborn and just make up," Jimmy said.

"It's been rough." I tried to defend myself.

"It doesn't matter. You can't keep putting us behind. I came here because I knew this would help you out. We're not to be taken for granted."

"Jimmy, I know how much it means to me that you came here. Thank you."

He waved me off. "You don't need to thank me. You're just paying for most of the road trip once we get to finally go." He walked past me.

"Where are you going?" I asked.

"You're not the only one getting some." He winked and walked away from me.

"I'm disturbed by that." I looked at Colby.

She shrugged. "I'm not really surprised. How's everything going?"

"It's been intense. I'm almost done with part three. I just look at the pain Caleb is going through and about to face."

She touched my face. "He went through it. He survived."

"He's dead."

She gave me a weak smile. "I don't know then. You need to finish it out. I've been saying that for a while." She ushered me to the desk. She pulled out my laptop from my backpack. "Finish it."

I looked at her. "I love you."

"Love you too." She walked into the bathroom and turned on the shower. She gave me the time I needed.

84

April 15th, 2014

The problem with me being drunk is that I make really stupid decisions. I ended up walking down the hall after classes were over. It was getting dark outside. I noticed all the professors were going home. I knew Jonathan was still here. He was always here working, planning, or writing.

I walked into his office. "Hello, hot stuff."

Jonathan looked at me. He was with a student. The student looked mortified. "Mr. Moore, it is extremely inappropriate for you to be here." I saw the anger radiating off of Jonathan.

I wanted to vomit. "I'm going to go." I turned and ran out of the office. I ran to the bathroom and started puking in the toilet. I didn't know if it was the sheer embarrassment, guilt, or the alcohol.

I raised my head and laid it against the cool tile. I needed to just sleep. I heard the bathroom door open. "Caleb?" I heard Jonathan's voice. I didn't want him to know I was here.

My stomach had another idea. I raised my head to vomit again. I heard the door to the stall open, and I felt his hand stroking me up and down my spine. "Are you okay?"

"I'm fine. I just drank way too much." I smiled.

"What was that?"

"I'm sorry. I didn't mean it."

"You embarrassed me in front of my own student. Do you know what would have happened if you tried to kiss me?"

I felt like a dog being hit with a newspaper. "I get it, okay? I messed up. I just wanted us to have fun like we used to. Like we did at the cabin last summer."

He sighed. "We can't go back to last summer. We have to grow up."

"Why?"

"Because that's how life works. We don't get to play pretend anymore."

I didn't want to believe that. I was only twenty-one. I shouldn't have to be an adult yet. I should be stupid and in love. "My feelings for you aren't pretend."

"You don't know what you want. You're just a child."

"But you fell in love with me."

"I thought you could handle a mature relationship. It's tiring being your boyfriend."

"Then just break up with me. It seems that's what you want."

"I never said that. Stop putting words in my mouth."

"Why are you here right now?"

"I was worried about you."

"You have a funny way of showing it." I looked away from him. I put my head on the tile.

"You don't get to call me a monster. You've done enough in this relationship to cause problems."

"Because I love you." I looked at him. "I wanted this great love that you promised me."

"The letter?"

I used the wall as support to get up. "Yes, the letter. You haven't measured up to it. I gave you everything that night."

"I was fool to write that letter."

I felt the dagger in my chest. "Do you even love me?" I asked.

"Yes."

"But?"

"I don't think I love you as much as you want me to. I don't think I'm this knight in shining armor you have me pegged to be. I wrote that letter because I thought I could be that man for you."

"And now?"

"I think I needed to grow up. I needed to realize my priorities. I was trying to be this young guy that could be stupid in love with you."

"What happened?"

"I grew up. I realized that the age difference between us is a problem. You're allowed to have those views because you're in your twenties. I'm in my thirties, Caleb. I need something more stable."

"I can be that for you." I grabbed his shirt.

He grabbed my hands. "I don't think you can. You're drunk and showed up to my office with my student being there. This isn't the first time you've done this. I don't think you're the man I thought you could be."

"And you're not the man I thought you were."

"I guess we both let each other down."

"Where do we go from here?" I didn't want this to end. I didn't want to say goodbye to Jonathan because I loved him way too much. I wanted us to fight for this.

"Call me when you're sober." He nodded and walked out of the stall. He left me alone like so many times before. I felt my heart break, and the hole I tried so hard to fill, get bigger. I slide down the wall and laid my head on the tile. I cried, not knowing if I would stop this time.

85

April 16th, 2014

I had knots in my stomach walking towards Jonathan's office. I knew I was in the wrong. I was the reason for this pain in my chest. I just wanted it to go away. I prayed that we could fix it.

He was grading papers. "Can we talk?" I asked him.

He looked up at me. "I don't know if it's necessary."

"Please." I begged him.

He sighed. He got up and went over to close the door. "What do you want to talk about?"

"I took some time to think about everything you said. I'm so sorry that I've caused all these problems in our relationship."

He shook his head. "I didn't want you to feel like you were. I was trying to bring up the point that maybe the age difference has become an issue."

"It doesn't have to be." I grabbed his hand. "I want this to work out, Jonathan. I know that I'm younger than you. I know that I've made mistakes, but I can change for you."

"Caleb, that's not the issue that I'm having here. That's not the reason that I want us to end. I need to make sure that I grow up. I can't sit here and believe in this fantasy."

"What fantasy?" I asked.

There was a knock at the door. I stepped to the side. A woman came in. She had long blonde hair. She had hazel eyes and a smile that had some years on it. "Jonathan," she said. She noticed me.

"I'm so sorry. I can come back in a little bit."

"Cheryl, we're almost done here. I'm just trying to finish up with his assessment." He gave her a warm smile.

"Okay, honey." She walked over and kissed him on the lips. My heart dropped in my stomach. I didn't know who this woman was, but it seemed that they were in love. He kissed her like he kissed me in the beginning. "The kids are in the car waiting for you."

Jonathan looked at me. "I'll be right out there." He waved to her.

She shook her head. "You never wear your ring. People are going to get the wrong idea." She walked out of the door with a laugh.

He went to lock the door. He didn't look at me. I knew he couldn't stomach the pain on my face. "That was my wife," he said.

"She seems lovely. It's shocking that you're fucking one of your students." I tried to keep the vile down.

"You don't get to judge me."

"You're married. You have a wife and kids. We've been together for almost two years, and it was never brought up. What the fuck!" I screamed

He turned around. "You don't get to judge me."

"I should have looked you up. I should have done my research. Why has it never been mentioned? How could I have not seen this?" I could have saved myself a lot of problems and a lot of heartache.

"Would it have mattered? You would have still come after me if you knew I had a wife. You would have still loved me if you knew about my family."

It killed me to know that he was right. I would have looked past all the red flags and still fallen for him. I've already been doing that now. "I loved you. I was faithful to you. I gave you everything."

"Don't put this on me."

"How isn't it on you?" I turned around. I fell to my knees. I let the tears finally out. "I knew that I couldn't be someone's love. I couldn't be someone's soulmate. I'm just the person that they toss to the side."

"Caleb, talk to me." I felt a hand on my back.

I stood up and moved away from his touch. "You don't get to touch me. You don't get to console me. You are nothing more than a piece of shit. I never want to see you again."

"I'm not the villain here."

"You have a wife and kids. You cheated on your family with me."

"It doesn't matter."

"Yes, I would have stayed. I hate to say that I would have just thrown myself at you. I'm just the mistress. It would have been easier because I would have known that it wasn't forever."

"But now?"

"I'm being dumped by you. I'm the one you cheated on your wife with. I was the fool to believe any words you said. I was the one that believed we could have been something. I'm the one that gave this everything."

"I did too."

"You have a wife and kids. You have people that look up to you and depend on you." I shook my head. "I can't do that. You talk about growing up. You talk about being an adult." I laughed. "You're just a fucking coward."

"You don't get to judge me."

"You have a wife and kids!" I screamed once again.

We looked at each other, and all I wanted to do was just cry. "What happened to the man with the letter in the cabin? What happened to all the promises and devotion of love? Where did he go?"

"He was never yours in the first place."

I smiled. "It's the first time that I truly believe you."

"Don't make me feel guilty."

"You cheated on your wife and kids-"

"You don't need to repeat it again." He snapped.

I walked up to him. "I'll continue saying it. You know why? I want you to feel guilty for the shit that you did. You have a wife and kids. You took a confused kid and made him believe that you loved him. You made him think you were a good guy."

"I am a good guy."

"No, you aren't. We're not the love story the broken hearted dreams of, or the love that inspires stories. We're the story that mothers and fathers fear for their children. We're the reason for all the ballads in the world. We're the tears that join the rest of the broken hearted."

"Don't say that. We had something special."

"I would have believed you if you dumped me. I would have looked back and said that it was all my fault. It wasn't. I was once again controlled by a man." I shook my head. "When do I get to control my life? When will someone love me and idolize me?"

"I never was that person for you."

"I know, and I made a stupid mistake hoping you were. Jonathan, you're just like every other fucking asshole in the world. You have a lot of words, but you're full of shit." I walked past him.

"Don't tell anyone. I can't have my life ruined."

I turned to look him. "My punishment is that you get to live with this guilt for the rest of your life. You get to remember this face because you broke me. Jonathan, I loved you, but I don't need to be some jealous scorned lover. I'm above that. Enjoy knowing you've killed a man's spirit to love."

I walked out the door. I never wanted to see him again. I wanted to look back at my relationship with Jonathan as this beautiful experience in my life. It kills me to know that it was all a lie. He never loved me. It was just words to keep me in. It's the problem with dealing with writers. They knew what to say to get you to give them your heart. It was just a sport to him. He gets to leave with a little sadness, while I'm completely destroyed. It's not the first time a man has walked out of my life. I guess I'm getting good at picking them out. I just wanted someone to truly love me for me. Was that so much to ask for?

86

"I've been waiting for you to get here," Aunt June said, placing two cups on the table as I walked into the kitchen.

"I told you that I was coming home."

She chuckled. She walked around the table and hugged me. "That's not what I'm talking about."

It felt good to be in her arms. It felt like home, and I could feel myself feeling like I wasn't falling apart. "I've missed you. I know it's been ten days, but I've missed you." I just needed to be around someone whose not judging me for every little thing I do.

I was surrounded by too much of Caleb's world. I needed to get back to being Colin. I knew coming home was the best option for me. Colby told me to do it on my own.

"I'm assuming the trip hasn't been the best. You sounded a little rough the last time we talked." She let go of me and took a seat.

I sat across from her. "I don't know where to start. I thought that I could keep it in. I thought that maybe if I just got through it then all the feelings wouldn't be brought up."

"You're learning about your best friend's life. I don't think feelings would be avoided." She took a sip of her drink.

"Colby and I fought. I got into a fight with Caleb's best friend. I've been drinking so much. I have no clue how I'm going to survive any of this."

"I can tell about the fight." She pointed the black eye. "Colin, I thought I taught you better than to fight."

"I saw him comforting Colby, and I lost it. Caleb talked about in the journal entries that I was being replaced. I thought that it still was going on."

"You do realize that those were feelings two years ago. You can't act like they're still around," she said.

"Aren't they?"

"How so?"

"Colby lied to me about knowing him or any of them. She kept it all a secret from me. How couldn't I feel like it was happening all over again?"

"Colby wouldn't do something unless it protected you. She probably assumed you would react like this. The girl is so stupid in love with you. She gave up an internship to make sure you were okay about your best friend."

"She told me it was pushed back two weeks?"

She grabbed my hand. "She turned it down. She came to me to ask if it was okay to give it up. She felt like she needed to be there for you. She understood it could be a stupid decision, but she made it for you."

I felt the guilt surge through my whole body. I covered my face. "I've been acting like a complete jackass to her. She should have left me."

I felt Aunt June's hand. "No, honey. You have a right to feel all these emotions. I'm happy you're finally feeling something. You've been holding it all in."

"I don't grieve."

"Yes, you do. You just take forever to do it. You still cry about your parents."

"I don't get how my dad, this incredible guy, could be such a bigot."

"I always hated your father for it. He was a good man, husband, and father. He just was stuck on his views. There is nothing wrong with that. I just think it wasn't right for you to be sucked into that world."

"Caleb had an affair with his creative writing professor."

"He always was meant to be with someone older."

"You don't sound surprised."

She shrugged. "Caleb always had an old soul. He deserved to be with someone that could properly take care of him."

"That's the problem. The guy didn't." I looked at my tea remembering all the words that Caleb said and all the times Jonathan was so cold to him for no reason. "He was so cruel to him. How could someone do that to a person they love?"

"Colin, you were blessed. You found the love of your life at such a young age. You don't know how hard it is to love someone."

I knew I was lucky to find Colby in my life. I didn't have to continue to wonder if I was going to find love, but Jonathan was this horrible villain to Caleb. No one deserves that. "He had so much hope for Jonathan. He stayed with him because he thought it could work out. Jonathan killed Caleb's spirit."

"That's the dark side of love. It's the worst kind to have, but so many people experience it. Caleb thought that he could give this man his heart then it could work out. I'm assuming it didn't."

"He was cheating on Caleb the whole time. He had a wife and kids. Caleb couldn't even get closure. His wife walked in and kissed him. That's how he found out."

"What was Caleb's reaction?"

"He blamed himself for the ending of the relationship. He wanted more than Jonathan could give. It was understandable. He had a wife; he couldn't give much more than what he was doing. Caleb felt lied to, and he didn't believe the relationship was a real one."

"Poor, Caleb." She shook her head. "Did he ever get closure?" She asked.

"I don't know. It's where part three ends. I needed some time away from the entries. I couldn't handle watching my best friend suffer."

"After all these years, you still care for him."

"He was my best friend. He helped me through so much. I think maybe I can help him now."

"What's stopping you from reading the rest?"

"I'm scared."

"Of?"

"Knowing how he died. Caleb knew he was being murdered. He knew his actions would lead to his death. I don't think I can handle that. I kills me to know he didn't get any kind of happiness."

"I wouldn't say that. He had some forms of happiness. He got to be friends with you."

"I ruined it by rejecting him."

"He got to experience love."

"Both guys ended up destroying him."

She sighed. "He still got to have those moments. Colin, he was murdered. He had a tragic ending, which means he had a tragic life. It doesn't mean he didn't have moments of bliss. He got to feel real love. It might have been a lie, but he got to experience it for even a moment."

"I just wanted to believe he was happy before he died."

"He might have been. It's still a mystery that you need to solve."

"Why?"

"Colin, you love mysteries. You want to be a detective of all things. Your best friend is going to be your greatest mystery to solve."

I looked at Aunt June, and I knew that she was right. I needed to figure out the last pieces of Caleb's life. I needed to get to the end of this journey. I knew I was close, and it scared me. I knew it wasn't going to get easier, and I wanted to believe it would. Caleb lived a tragic life until his death. No one can argue that, but maybe he did get some kind of clarity or hope at the end.

87

I knew I needed to drive up to my parents' gravesite. It had been a long time since I've been here. I said goodbye to my Aunt in the morning. I told her I would call her when I got back.

I drove up the same path that I used to drive through all the time. It had been so long since I had gone to see them. I think it was the summer before I left for college. I knew my father would be proud to know that I went into the same path as he did.

I parked my car and walked down the rows of graves. It was always a favorite thing of mine to see read the names and see how old they were when they died. I found happiness for people with long lives and sadness for the short lived.

I stopped at the usual spot. I read the tombstone once again. *Ron and Martha Wilson. Parents, Friends, and Amazing Souls. They were taken too soon, but we will never forget them.* I always felt myself unravel a little when I read it. I chose the words with my Aunt's help. I missed them way too much, and it killed me to know they were still gone.

"Hey guys. It's been a while since I've been here. I guess four years. I remember coming up here with Aunt June all the time. She would always talk to you. I thought it was a bit silly. She said you were still around. I guess I never lost the idea of it."

I looked at the tree we planted right when they died. I smiled. "I see the tree is alive and well. It's gotten so big. I remember planting it when it was just a little sprout. I guess it makes me realize how long you've been gone."

I felt the wind blow. "I've missed you guys. I just don't know if I could have agreed with you. I wish I could have seen your faults. I wish that I could have known you weren't super heroes when you were alive. I think maybe I would have disagreed with you on your views. Maybe I wouldn't have hated Caleb when he came out."

I walked over and touched my dad's name. "I knew you as this incredible, strong person. I didn't see you as a human. I thought you were God in a way. I guess it took me growing up and even the past couple of weeks to realize you had your faults. I remember walking with you one day to the grocery store, and we saw a gay couple holding hands. You told me that it was disgusting and wrong. I never questioned you, and I should have. I should have thought you were wrong. There was something wrong with you because love is something everyone should have. I wish I learned that sooner."

I felt like it always needed to be said how much my father influenced me. I never will regret having him on such a high pedestal, but I needed to make my own views and opinions. I think I had to grow up to realize that.

I looked over at the tree again, and I saw something tied to it. It looked a little ruin, but it was an envelope in a plastic bag.

It was a little torn, but I could see that it was addressed to my parents. I pulled the envelope off the tree and took it out of the plastic bag. I opened the letter. I knew the handwriting right away. It was from Caleb.

Dear Ron and Martha,

I never knew you and you never knew me. I didn't even know you two existed until I met your son. I know the past couple of years we haven't gotten along. I guess it has something to do with you, Ron. I think you had a problem with homosexuality. I don't blame you because you come from a different time. I want to hate you. I wanted to know you as you were alive to argue with you. I wanted to change your mind about how wrong you were. I think that it would have made it easier for Colin to accept me for me. I don't think we could ever change or go back. I'm okay with that though. You did raise an incredible son, who is still my best friend. I miss him terribly, and I think that in the past couple of weeks I have really understood our friendship. We were each other's foundation. We inspired and gave each other hope. I knew he didn't get my lifestyle, and I'm okay with that. I just want to say thank you for giving me your son. Thank you for making him who he was. We didn't agree fully, but he was always there for me. He always made me feel like I mattered or belonged. I didn't get a lot of that in college. I was hurt by a lot of people that I truly loved. Colin wasn't one of them. He was your foundation, and he was mine. I think that's why you two are part of my foundation. You two made him who he was, and he turned into an incredible human being. I hope to see how he grows, and I hope he realizes how wrong it is to hate people for loving someone.

Love,
Caleb.

I folded the note and took in a shaky breath. "You son of bitch." I laughed. I didn't now how he found where my parents were buried, but I wouldn't put it past Caleb. He always seemed to find things out about people. I probably talked about it in passing, but he came to see my parents. He wrote them a letter. I knew my dad and Caleb wouldn't get along, but it would have been okay.

I would have realized it was okay to stand up to your parents. It's okay to have different views. It made me feel at home knowing that after everything, Caleb still viewed me as a best friend. He still viewed me as his foundation. "Foundation," I said out loud.

I pulled out my laptop and clicked on the fourth key. "Our foundation." I put in multiple people's names, but I never got anything back.

I typed in my parents' names, and it unlocked the next part. I didn't see how they were our foundation until now. The people that influence us help us influence others.

88

Dear Colin,

So yeah, I slept with my professor. I fell in love with my professor. I chased my professor, and he had an affair. You can judge me all you want, Colin. I don't regret it. I loved that man even though he broke me. He destroyed everything I built up about love. I'll never know why he did what he did, but I don't think I need to know. I should have taken the higher road, but I just wanted someone else to be in pain with me. Maybe that's why I did what I did.

Love,
Caleb.

April 23rd, 2014

I walked out of my room with the bottle of whiskey in my hand. It was half the bottle since I curled up to it like my lover last night. It's the only thing that hasn't abandoned me. It's the only thing that hasn't lied to me for years.

I didn't want to think about Jonathan. I just wanted to run from all those problems. He tried to apologize to me, but what was the point? It wasn't going to change anything. Our whole relationship was a fucking lie. I was used and tossed to the side. My feelings were ignored.

I walked into the living room to see Drew, Cameron, Beth, and Shawn standing there. They had concern written all over their faces. "This is going to be fucking great." I took another swig of my bottle.

Drew walked over and tried to grab the bottle out of my hand. "Caleb, you need to give me the bottle."

I laughed. "Why because you're so worried about me?" I rolled my eyes. "Please, no one cares about poor defenseless me. I'm just everyone's fucking punching bag." I took another sip, but he ripped the bottle out of my hands.

I tried to grab the bottle, but Cameron and Beth grabbed my hands. "You're done. We're going to talk to you," Beth said.

"I don't want to do feelings. I don't want to do this bullshit." I tried to struggle until they pushed me onto the couch.

"What the fuck has been going on?" Beth asked. "You've been drinking the past week. You've been rude. You haven't talked to any of us. We're freaking out because of you."

"Oh look, the bitch cares. How adorable?" I clapped my hands together.

Beth leaned forward and slapped me across the face. She got into my face. "You want to be an asshole, that's fine. You think it's going to push me away? You want to push my buttons? That's cute, because I used to be the same way. I came here trying to keep people away. It didn't work for me, and it's not going to work for you."

I leaned forward. "What do you want me to say?"

"What's going on?" Shawn asked.

I looked at him and then everyone else. "Should we tell him the dirty little secret we've been keeping from him? Should we break his heart? Hey, he can join the club. I've been broken so many times."

"What is he talking about?" Shawn looked confused.

I laughed. "I think it's time we told him." I got up off the couch. Beth and Cameron tried to stop me, but I just pushed them. I got in Shawn's face. "I've been banging Jonathan for almost two years now." I laughed.

He looked confused. "He's married and has kids."

"You knew?" I screamed. "You knew, and you never told me." I felt Drew pull me back. I had so much rage in my body. I could have been saved from all this heartbreak. I could have gotten out of this misery.

"I thought everyone knew. His wife comes to campus all the time. She's really nice."

"I don't fucking want to hear that!" I screamed. "I don't care how nice the bitch is. She took him away from me." I leaned down and felt the tears fall down my face. "She took him away from me."

"Caleb, what's going on?" Cameron asked.

I looked up at everyone. "He dumped me. He said that we couldn't be together because of the age. I was drunk and walked into his office to have sex with him."

"You were serious?" Shawn asked.

"Shawn, this isn't the time," Beth said.

He shook his head. "You've been sleeping with our professor. He's been your secret boyfriend. I've been giving you advice on how to sleep with my idol. The guy I'm madly in love with has been sleeping with my hero. I can't do this." He walked out of the apartment.

"I told you we shouldn't have told him. I'm glad I'm not the only person that is destroyed in this." I stood up.

"What happened?" Drew asked.

"I went to go apologize. He ended it right before his wife came into kiss him. She told me that the kids were in the car waiting for him." I threw my hands in the air. "How adorable is that? He cheated on his wife and kids with me. I'm just some easy fuck for him." I grabbed the bottle out of Drew's hands. I sat on the couch.

"I'm so sorry," Cameron said.

I shrugged. "It seems that's my life. I get used to it real quick. Why doesn't one of you check on Shawn?" I asked taking another sip.

"We're focused on you," Beth said.

"Why? It's not going to matter really. Do you think we're all going to be friends once we graduate? Do you think we are all going to be super close?" I rolled my eyes while taking another sip. "Please, it's all bullshit. None of us will be friends. You four might because you get to feel love. I don't."

"That's not true." I saw the pain in Cameron's eyes. "We love you so much, Caleb. We know it's been hard for you."

"You know? You don't know the shit I've been through. I lost my best friend. I lost both boyfriends because they couldn't handle being in a relationship with me. What? I'm so horrible to be with that you need to end it when I want to take it public? I'm just this guilty pleasure people like to fuck, but it's horrible to be committed to me." I looked at them for ideas.

"We don't know what you're going through," Drew said.

"We're trying to help," Cameron said.

I stood up. "Stop trying. I just want to drink my pain away. It's the only thing that I get to control in my life. It seems everything else I just get to deal with the aftermath." I walked past them to my bedroom.

I took the bottle in bed and curled up to it. I felt my heart begin to hurt, and I cried. I cried replaying the day in my head. I couldn't get the joy on their faces or the kiss they shared out of my mind. I wanted that for my life, but I almost took it from someone else. She had no clue that he was cheating. He was destroying what they shared, but it didn't matter. He got to be happy with her, while I lied on my bed drinking the pain away.

I looked up when the door opened. Drew walked in. He came over to my bed and climbed over me. He pushed me so his back was against the wall. He pulled me into his arms. "This is the second time we've done this."

"I don't care. You need this. You need someone to hold you together."

I grabbed his hand. "Thank you." I choked out before I just lost it.

Drew never talked about it or judged me for crying in his arms. He never thought it was weird, and I thanked him for that. I just needed to be in someone's arms that I knew would tell me it was all right. I needed someone to remind me that I was loved. I knew being in Drew's arms was going to help me, but it wouldn't put my heart back together

89

May 3rd, 2014

It was another bleak day in my life. I was rather tragic how people woke up every day to just be hurt by people. We do the same thing over and over again thinking it will lead to our happy ever after. They don't realize that it's just the tragic ending of their pathetic lives.

Drew, Cameron, Beth, Shawn, and I were around the fire for our annual bonfire. It was nice to know I still had friends who would stay with me through all the shit that's been going on in my life. I know it will eventually end, and I was waiting for that to happen.

I took a sip of my whiskey when I noticed Shawn coming over to talk to me. He took a seat next to me and didn't say anything. We looked at the fire. I continue to drink because I didn't want to be here. Drew said I needed to get out. I was, and I hated every moment of it. I noticed Drew, Cameron, and Beth were watching us.

"I'm sorry I reacted the way I did. I guess it took me a minute to digest the news that you were sleeping with Jonathan," Shawn said.

I laughed. "Trust me, you weren't the only one that freaked out. I guess no one suspected it. We did a great job of hiding it from everyone."

He grabbed my hand. "You shouldn't have gone through that alone. You should never have to feel broken. He wasn't a good man to you."

It was a nice set of words, but it didn't matter. What could have he done? Jonathan was the only one that could have made sure I didn't break the way I did. He's the only one that could have made sure I didn't feel like this black hole was swallowing me up.

"Thank you. It's nice to know I have someone." I didn't look at him. "I should have just looked him up."

"Yeah, but there are a lot of moments in life that you wish you could change."

I nodded. "That's true. I wish I never fell in love with him."

"Love does that sometimes. You don't get to choose who you love."

"Yeah, you don't. I just wish he was a better man." I turned to look at Shawn.

He turned to look at me. "I wish he never hurt you."

"I wish I was in love with you." I touched his cheek. He was so adorable with his naïve eyes. He had no pain on his face, and it killed me. He lived a good life, and I wanted that for myself. I didn't want to be the only one in pain.

Shawn smiled. "I can fix you. I can show you that love doesn't have to be wrong. Caleb, I've loved you for so long. I've wanted this to happen between us. We don't have to hide our relationship. We can actually be together. I can love you properly."

I heard every word that Shawn had said. I wanted to believe it, but I couldn't. I shut off my heart to the world. It was easier this way. It was better to know that no one could hurt me.

"I need this." I leaned forward, so did he. Our lips met. It should have made everything better, but he could never make me whole again. I don't think anyone could.

We separated and looked at each other. I saw the light in Shawn's eyes. He finally got what he wanted. "Does this mean we can try?" He asked with hope in his voice.

I gave him a gentle smile. "Yes." He had no clue that I was going to destroy him. I was going to leave him broken on the ground like Jonathan left me. I wouldn't be alone in this pain. Why should I be?"

May 4th, 2014

I woke up to someone banging on my door. The hangover was real from last night. I ended up making out with Shawn and pounding shots. I lifted my head to Drew and Beth walking into my room. "This can't be good."

I sat up and had both of them in my face. "What the fuck were you thinking?" Beth asked.

"With?" I was playing dumb.

"You made out with Shawn. You can't do that to him," Drew said.

"Why can't I? He told me that he could fix me. He could make the pain go away," I said.

"Shawn is too fragile. He's with Dylan."

I laughed. "He's the one that initiated the kiss. He's the one that wanted to be with me. Dylan knows that Shawn is only with him because he couldn't be with me. He can be with me now." I stood up. "I don't see a problem with it."

"The problem is that you're not in the right state of mind. You have no clue how much this is going to hurt him," Drew said.

I turned to look at him. "Everyone is so worried about Shawn. We keep coddling him. We have to make sure we don't hurt his feelings. We have to make sure that he feels belonged. He's a grown-ass man. He knows what he's fucking doing. This is all bullshit. What about me?" I looked between them. "What if he is this guy that will make me happy? Have you thought about that?"

"You don't honestly believe that you two will work out?" Beth asked.

I shook my head. "I don't know, but we will see what happens."

Drew grabbed my arm. "You're still a fucking mess from Jonathan. We love you, but we don't think this is a good idea. You shouldn't bring Shawn into this mess."

I grabbed Drew's hand and ripped it off my arm. "He knows what he's getting into. He's equally in this like I am. You can't blame me for that." I grabbed my bottle off my nightstand and walked out of the room. "I have to ask Shawn on a date," I said walking out of my bedroom.

They were trying to protect Shawn from me. I was his drug, and I was giving him all the doses he wanted. No one stopped me from falling with Jonathan. Why should I give Shawn that courtesy?

90

May 15th, 2014

I felt someone shake me, and I had no clue who it was. "Leave me alone."

"No, you're getting your ass up," Cameron said.

"Why?"

"You're missing your fucking date with Shawn." She pulled me out of my bed. The room was spinning. I spent last night and early this morning drinking because I was now a senior. Drew thought it was a bad idea, but he couldn't deny that we had three years down. I almost failed my classes, but I didn't care. I moved on to my last year, then I would be out of here.

"That's tonight."

"It was supposed to be an hour ago. Shawn called because he was worried." Cameron pulled me up. "Get in the shower."

"Can't we just drink instead?" I asked.

She smacked me across the face. "I fucking can't believe you. You are already late for your dinner with Shawn, and you want to drink. You need to get your shit together. I don't know what you plan on doing with Shawn, but I'm not going to have you stand him up." She pushed me into the shower.

I let the water sober me up. I should have never agreed to go on a date with Shawn. I should have told him that it was wrong for us to do anything more than the kiss.

I got ready and called a cab to pick me up. We were just meeting at an Italian place down the street. I walked in to see Shawn sitting alone. He looked a little hurt and humiliated. He looked up and saw me. His whole face light up, and I felt a little ting of guilt. He was so happy to see me. This is what he wanted for the past three years, and I couldn't give it to him. I couldn't give him the love he deserved because I had nothing left. The sad part is that it didn't mean I was going to stop. I would still continue with all of this because at least someone gave me attention.

"I didn't hear my alarm go off. I've been in bed all day," I said walking over.

He got up and gave me a gentle peck on the lips. "It's all good. You're here now."

"Cameron shoved me out of bed and into the shower." I took my seat.

He grabbed my hand. "It's all good. You're here. I just didn't want to get humiliated." He didn't look at me.

The waiter came over, and we both ordered drinks. I looked at our fingers intertwined, and I saw how wrong it was. These were the same fingers that Jonathan would kiss. These were the same fingers that were held by Jonathan's. These were the same fingers that I used to dig into Jonathan's skin when I thought he was loving me.

I looked away from our hands and pulled back. I saw that Shawn looked a little hurt. "I'm sorry if that was too forward."

I shook my head. "It's okay. I think that it's just all a bit too much right now. It's a lot of adjusting."

"We don't have to do this," he said.

I could have stopped it right then. I could have said no that this was all too soon. I could save him from the heartbreak that would eventually happen, but I didn't want to do that. I saw the innocence in his eyes. It was time for Shawn to grow up. He needed to realize that this world was dark. I would teach him.

"No, I want this. I think it's going to take time to adjust."

"Things are changing. I get that. I guess it's all surreal."

"What is?"

"We're here. I'm finally with you. I can kiss you." He leaned forward to give me a chaste kiss. I let him. I had to give him some benefits before I broke him.

He smiled. "Yes, you can do all of that." I took a sip of my drink. "What happened to Dylan?" I asked.

"We never were in love. We never were meant to be together."

"But you were with him?"

"We understood why we were together." Shawn was open and honest with me. I've never had someone do this. There were no games with him.

"Isn't that a waste of time?"

He shrugged. "Not really. It was nice to have someone there. I couldn't deal with the fact that you were in love with someone else. I always knew that it was supposed to be with me."

"Jonathan broke me. He dated me, lied to me, used me, and tossed me to the side. He fucked me up. You do realize that."

"I know this, but I've been in love with you since the day I met you. Caleb, you're this incredible light that I've never experienced before. I know it's not going to be easy, but you're worth the wait."

"Why?"

"You're a good person."

I laughed. "I'm not."

"You might not see it, but I do." He grabbed my hand again. "I believe in you."

"You're a fool then."

"Let me be one. There's nothing wrong with being a fool."

"I was, and here we are."

"You don't want to be with me?" He raised an eyebrow. The opportunity has present itself. I could run once again, but I wouldn't.

"I didn't say it like that."

"I know what you meant."

"I just want you to know what you're getting yourself into."

He nodded. "I do, and I know it's going to be okay. I love you too much, and I want this to work out. I know it's stupid and crazy, but shouldn't love be that way?"

"You have an idealistic view on love."

"And you have a pessimistic view."

I raised a glass. "Let's see who wins."

91

June 3rd, 2014

Shawn and I dated, drank, and hung out. I always had to deal with the constant fear on my friends' faces, but I didn't care. I had someone who was devoted to me, and I couldn't let that go to waste. We were at a club drinking and having a good time. My hand was squeezing Shawn's thigh.

I felt a shaky breathe out of him. "I'm getting aroused." He winked.

I smiled. "I want you to be aroused. We should get out of here." I bit down on his earlobe.

He pushed me back. "No, we're not going to do that."

I've been trying to have sex with Shawn for the past week. He says that he wants to wait the right time. I wanted to wave him off. There was no point in waiting for the right time. It was all bullshit. I waited for the right time with Jack and Jonathan. It didn't do any good.

"That's boring. I want to have fun with you."

"Caleb, you're drunk. You're not thinking clearly."

I pushed off of him. I stood up. "I'm not listening to you. I'm not going to have you give me the same bullshit speech that Drew, Cameron, and Beth have been beating me with."

I started walking away, but he grabbed my arm. "Caleb, it's not what I'm trying to say."

I turned around to look at him. "What are you trying to say? I'm too fucked up."

"No, I have this whole relationship pictured in my head."

I laughed at him. "You want this to be a romance novel, don't you?"

He looked a little humiliated. "Maybe."

"It doesn't work like that. The guy doesn't get the girl, or the guy gets the guy. What happens is the guy gets the guy who lied to him the whole time. You will never have a happy ending."

"Do you believe that for yourself?"

"You need to wake up, Shawn. I'm not that stupid kid you knew freshman year."

"I never said you were still him. I think there is still a part of you that hopes. I see the Caleb that I grew to love. I want him back."

"He's not coming back. You better fall in love with me. It's all your going to get." I didn't want to talk to Shawn anymore. I didn't want to feel like I needed to play. I was drunk and horny. I wanted to have sex with someone and completely forget about it.

I walked to the center of the dance floor. People were looking at me, but no one was really appealing to me until I saw a guy with a million dollar smile. He was walking into the middle of the dance floor. He had dark skin and looked like he could break me. It was exactly what I needed.

I walked towards him. "You look fun," I said.

He chuckled. "I've been told that I can be."

I ran my fingers down his arms. "I would like to see that come true."

He raised an eyebrow. "Don't you think that's a bit forward?"

I rolled my eyes. "I don't have time to waste on bullshit formalities. I want to have fun. It's a club. Isn't that the point of them?" I asked.

He wrapped his arm around my waist and pulled me close. Our bodies were grinding against each other. "I like a guy who goes for he wants."

"I like a guy who I'll regret."

I looked over to see Shawn looking at us. I saw the hurt in his eyes, but I wanted him to know that I wasn't the stupid Caleb anymore. I have edges and scars. I've become more realistic. I pulled the guy in for a kiss, knowing Shawn was watching. Shawn needed to see this. He needed to know that I wasn't a fool looking for love. I was looking to cause pain.

June 6th, 2014

I needed time to actually get some sleep without waking up to throw up. I hadn't seen Shawn or the guy since the club. Shawn had been radio silent, and I was hoping that he finally got the message.

Drew walked into the apartment and looked at me. He walked over and sat down on the coffee table a few feet from me. "You want to explain to me what happened?"

"With?"

"You and Shawn since the club."

"I haven't talked to him. Have you?"

"He's been holed up in his apartment since he saw you kissing another guy."

I knew this was going to turn into a fight. I got up and walked over to the kitchen. I needed a drink. "I'm not going to argue with that."

"Why not?"

"What's the point? Why should I argue with you?"

"What the fuck's wrong with you? I get that Jonathan broke you, but you're doing the same thing to Shawn."

I poured myself a drink. "You don't get it. Jonathan never was honest with me. He never showed his true colors until the end with me. By the time I knew him it was too late. I was so deeply in love with him that it killed me to watch him kiss another person."

"So you're doing the same thing to Shawn?"

"I told Shawn straight up that I was fucked up. He knew that I was damaged goods. I never lied to him about that."

"But you're still playing games with him."

I laughed. "That's the whole point, isn't it? We're all just playing games until we get ahead."

"Caleb, that's not what you believe in. You've always loved the idea of connecting truly with someone. You've always been the guy that wanted to have a happy ever after."

I slammed my glass on the counter. "I'm not that guy anymore!"

We looked at each other. "Caleb."

"Don't Caleb me. You don't get to judge me or give me advice. You've lived in this perfect damn world for the past three years. I've seen you easily go through the relationships. I'm the one who got hurt. I'm the one who ended up crying in my bed curling a bottle of fucking whiskey."

"With me holding you together."

"Shawn knows what he's getting into. You want me to give him the happily ever after. You want me to be the fucking Caleb everyone knows and love?"

"I want you to be happy."

"I'll put that big smile on my face. I'll fucking fake it for all of you." I walked away from him. I walked into my room and slammed the door. I sat down at my desk. I opened the drawer to a letter Jonathan had sent me. It was last summer, and it killed me that this summer we weren't together. I wanted him to know that I missed him. It killed me that I couldn't be with him. I wanted him to fix it. I wanted him to choose me. I wanted to be rightfully loved.

92

Dear Jonathan,

You'll never read this, or you might. I don't see the point if you did. I just want you to know that you really screwed me over. I've never been more in pain than I am by you. You tried to explain it to me, but I can't get the image of you kissing your wife out of my head. I can't get the idea that I was just a pawn in your fucking game. It doesn't matter anymore. I've moved on from you. I've got a new boyfriend. I'm happier without you.

Love,
Caleb.

June 12th, 2014

Dear Jonathan,

I can't get you out of my head. I can't get you from appearing in my dreams. My friends are worried about me. They have always been concerned, and it's getting pathetic. I want them to focus on their own lives. It's hilarious that Shawn forgave me. He forgave me for making out with another guy at the club. Yeah, I'm dating Shawn. The guy had no clue we were together. He still has hope that we will make it through it all. He believes he can change me. How pathetic?

Love,
Caleb.

June 17th, 2014

Dear Jonathan,

I'm back in therapy talking about you. She thinks that it's a horrible idea that I continue to write you, I should move on with my life, and I need to realize that it's over between us. I don't need some stupid bitch telling me that it's over between us. I don't even know why I continue to send these letters. I know I won't get a response back. I just want you to know that I'm still thinking about you.

Love,
Caleb.

June 23rd, 2014

Dear Jonathan,

I'm drunk and looking at all our photos. I'm looking at how happy we were. I found the box filled with all our letters. I found everything we were going to do last summer. It was full of promise and hope. We could have been something. I hope you know that. I hope you go to bed every night missing me. I hope you feel pain in your chest because of what you did to me.

Love,
Caleb.

June 29th, 2014

Dear Jonathan,

I'm playing nice for everyone. I'm being the guy that they want me to be. I'm giving them fake laughs and smiles. I'm giving them everything they wanted because they think this will make me happy. They think going to the beach is a great idea. I spent the day tanning, grilling, and sitting at a bonfire. Shawn continues holding my hand, kissing me, and telling me how happy he is. I had to reply the same, but I didn't feel the same way. It was all for you. I wanted you there. How messed up is that? I wanted you there.

Love,
Caleb.

July 4th, 2014

Dear Jonathan,

I watched the fireworks with Shawn. We kissed when the fireworks went off. We went on a double date with Drew and Cameron. I remember last year that I hoped it was you. It's not fair how much changes in a year. It's not right that we couldn't get a kiss under the fireworks. I think maybe it was for the best. You couldn't have lied to me. You didn't get to ruin this experience for me, but it felt wrong with Shawn. I knew everything was wrong with Shawn, but it felt so good having someone love me.

Love,
Caleb.

July 9th, 2014

Dear Jonathan,

Shawn and I rode bikes in a field. We found an old barn and had a picnic. It was the best date I've ever been on, but it didn't make me truly happy. I thought that maybe Shawn could break me from this spell. We curled on the blanket and watched the fireflies and sunset. We played music and danced under the stars. It was a stupid romance novel moment, but it didn't fix anything. It wasn't with you. It was your arms I wish I was in when dancing with him. He wasn't the one I wanted to tell that I loved. He's being perfect for me, but I couldn't fall for him because of you, and it will always be because of you.

Love,
Caleb.

July 23rd, 2014

Dear Jonathan,

I'm sorry I haven't written in a while. I don't think that it actually matters really. My parents came to see me.

They've been worried, and it was nice to be in the arms of the people I love. Drew thought that I should have told them what's been going on. They could have given me advice or gotten me out of here. It was wrong lying to my parents the whole time, but I needed to do this on my own. I had to keep secrets from my parents. They thought I was perfect, and I didn't want to ruin that image for them. I never could tell them that I was in love with my professor. I sobered up and acted like this character for them for two weeks. It didn't stop the dreams about you or the tears I shed alone at night thinking about you. I hate you for everything.

Love,
Caleb.

August 1st, 2014

Dear Jonathan,

I couldn't avoid you. I know you now know that I'm having a class with you. I tried to rearrange my schedule, but I have to take your class. I need to graduate and focus on my future. It's odd that it's senior year. I'm about to start the beginning of the end for me. I'm about to close this chapter of my life and never think about it again. Shawn liked the idea of us having classes together, but I didn't care anymore. I couldn't be with him. He tried to be the perfect boyfriend, but he wasn't meant to be with me. I just wanted it to end, but I wanted to feel a connection with someone again. I wanted to be loved. I've been writing you all summer, and I've gotten nothing back. I haven't heard a word from you. I should have known that this was going to happen. I don't know why I get my hopes up. They end up getting crushed. You've done it so well before.

Love,
Caleb.

93

August 15th, 2014

I still didn't get anything back from Jonathan. I didn't know why I bothered anymore. I just continued to drink my bottle of whiskey looking at all the stupid letters I got from him. I heard a knock on the door. Drew walked in. "Shawn's here to see you." He was dressed up in a suit.

"Why are you dressed up?" I asked.

He rolled his eyes. "You've been completely forgetful lately. Cameron and I are going to the Psychology Benefit."

"That's tonight?"

He nodded. "I'll see you later. Have fun tonight." He winked while leaving my room.

I got up and walked into the living room. Drew and Cameron said their goodbyes to Shawn and left out the door. Shawn looked at me and smiled. "We have the whole place to ourselves." He walked over and kissed me on the lips.

I gave him a smile. "Yeah, we have no one distracting us."

"You want to watch a movie?" He asked.

I nodded. It's how we spent the next couple of hours curled up on the couch watching stupid movies. I continued to drink thinking about how I used to do this with Jonathan. We would sit for hours curled up just being there for each other. Shawn played with my hair. I knew he was content with this, but I couldn't.

I didn't even let the movie finish. I got up and walked away from the room. I walked into my room to get my shit together. I wanted to forget all about this. I didn't want to be just some stupid person anymore.

I heard a knock on the door. I turned to see Shawn walk in. "Are you okay?" He asked.

"Yeah, I'm fine. I just needed to walk around."

"I don't think that's true." He walked towards me.

I grabbed the bottle on my desk and took a swig of it. I drank the pain and thoughts of Jonathan away. I looked at Shawn. I had to admit he was looking good. I think he was working out. I wasn't going to forget about the benefits of a boyfriend.

I walked over and pushed him against the door. "I think we shouldn't talk about feelings right now. I think we should have some fun." I crushed my lips on his. It was a bit abrasive and sloppy, but it was working for the purpose.

Our lips moved together. I began to kiss and nibble on his neck. "Caleb, I don't think this is a good idea."

"Oh come on. I know you want this, Shawn. Why are you trying to deny it?" I asked. I lifted the hem of his shirt and ran my fingers down his stomach. I heard a shaky breath.

"Caleb." I swallowed the rest of the sentence in my mouth, so he couldn't object anymore. I felt his hands go under my shirt, and I was pleased that he was finally getting the picture.

"Less clothes now." I ordered. I pulled the hem of his shirt up and helped him take off his shirt. I looked at the more muscular Shawn. "Has someone been working out?"

He blushed and looked away from me. "I thought that you would enjoy it."

I ran my fingers down his muscles. "I can't deny that it's a great turn on." I pushed him against the door again. "I think we're still talking to much." I attacked his mouth again.

His hands started roam to my ass and felt a tight squeeze. I began working with his belt until I had it unloosened. I began to unbutton his pants and slide my hands into his boxers. "You're going to make me forget all about that silly professor," I whispered into his ear.

Shawn stiffened. He grabbed my hands and pushed me off of him. "I can't do this."

I was a bit startled that he just abruptly stopped us. "What?"

He shook his head. "I can't be with you. I can't let this continue. This was stupid. I thought you were better than this."

I felt in that instant another moment of rejection. I found another person that didn't want to love me. Shawn had always loved me. He had always been obsessed with me. He didn't want me anymore. I was just trash to him too.

I walked over to my desk and grabbed the bottle of whiskey. "I guess I'm just trash to you."

"I didn't say that."

"You implied it."

"Caleb, I love you."

I felt the rage build up in my body. I threw the bottle towards him. "No, you don't." He ducked, and the bottle shattered against the wall. "No one loves me. If they did, they wouldn't have abandoned me." I felt the tears fall down my face. I felt it all completely come out. "No one would have made me feel like I didn't matter. If people loved me, I wouldn't feel like trash."

I saw the concern and pity in Shawn's eyes. I didn't want them. I didn't want to break down in front of him. I wanted to keep it all built up. I wanted him to be the broken one. I was once again alone. I had no one.

He walked over and pulled me into a hug. "Let me go." I tried to struggle.

"No, I'm not going to do that. I'm not going to let you feel like you have no one in your life. Caleb, I'm not going anywhere."

"You're just like the rest of them." I looked at him. "No one can love me."

"I thought for the longest time that we could be something special. I've had you as this amazing ending for my life. I saw so much potential with us. I really loved you, Caleb, but this isn't what I wanted. I didn't want games."

"You can't handle me at my worst. That's cute."

"No, you just aren't over Jonathan. Your heart still belongs to him. I never had it in the first place."

"Why are you being so understanding? You should hate me. You should tell me that I should rot in hell."

He shook his head. "What's the point of that? I realized that I loved the idea of you, not you. You were the hope that I would find someone to love me. I just realized we're better off friends."

"I have no one in my life. I'm just getting abandoned by everyone else." I pushed him off of me. "I don't want to see you anymore. I want to be left alone."

Shawn stepped forward. "That's not what you want. You want to be left in this self-pity. I'm not going to do that. I'm not going to let you destroy yourself. Caleb, you're better than this." He grabbed my face. I tried to look away. "Look at me."

I looked up at him. "What do you want me to say?"

"Tell me the damn truth."

"I've been rejected by everyone in my fucking life. People don't care about me anymore. I don't feel like I'm loved. That's how I feel."

"That's a load of bullshit. You have your friends. We're all here for you."

"No, you're not. I hurt you, Shawn."

"I'm a big boy. I can handle it. I'm tired of people thinking that I'm this quiet, shy guy in the corner. I'm adult, and I know what happens when I get hurt."

"I don't want to be broken anymore," I said. "I'm tired of feeling in pain. I'm sick of feeling alone."

"Caleb, you've never been alone. You've always had Drew, Cameron, Beth, and me. We've always been here for you."

"I don't think I have you guys anymore."

"You've made a mess for yourself this summer, but we understand what happened."

I wrapped my arms around Shawn, and I needed his comfort. I needed to feel like I wasn't a mess. "Where do we go from here?"

"We become friends again."

"I don't want to be broken anymore," I said again.

"You won't eventually."

I don't know how long we stood there, but I was okay with it. I felt like my friends were keeping me together. I wanted Shawn to be broken like me. I wanted him to feel the pain I've been going through. It seems that I was wrong to think that. I was wrong to wish that upon him. I just needed friends to keep me together. I needed people to make sure I wasn't falling apart. I knew Shawn and I wouldn't work out, and he felt the same. We were perfect on paper, but that's it.

94

I drove as fast as I could to get back to Grover. I knew there was
one person I needed to see before I continued. I parked my
car in front of the library. I walked down the halls to the same
radio station.

I walked in to see Drew, Beth, and Shawn talking. They all stood
up when they saw me. I walked over to Shawn. I pulled him into a
hug. He was a bit startled, but he wrapped his arms around me.

"What's going on?" Beth asked.

"I'm sorry for all the things that Caleb did to you. I'm sorry that
he would hurt you like that. I'm thankful that you were there for
him. You didn't give up on him." I looked at him. "Why?"

"Because he was my best friend. I could never give up on him."
Shawn turned to Drew and Beth. "None of us could give up on
him."

I stepped away from them. "I did. I abandoned him."

"You didn't understand him. You lived in this world where you thought homosexuality was a sin. You're here now. That's all that matters." Shawn smiled.

I looked at him. "You really loved him."

"I didn't."

"What?"

"I loved him as a best friend. I loved what he stood for. He's always been the guy that gave me hope for something more for my life. I looked at Dylan as a guy that was just there for convenience. Caleb was right."

"With what?"

"I didn't love him in that way where I could be with him. I knew falling in love with Caleb would be jumping in the fire. I would go down in flames, but we would do it together. The problem is that I was there to make sure he didn't burn alone. We all were there to make sure of that."

"How didn't you guys hate him?"

"Because we knew he was in pain. We saw how much he loved Jonathan, but it didn't make sense to fight with him. We needed to let him get it out of his system," Beth said.

"Even if it hurt you guys?"

"Caleb has always been there for us. He has made sure that we weren't alone. He was always there when I needed him the most.

I thought I was just a fucking whore because of Alex. We got into some shit, but Caleb was there for me," Beth said.

"He was there for me when Cameron and I fought. He was there when I just needed a friend to go to. We might have disagreed on some things, but we had each other's backs. I knew it's weird that I would lie in his bed to make sure he was okay. I would try to be the one to hold him together. I think he did that for us too," Drew said.

"Caleb is the reason I write. He's the reason I know that I'll be okay in this world. He didn't have to be there for me all the time. I know he made some really messed up decisions, but it was okay. We all have fucked up, but he was there. It was all we could ask for," Shawn said.

I pulled them into a group hug. "I don't want to ever forget him. I just wish that I got to know him like this. I hear all these great stories about him, but I feel like I don't have that for myself."

"Caleb and you had a special bond. We didn't know it, but we got an understanding of it," Shawn said. "He always wrote about it in his works. He talked so highly about your friendship. You're here after not talking for almost four years."

"I just never thought he would be fully gone. I remember when we were little. I was the shy little kid in the corner. I had no clue how to make friends. I was so alone because my parents were gone. I was the freak with no parents." I looked at my hands. They were shaking. "I had so many walls up. I still have those walls up. He didn't care. He pushed through it all and came to talk to me." I laughed.

"Caleb did that to all of us. He made sure that we knew we were loved. That son of a bitch made damn sure we had people around us," Shawn said.

"Even when he thought he was alone. He didn't feel like he could talk to anyone or believed that he would be loved," I said.

Beth grabbed my hand. "I think if he knew how much he was loved, he would still be with us."

"I guess that's the problem with our flaws. We don't think anyone could love us because of them. We're defined by them, but it's what makes us beautiful," Shawn said.

"He had so many walls up. He was hurt and became jagged," I said thinking about all the pain he's been through in his life.

"He was protecting his heart. We were lucky to have experienced his love," Shawn said.

I looked at Drew, Beth, and Shawn. Caleb wasn't perfect. He made a lot of bad decisions in his life, but he made sure that people were loved. He gave them everything he had, and it killed me to know that he felt like no one loved him back.

95

August 25th, 2014

"I think that will be an excellent story. Hopefully you can have it done by the end of the year," Dr. Delilah said looking over my outline for the novel I needed to write for my senior capstone.

I nodded. "I think I'll be able to finish it." I had eight months to write my novel before it was presented to the boards.

"What's the inspiration behind the novel?" She asked.

"Getting my heart broken. I feel like that's inspiration for anyone." I chuckled.

She nodded. "It's very universal. I think you've grown so much over the summer as a writer."

The past weeks have given me so much clarity. I made amends with Drew, Cameron, and Beth. They forgave me in an instant. They knew I wasn't in my right state of mind. I don't think anyone could be after what I've been through. I knew it would take some time, but I would be able to get there. I think my biggest support was Shawn. We might have had a mess of a relationship, but it was okay. We knew that we weren't right for each other in that way.

I walked down the hall when I heard his laugh. I looked at him smiling with another professor. He looked happier than I've seen him in months. I saw the ring on his finger. He was finally showing the world that he was married.

It felt like a knife went through my whole heart. I've been trying to build up these walls, but they were being destroyed. He instantly had his hand around my heart. I needed to be away from him.

Our eyes met, and I was stuck there. I wanted to bolt. I wanted someone to kidnap me or give me an escape route. He nodded at me. He said something to the gentleman and walked towards me.

He stood in front of me. We hadn't spoken all summer. I felt like a fool to believe that he would have written me back. I knew that I would eventually need to see him. I was in his fucking classes this year. We were standing in front of each other. He had no clue how much he broke me. He had no clue how long it took me to build up walls of paper against him.

"You look good." He smiled.

"It seems you got a lot of sun this summer," I said.

"Yeah, I went to the beach."

"With your family." I put venom in my voice.

He sighed. "I see you're in my classes this year."

"I had to be. How else would I graduate? I tried to get out, but it was too late."

"I don't want things to be awkward between us."

I looked down at the paper in my hand. "You broke my heart. You lied to me. You cheated on your wife with me. I don't think we could be normal with each other."

"Caleb, look at me." He commanded.

"I don't want to look at you. I know that it will bring up all the memories of what we shared together. I'll have to look at the man that broke my heart. I'll have to look at the face of the guy who I wrote letters to all summer with no response. I was an idiot, and I don't want to be reminded of that by looking at your face."

"That's not fair."

I looked up at him. "You know what's not fair. I'm the one that lost in all of this. I'm the one who went home and drank myself to sleep for months. I'm the one that pushed my friends away and tried to break my best friend's heart to not be alone. That's not fair. You got to keep your wife and kids. You got to still be in love. You don't get to tell me what's fair." I looked him right in the eye.

He stepped back. "I didn't-"

"You can keep your bullshit apology to yourself. I want nothing to do with you. I'll see you in class, Professor Lancaster." I didn't give him a chance to say anything else. I walked away from him.

I kept it in until I got back to my apartment. I grabbed the first bottle of whiskey that I could find. I tried to open the bottle, but I had voices in my head telling me that I shouldn't be doing this. I remembered Drew, Cameron, Beth, and Shawn's faces as I broke their hearts. I had flashbacks to when I tried to break Shawn. I looked at the evil man that I was only a couple of weeks ago. I wasn't trying to go there.

I slapped my hands on the counter and cried over the unopened bottle of whiskey. "This isn't fair."

I heard footsteps. Cameron was standing there. "Caleb, what's wrong?"

I wiped the tears away. "It's nothing." I didn't want to get into it again. It was the same thing it's been for so long. I was tired of the fact that Jonathan has had my heart for almost two years. I wanted to put him in the past.

She walked over and pulled me into a hug. "What's going on?"

"I saw him. I knew I would have to see him. I just didn't think it would hurt this much. I hate him. I hate how much he got to be happy after all of this. Why do I still hurt?" I cried into her arms.

"Caleb, you loved him with all of your heart. It doesn't mean it's going to be easy for it to go away. You'll get through this."

"I don't think I can. I don't know if I'll ever stop loving him. I don't know if I could ever get over him."

"You will. You're going to find some one who loves you more than anyone else in the world."

"I want to believe you, Cameron. I just don't know if I'll ever able to survive this. He was everything to me. I want him to be miserable without me in his life. I want him to know that he can't get away with this."

"What are you going to do?"

"I don't know, but I'm not going back to that time. I'm not going to ruin what I've tried to rebuild. I might have stumbled because of him, but it won't define me."

"Do you believe that you can?"

I couldn't answer her. He was the definition of my life. I don't know if I'll ever move forward from him. He was the happiest I've ever been. I wanted that joy back in my life.

96

October 7th, 2014

I spent the past months trying to forget about Jonathan and everything associated with him. I sat in the back of the class. I didn't participate or really care what he was discussing in class. I only talked if he needed me to give my opinion.

It was nice because most of the classes were spent working on writing exercises. I thought that I only had a couple of months until I was done with Jonathan. I would be able to take Dr. Delilah's senior class, and I would put him completely in my past.

Jonathan ended the class. "Caleb, can I speak to you for a moment in my office?" He asked.

"I have another class right after this."

"I looked at your schedule. You're free after this."

I didn't have a response. I nodded and followed him to his office. He closed the door and took a seat behind his desk. I crossed my arms and stared at him. I thought this was a waste of time. We both didn't want to be here.

"What happened to you?"

"What do you mean?"

"You used to love talking during class. You were the type of guy that always loved giving his opinion. You were a joy to have in a classroom. You've become this shell."

I rolled my eyes. "You don't get to talk to me like you don't know me. You don't inspire me anymore. You've become someone I use to write about. You're the monster in my life. You're the reminder of how low I thought of myself."

"Do you really think of me like that?"

"You cheated on your wife with me. You lied to me the whole relationship. You promised me forever, and it was all bullshit to you. I'm not going to be lectured by someone as cruel as you." I stood up.

He stood up too. "I'm trying to move forward. I'm trying to get you to see that I'm not this horrible person. I made a mistake. I understand you're still hurt. Why can't we move forward?"

"Why didn't you write me?"

"What?"

"Why did you never answer any of the letters I sent you? Why did you ignore me?"

He sighed and looked down. "I thought it would hurt you more if I answered you. I knew there was no point in answering them. It would give you this hope we would get back together."

I nodded. "I figured as much." I needed his words as verification that I was nothing to him but a messy memory. "I'll talk more if you need me to. I'll give you everything you want because you still have fucking power over me. It's fucking pathetic." I screamed.

"I'll never stop having a spot in my heart for you." He looked at me. "I'll always deeply care for you. We were good together. I'll never let you forget that. We were something magical."

I shook my head. "I don't believe you, and I never will again."

There was a knock on the door before Cheryl walked through. "I really hope I'm not interrupting anything. Jonathan, we have Blake's football game to get to. You promised you would be there."

He nodded. "I'll be right there."

She smiled and left the room. I looked at him. "That's exactly my point." I turned and walked out the door. I saw Cheryl standing there. She looked up at me. "Is my husband giving you a hard time?" She asked.

I didn't want to strike up a conversation with her. I gave her a weak smile. "It's nothing that I can't handle."

"He's a good professor. He loves his students. I'm pretty sure you see how dedicated he is to everyone."

"Yeah, he really devotes himself to us." I tried to keep my calm with her. I could have told her right here that he had an affair. The man she had in her mind was just an illusion. He wasn't a good man.

I saw the smile on her face. "He's always been a good man. I'm blessed to have him. He's always been so kind to me, and I've seen how he is with the kids. I see how he is with his students. He talks about you guys all the time. He's so impressed with how much his students have grown. I see the light in his eyes, and I know he's a good person. We're lucky to have him because there is no one like him in the world. I don't know why I'm telling you this."

I knew I couldn't tell her. She had a perfect view of this man. I knew telling her would shatter that veil. Someone should be able to keep up the illusion of him. "Yes. He is one of a kind. He's a good person to have around. I better get to class. I'll be late."

"Okay, honey. I hope he helped you."

"Me too." I walked away from her. I felt sick to my stomach, and the voices were coming back. I could have ruined everything right there. I just needed to show her one little letter, and his life would be ruined. I needed to stop myself because it would ruin her life too. His family would be broken, and I couldn't do that. He might have caused me so much pain, but his family didn't deserve that.

97

November 24th, 2014

I spent the next couple of weeks focusing on my writing. I got my feelings out in poetry. I got my closure out in short stories. I focused on going to bars with Drew. I went to concerts with Beth. I cried to stupid romantic comedies with Cameron. I went to poetry readings with Shawn. I saw Jonathan, but it started hurting less. I could do this. I was going to be okay.

Shawn walked up to me after our poetry class. "That poem you wrote," he said.

I looked at him. "I wanted to talk to you about it before I presented in class, but I felt that I needed to just do it."

"A friend, my rock/ I backstabbed you, but you forgave me as you took the knife out/ I loved you but not the way you needed me to/ I hope this makes me no longer a God in your eyes/ I'm among the commoners now," Shawn read part of the poem to me.

I blushed and looked away from him. "I never wanted to hurt you."

Shawn rolled his eyes. "Caleb, I never thought you were trying to be vicious to me. I knew you were going through things in your life. I understand that. I did things I'm not proud of."

"How so?"

"I was with Dylan. We both knew that it was going to be a quick fling, but it turned into a relationship. I got to be with the guy I wanted to be with. He didn't."

"Have you spoken to him?"

Shawn didn't look at me. "No."

"Shawn, I want you to stay open."

He shook his head. "I don't like causing people pain. I think staying on the sidelines is best for me."

"I liked this new confidence in you."

"I know, but it's not for me. I don't get to be like you or Drew. I can't just be the center of attention. Dylan was a great guy for me, but he wasn't you."

"But I-"

"I know you aren't that guy anymore. I think it's better to live with the ideas of something than deal with the reality. I watch you guys dance and live your lives. I don't want to deal with the hardships."

"But won't you be running from your problems."

Shawn shrugged. "It's better this way for me."

I didn't know why Shawn was protecting himself from the world. I knew that I was in pain from Jonathan and guilt from Shawn, but I wouldn't regret living with it. I've always wanted to have these experiences. I didn't want to look back on my life wondering about the fantasy. I knew Shawn was protecting himself, but I wanted him to know the joy I felt being loved, even if it was a lie.

December 10th, 2014
"And with that, you're all set for your final semester of college," Dr. Delilah said. She handed me a stack of papers.

I looked at the piece of paper in front of me. "It's weird to think that it's here."

"You've grown a lot over the past three years."

"I don't know if it's for the best."

She shrugged. "I think that you'll look back at your memories, and you'll be proud of everything you've accomplished here."

"I don't know if I've accomplished a lot here."

She shook her head. "That's nonsense. You've been published."

"By a crappy little literary magazine."

She leaned over and grabbed my hand. "Who told you that you weren't a good writer?" She asked.

"My ex-boyfriend."

"They're clearly an ex for a reason. I wouldn't listen to a word they've said. Yes, they're small accomplishments, but they're still your accomplishments. I don't see how you could think so negatively about it. Do you love writing?"

"More than anything in my life."

"Are you writing?"

"My ex destroyed me. He took away my heart, and I lost my spirit to write. I'm getting back into it the past couple of months."

"That's all that matters. You need to be happy, and you found your voice again."

"I'm worried that my voice and heart are too broken."

"He really destroyed you?" She asked.

I felt the emotions boil over. "Yeah, I don't think I'll ever be over him."

She nodded. "It's okay. I've read some of your recent work. I think it's the best I've ever seen of yours. You can be the voice for the broken hearted. This might be what you need."

"I hope you're right." I knew this wouldn't be the end of the pain. "I just never want to stop writing. I think it would have been my biggest mistake, if I listen to the person I loved."

"That will always be a writer's mistake. Those are your words. You need to wonder and figure out what to write. I don't think there is anything wrong with stopping for a while."

"I did because I loved him."

"You did it out of love. You should always make foolish decisions because of love. It causes you to be a better human being. There are so many times I did some really hasty decisions because I was in love."

"Do you regret them?"

"No, but I learned so much from them. I'll never forget them, and I don't think you should either. You've reached the end of your college career. You're going to make more mistakes, but you'll do incredible things for this world. You have to just believe in yourself."

I knew she was right. I gave up everything because I was madly in love. I learned a lot, and I would continue to grow. I just wished my time at this school wasn't coming to an end.

December 21st, 2014
"I can't believe we got a tree this year," I said putting up another ornament.

"For a gay guy, you aren't into all this shit," Drew said.

"For a straight guy, you really are." I shot back.

"You two need to grow up." Beth walked into the living room with a glass of wine and a bowl of popcorn in her hand.

I turned around to look at her. "Why aren't you helping?"

She put more popcorn in her mouth. "It's not my place."

"Why didn't we do this at your place?" Drew asked. "It's already decorated."

Cameron put plates on the table. "Because your place is bigger, plus we didn't want to make a mess."

Shawn placed the turkey on the table. "It's also got a better kitchen. I don't feel like dealing with their annoying neighbors."

"Ron isn't that bad. Sure, he likes to drink a lot, but he's nice." Beth defended him.

Everyone laughed. "Food's ready." Shawn announced.

We all took our seats around the table. I looked around at my group of friends. It had a bit of sadness for the dinner because this was our last holiday together. We would all be graduating in five months. We would be going to different places, and I didn't know if I could handle that.

"It's insane to think that we've been friends for so long. It's sad to know that we're going different ways."

Drew nudged me. "We're not going that far. You, Cameron, and me in California."

"I'll only be in London for a year, then I'll be with you guys," Beth said.

"I might be in New York, but it doesn't mean we won't see each other all the time." Shawn grabbed my hand.

"I just want to say thank you for being there for me. I guess I just didn't believe that I would find such a good group of friends. I know it hasn't been easy being friends with me, but thank you for sticking it out with me. I didn't fall apart because of you guys. I've never felt loved like I do now."

I raised my glass. "To our group."

"To our group." We toasted to what we'd experienced the past three years. It might have been with ups and downs, but here we were. They were always by my side, and I'm blessed for that. It just seemed that we were getting to the end of the road. I didn't know how I would be okay without them in the next couple of months. I knew I would have Cameron and Drew, but I've realized all five us needed each other, or we wouldn't be whole.

I guess through it all I did have these people in my life. I didn't know what the last semester would bring, but it would hopefully end on a high. I knew it would be a lot of tears and worry about if our friendships would survive. I didn't want to believe that we were heading to our end. I wanted to believe that our lives would always intertwine. Our friendships have left impressions on each other, and I'm thankful for every second of that.

98

"**I** wanted to talk to you about getting some of Caleb's writings that you kept," I said to Shawn. I wanted the broken Caleb. The one that felt love and let it consume him.

Shawn pulled out papers from his backpack. "I've been waiting for this."

I raised an eyebrow. "What?"

"I didn't get it until a couple of days ago. Caleb came up to me before he died. He told me that he was going to give me stories that were going to be given to his family. I thought he meant his parents, but I read them."

He pulled out one story that was titled, *Thank You*. I knew this wasn't about his parents. Caleb always talked about you. He tells me that you were the one that has been there for him. You were the first person he told about his father.

I smiled. "Yeah, I was. He broke down in front of me, and I think it brought us closer together."

"So close that he told you about him being gay?"

I nodded. "Yeah, and I fucked it up."

"It's weird how much Caleb remembers. He keeps the positive to his heart, and he keeps the negative to his brain."

"He knew that I always did love him. I never stopped caring for him, but I just didn't know how to change our friendship. It evolved into something else, and I had no clue what I was supposed to do about it all."

"I think he just needed a best friend."

"I'm going to agree with you." I looked at *Thank You* and saw a line that was highlighted. *I'll never be able to say thank you. I took a risk and told you my soul, but you couldn't accept it. I don't think it was anything we could have changed, and I'm okay with that. We needed to go our separate ways, but we will meet again. I will push the anger I have to the back even if it's to say thank you.*

It was what I needed to read from Caleb's writing. We did have a moment together before it went to shit. He told me that his father wasn't his father. It was the closest we had been ever, and I was grateful for that time together.

"He knows how to use his words."

Shawn grabbed my hand. "You know it's okay to cry."

I looked at him. "What?"

"For someone who lost his best friend, I've noticed that you have never cried. You always keep it in. You can finally let go."

I nodded. "Thank you, but I think I'm going to be okay. I know that I need to let it out, but I will once I finish this. I have one last part to figure out, and I'll be able to finally understand what happened to Caleb."

"Do you still believe that it's about finding out who killed Caleb?"

"Yes, it's always been about that. I know that I'm learning more about Caleb, but I still need to find out who killed him. It's wrong that they took this incredible soul out of our lives. It's wrong they get to walk around freely knowing that he's gone."

Shawn shook his head. "You came here to learn about your best friend. I think maybe that's what you should be focusing on."

"It's made me realize how much he was valued to this world. He would have made everyone feel comfortable being here. It's not right that people didn't get to experience that side of him. He deserved happiness."

"I hope that he found some before he died."

I gave him a weak smile. "I do too." I turned back to the works. I always wondered if he found out more about his real father. I prayed that door was finally closed.

99

Four Years Ago

"Caleb, are you okay?" I asked as he was pacing back and forth in front of the tree house.

"I don't know if I can tell you this."

"Caleb, what's going on?"

He looked at me. "Have you ever been lied to?"

I saw the pain in his eyes. "What's going on?"

"Colin, I don't even know how to process it right now. I don't know what to even think. I've lived my whole life this way, and it's been all a lie."

I pulled Caleb into a hug. "Caleb, breathe."

He took in a deep breath and exhaled. He wrapped his arms around me. "I don't know what to do."

"What's going on?"

"My parents lied to me. They wanted to tell me before I went to college. They thought it would be best when I was older. They think I would have handled it better. How can you handle this better?"

I backed up a little to look at Caleb. "What?"

"My father isn't my real dad."

It was like a bomb had been dropped. I always knew how close Caleb was to Vince. They were the same person. "What?"

"They sat me down. They told me that my father left when I was born."

"Why would they tell you this?"

Caleb backed up with tears in his eyes. "I don't know. They thought it was time for me to know. Why couldn't they let me live in the lie?" He wiped a tear away. "Why did they have to shatter my whole life?"

"You can't think like that."

"It's how I fucking feel." He screamed. "My parents kept this from me. I looked at this man as my father figure. I thought through it all I had a good support system. I believed that I knew my roots."

"And now?"

"I wasn't loved by my father. He looked at me, and he realized I wasn't worth it. My real father didn't want me. I was just a piece of trash that he tossed to the side. Why would I matter to him? I was going to grow up to be nothing. Colin, I'm nothing."

It was like knives were being cut into my soul. I saw the destruction that this asshole did to my best friend. I walked forward. "Caleb."

"Colin, I don't want to be touched."

I ignored his protest and pulled him into a hug. He broke down in my arms. "I'm trash. I'm worthless. I don't mean anything to him. How could someone hate me so much even when they don't know me?"

"You can't believe that." I said.

"Why?"

"Because. Your real father wouldn't have left you if he knew how special you were. He wouldn't have abandoned you if he knew what an incredible son you would become. Caleb, you're a blessing in my life."

"Colin, I don't feel loved."

"I'll love you for him."

"I feel lied to."

"They were protecting you."

"I feel completely broken."

"Then I'll be here to piece you back together."

He backed away to look at me. "Why do you care so much?"

"Caleb, you came up to a shy kid with no friends. You asked me to play when I was known for being a freak. You made me feel like I could make it here."

"That was so long ago."

"It doesn't change that you've been here for me since. You're there for when I break down about my parent's death. You've made sure I was okay after my first date with Colby and our first time. You promised we would stay friends, even though we're going to different colleges. Caleb, you're my brother, and I'll protect my family."

"I just don't want to feel like I'm worthless."

"Caleb, you'll never be worthless. I'll always love you. I'm not going to give up on this friendship ever. You feel like you don't have a foundation, well you have it now. You feel like you don't have a family, but we're family."

I pulled him back into the hug, and I held him as he broke down. I'll never give up on him. He's made sure that I didn't feel alone or lost. I would give him the same respect.

I don't know how long we stood thee, but we eventually ended up in the tree house as it was raining. "I know that Vincent isn't my father anymore, but I don't want to look for my real father."

I turned to him. "Why?"

"Vincent is my dad. I have so many questions why my father left me. I can feel myself succumbing to the negative thoughts, and I can't do that. I won't do that for myself. I had to believe that he did it for a reason."

"You should look for him."

"Wouldn't that be wrong?"

"Why?"

"Vincent has been my dad my whole life. I know that this stranger was a sperm donor, but Vincent has never given up on me."

"I think you will always have a hole in your chest unless you go searching for him."

He wrapped his arms around his knees. "I'm scared."

"I would be too."

"How can I stop it?"

"You should always keep that fear." I looked at the rain. "It makes you realize how important it could be to you."

I heard Caleb whimper next to me. "I want to stop feeling like I'm not good enough."

I wrapped my arm around his shoulders and pulled him closer. "Caleb, I'm never going anywhere. I'll tell you if you need me to. I will. You're never worthless even if your father left. He missed out on someone special. I don't want you to ever forget that."

"Thank you, Colin."

"It's just what best friends do."

We watched the rain, and he cried more. I let him get it out of his system because he needed to. He needed to know that he was loved, and I would keep the pieces of his broken soul together. I would stay in Colin's corner because it's what best friends do. It's what humans do. We protect the hurt, and we love them when they feel lost.

100

"I don't know his father's name." I screamed into the computer. I shut my laptop and threw it across the room. I crossed my arms and looked at the blank wall.

"You want to explain to me what's going on?" Colby asked.

"I'm trying to figure out the last code. The clue is real father."

"So it's his real father's name?"

"Yeah, but I don't know it. I knew he was scared to talk to his real father, but I didn't think he actually talked to him." It pissed me off that I missed that moment of Caleb's life. He found his real father. He went on that search all by himself. Why did he never mention it in his journal entries? He always kept secrets to himself. I guess this was another test for me.

"Have you thought about calling his mom?" Colby asked.

"I don't want to bring her into all of this."

"Why not?"

"I can't hear the pain in her voice anymore. I can't hear her tell me one more time that we should have stuck together."

"You're going to need to deal with your guilt eventually."

I shook my head. "We should have stuck together."

She kissed me on the cheek. "You're not going to feel guilty anymore. You're going to call her, and you're going to finally talk to her. I know you've been avoiding her since you went to his place."

"I just have nothing to say."

"How about you get the answers you need?"

I looked up at her. "We should have stuck together. It would have fixed everything."

"I think it was all supposed to go down this way. I know it's messed up to say, but I think this was the right path for all of us. We're becoming the right people."

"Even Caleb?"

She gave me a weak smile. She handed me my phone. "Even Caleb." She turned and walked out of the hotel room to give me some privacy.

I dialed Mrs. Moore's number. She picked up. "I've been waiting for your call, Colin."

I laughed. "You've always known when I needed you the most."

"You've been avoiding me. I figured I would have heard from you by now."

"I guess I didn't want to be reminded that I abandoned your son. I'm the reason he's dead." I admitted to her.

"Do you believe that?"

"I think you want to blame me for his death."

"Colin." Her voice broke. "I could never blame you for Caleb's death. I do wish you both didn't have a falling out, but I can't blame you for his death. You both were brothers."

It was a relief to know that she didn't hate me. "I guess I've been worried that you did."

"Colin, I couldn't hate you for breaking Caleb's arm in eighth grade. I don't hate you now."

I laughed. "I guess that makes it all the better. I missed you. I know I have Aunt June, but you've been like my second mother."

"I've always seen you as a second son. Why are you calling?"

"I'm trying to find out if Caleb ever went to see his father."

"His biological father?"

"Yes."

"Why are you asking?"

"Caleb has mentioned to me before that he was scared to look for him. He didn't want to find out the truth about why his father left him. I guess it was one of the questions he had before we fought. I guess I want to know if he ever got those questions answered."

"I knew Caleb was acting funny right before his death. He came home, which he never did. He hugged Vince and I. He looked at both of us and told us he loved everything we have done for him. He knew that we were his parents, but he wanted to find out about his father."

"Did you tell him?"

"It was hard to tell him that his father didn't want him."

"Why didn't he want him?"

"He wasn't ready to be a father. He wasn't ready to be a man. He just wanted to continue to live the life of a rock star. I know its cliché I fell in love with a drummer. He was such a lover, and I see so much of Caleb in him. They believed in loving everything about the world."

"So he left?"

"I wanted him to grow up. I fell so stupid in love with him. It's really so sappy to know that he picked a quiet girl to play his drums to. We would talk for hours about everything under the sun. We talked about marriage."

"You did?"

"Honey, I was in my mid-twenties. I was fresh out of college. I had no clue what was going to happen in my life. We had the greatest sex because it was two souls coming together, not bodies. I found out I was with Caleb, and he ran."

"Because he couldn't be a father."

"He told me that he had been cheating on me the whole time. I was devoted to him, but he was devoted to love. He wanted to find every form of it, and I would hold him back."

"Loving your son is a form of love." I snapped back.

"Trust me, I've tried with the asshole. I thought maybe he would grow up and still see Caleb. I knew once Caleb was about to go to college that he wasn't going to show."

"Is it why you told Caleb about his father?"

"No, I wanted to tell him because I got the news Randolph had died of a drug overdose." I heard the pain in her voice. "I knew that I needed to tell Caleb about him."

"He never met him." My heart broke a little bit.

"No, he never did. It killed me telling my son that he would never meet his father. He had passed, and he couldn't get the answers he wanted. I saw a change in Caleb that day I told him about Randolph. He had a dark side in him that finally revealed itself. I saw the doubt splashed across his face."

"Was it worth it?"

"I cried myself to sleep so many nights because I didn't tell him. He needed to know about his father. I love Vince with all my heart, but Randolph, still to this day, has my heart. I'll always love him, but he wasn't the man Caleb needed as a father figure. Vince was. I think keeping it a secret was wrong, but I was protecting Caleb.

"I think we all were. We didn't give Caleb the credit he deserved. He was stronger than we all thought. I just wish I knew how he was when you told him."

"He found clarity in it all. We sat down for several hours talking about him. I knew Caleb was upset that he would never meet his father, but it was all he could ask for. He told me that Vince was his real father, but he found common grounds with Randolph."

"Why do you think he asked about Randolph?"

"I think with everything changing, he wanted to close doors. I know he wanted to make amends with you."

"Really?" I was shocked by the news.

"Yes, he said that you were there for him during this time. You were the one that kept him sane. He would never forget that. He was saddened that things had completely went away with you two, but he was hopeful it could change."

"But it's too late."

"I don't think it matters. You can still learn and connect with someone after they've passed. You're finding out about Caleb now. You're learning to love him again. You can never stop that."

"I miss him." I admitted.

"We all do, but he's in our hearts. Our hearts are like lockets."

"Thank you for everything."

"Thank you for loving my son and still doing it now. You two were brothers, and it never will change. We can't change the past. We all have burdens to carry, but you're fixing yours now. I'm always a constant reminder of how much Caleb loved you. Call me when you need reminding."

"I will."

"I hope this call helped."

It helped more than she could know. Caleb was still this incredible asshole that got attached to everyone's hearts. It's why so many loved him. It's why so many want answers. I found the final clue, and I was hoping to finish my burden. "It did." Mrs. Moore would always been an incredible woman that helped shape Caleb to who he was. I would never forget her like I would never forget him.

101

Dear Colin,

I don't think I can ever say I was a saint. I'm not this grand hero or this lovable character. I've made so many mistakes in my life that I wish I could change. I guess what it all comes down to is how much Jonathan hurt me. I never thought that I would love a man so much like I did. I think he just shifted everything that I was as a person. I think that's what love is supposed to do for you. You need to be someone different after you deeply love someone.

I also want to apologize for hating you after what happened between us. I think you slowly faded in the background of my heart and mind. I should have understood you. I think life would be easier if we understood the other person. I want you to know that I'm sorry for the words that were said during our fight, and I forgive you for not accepting me right away. I know you hold a lot of guilt about everything that has happened in my life. It's not your fault. I've done all of this on my own. I knew what I was doing, and I wouldn't change a thing. It might have seemed tragic, but I still got to love. I got to have a group of friends that I was blessed to have in my life. I don't cry for how my life ended. I'm joyous how my life was.

Love,
Caleb

March 12th, 2015

"I'm surprised to see you called me," Colby answered the phone.

I smiled. "I guess I just needed someone to talk," I said. Colby and I sent the occasional text, but she was focused on college and Colin. I was dealing with things.

"What's going on?" She asked.

"We're about to graduate college."

"Yeah in two months. I can't believe we've finally got here. It seems like yesterday we were opening our acceptance letters."

I chuckled. It seemed like a foreign memory. "Yeah, and now were going to separate again."

"You're not going home?" She asked.

"No, I'm moving to California. Drew, Cameron, and I want to get away from the East Coast. We want to see what else's out there. We like the idea of moving somewhere that we don't know anyone."

"That's sounds nerve-wracking."

"Yeah, I'm freaking out, but I know I have so much left to finish here."

"Like what?"

"I want to make amends with Colin. I don't want to hate him anymore. He was such a big part of my life, and it kills me that we don't know anything about each other anymore."

"I don't think you could ever be the old you, but you can be a better you guys. He misses you, and I know he regrets how everything went down between you two."

"I do too. I just didn't know it would be this long without each other talking. It seems like I had a relative die. We never talk. I look at memories of each other, and he's there. But he's not here now."

"I know. I think it's time to make amends before you leave for California."

"I also want to find out who my father is."

"Your biological father?"

"Yeah."

"I thought you didn't want to know the man that treated you like trash."

"I thought so too, but like I said, I want to have closure before I move. I don't want to be scared to come back. I want to know that I've left on good terms."

"How are you going to do that?"

"I'm going home this weekend, and I'm going to talk to my mom about everything. I need to know who my father was."

"I think it's time. You've been running from it for so long. We've all be running from our issues."

"I just want to be whole again." I knew that Jonathan had caused so much damage in my life, but I could fix other aspects of my life. I just wanted to know that I wasn't this confused scared boy anymore.

"You will be. Do you want me to talk to Colin?" She asked.

"No, I want to do it all on my own. I'll wait until I get home. I think it will be best once we're in the same town."

"Back at the tree house?"

That tree house held too many memories. "Yes, at the tree house."

"It will be nice to have the group back together."

I knew that things would never be the same with Colin, Colby, and I, but it could work. I knew that I could finally have my hometown friends back. I didn't want to look at those memories with pain anymore. I want to know that we loved each other. We ended this chapter on a new good note before California. I hoped things with Jonathan would be resolved, but I don't think they ever could, and I would be okay never seeing him again.

102

March 14th, 2015

"It's so good to have you home." My mom hugged me again.

"I guess I needed to come back before everything got a little hectic at school. It's still surreal that I'm almost done with college."

"You should be proud of yourself. You've come along way since you left almost four years ago."

I gave her a weak smile. "Yeah, I don't know if I should be proud of all the things that I've done since I left."

She grabbed my hand. "It's all part of growing up." She took a sip of her tea. "You want to explain to me why you're here."

"I came to see you."

She looked at me skeptical. "I don't believe you."

I hated how much my mom could call me on my bluff. "I want to know about my father."

"Vince. You know everything about him."

"Mom, I meant my real father."

She looked hesitant about telling me. "Honey, he's in the past. I don't see the point of bringing him up."

"Mom, you don't like talking about him. You said he left before I was born. Am I like him? Am I going to leave the first sign of commitment?"

She grabbed my hand. "You'll never do what your father did. You'll never destroy a family like he did."

I wouldn't be so sure. I did have an affair with a married man. I have the potential to destroy a family. "Mom, I just want to know him."

She got up. "What's the sudden fascination with the topic?"

"I'm moving to California in two months. I want to be able to have some closure here. I want to fix all the wounds before I leave."

She turned to look at me. "The wound will always be there."

"I know, but I want to know my father. I get that Vince is my dad. He raised me, and I'll always love him as my dad, but I do have another father."

"He's gone." I knew she was trying to be gentle with me.

"I know. I get that he's dead. I won't get all the answers because he's gone, but I can get some from you. What was he like?

What did he do? Why did he leave? You only told me that he left when I was born and that he's dead. It's all you've given me."

She sighed and walked out of the room. She walked back in with a book in her hand. She sat down next to me. "Do you want to know your father?"

"I do."

She placed her hand on the book. "Your father was an incredible person. He made me believe in love and fate. He was such a bright soul that my life belonged to him. I gave up everything to be with him. I dropped out of college to follow his band."

"Was it worth it?"

She smiled. "Every second. We would be high on his bus talking about life. I would catch him staring at me and ask him why he was doing it. He said that he wanted to always stop and look at the beautiful moments in his life."

"He was a romantic."

She opened the book that contained letters, bus tickets, concert tickets, and pictures of them. "He would always write me letters when I couldn't go with him on tour."

"Really?"

"Yeah, he thought that letters were your heart trying to communicate. He wanted me to always cherish these letters from him because it was something we shared."

"Why did you keep them? He hurt you."

"He might have turned out to be a heartless asshole, but he made me feel love for the first time. I can never thank him enough for that."

"Really?'

She turned to look at me. "Caleb, you're going to find a love so profound that it's going to consume you. You're going to get wrapped up with that person to the point of obsession."

"I shouldn't do that."

"No, honey, you should. I gave everything up to be with the man that I love."

"But he left you."

"I will never regret those years we were together. We had no clue where our lives were going to take us. We could end tomorrow, and I would return home. He could cheat on me with some groupie. We could have overdosed and died. We didn't know what life had for us, but we were doing it together. We had our love. No one could take that from us."

I looked at the pictures and read some of the letters my father wrote her. "Why are you being so open?"

She grabbed my hand. "Because you've fallen in love."

I looked at her. "How?"

"You have your father's romantic side, but you have my mannerisms when you're in love. I could see it written all over your face. I noticed the light you gained from that experience is gone."

"Our relationship was a complete lie. It's been over for almost a year now."

"But you're not over him?"

"He will always have my heart. I don't think I'll ever get over him. I thought he was the one for me. It was supposed to be us against the world. It turned out to be just me against him." I felt the tears forming. "It doesn't matter. It's never going to work again."

She kissed me on the cheek. "I'm so sorry you had to go through that kind of pain. No one should do it. I wish you could have had a forever with him."

"Do you feel like that with him?"

"Randolph and I?"

"Randolph?" I asked.

"Yes, Randolph."

"Is that why my middle name is Randolph?" I asked.

She kissed me on the forehead. "Randolph is for your biological father. Moore is for your dad. Those two men created you, and I wanted to honor them both."

"Do you wish it could have worked out with him?"

"I sometimes go to sleep crying because I think back to my time with him. I think back to telling him I was pregnant. I saw him change in that moment. He was cold and I lost the guy I fell for. He left me alone. I cry, but Vince is there to take care of me. He holds me and keeps me together. I loved your father, but Vince is who I'm meant to be with. He fixed all those broken pieces."

"Will I get that?"

She grabbed both sides of my face. "Yes, you'll find a love like Vince and I. You'll find someone to pick up all the broken pieces. He will make you whole. You'll find someone to really love you. You will still have pain from your first love, but it will be fond memories. You just need to get give it time."

I looked at the love my mom and Randolph shared. I saw the looks they gave each other, and it reminded me of Jonathan and I. This gave me hope that I could move forward from Jonathan. I could find my Vince, and we would live happy ever after. We would fall in love, and Jonathan would be just a memory. I put my hand over my heart and I prayed for that story for me.

103

March 31st, 2015

I heard a knock at my door. Drew and Cameron were on date night, so I had the whole place to myself. I opened the door to see Jonathan standing there. My whole heart dropped, and I had no clue why he was here. He had no right standing at my door. I was trying to put him in the past. I was about to graduate in a month in a half. I was saying goodbye to him.

"What are you doing here?" I asked.

"You're graduating."

"Yes, I got the confirmation letter this morning." It was a relief getting the email that if everything goes according to plan, then I would be walking. "Why are you here?"

He stepped closer to me. "You're leaving in a month. You will be moving on from this place. We will never be able to reconnect."

I looked at him in the eyes. I felt knots in my stomach. My mouth was going dry. "It doesn't affect you." It barely left my mouth.

He grabbed me in for a kiss. It had been almost a year since I found out about his wife and kids. It had been almost a year since my whole world was turned upside down. Here he was kissing me. Here he was putting the pieces he broke back together.

I wanted to protest. I wanted to remind him of his wife and kids. I wanted to do so many things, but it felt right. I had been missing Jonathan, and I felt my heart beating for the first time since he walked out on me.

I wrapped my arms around his waist and deepened the kiss. I let a soft moan escape from my mouth. "You don't know what you do to me," he said. "I've missed this so much."

I smiled. "Me too. I never wanted this to end." I looked at him in the eyes and touched his face. "I want this to be real."

"It is." He then towed me to my bedroom. I wanted to be rational. I wanted to tell him that we couldn't do this. He broke my heart so many times, and I couldn't just get back into bed with him.

He turned to look at me. "Caleb, it's me."

I backed against the closed door. "That's the problem."

He walked over and gave me a reassuring kiss. "I won't hurt you."

"You told me that before."

"I made a mistake letting you go. The past year of my life has been miserable. I want you back. I never stopped thinking about you."

I shook my head. "You lied to me. I thought we had something special. You told me I was never yours. Do you know how much that destroyed me? Do you understand what kind of wreck I became?"

"I didn't mean to hurt you. I wanted us to work out, but I couldn't have my wife and kids finding out. I couldn't lose my family. I had to give up love for my family. I needed to hurt the person I wanted to be with to make sure everyone around me was happy."

"What about now? Why are you here then? Tell me the truth."

"Because I lied to myself that I didn't love you. I didn't know how much your presence is needed in my life. I don't ever want to lose you again. I saw your name come up as those who were accepted to graduate. It made me realize that my heart was walking out of my life. I couldn't do that again. I couldn't say goodbye to the man I want to be with."

I knew that he had my heart right then. I saw the yearning in his eyes. I could hear the desperation in his voice. It's all I ever wanted. I needed to know he loved me, and he didn't need to say it. I felt it. I pushed him on my bed. "Jonathan, I love you. I never stopped, and I don't think I ever will. I want you, but I'm not staying for you. I'm leaving after graduation."

"What about us?"

"You have a family and kids. I need to focus on my future."

"I don't want to lose you."

"You lost me the moment you lied to me. My walls are up because you broke my heart. I gave you everything of me, and you didn't give me anything. Why should I do it all over again? Why should I give up the walls I've built this past year against you?"

"Because you never stopped loving me, and I never stopped loving you." He grabbed my arm and pulled me on the bed. We continued to kiss. I wanted to fight it, but I craved this. I missed him opening me up only to take care of me. I missed being this close with someone. We were connected, and I loved every second of it. I didn't feel like trash or replaceable. I was addicted to the attention, and I would do anything for it. I got my fix with Jonathan, but I knew there was going to be a catch. There always was.

April 1st, 2015

I woke up to arms wrapped around my body. I heard light snores next to my ear, and I felt my whole body vibrating. Jonathan was in my bed with me. He came over and confessed his love for me. I would be a fool to believe that we would get right back into the swing of things. I thought maybe we could have the closure we needed. I would be leaving for California soon, and he would be in my past. I knew I would always love him, but we wouldn't last.

I rolled around and looked at him sleeping. I didn't think this was real. Here he was in my bed with me. I saw him open his eyes and smile when he saw me. He wrapped his arms around me and pulled me closer to him. "It's creepy that you're looking at me."

"I think it's adorable."

He chuckled and kissed me on the lips. "I've missed this." He kissed me again. "I've missed you."

It had to be a dream that I didn't want to wake up from. He was in my bed with me, and I never felt more love than right now.

"I've missed you too. You have no clue how painful the past year has been without you."

"I'm sorry for that."

"Why did you lie to me? Why didn't you tell me?"

"I knew how much of a romantic you were. I couldn't do that to you."

"You promised me forever and then told me that was bullshit. You said that I never was yours in the first place. Was it true?" I looked at him in the eye.

"Caleb, I'm here now." He leaned in for a kiss.

I stopped him. "Jonathan, answer the question. Do I have you now? Can we be something?"

"I don't want to lose you. I can't lose you. I need you in my life, Caleb. I love you too much. I'm yours."

"I can't just jump back into it with you, Jonathan." I wasn't going to be a fool again. I gave him everything. I didn't want to make the same mistake.

"Caleb, I'm here. Doesn't that matter?"

"Where were you when I was crying myself to sleep? Where were you when I tried to break my best friend's heart because I didn't want to feel alone? Where were you when I drank myself to sleep every night because you weren't here to stop the pain?"

He tightened his arms around me. "I never meant for any of this to happen."

"But it did. We can't reverse time. I will never stop having these scars, but I can't stop loving you. I've tried so hard to put you in the past, and I can't. It kills me to know that."

"Why?"

"You're going to hurt me again. You're going to break my heart, and it's going to hurt worse the second time around. You're going to go back to your wife and kids. You're going to leave me."

He kissed me hard on the lips. I knew he was trying to get his point across. "I'm not going to leave you. I promise to be here as long as you want me. I know you're going to California, but I want as much time as I can with you. Caleb, I'll do anything for you."

"Don't make me second choice. I don't want to be a skeleton in your closet anymore. I want to know that you love me."

"I love you now and forever."

It was all I needed to hear. I leaned forward and kissed him on the lips. I wouldn't have my heart fully open to him, but I could give him something. I think it was good we were separated for a year. We can realize that we do care for each other. I love this man, and I don't want him out of my life. My story with him wasn't over yet. I hope it has a happy ending.

104

April 11th, 2014

I was sitting alone at a restaurant a couple of miles away from town. I felt like a complete jackass because I was waiting for Jonathan. He was already twenty minutes late. This was his make-up dinner to me. This was his chance to prove himself to me. Here I was alone being stood up.

"Where are you?" I texted him.

It was a couple of minutes before he responded. *"I'm so sorry I have to cancel. Something came up."*

I felt the tear in my chest. He was doing it again. He was breaking all of his promises. *"You promised me."*

"I didn't mean for it to happen."

"Like you say all the time. I look like an idiot right now."

"Caleb, you have to forgive me."

"Jonathan, I don't have to do anything. I'm so sick and tired of your bullshit. You do this to me all the time. How dare you?"

"Please forgive me."

"I don't think I can." I closed my phone. I deleted Jonathan's number out of my phone. I deleted all text messages and pictures I had of Jonathan. He was dead to me.

I picked myself up. I wasn't going to give him the last laugh. I grabbed a cab and went home. I got inside, and I was alone. I went straight for the bottle of whiskey. "Hello, old friend." I had been trying to stay sober. I've been trying to forget about drinking because I knew it would bring up all the demons. I was trying to be a better person.

I opened the bottle and started taking swig after swig. I walked into my room. I grabbed all the letters Jonathan had sent me. I ripped every single one of them up. He was worthless to me now. I was just a fool to believe that we could be something. I thought he loved me, but I was just a fucking booty call to him.

I lied on the ground surrounded by the bullshit love story that Jonathan tried to convince me of. I finished the bottle of whiskey and cried. I let it all out. I wanted nothing more than to just forget about everything. I wanted to believe that he could be someone. I wanted to believe he was the one.

"When do I get love? When do I stop crying?" I curled the bottle of whiskey in my hand, and I closed my eyes. I hoped that I never had to open them back up because then I wouldn't have to feel anymore. I wouldn't be reminded of my broken heart.

April 13th, 2015

I had everything collected. I was supposed to be focused on my future in California. I was supposed to be focused on graduating college. I had my closure with my father. I was going to have closure with Colin when I went home. I put Jonathan in the background. I spent the past year getting back to who I was as a person.

It took one night of him confessing his love for me, and a night of him disappointing me to bring it all down. What was the point of being happy? It was all a bunch of bullshit. You let someone in your life, and you believe they would be good for you. It turns out all they're good at is destroying everything about you.

I knew Drew, Cameron, Beth, and Shawn were worried about me. I lied and said it was about finding out about my father. I didn't want them to know it was about Jonathan. I didn't want to sound like a broken record.

"Caleb, are you with me?" Shawn asked.

I spaced out. I turned to look at him. We were on our way to class. "What?"

"Did you want to come over later and work on our last show?" He asked.

I nodded. "Yeah, sorry. I have a lot on my mind."

"Is it about your dad?" He asked.

"Yeah, I guess I'm still trying to digest everything my mom told me about him." I gave him a weak smile. "I thought I would hate him for leaving me, but I see a lot of him in me. My mom could have hated him, but she still loved him. I guess I need to forgive him."

"It's weird to think about that. Your mom was the most hurt by him. She could see past it and see that the love they shared was so profound. I guess she wanted to focus on the positives."

I looked away from Shawn. I wish I could do that with Jonathan. We had this great love together. I wish I could have some fondness about our relationship. Maybe we could have left it the last night we were in bed together. We could have had hope of reconnecting, but there wasn't any disappointment. The tragedy was he tainted it.

"I just wish I could do the same thing."

Shawn grabbed my hand. "You will eventually. You'll be able to look at your love as something special. It's been a year."

"The wounds haven't healed even after all this time."

"Just think, California is around the corner. You're about to put this all behind you."

"I hope so." I really wanted to believe that Jonathan was behind me. I wanted to make Jonathan a lesson in my past. I needed to believe that he could be something of a past ghost. I would be stronger when I saw him again.

"Let's talk about the radio show?" I asked.

I smiled. I needed to focus on this. It was our last radio show. It was going to be another point that's ending. It reaffirmed that I would be moving away from here. I was getting away from all the pain that's happened in my life the past four years. It would stick in the past.

We walked down the hall until we spotted Jonathan and his wife kissing. I felt numb to it. I looked away. "I can't watch this."

He grabbed my hand. He towed me around the corner to the bathroom. I felt my chest tightening. I couldn't do it. He broke my heart over and over again. I was fed up with it. He got to the bathroom and locked the door. "I can't." I ran to the toilet and threw up.

I felt Shawn's hand rub my back. "I'm sorry it's still painful."

"I just want it to be over with. Why can't I stop loving him? Why can't I get him out of my mind?"

"It's not right that he put you through that pain."

"He's still fucking doing it." I laughed as I leaned my back against the wall. "I can't get over him. I can't put him in the past."

"It's good you didn't go to the banquet this past weekend."

I raised an eyebrow. "Why?"

"He announced him and his wife were expecting a third kid."

I felt my heart drop. I felt my whole being shatter. He stood me up because he was announcing he was going to have a third child. "He's having another kid." I had to force it out of my mouth.

"Yeah, it's still really early. They couldn't contain their excitement."

I felt the walls getting smaller. "I need to breathe." I got off the ground and ran out of the bathroom. I ran out of the building. I ran into the middle of the grass area. I just screamed everything out. I screamed about the pain, love, confused, lost, and lonely feelings I've had surging through my body the past three years. I released all of the anger that I've kept in my body. I've always taken the higher road. I've always been the victim, and I was done with it.

I wanted him to know what it felt like to be in pain. I wanted him to know what it meant to have your whole world shattered. I was tired of being the one left broken while he got to be in love. He was having a third child. He toyed with me once again, and I was left to the side. I was just a quick fuck for him. I'm not going to be his skeleton anymore.

I walked myself back to my apartment. I ignored Drew's concerns as I went into my room. I sat down at my desk and wrote the letter. I wrote my final letter that I would ever write to Jonathan. I knew it was risky to write it, but I was done thinking about the consequences. I knew I was about to get my closure, and this was the final piece.

I got everything I had for Jonathan down on paper. I've spent almost three years of my life on this man. I loved him with everything I had in my chest. I learned so much from that man, but it wasn't positive. I didn't get a happy ever after, and I don't think he should either. He got to continue to be loved, and it wasn't fair.

It would be one of my greatest mistakes writing this letter, but I didn't care. I was tired of having no control of my life. I was tired of being in the closet for these men. I'm not someone you could toss to the side. I was someone you fucking love. I was special, and I knew it. I meant something to people, and it was time that I was heard. It was time for people to know who Caleb was. I wasn't going to be forgotten or abandoned anymore. I was going to be loved. I was going to be something.

105

"I can't believe we're doing this," Colby whispered.

We walked down the halls of the Liberal Arts building in the middle of the night. We walked down the halls until we reached Jonathan's office.

"We need to know if Jonathan killed Caleb."

"Why would breaking into his office prove that?" She asked.

"Caleb hinted in his last journal entry that he wrote a letter to Jonathan."

"So?" Jimmy said.

"So, if there is a letter that Caleb threatened to expose their relationship it's the cause of motive. Do any of you watch any criminal shows?"

They both shook their heads. "I don't see the point in them," Jimmy said.

I groaned. "Caleb wrote a letter to Jonathan. He had to have done it." I knew once I found the letter that Caleb wrote to Jonathan than it would be all over. It would prove Jonathan murdered Caleb. It would mean all of this would be over, and I got the answers that I needed.

I took a deep breath. This was the moment I've been waiting for. The door wasn't locked, and we walked in. "I guess we can start searching his drawers." We started looking through all of his files, papers, and drawers to find anything that could resemble the letter.

We searched for an hour and found nothing. I slammed the last folder down. "It has to be here. He had to have kept it."

Colby walked over and rubbed my back. "Maybe he didn't do it."

I whipped my head to look at her. "He did it. I know he did. He's the reason that my best friend is dead. He's the reason for all the bullshit that Caleb went through. It's here."

"I hate to tell you, but it's not here," Jimmy said. "We've looked everywhere."

I looked up and around at all the bookshelves. I scanned the titles of all the books until I stopped at one. *Love Letters*. It was the title of the book that Caleb and Jonathan read during class. It was the book that started it all.

"I might have an idea." I walked over and grabbed the book. I opened up the book to see an envelope. It was time stamped April 17th, 2015. It was right around the time Caleb died.

I felt my whole body shaking. This was the moment that I had been waiting for. I had been going through all this bullshit for this one stupid letter. Caleb could have just given me this letter. He could have shown me that this asshole was the reason for his death. He didn't need to send me on a wild goose chase.

"Did you find something?" Colby asked.

"I think I found the letter." I opened the envelope and pulled out the letter. I started reading the letter.

Dear Jonathan,

You will always remember your first love and your first heartbreak. They'll be a scar on your heart forever. Jonathan, I believed we had something real. I thought we were going to be one of the great love stories. It's what you told me. We were the ones broken-hearted people dream for. You were a nice guy with a bunch of fancy words. You never wanted to be alone, and I can see that. You've left me alone too many times. You have broken me. There were too many nights that I curled up to a bottle of whiskey praying that the pain would go away. I prayed that I would never wake up because of you.

I had so many dreams and hopes for our relationship. I wanted nothing more than to spend those summer days at the cabin by the lake. We would just hike, ride bikes, and we would just get lost in our love. We wouldn't worry about anything else in our lives because it was just us. I miss that week more than anything else in the world. You gave me hope for a future with you.

I look back at my time with you, and I see how much of a liar you were. You told me over and over again that you loved me. I mattered to you. That I was someone you could spend the rest of your life with. Why would someone do that to the person that had their heart? Why would someone be so cruel?

I should tell you thank you for helping me with Colin. I realized that he wasn't a monster or a villain. It's the guy with all the right words who likes to break people. Colin didn't understand me because he was raised not to. I hope that he eventually understands that I was always the same person. I hadn't changed since we grew up. We would always be best friends, and I hoped we would get back there. It would take time, but I would have my best friend back. I would have my brother.

You will never know what it means to have close bonds with people. You've manipulated your way through life, and that's pathetic. You say you love your kids, but where is the proof? Where is the love for them when all you did is hurt? I hear congrats are in order. You're going to have another kid. It's tragic that child will have you as a father. You're a heartless son of a bitch.

You destroyed me over and over again. You got to go home to your family. You got to be in love and have kids. I didn't get any of that. I almost ruined all my friendships. I almost ruined my life because I fell in love with you. I don't want that anymore. I don't want to be the only one in pain. I should just put you in the past, but I know you need to learn a lesson. You need to know that your actions have consequences.

I'm going to tell your wife everything about us. I hope I'm there to see the look on your face when she leaves you. I pray that I get to see the pain in your children's eyes. You killed me, and I'm going to kill you. You don't get to be happy anymore. You don't get to smile. It's not right that I get to be alone. It's time you feel the same.

Jonathan, I wanted this to work out between us. I wanted nothing more than a forever with you. I gave you my whole world, and I don't regret it. I will never regret the time that we shared together because you taught me a lot. I'm just tired of you getting away with it. I'm tired of you having no guilt for all of the things you've done. You'll always be my first real love, but you were my first real heartbreak.

Sincerely,
Caleb

I dropped the letter on the ground. "Jonathan did it."

"Are you sure?" Colby asked.

I turned to look at her. "Caleb was going to expose their relationship to his wife and kids."

"Caleb would never do that."

I bent down and handed her the letter. "It's in the fucking letter. He was going to tell her. He wanted Jonathan to be in pain like he was. He wanted to hurt him."

"So he did it?" Jimmy asked.

"Yeah, he did it. Jonathan killed my best friend. Mystery is solved." I felt a weight on my shoulders lifted. I solved the mystery. Jonathan murdered Caleb. I figured out the last four years of Caleb's life.

I smiled and turned to Colby. "I solved it."

She gave me a weak smile. "You did."

It came crashing down after seeing the pain in Colby's eyes. This didn't change anything. This didn't bring back my best friend. This just made it more real. "He's dead." I broke.

Colby looked at me. "Yeah, he's gone."

I felt my whole body tremble. "This isn't fair. I figured out who killed him. He should be back. He should be coming through those doors. He should be telling me that he's proud of me."

Colby walked over and wrapped her arms around me. I held her close to me. I felt the tears that have been stored up finally coming out. "He's dead and never coming back."

"He's gone," Colby said.

"No, it's not fair. He didn't deserve this. He didn't deserve to die."

"Colin, he's in a better place."

"I never got to apologize. I never got to tell him how proud I was of him. I didn't get to say goodbye. He will never know that I love him."

"He knows, Colin. He knows."

"Why did I have to be an asshole all those years ago? Why did I stop listening to him?"

"We all make mistakes."

"He's gone," I said again because reality finally caught up to me. Solving this mystery did nothing. I found out the bastard who killed my best friend. I figured out what happened to him, but it didn't change anything. Caleb was dead, and he was never coming back. I lost my best friend because of me. I'm the reason he walked out of my life. I'm the reason he's gone, and I'll never get him back. I caused the tears to come out of my eyes. I caused the pain in my chest. I caused his death.

106

Four Years Earlier

"Caleb, why am I here?" I asked as I walked towards the tree house. I needed to finish up packing since I was leaving next week for college.

Caleb turned around, and I saw that he was crying. "I needed to tell you something."

I walked over and pulled Caleb into a hug. "Caleb, what's going on?"

He could feel his body shaking. "I'm nervous to tell you this. I don't know how to."

"What is it?"

He looked up at me. "You've been my best friend since we were six. We've always been there for each other. I can't thank you enough for having my back when I found out about my real father. You've always been my rock, and I can't live without you. It's why I wanted you to be the first to know."

"What is it?" I asked.

He looked at me in the eyes. "I'm gay."

My whole body stiffened. "What?"

"Colin, I'm gay."

I stepped away from him. "No, you're not. You were in love with Tracy and Sarah."

He shook his head. "It was all a lie. I knew I was gay, and I didn't know what else to do. I knew I couldn't come out. We live in a town that rejects it, but I just didn't feel like myself. I want to be me."

"Why are you doing it now? You should have stayed in the closet." I felt so much vile in my mouth. My best friend was gay.

"Colin."

"Why would you tell me this?"

He tried to move closer to me, but I stepped backwards. "Because you were there for me about my dad. I thought you could understand this. You've been there for me through everything. I need you for this."

"No, I can't. It's disgusting to be gay." My father raised me to know that homosexuality was wrong. I saw the disgust on my father's face when we saw the gay couple in the grocery store.

"Colin." His voice broke.

"It's true. Caleb, you should have stayed in the closet. I can't be friends with a homosexual. I was raised better than that. You've been a lie to me."

"I'm still the same person."

"No, you're not. It was all a lie. You can't be serious that I've known you my whole life. I would have known you were gay."

"Would you have been friends with me if I told you sooner?" Caleb asked.

Caleb had been my best friend through some of the darkest times of my life. He had always made sure that I didn't feel alone and ashamed. He had been my brother, but I couldn't do this. I couldn't accept that my best friend was gay. "No, I wouldn't have."

He nodded. "I wish I never talked to the freak with no parents."

"Excuse me?" I felt the anger forming.

"I mean it's why your parents died. They didn't want to be known as your parents anymore. They would have been disappointed to know their son has so much hate."

"Fuck you!" I screamed. "You don't know anything."

"I know enough to know that you're a fucking monster. I've been nothing but a good friend to you. I guess I just felt sorry for you. I saw the reject in the corner by himself."

"You're the fucking reject. No one is going to love a fag."

"Least I have parents to be there when I deal with ignorant ass-holes like you."

I walked over and grabbed a fistful of his shirt. "I'll fucking punch you in the face if you keep talking."

"Do it. I bet you won't. You're just the pathetic loser with no parents."

"And you're the fag." I shot back.

We looked at each other for a moment. I felt our friendship ending. I felt the pain in my chest. I never knew what it felt like to have your heart broken, but this was one of those moments. I was losing my best friend, but I didn't care. He was gay, and I couldn't accept it.

"I guess it's good we're going to different colleges," Caleb said.

"Yeah, I won't ever have to see you again." I let go of his shirt.

"I'm happy I never have to see you again." Caleb turned and walked away. "Good luck with your life."

"I hope a man breaks your heart. I hope someone ruins your fucking happiness. You deserve to know what it feels like to be in pain," I screamed.

He turned around and looked me. "Trust me, I know what it feels like to be in pain. I'm doing it right now." He turned and walked away.

I lost my best friend right then. I watched, as he walked away from my life. I couldn't be friends with him after everything that was said. I could never forgive him or be able to love him the way I did. I was starting a new chapter, and I didn't need Caleb in my life anymore.